DROWNING

MERMAIDS

Book One of the

Sacred Breath

Series

By Nadia Scrieva

ISBN-13: 978-1469932736
ISBN-10: 1469932733

For Samantha Major; the girl with the mermaid tattoo and unquenchable zest for adventure.

TABLE OF CONTENTS

We are tied to the ocean.
And when we go back to the sea, whether it is to sail or to watch—
we are going back from whence we came.
John F. Kennedy

Chapter 1: Change in the Seas

"To our lost friend."

"To Leander. I hope he's in a better place than this—one with more tolerable temperatures."

"So anywhere? Including hell?"

"I'm not sure what I believe about the afterlife," the young man responded thoughtfully, "but I am positive that the fires of Hades are a tropical paradise compared to Alaska."

The older man laughed at this, temporarily transforming his sorrowful face. "Cheers, kid."

"Cheers, Captain." The two men nodded at each other solemnly before clinking their mugs together. The younger one took a long, satisfying swig of the brew before smiling in appreciation. "You know, this club is a lot wilder than I expected. I figure if I'm going to kill myself for money, I might as well spend it on some quality entertainment in the downtime."

"Kid," said the grey-haired man, shaking his head disapprovingly, "too much of this kind of 'entertainment' will be the precise thing that gets you killed on the job if you're not careful."

"I've been lucky in my life so far. I don't intend for that to change. Want to get a seat closer to the stage, Captain?"

"No, thanks, Arnav. You go ahead. My leg's aching something awful."

"An excellent excuse to save your dollar bills!" Arnav joked before clapping his friend on the back and heading to the center of the action.

Captain Trevain Murphy leaned back in his chair, mulling over the details of the previous days. He had always been fortunate on the waters; he had always somehow scraped by until the end of the season without a single casualty.

He was a firm believer in not allowing the sea to collect the souls of his men. Although they took their food from the sea's open mouth,

1

he did not believe it was necessary to offer up human sacrifices for this privilege. He had stayed in business long enough without appeasing any pagan gods—and he was quite certain that the gods did not pay close attention to Alaska anyway. Trevain did not accept that losses were bound to happen as most others did. He held that they were the result of carelessness and inefficiency, and he chose his men cautiously to avoid having either of these blights on his boat.

The conditions of Leander's demise had been strange. The captain had begun to wonder in the moments before the incident whether the man had been feeling all that well.

"Did you hear a strange noise, Captain?" Leander had asked in his suspicious but respectful manner.

Trevain had briefly paused, as if to listen, to satisfy the man. Perhaps his mind had been too occupied with the remaining tasks on board, but he had heard nothing. *"Just the whistling of the wind, Leo. A storm's not far off, but we'll be home long before it hits. Why are you so agitated?"*

"I just… I swear I saw something in the water earlier."

"Like what?"

"I don't know." Leander had been so tense that he twitched when Arnav dropped a coil of rope a few feet away from him. *"I am a bit tired and feverish. Might just be coming down with something and seeing things."*

"Just relax—we'll be back to shore soon. A hot meal and a warm bed will fix you right up, son." Now, in retrospect, his own words made him cringe.

The weather had been benevolent while the day had unfolded smoothly. There was no way that Trevain could have expected anything unusual on such a humdrum fishing trip. After hauling up the pots and completing all of the most grueling tasks, the crew had begun to bask in their communal sense of accomplishment and good cheer. They had been turning the ship around and preparing to head home when the first mate, Doughlas, had noticed that Leander was missing. None of the men could find him below or above deck, and no one had shouted for a man overboard. Everyone had been puzzled, and Trevain had felt the first pangs of true panic he'd experienced in over thirty years. Leander had just seemed to vanish.

The crew had suggested that the young man they fondly called "Leo" might be taking a nap somewhere. It had been a long trip on the water, and the seasoned seamen were used to working inhuman hours. They had considered that he had been hiding or trying to pull some strange kind of prank. It had only taken a few hours for the *Magician's* temperament to progress from mildly amused to generally annoyed and finally to disbelieving and appalled. It was hard to accept that a man was dead when there were no details to process regarding the incident. Nothing to examine, nothing to understand.

The last person to speak with Leander had been Edwin, the Canadian. When asked about the conversation repeatedly by the crew, Edwin lost his cool at having to revisit, dozens of times, that Leander had only told him that he was going to take a leak. The Canadian had cursed incessantly, while wiping tears from his eyes with his sleeves. *"I thought it was safe enough for him to go to the fucking washroom on his own. I didn't think he was in danger of drowning while urinating! Toilet monsters that grab you by the wang and pull you down to a horrifying death-by-piss haven't exactly been my major concern since preschool."*

Now the men were drowning their woes in women and booze. They loved the occasional sojourn in Soldotna for that purpose, but their woes usually did not require such a substantial sloshing to be adequately submerged.

As Captain Murphy sat in a secluded corner of the strip club, he frowned until his face creased with dozens of dismal trenches. The lines deepened and intersected to create a roadmap leading to nowhere as he inwardly labored to find the path to understanding how he had lost a man. He had always prided himself on being able to bring men home to their wives and children at the end of the season. Leander had been young, and had no children depending on him—but he had a girlfriend that he had spoken of often, one whom he had hoped to marry. He also had loving parents. There had been an established place for him in the world which had now collapsed.

No obvious, detrimental mistake had been made and no miscalculations could be identified. There was no one to punish or blame. Trevain could not yell at the men to reinforce or avoid a certain action in the future to prevent this from occurring again. There was nothing to correct, there was no lesson to be learned. Nothing had really gone wrong. It had been a random, quiet, shadowlike loss.

Had Leander just decided to dive off the side of the boat when no one was looking, just for the hell of it? Had he plunged himself into the cold depths to see how far he could swim down into the sea before he sucked in a breath of saltwater? These were the types of scenarios that floated through the captain's mind as he tried to imagine what had happened to the deckhand. The situation seemed *that* crazy. Trevain couldn't shake the feeling that something had changed. There had been some kind of major change in the seas since he was a boy, and he no longer knew the waters as well as he always felt he had.

The ocean was not usually quiet and mercenary-like in her brutality. There had always been plenty of fanfare to announce her burgeoning rage. The sky would use its whole canvas to display a bloodbath of remarkable colors in unmistakable warning. Trevain had always interpreted the message correctly: "She is ravenous. Do not go out to fish today. She will rape you." It had very little to do with the weather—of course bad weather presented a technical danger. Trevain was more concerned with some quality he could not quite describe, but could intuitively feel and gauge—bad energy, perhaps.

Oftentimes the crew would call him silly and superstitious. Trevain would patiently point out other signs of trouble as he sternly forbade the men to sail. Large, dark birds like falcons and eagles would leave their secret roosts and venture out, flying in erratic and confused patterns over the shoreline as if trying to discern the source of an unknown crisis. There might be a certain mournful sound in the wind or a certain morbid chill in the air. It was as if everything on the planet was privy to some knowledge that escaped Trevain. Everything was pulsating with the excitement of some indefinite impending carnage. Trevain felt that being human automatically precluded him from being on nature's mailing list for memos about this sort of thing, but he would not allow that disadvantage to cripple him.

"We have all lost touch with nature," Trevain would lecture threateningly, pointing at his only Inuit crew member, "yes, even you Ujarak." The accused man would shrug his innocence and chomp down on his cigar nervously as the captain continued his tirade. "If your greed for a few dollars is greater than your inclination to live, then by all means, go out and fish! Be my guest, take the boat." Trevain would turn around and march away from the docks, with a parting wave and a mocking challenge, "Go out and fish!"

Of course, no one did.

One by one, the crew would lose their motivation for the intended trip. Without a tenacious leader to rally them, they would disband within minutes and trickle off into homes, bars, and hotel rooms. Sure enough, by the time they gathered again they would have heard of at least one accident or casualty on another fishing boat. They would return to work with the high morale that came from knowing they had escaped the ultimate misfortune. They would hastily remove their hats when speaking of the lost or injured man, and have their faith in their captain renewed to the greatest magnitude.

For decades, although men had come and gone from his crew, that was the way things had worked. Until Leander. Until a few days ago when Captain Murphy had been unable to inform his crew of impending danger. He had not noticed any distress in the birds, the sky, or the winds. His usual indicators had failed him. It was as if even *they* had been unaware of the ocean's ire.

Maybe Leo was just mentally unstable, the captain thought to himself. *I could have overlooked something when I hired him—maybe he was hallucinating, and he saw or heard something which caused him to jump overboard and dive to his death when we were all occupied. Maybe it was just a singular event. Something out of my control.*

As he tried to mentally reassure himself, he leaned back and drank deeply of his cold beer. He did not feel very reassured. Smiling wryly, he imagined that he suddenly understood what it was like to be a veteran master of some now obsolete technology: that which he had been most intimate with had gone and innovated itself on him. Yes, he was fairly certain there had been some kind of eerie change in the seas he had come to know so well, and he was pretty sure that it did not have anything to do with global warming.

Chapter 2: She Danced Power

Captain Murphy had not intended to even glance at the stage.

While his shipmates found the hollering and raucous energy of the crowd distracting and healing, he felt that remaining silent in a corner while slowly nursing his drink was a better way to pay homage to the memory of his shipmate. Staring very hard at the droplets of condensation gathering on his glass, and following them as they trickled down into a little pool on his coaster, was his manner of protest.

Why should he seek to experience anything resembling fun when Leander no longer could? The man had been robbed of his life while working under *his* watch. Trevain was the ship's captain—the ultimate authority: God of his boat. This made him ultimately responsible. He felt it more than ever as he lifted the cold beer to his lips again for a long swig.

The last simple, coherent thought he would remember having before his mind was plunged into a war with itself for fourteen minutes and twenty three seconds was that he definitely needed to get something stronger.

He really had not meant to look.

However, sometimes a word of certain significance can draw a man out of his reverie. When the DJ announced her name, it brought back the memory of his mother's voice reading to him when he was a child.

"Now gentlemen, get ready to be blown away by our mysterious newcomer. She's the girl you've always dreamed of, but never thought you'd actually meet in the flesh: *Undina!*"

He glanced up for a moment, his eyes falling upon the dark-haired woman who was slowly ascending the stairs to the stage. The length of her hair was astonishing—it flowed almost down to her knees. He felt immediate curiosity about the way her stormy eyes were downcast and her mouth set in a grim line. He felt further curiosity when he saw her light graceful steps—she was wearing ballet slippers!

Not eight inch heels that made her steps awkward and clunky, but real dancing shoes.

Despite his escalating curiosity, Trevain managed to yank his eyes away from the stage and focus again on the droplets sitting on his beer glass. He had no business looking at such a young girl, he told himself. She might be an adequate dancer, someone moderately trained in ballet but not skilled enough to be a prima ballerina. She might have chosen an interesting stage name which suggested she had some mild knowledge of art or literature, and it might be entertaining to speak with her...

Trevain clamped the thought by the neck before it could gasp its first breath. He would not, absolutely would not, even *consider* speaking with such a young girl. He would not behave foolishly like the other older men who frequented this club and places like it. He was here for the sake of his crew's morale. He was not even a patron of this place, not in the traditional sense, not really. He would not sit with her, converse with her, and tentatively place his hand on her knee in desperation to touch her to be assured that she was real. He had just about as much business doing so as the disinterested droplets of condensation on his glass.

Why was it so quiet in the club all of a sudden? Several strange, hushed seconds of silence made Trevain wonder if he had been transported to a different venue. Was this the same rowdy, vulgar club that he despised? What was happening on the stage? An asymmetrical bead of water joined with its neighbors and slowly began its descent. Trevain put his finger on the glass, destroying the slow moving droplet and quickly tracing its path with his roughened skin.

I will not look. I will not look. He mentally chanted a mantra of encouragement to himself, trying to gain strength from watching the apathetic and asexual water droplets and participating in their gravity-induced activities. Carefully picking up the glass and bringing it close to his face, he could almost successfully pretend he was one of them. He clung to the glass in a strange suspension. Until the silence ended.

One massive, powerful voice filled the club—only overwhelming, bewitching soprano vocals, no music. There was no need for music, for the voice itself would have shamed a harpsichord. Trevain's first instinct was to close his eyes and let the voice wash over him, but he had been struggling so valiantly to do the opposite of what he most desired that he instead savagely lowered his glass to its coaster and turned his head toward the stage. He looked.

Later he would not be able to describe exactly what he saw, or how it affected him. A slender gracefully extended arm, an expression contorted with longing and yearning of the truest kind. Eyes flashing like lightning, lips parted with vulnerability.

The woman's feet moved across the floor with such ease and liquidity that he could have believed she was flying. Yet when they hit the ground after certain spins or jumps, he could hear the solid sound they made, even over the enchanting volume of the music. Those long, slender, girlish legs were deceiving in the strength and flexibility they possessed.

She danced power. Yet there were moments of such tenderness! She would pause, and hesitantly beseech the audience with a pleading look. It was heartbreakingly poignant—as though she were seeking wisdom to correct the error of her ways. Then she would suddenly be fierce, and her movements would be so sudden and quick and sure that he had to hold his breath to properly absorb her furious, vengeful sequences.

Absorb he did, and consumed he would have if it were possible.

Oddly enough, he recognized the first two of the songs she danced to. One was from the opera *Rusalka*, and another was from an opera called *Undina*, which must be her namesake. Trevain's mother had loved obscure pieces of opera, and on any given day in their household when he was growing up such songs could have been heard playing as Alice Murphy had gone about her housework.

He was startled as the woman on stage fell quite suddenly to a lowered position, and continued to dance from her knees. She was sometimes so still, stationary, and quiet, and then she would be explosive—she would be everywhere at once. Every single moment of her dance had him fully engaged, and he could not have looked away if he tried. He did not even realize that he was craning his neck for a better view.

When she gracefully lifted her dress to slowly remove her lace panties, Trevain was again surprised. She did it in a manner which was so relaxed that she could have been in her own bedroom, yet so careful that no skin was yet exposed. She was fulfilling the requirement of removing an article of clothing during the second song, he knew. However, the article she had chosen to remove showed nothing. As

8

she continued to dance without her panties, her skirt swirling around her thighs was suddenly tenfold as tantalizing.

He found himself staring at the glittering red fabric as it billowed in the breeze created by her motions. He found himself staring at her smooth tanned thighs, illuminated by the flashing lights, and hoping for a glimpse of more of her skin. He found his lips had become very dry, and he licked them to moisten them. Trevain thought he imagined for a moment that the woman, Undina, cast a smug and proud look in his direction, as though she knew how impatient he was to see more— as though she knew the effect she was having on him. She was far too young to exhibit such confidence. Also, there was no possible way she could have known the true extent of what her dance made him feel. It was beyond anyone's comprehension, including his own.

Before long—it certainly felt like an instant, the woman on stage was removing her dress. Trevain felt his heartbeat quicken, and almost thought he should look away. She was too young, too young for him to behold in the nude! Yet it was the nature of the establishment, and although the girl had perhaps taken refreshing liberties with her choice of music and her style of dance, she conformed to the basic rules of the job.

As the melody played, whimsical and feminine, Undina stood with her back toward the audience. She glanced back at the enrapt onlookers as she slowly, *achingly* slowly, slipped one scarlet strap of her dress off of her right shoulder. Her fingers were extended to emphasize the drama of the gesture. She smiled then, one of those carefree smiles of youth, and her once stormy eyes seemed to twinkle with mischief and delight. She did the same with her other shoulder, yet it was somehow different. The subtlest change in her expression seemed to change the mood from light and airy to somber and sultry.

She tossed her impossibly long dark hair to the front of her body and began sliding the crimson dress down her back. Trevain watched closely, drinking in each new inch of velvety tanned flesh that Undina exposed. Her skin was flawless as it hugged the sinews and contours of her back, and in the atmospheric lighting of the club, almost luminous. The contrast of her skin against the bold burgundy hue of the fabric was striking. She arranged her dress around her hips before slowly turning to face the audience. She crossed her arms over her chest in a display of modesty as she moved forward, gentle steps in time with the music.

Then her arms were gone, and her face was proud and bold as she bared her breasts—unbearably round and firm collections of flesh. As she moved back into her dance, using one hand to hold her dress around her hips, Trevain wondered at how impressively young her body was. He marveled at her athletic silhouette when she arched backwards with extended arms, and he marveled at how she seemed conscious of her motions to the perfectly extended tips of her fingers and pointed toes.

She danced not only shamelessly, but proudly when she was nude, and had cast the dress completely aside. Her motions were not as wild and powerful, but they were careful and precise. Her steps were so controlled and gentle that her breasts did not shake when she moved. She moved as though her limbs were cutting through a substance far more viscous than air—almost as if she were underwater.

She was dancing the nighttime. She had taken them through the course of a full day, through energetic mornings, brilliant noons, mellow evenings, and now it was the quiet, peaceful night. Or perhaps she was dancing the winter. Having already paid homage to the midnight sun, she now saluted the midday moon.

Then it was over, as solemnly as it had begun. Undina stood completely nude, with a hauntingly serene and satisfied expression on her face.

The crowd erupted in applause, in thundering, most appreciative applause. Undina inclined her head in polite acknowledgement. In the midst of the loud clapping and cheering, she looked up at the audience, and her eyes met with Trevain's. She gazed at him, and he gazed back at her, enraptured. Their eyes were locked for a moment in a quiet, private intensity. As the music and applause subsided, her expression darkened once more and her eyes lowered. She quickly gathered the garments she had disposed of, and in an instant she had disappeared backstage.

Trevain used his tongue to moisten his dry mouth. He exhaled. He mused at how shaken and affected he was. *It was a work of art,* he told himself. *It was just as if I had entered any museum and observed... some work of art.*

He felt emotionally drained. Grasping his beer once more, he brought it to his lips and poured the remaining contents down his throat. As he lowered it to the table, he noticed a particularly large droplet sliding down the glass. A tear.

He moved his hand to his eyelashes to scrape away any others that threatened to fall. *One tear is acceptable,* Trevain reasoned, *considering that a man just lost his life. One tear is acceptable.*

He knew quite well that Leander had not crossed his mind for what must have been over fourteen minutes and forty-six seconds.

*   *   *

Her cheek grazed her knee as she waited backstage, doing simple stretches. A woman with large fake breasts tottered by shakily on towering heels, sending her a suspicious glare. Aazuria was stricken by the disproportionate size of the woman's breasts with respect to the rest of her emaciated body; she remembered something her personal doctor had told her about new procedures which augmented certain physical attributes. It was fascinating, but not really of much significance to her, and she returned to pressing her forehead flush against her leg.

The carpet under her bare legs was rough and abrasive. She imagined that it was already leaving ugly scratches on her newly-tanned skin. As she straightened slowly from the stretch, she stared at the unfamiliar color of her knee. She missed being underwater. More women strolled by, sending her more distrustful and disdainful looks. Aazuria sighed to herself, and continued to pull her muscles taut. She focused on the comforting ache in her tendons as she tried to bury her homesickness and override the upsetting images from her recent past which flashed just behind her eyes.

A redheaded woman burst into the room, strutting buoyantly on her six-inch pumps as if they were springs. Her whole body was finely toned and her height was intimidating; at six feet tall she towered over the other women in the room who barely came up to her chin. Her pleasant laughter rang out loudly in the dressing room.

"For Sedna's sake! Zuri, you really don't need to stretch. Don't bother giving this any effort! It's supposed to be a low-class, inferior form of entertainment." The redhead turned to the women who had been watching Aazuria with airs of superiority and glared at them. She flung her hand towards the exit as she barked an order, "Skedaddle, bitches."

The women quickly complied. Aazuria smiled up gratefully at her protectress. "It is not worth doing unless it is done properly, Visola."

"Then show me how it's done, Princess," Visola said with a wink. "Just be careful not to overexert yourself. Those lovely legs of yours aren't used to these ghetto conditions."

"Are you referring to the club or the land?" Aazuria asked as used a knuckle to knead her thigh.

"Both. I'll be watching."

"You have always been watching," Aazuria said fondly. She heard the first few notes of her song begin, and she rose to her feet nervously. She took a deep breath, feeling the unfamiliar air fill her lungs—it felt extraordinarily empty. The muffled voice of the DJ filtered backstage:

"Now gentlemen, get ready to be blown away by our mysterious newcomer. She's the girl you've always dreamed of, but never thought you'd actually meet in the flesh: Undina!"

Visola smiled. "Not a bad introduction. Why did you choose to use your mother's name?"

"It was the first thing that came to mind when they asked." Giving her friend a gentle shrug, Aazuria glanced at the exit with foreboding. "Well, here I go."

"Break a le—"

"I would much rather not." When she pushed past the beaded curtains, Aazuria immediately felt the vibrations of music seeping into her bones. Her fingers twitched with the desire to move before she had permitted them to do so, and she exercised discipline to quell them. *To do this correctly means moving precisely when the music commands me to—I will not waste a single motion.* Her eyes were downcast as she ascended the stairs, feeling a strange sense of simultaneous nervousness and excitement. She had always been confident in her dancing technique—she had studied various styles on various continents, and she had practiced for hundreds of years. She usually trained in water, and it was far more difficult to dance in water than it was on land. By all accounts, this should be a cinch.

The familiar vocals began, and Aazuria finally surrendered to the yearning of her limbs and plunged them into motion. A burst of energy began in her chest, and visibly traveled throughout her every cell. Indescribable sensations of loveliness washed over her, as they always did when she began dancing, reaching her lips to settle there in a subtle curve of pleasure. Once she had expertly commenced her art, she turned to gauge the reaction of her onlookers.

The audience was a sea of eyes. Adoring eyes of those seeking something from her dance which she would never be able to give them. They were seeking the things which they did not really need. They sought sex and excitement or momentary stimulation, but her every gesture and expression, her every step, was dancing in homage to something transcendent and everlasting.

Slowly, the audience was pulled out of the realm of their own expectations and into the realm of her creation. Yes, she could hold them spellbound with a little help from the haunting sound of her sister's recorded voice. Aazuria was strong enough to guide them all— she had always been in a position of leadership, and this was no different. She created the atmosphere; she poured her personality and her principles into it, and she invited them inside for a moment to glimpse the décor of her soul. She felt like she was challenging their roughness with her grace, and ultimately, she was winning. She was overpowering them.

She spun, and spun, until she felt windborne. There was an impossible fire within her which seemed to radiate forth from her center. All of the elements coalesced in her emotions, and as always, she felt far greater than herself when she danced. Aazuria felt a memory of her father's face return to her, but she flung her head to the side, casting it away from her thoughts before it could cause her harm or interrupt the flow of her kinetic thrill.

There might be other moments of her life when she was twisted into various uncomfortable shapes by exterior forces, but for now, at least, she was in complete control. The stage was hers, the audience was hers, and time was hers. She could bend it and make the moment last an instant or a lifetime, depending on her whim. She could manipulate all of their hearts like putty, just as long as she kept moving—and as long as the poignant music played, she had no intention of stopping. Each moment was a crescendo, overpowering the last.

She revelled in this complete control until *he* looked up from his drink. Aazuria paused for a millisecond, nearly missing a beat. She felt shame at what had almost been a misstep, but certain that no one had noticed. Turning her gaze away, she tried to focus on the perfection of her lines. But she could feel that the dramatic expression on her face had lost some of its conviction, having been replaced by curiosity. She hoped that the flaws in her dance were imperceptible.

Aazuria did not mean to make eye contact again, but she could feel the force of his scrutiny like a warm stream gushing toward her. Even from a distance, she could discern a hue of sadness in somehow familiar jade irises. In the midst of this strange new environment, and this even stranger establishment, something shone in that expression which she felt she knew. She was suddenly safe in the comfort of a warm lagoon as she beheld the unmistakable intelligence glinting at her from across the room.

She had to remind herself to keep moving—for her hand had paused without her consent for a fraction of a second. The eyes had seemed to notice even that tiny hesitation, for they flitted to her fingers vigilantly before returning to her face. What did it mean? Admiration? Loneliness? Loss? Her chest constricted as she tried to explain the connection—the man's contemplation hit her like a tidal wave and nearly knocked her off balance. All she could do was hang on for dear life, as she pushed her body onto automatic mode. At the same time that she moved thoughtlessly, she was doubly conscious of her postures. She tried a little harder because she knew that there was at least one person in the room who could distinguish the quality of her execution.

The rest of her dance flew by in a blur that she could barely remember. Her heart was beating unusually quickly under the keen inspection. Every moment she could justifiably spare was spent glancing at the sharp gleam unnaturally present in those olive green eyes. The person they belonged to was the furthest away from her, concealed in an extremely dark-lit corner. Luckily, her vision, especially in the dark, was better than most. There were dozens of men, probably handsome young admirers, clustered around the stage; she was not sure why her attention was held rapt by this distant, intense gaze.

As the world churned about her in a mess of sea foam, those green eyes were a solid island. How sweetly they shone, and how firmly they were grounded. She could not resist being drawn to them as a windswept ship eagerly seeks a harbor. She could not resist the immediate intimacy that was provoked in her chest, completely unbidden and unanticipated.

When she had finished her dance and retreated backstage, she stood naked against a wall, trying to calm her racing heart. She sucked in gulp after gulp of the air which no longer felt empty. Each breath was laced with electricity. A surge fizzled through her scalp and neck, and she reached up to touch her skin soothingly. Underneath her fingers, her skin still tingled with triumph. The audience had loved her; she had sensed it. She felt strangely affirmed by this—she was by no means a young woman anymore, despite her smooth skin and physical appearance.

But that man! She closed her eyes as she leaned her head back against the wall, remembering his gaze. Imagining that she might never again feel such an intent and private gaze, she tried to commit the feeling to memory.

"How was it?" came a soft voice from the shadows. It was Visola, of course. The red-haired warrior woman never strayed far from Aazuria's side.

"Oh, Viso," she said, her chest heaving with exhilarated breaths. "It was divine. There was a man…"

"There were many men, darling."

"Yes, but this one… I saw the sea in his eyes."

Visola released an incredulous grunt before scowling. "Princess Aazuria! I have never known you to spew such a load of romantic whaleshit."

"I am not being romantic, General! You know that I have a knack for judging people." Aazuria had straightened her posture in order to defend herself. "There was a unique quality—something that I have never seen before, and yet it was familiar..."

Visola reached out and grabbed Aazuria's naked shoulders. She gave her a violent shake. "Listen to me. I know that home is a distasteful memory you want to escape right now, but you can't deceive yourself with fantasies about this place. This is a cruel, disgusting world. The atmosphere isn't the only thing you need to get acclimatized to—it's the people. You must stay on guard."

"I have lived among land-dwellers before," Aazuria argued, reaching up to remove Visola's hands from her shoulders. "I know how to interact with them."

"Things have changed in the last hundred years that we've been cooped up in Adlivun. Culture, technology, weaponry…" Visola was speaking in a low voice, but when a dancer walked by with a heavily painted face, she relaxed and hit Aazuria in the arm. "You should go talk to this guy! And for Sedna's sake, try to smile a little. You look like someone died."

"Someone did die."

Visola waved her hand casually. "That's irrelevant. We're here to collect copious amounts of this nation's currency with minimal interaction. We make our money and get out." Visola's voice was stern, and she raised a finger to add emphasis to her next words. "You cannot get attached to these land dwellers, Princess. We have a mission to complete."

"I have no intention of veering away from your directions," Aazuria said with a nod. "You are the strategist. By the way—where is Sionna?"

"Around here somewhere," Visola said with a shrug. "Off making tons of cash, no doubt. She keeps trying to convince me that we should purchase medical equipment instead of firearms. That's my sister and her screwed-up priorities for ya! I tried to tell her that if we have a good offense we won't need... hey, Zuri?" Visola paused, studying her friend. She noticed that her friend was idly fingering the back of her neck and glancing toward the beaded curtain. "I've never seen you so distracted. What did this man of yours look like?"

Aazuria stared at the redhead blankly. She tried to picture his face and frowned when her mind faltered. She could not remember a single attribute of the man—not the color of his skin, his hair, his clothing, or even his height and build. Nothing came to mind. But burned into her memory was his peculiar pair of emerald eyes, and the odd feeling which they had stirred in her breast.

"I do not know," she said in confusion. "He was interesting."

"Interesting!" Visola barked as she recoiled. "Darling, 'interesting' is tantamount to 'deadly.'"

Aazuria smiled at her friend. "Just because you married a demon..."

Visola stiffened at the mention of her husband. "I know. Not all men are mass-murdering monsters—just the ones I like. Come to think of it, I don't even know what type of fella you like. You've always been so disciplined. I haven't seen you display interest in someone since 1910."

Aazuria shook her head. "The Rusalka prince? That was diplomacy, not romance. I was being cordial for the sake of the alliance."

"Good. If you can be polite to the Russian sea-dwellers for our country, maybe you can be friendly to American fisherman." Visola grinned and reached under her skirt, revealing a giant knife. "I've got your back. Go out there and have fun! I can't wait to see what this guy looks like—he must be a total hunk if he managed to get your attention."

"Perhaps," Aazuria said with a frown. It still bothered her that she did not remember what the green-eyed man looked like. She could recall the general area where he had been sitting, but it was possible that he had already left the club. If he had moved to another location, she might not even recognize him. "He could be hideous," she mused.

"Well, go find out," Visola encouraged, nudging Aazuria playfully. "Remember, the most important part of a man's appearance is the girth of his…"

"Visola!"

"…wallet."

Chapter 3: Wealth of Emotion

As the hours slowly ticked by, Trevain found himself lost in drink and observation. He had switched over to brandy after watching the dance of the woman called Undina. He could not help but notice when she re-emerged from backstage and seated herself in an isolated corner of the club. In order to quell his natural desire to go over and speak with her, he had taken to carefully monitoring the way his crew members were interacting with the various women in the club.

The captain's younger brother, Callder Murphy, had already guzzled down far too much beer. He was puffing out his chest and doubtlessly boasting of grand, falsified exploits to the girls who flocked around him. Even watching his body language from across the room made Trevain exhausted. He was fairly certain that his brother would convince one of those girls to accompany him home at the end of the night. To Trevain's home, anyway, where Callder parasitically stayed.

Rolling his eyes at Callder's behavior, he sent a fleeting curious glance in Undina's direction before turning back to his men.

His eyes settled on his young protégé, Arnav Hylas. The boy was a college student from New York who had grown tired of the burden of his sky-rocketing debt. He had researched the position in which he could make the most money possible in a few short months, and here he was, giving it his best shot. Trevain felt protective of the boy. For all his cosmopolitan cleverness, he still had a youthful recklessness about him which was hazardous in a place like this. Trevain wondered, as he watched a blonde seat herself on Arnav's lap and whisper in his ear, whether the young man really understood the danger he was facing. Not from the blonde, who was only a danger to Arnav's heart and bank account, but from the job.

Arnav had not actually seen Leander die. Neither had he seen the man's body—they had not been able to recover it. Perhaps a gruesome, visually violent death would have been healthier for the boy's deficient sense of caution. Then again, most young men carried themselves about with an aura of immortality and invincibility. Trevain wondered why he had never felt that way himself.

He discreetly looked over at Undina's corner once more. Trevain felt an inexplicable pang of jealousy when he saw a man approaching her, and an even more peculiar pang of pride when he observed her crossed arms and reproachful body language.

He turned back, casting his gaze on Ujarak—the brawny man of Inuit descent who was always chomping on something. A cigar, a toothpick, a pen, a piece of rope. He was sitting with Edwin, the Canadian, and the sentimental ex-marine Doughlas. For a supposed war hero and someone who was self-proclaimed to have "seen it all," Doughlas was not taking the situation well. He was essentially sobbing as Edwin and Ujarak consoled him.

Not far from those three sat the brothers from Seattle—Wyatt and Wilbert Wade. For being such very different people, the Wade brothers were fiercely loyal and devoted to each other, and they got along far better than Captain Murphy and his own brother. Wilbert, called "Billy" by the crew, was somewhat effeminate. He was never the butt of any jokes or teasing, for Wyatt was extremely defensive and always joyously ready for an excuse to deploy his fists. Trevain could not resist a small smile as he observed Billy interacting with a pretty dancer. He was doubtlessly complimenting her clothing and sense of style and confusing the poor girl.

Again, the captain looked over at Undina. A gorgeous redhead passed close by her, being pulled to the private dancing area by a young man. The redhead looked at the seated dark-haired woman, and quickly made a complex hand gesture as she passed her. Undina responded with a hand gesture of her own. Trevain frowned thoughtfully. American Sign Language? Could one of the girls be deaf or mute?

He was positive that Undina could not be deaf—at least not completely. She had danced too perfectly to the time of the music to be unable to hear it. Yet it was possible that she was mute. He had not once seen her lips move in speech; those sensuous, reddened lips, which contrasted sharply with her impressive mass of dark hair. Undina's head turned towards him sharply, as though she could feel his inquest. Her dark eyes locked with his hesitantly, and he looked away in embarrassment and dismay.

Trevain began to scan over the activities of his men once more. After a few minutes of this, he began feeling a bit like a hovering father. He knew that his tendency to be overprotective had been amplified by Leander's death. He tried to tell himself that he was not at the club to supervise a daycare, and that the men were all adults who could take care of themselves. None of them would fall into any kind of jeopardy if he looked away for more than a few seconds. But he did not look away.

Only one of the living members of the crew was missing from the club. Trevain sighed and took a swill of his brandy, thinking of their only female shipmate, Brynne. She had taken the weekend off work to attend a family member's wedding in Florida. While many crews still archaically maintained that a woman on the ship was bad luck, Trevain felt the opposite—if the woman was tough enough she could help to keep the men in line better than his authority alone ever could. Now, his superstition was confirmed, and he already dreaded having to tell Brynne about Leander's demise. She would be furious.

It occurred to Trevain, as his eyes wandered over the crowd, that it was a certain specific type of person that was drawn to a place like this. Some of the folks, like himself, had the misfortune of having been born and raised in Alaska, but the majority of the crowd, especially during the fishing season, was not local. Both the men and the women, the patrons and the dancers, probably had pasts which were darkened by financial difficulties. Something awful had happened to many of them, or they had somehow been pushed to the realization that they needed to make a drastic change and take drastic action. They had somehow decided that fast money was worth very high risk or high levels of discomfort. Then, once they had ventured into the world of large gains and large losses, they had been unable to turn around and return to wherever they hailed from.

They were the same type of people who frequented casinos. The same type of people who drove their cars a little too fast for the sensation it gave them. The same type of people who experimented with substances which allowed them to step outside of themselves for a moment. The same type of people who did not file their income taxes. The same type of people who ventured to Alaska to fish for king crabs.

Everywhere he looked he could neatly categorize the humans into little mental file folders for future reference. He could easily place them above captions and under subheadings; except for that girl, Undina. She struck him as tremendously different and out of place. Even from his infrequent, uncertain glances at her, he had gauged that she did not have the air of desperation that most of the females in the place exuded. After her dance, she had found a quiet place to sit which strategically overlooked most of the club, and she seemed to be observing people and their interactions just as much as he was.

He felt inexplicably drawn to her. He felt kindred to her in that they were both withdrawn onlookers, not active, wild participants in the madness of the establishment. He wanted to go to her, but her perfect young body repulsed him. Perhaps he could relate to her in certain ways, but his age was a greater disability than even his physical impairment. The combination of the two tarnished any feeble chance he had of being remotely attractive to a young girl.

He knew that she would take one look at his grey hair and his limp and her smile would disappear in disappointment. That extraordinary dancer deserved an energetic young man like Arnav.

"Captain Murphy!" a voice bellowed. Trevain looked for its source, and saw Arnav holding up a bottle of beer in each hand as he slurred his speech, "Captain, come party with us!"

Trevain shook his head and held up his hand to politely decline the offer.

"Why's my big brother alone?" Callder shouted, leaping up from his seated position and swaying slightly on his feet. "Don't sit there in the corner all gloomy, Trevain. You gotta have some fun tonight!"

"Yeah, let's hear it for the captain!" shouted Edwin, the Canadian. The men all cheered and drank from whatever glasses were close at hand. Trevain couldn't help but notice that some of the men had picked up their neighbor's glass instead of their own. He had nightmarish visions of having to carpool the men home to their various locations and drag them all in to their beds. He imagined having to tuck them in and listen to their crying about Leander.

This is sometimes like running a preschool, he thought to himself in mild amusement, *but I suppose they're all just miserable and scared under their drunken party-animal disguises. I guess it won't hurt me to play governess to the kiddies in the nursery for one night.*

"Big brother! Come over here and have a drink with this pretty girl!" Callder shouted as he stumbled over furniture while navigating the room.

Trevain cursed softly, feeling a sickening feeling in his stomach as his head snapped around to witness his brother approaching Undina.

Of course. Why? Of all the women here? When Callder began trying to wrestle Undina out of her chair, Trevain leapt to his feet and crossed the room in as few strides as possible. He firmly wedged himself between his brother and the dark-haired woman, and glared at the younger man sternly.

"Callder, relax!" He forced his brother into a nearby chair and pinned him to it. "Sit here and try to calm down, okay?" Trevain turned to Undina in embarrassment and began to apologize when Callder cut him off.

"I saw you looking at her," Callder accused. "You're not a complete fucking robot, even though you pretend to be! I just thought you should meet her. I know you like her. Since you wouldn't get off your ass I was going to bring her to you."

Trevain shook his head and exhaled. "Callder, you're out of line…"

"No!" he hissed, leaning forward and staring past Trevain at the girl. "Look. Undina, that's your name right? Undina?"

She lifted an eyebrow and gave the slightest of nods.

"Okay. Undina," Callder tried to straighten his sloppy posture and gesture toward Trevain. "This is my brother: Captain Trevain Murphy. As you can see, he and I don't really get along. It's not because we don't love each other. It's because he's, like, some big-shot crab fishing tycoon, and I'm just his stupid kid brother who gambles away every penny that he pays me."

"Callder," Trevain said in warning, but the drunk man continued ranting.

"But you gotta meet him, Undina. He's, like, the richest man around for hundreds of miles, probably. He's a good guy, really, I promise," Callder emphasized this point by throwing his arm around Trevain in a lopsided, meager attempt at a hug. Trevain pressed his palm to his forehead as his brother continued on boasting proudly. "He worked as a deckhand when he was just a kid, like forever ago. He's been in charge of a boat since he was a teenager. You can do the math: now he's like… a millionaire, and a couple centuries old or something."

"Oh?" the dark haired beauty remarked with a shy smile, glancing at Trevain. "How many centuries?"

It was the first time she had spoken. So, she was able to speak.

"Lots. Like two or three," Callder boasted, "he's ancient."

"Hardly," she responded. "You could live on this earth for a millennium and still be surprised on a daily basis."

When her lips opened to allow the phonemes to travel forth, they emerged with a slight accent Trevain could not place. His brow creased slightly, and he found himself leaning forward to better hear her lilting syllables over the unpleasant thundering of noise which was considered music.

But Callder had already begun ranting again, obviously enjoying the sound of his own gruff voice. "Trevain is so wise and amazing. He never makes mistakes, ever." Callder was gesturing at the older man wildly as tears gathered in his eyes. "That's just my big brother. Just the way he is! He should hate me for what a screw up I am, but he doesn't. You wanna know how I know that?"

"Hush now, Callder," Trevain said, trying to pull the man away from Undina, "quit bothering the girl."

Callder shrugged his brother off and leaned closer to the dark-haired woman, speaking in a conspiratorial tone, "He doesn't fire me. He keeps me around so that he can watch over me and make sure that I'm safe. He continues to pay me a salary. He's always looked out for me like that, even though I'm a shitty sailor. I'm pretty much useless on the *Magician*, and I waste all of the money he pays me. Do you want to know what I'm good for? I scrape ice off stuff. That's glamorous, isn't it?"

"Quite glamorous," she answered with the friendly smile one would give to a stranger's adorable infant. Trevain frowned and wondered how she could possibly find Callder's lewd behavior charming.

"But you know the worst part?" Callder moaned. "I failed my brother. I totally screwed him over this time. Because if I wasn't such a deadbeat, and I paid any attention to what was going on around me, Leander would still be alive and drinking with us now. He used to drink gin and tonic. The stuff tastes *terrible*, but at least he'd be alive to drink it. It's my fault that he drowned, because I'm such a fucking loser…"

Callder had excited himself into a torrent of tears, and Trevain looked on in silent sadness at his emotional display. The woman called Undina seemed troubled at the knowledge that someone had drowned.

"I killed Leo. I killed him with my laziness!" Callder sobbed, smashing his fist down onto the table. His shoulders began to shake.

"My own brother can't even enjoy himself in a strip club, and it's all because of me. I ruined everything."

Callder suddenly slumped into his chair. It was a moment before they realized that he had only gone quiet because he had passed out.

"Thank God that's finally over," Trevain murmured, rubbing his temples. "What a fool."

"He may be weak of heart," Undina noted, "but he has great respect for you. He seeks your approval."

"Well, he'll never have it if he keeps drinking himself into oblivion!" Trevain said sharply. He turned to Undina, shaking his head wretchedly. "I'm so sorry you had to deal with this tonight…"

"Do not apologize," she answered softly. "He was so honest and exposed. He was temporarily ignited with such a wealth of emotion. It was refreshing."

Trevain looked at her curiously, and then back at his collapsed brother. "He was just being a drunken idiot."

She nodded staring directly at Trevain. "I can see that. Nevertheless, I appreciate that he was thoughtful enough to introduce us, however clumsy his methods may have been."

"Undina," Trevain began, testing the sound of the name which was obviously false. He was intrigued and pleasantly surprised by her personality, and wished to engage her further. A thousand sentences threatened to spill off the tip of his tongue, and tumble forth toward this young woman warmly. He just wanted to speak to her—he just wanted to continue to hear her carefully woven words, curled up in her rich accent. Yet he knew he could not. He cleared his throat. "I'm sorry about this again. I'll take him away and I promise he won't bother you anymore."

As Trevain moved to pull his brother out of the chair in which he had collapsed, the woman called Undina gently touched his sleeve near his elbow. Although her hand had not even grazed his skin, he was startled by the intimacy and felt his whole body grow tense.

"Please," she said quietly. "You and I have been sitting alone all night. Life has been happening all around us. I would like to partake of it. Would you please sit with me for a little while?"

He stared at her, searching for any sign of humor. She did not seem as put off by his grey hair and his limp as he had thought she would be. On the contrary, she seemed to hardly notice.

"I have two younger sisters as well," she was saying with a ghost of a smile on her lips, "perhaps I could tell you about them."

Against his better judgment, Trevain found himself using his foot to slide his snoring brother a few feet away before seating himself closer to Undina. He could not believe she had invited him to chat. A smile threatened to reveal his gladness, but he counseled it to desist.

"I enjoyed your dance so much. More than I can tell you," Trevain admitted to her.

She looked at him appreciatively and nodded. "Thank you. It is so invigorating to dance for an audience."

"Where are you from?" he asked her.

Her eyes widened slightly in surprise at his direction of questioning. "Not far from here," she answered. Then in a low voice which he imagined she thought he could not hear, she added, "But also quite far from here."

In fact, he could not hear those last few words, but luckily he had a knack for reading lips. "I see," he answered, "are you from Canada?"

She raised an eyebrow, hesitating before casting her eyes downward, "Uh, something like that. How did you guess?"

"You have a slight accent," he said. "I can't quite determine what it is, but… never mind. So, what brings you to these parts?"

Her slender shoulders rose in a carefree shrug and her eyes lit up as she smiled. "I have chosen to follow the waves and see where they take me."

"Well, they've taken you to a strip club in Soldotna, Alaska," he said, leaning forward. He studied the curve of her cheek and chin, and returned his gaze to her compelling dark eyes. They were hypnotizing at close range. "Those waves may be mighty but they don't have magic in them, child. You need to master them and choose where it is you want to be."

She looked up at him harshly. There was a flash of anger in her murky irises as she answered, "I think you and I must be acquainted with very different waves."

"How is that?" he asked.

"The ones I know do have magic and cannot be mastered." Her serious expression disappeared and her smile returned. "Anyway, I do not think you should be calling me 'child' since we already established that I am older than you."

"I'll be fifty next year," he admitted in a crestfallen voice. "What are you, eighteen?"

"Six hundred and three," she answered, wrapping a strand of her dark hair around her finger. There was something whimsical about the way she moved.

"I see that you're protective of your personal information," he observed. "That is very wise in a place like this. I didn't mean to offend you, but compared with me, you are really but a child, Undina."

She closed her eyes for a moment. "I may seem young, Captain Trevain Murphy, but my life has been very difficult. I have experienced a lot of hardship and I do not feel like a child."

While her eyes were closed, he used the opportunity to drink in the oval shape of her face, allowing every precise word she spoke to register in his mind. Her eyes opened and she looked out across the room at the silhouette of a tall redhead.

She turned back to him and gripped the arms of her chair abruptly as she pushed herself into a standing position. "It was a pleasure to meet you, Trevain, but I should probably go."

He nodded, feeling his stomach sink. He knew that he would scare her away. He half wished that his brother had not initiated the irrational introduction to begin with; he should not have ever spoken to her. Trevain had never been a very sociable person since he spent most of his time buried in his work. He did not possess any friends who were not paid employees, and his only family was Callder, who was also a paid employee. Every interaction in his life centered on his financial arrangements, and he only knew how to speak to someone when their livelihood depended on their cooperation with him.

The woman called Undina had stepped around the table, and was moving past him to surely disappear from his life forever. This thought made him reach out to gently catch her wrist within his hand. He marveled at the feel of her tiny bones as his longest finger and thumb overlapped each other. She had paused in her departure, awaiting his words.

He hesitated, deciding what he should say to her. They could be the last words he ever spoke to her, and they were important. Since Leander had disappeared, Trevain's mind had been filled with all manner of darkness. His thoughts had been chaotic and racing as logic and emotion waged a painful and confusing battle over trying to make sense of a man's unnecessary death. However, since he laid eyes on Undina, his mind had felt clear, purified, and temporarily relieved of strain. She had filled every aching corner of his soul with the tenderness and strength of her dance. He would do anything to hang on to that feeling. Her mysterious nature occupied every spare effort of his mind as he tried and failed to make sense of her.

He opened his mouth, intending to apologize, or perhaps compliment her—anything that he could think of to make her stay a moment longer without sounding too desperate. He believed he should say something so profound that it would leave an impression on her, and inspire her in some way, since he would never see her again.

Instead, the words that left his mouth inquired, "Would you please dance for me in private, Undina?"

Chapter 4: Witness Her Being

They sat together in the private booth. It was not completely closed off from the rest of the club's VIP area, but a beaded curtain over the only exit gave a sense of privacy to the small room. The dark-haired woman glanced up apprehensively whenever someone walked by the curtain, almost as if she was expecting to be attacked at any moment. The tall redhead that Trevain had noticed earlier was lingering not far away.

Trevain was wondering why he had thought to purchase private dances. He had not asked a girl to dance for him in close to thirty years. The initial experience had been a rather boring and expensive one that he had chosen not to repeat. Now, he knew that he would have done just about anything to secure a few more moments of being close to the woman called Undina. Yet another one of his relationships was now dependent on money, but he was more comfortable that way. Trevain felt it was worth having the security that she would not leave— he gained something from their interaction that he could not place a price tag upon. He just needed to sit with her and witness her being. The reassurance of her existence somehow swelled his courage.

"Would you like me to begin?" she asked softly. The section of the club that they had moved to was much quieter, and Trevain could hear every nuance of her enigmatic accent. He could have sworn that he had heard similar pronunciation before, although he could not determine where. It did not sound Canadian.

"You don't have to actually dance for me," he said, lifting his hands as he explained. "I would prefer if we just talked. Is that okay with you?"

There was skepticism in her shadowy eyes. "I would love that, but I should probably return to work." She glanced up at the curtain, as if considering leaving. There was a look of purpose on her face.

Trevain reached into his jacket for his wallet. Unfolding the creased leather with his work-roughened fingers, the captain deftly counted out some bills and extracted them. He handed them over to her with a smile. "A thousand dollars for the pleasure of your company. A thousand dollars if you'll sit with me and tell me about yourself and your life until the end of the night."

She stared at the money, and then back at his face hesitantly. "Trevain, I am not sure…"

"Please," he said, grasping her hand and pushing the folded bills against her palm. He closed her fingers around the bills and held her small hand in his larger ones. "I don't get a chance to talk to someone with a brain very often. You've seen the morons I work with! I feel like a good conversation with you could be really rejuvenating."

She smiled at him weakly, and gave him a gentle nod. "Thank you," she whispered, "this is so kind of you."

"Nonsense," he said, gesturing back to the main area of the club where his brother was being taken care of by the other deplorably drunk sailors, "Callder boasted about my finances enough for you to know that I am quite comfortable. These aren't my last pennies, dear. I want to know more about you."

As he spoke, she observed a twinkle of mirth in his eye. It pleased her enough to feel comfortable in accepting his gift and opening up to him.

"I will tell you as much as I can," she conceded, graciously tucking the money into her purse. She glanced up through the beaded curtain where a swift flash of wild red hair was visible. She turned back to Trevain, and seemed to force herself to relax, making an effort to smile. "I must admit that I am not sure why you are so curious about me. Your life must be far more interesting than mine."

"I would like to know why a talented young woman like you is dancing in a strip club in Soldotna."

She flinched, but instantly recovered herself and nodded. "For the most part, I am here to learn about people and the world. I have lived an unusually restricted life, caged up for far too long."

Trevain mused over her words. He stared down at her long, slender fingers which rested lightly on her thigh. While he wanted to learn about her, he did not want to press too far or make her uncomfortable. He decided to prompt her with an open ended and vague question. "Caged?"

"Yes." The woman called Undina looked up at him with a guarded expression on her face. She could see that he wanted to know

29

more, and she did not want to disappoint him. She struggled to speak the difficult words. "He kept me imprisoned for a very long time, along with my two sisters. I had no connection to the outside world for many years, and I lost track of time."

"Your father?" he inquired, prompting her again.

"Yes." She lifted her hand to her neck, rubbing her throat nervously. "My father was the sort of man who made fairytale villains look like gentlemen. Very powerful and very overprotective. He was a man of the sea, much like you are… but he was not kind. He was commanding and everything *had* to go his way. I have been well educated and have many skills, but until recently, I have had zero practical application for them." Her expression darkened and her tone grew harsh. "If my father was successful, I would never have seen any portion of the world again. I would never have felt the midnight sun tanning my skin."

"So this is an act of rebellion against him?"

She grimaced. "No. No. My father is dead now. This is my first very small, rather silly act of freedom."

The captain shook his head, beginning to understand. "I'm sorry for your loss. My dad died when I was very young too."

"How old were you?" she asked him gently.

"Seventeen. My father was the captain of the original *Fishin' Magician*. When he was killed in a senseless accident, I took over. I vowed I would never let another sailor die on my boat." Trevain gritted his teeth. "And I didn't… until two days ago."

She placed her palm against his cheek. "Do not blame yourself. The sea takes lives callously."

He seemed surprised by the touch of her soft hand against his face. He immediately felt self-conscious and wondered when last he had shaved his face. He was sure that his stubble felt rough and prickly against her delicate skin. He cleared his throat, in discomfort at her attentive affection. He did not know how to respond. "Anyway, my dad died a very long time ago," Trevain said. "Your loss is much fresher, and I should be comforting you, not the other way around!"

"No," she responded, withdrawing her hand and clenching it into a small fist. She shook her head fiercely. "It sounds like your father was a good man that you regretted losing. I cannot say the same for mine. What about your mother—is she well?"

Trevain stiffened slightly and stared at the pattern on the tacky wallpaper before giving a small shrug. "I hardly know, to be honest. She was committed to a psychiatric hospital when I was twelve. I used to visit her frequently, but as I grew older and her health deteriorated, I began to visit less and less. It's hard to see her falling apart the way she is."

"My sympathies are with you," the woman said in a low and gentle tone. Her voice sounded like it was made of wind. "Your youth must have been difficult."

"It was harder on Callder than it was for me," Trevain said, gesturing to the main area of the club. "That's why he is the way he is. I couldn't take care of him as well as our parents would have been able to."

She smiled. "I think you did a great job. Forgive me if this is too familiar; I hardly know you, but I believe Callder could not have asked for a kinder or more capable big brother."

The compliment moved him. He felt suddenly embarrassed to be revealing so much of his life, and he felt the need to distract himself. She was sitting very near to him, and he felt the desire to touch her dark hair. Pretending to have an excuse, he gently reached out to tuck a few strands behind her ear. He marveled at the silken texture; even her hair seemed too velvety and luminous to be real. Of course, he had not touched a woman's hair in as long as he could remember, so perhaps there was nothing special about the texture. She seemed surprised at the boldness of his touch, but not offended. As his fingers brushed her ear, he felt himself swallow.

"Undina," said the captain quietly, "I also hardly know you, but I think there are much better things that you can do with your newfound freedom than *this*."

She bit her lip and gave him a hard look before responding. "I have two younger sisters who are now under my care. I am sure you understand this. I want to do the very best I possibly can for them, and I want to be able to keep them safe from future harm."

"I'm sorry," Trevain said. His fingers ached to reach out and touch her again, but he could not find a good excuse. He did not want her to be upset with him. "I don't know your situation."

She nodded in acknowledgement, giving him a small smile. "There are many positive aspects to this job. I have to look at it that way. It is a way to learn about the world. It is a way to meet interesting men like yourself, and a way to interact with other human beings. It may not be the best way, but I am just grateful to be free to make my own choices and live my life… even if I choose poorly."

"I understand," Trevain answered thoughtfully. He surrendered to the urge to touch her shoulder. Resting his elbow on the back of the sat behind them, he brushed his thumb lightly over her collarbone. Her skin was so thin there; as thin as silk or gauze.

"The world is so large," she murmured, enjoying his caress. "There is so much land, so much sea. I have been yearning to experience life for the longest time."

"Life is a good thing," he answered. As he gazed down at her half-lidded eyes and somehow melancholy smile, Trevain was overcome with the urge to kiss her. His self-control was weakened by the moisture of brandy and beer, and his torso seemed to be inching forward without his permission. He was a few inches away from her lips when he was suddenly distracted by movement on the other side of the beaded curtain. A redhead's piercing green eyes sent him a wary look of appraisal. He was startled by the distrustful look in that fierce face. The fiery glare quickly disappeared, but not before it had instantly reacquainted him with reality. The redhead's eyes had a strange quality about them, gleaming almost in the way a cat's eyes did in the dark.

He pulled away from the girl that he had been intending to kiss a moment before. Trevain inwardly cursed himself. Undina's manner of speech had made him feel more comfortable with her than he could have imagined. He had forgotten to remind himself of how young she was, and what a lecher he would be if he made any sort of advance on her. Although he did not *feel* much older than she was, and he did not *feel* like she was mentally or physically juvenile in any way, he had to remind himself of his age. He chastised himself for nearly crossing his personal boundaries of courteous conduct.

"That redhead; she's a friend of yours?" Trevain asked, clearing his throat. "It looks like she doesn't trust me."

Undina's eyes shot wide open in surprise. She squinted out of the small room before releasing a tiny burst of laughter. "Yes, she's just paranoid about everything. She likes to keep aware of her surroundings."

Trevain had never heard her laugh before, and it was just as powerful and pure as her dance. She threw her head back slightly, and opened her lips, and let the laughter bubble up from deep within her. It

stirred him. What he would not give to see her laugh like that more
often! He decided then that he would find a way to hear that laughter
again.

"Where are you and your sisters staying?" he asked. "Do you
have friends or relatives in Soldotna?"

"No. I am renting us a room in a nearby motel. Not the best
accommodations, but we are grateful. It is so good to be far away from
home; away from all the depressing memories..."

"How old are your sisters?" Trevain asked.

She hesitated. "Elandria is only slightly younger than I am,
although she is far more mature. Corallyn is... much younger. She is
just a child."

He wondered why she was not giving specific ages. He did not
care. "Undina, forgive me if this is too bold and presumptuous..."
Trevain tried to stop himself from saying the words as they spilled
forth. Was this the brandy talking? What was he thinking? "I feel
strangely connected to you because of what you're going through. I
know how hard it was to raise Callder when I was just a kid myself. I
can help, if you'd let me."

"How?" she asked.

"You're going to think I'm crazy," he said. In fact, he already
considered himself crazy for what he was about to suggest. But he
wanted it to happen. He wanted it more than anything, and knew he
would continue to want it even after the brandy had been purged from
his system. "I would like to offer you to stay in my home, and you can
bring your sisters along. I have a massive house, with far more room
than Callder and I have any clue what to do with. We're gone out to sea
for several days at a time anyway, and the place is cold and empty. I
have many spare bedrooms, and I can offer you one for each of your
sisters..."

Some of the shadows had retreated from her eyes, replaced by
the light of curiosity. "Are you serious?"

"Sure. We have an old friend of the family who helps out around
the house and does all the cooking and cleaning. You girls wouldn't
have any responsibilities, and you could focus on your education. You
wouldn't have to work in this place."

"Trevain, do you really mean it?" The dark haired woman had
clasped her hands together in surprise.

"Of course," he answered, swallowing and desperately hoping that she would agree. "I understand if you find it difficult to trust me. I promise, I'm not asking you for anything in return. I just want to see you settled, comfortable, and happy. Living out of a motel is not the best arrangement for young ladies. I can offer you access to all the money you could possibly need, meals, clothing, books, computers, tutors…"

"Trevain," she said quietly. She contemplated him for what felt like a very long time. He fought the urge to shift in discomfort, remaining motionless as she studied his face meticulously. The young woman's dark eyes bored into him; he tried to imagine what was racing through her mind. When she spoke, her voice was choppy and wavering. "How is it possible you can be so kind? To a complete stranger you have only just met? I could be… I could be a murderer. I could be… some kind of inhuman beast."

It was Trevain's turn to throw his head back and laugh. "I highly doubt that you're a bloodsucking vampire."

Mirth danced in her mysterious black eyes. "I could be something far worse."

When his laughter finally dissolved, Trevain ran a hand through his grey hair sheepishly. The motion of laughing had felt so good in his chest that it had been difficult to stop. The merriment was therapeutic, mending all the brokenness his insides had accumulated. Even deeper than that, the rusted gears turning in his mind felt like they had been newly oiled. It was her company that had this effect on him, he knew.

Trevain suddenly felt like he was sitting with an old friend. He smiled and spoke with greater confidence. "You don't belong in a place like this, compromising yourself to make ends meet. The kind of life you should experience, now that you're seeking to experience life, is one in which you will enjoy every single moment—one where you can trust that your sisters will be provided for and happy, and that they won't turn out like my nutcase of a brother."

His comfortable new manner was infectious. The rigidity of her limbs had released along with the tension around her lips and eyes. She gave him a look of sincere gratitude, and placed her fingertips lightly on his forearm. Feeling emboldened, she squeezed his arm affectionately. "Will you let me talk it over with my sisters tonight and see what they think? I do not want to force them; we have just been liberated from living under tyrannical male authority. They may not like the idea that it could happen again."

Trevain shook his head emphatically. "I promise that it won't be like that."

Her obscure eyes moved toward the beaded curtain, evidently searching for her red-haired friend. She took a moment before she spoke. "If we become dependent on you, we will owe you everything. Our freedom will be yours. But I have seen that you are beloved among your crew; they adore you and your guidance, so I have no reason to imagine that you would not be caring of us as well."

"Those are my employees," he explained, "but they are my only friends. They're the closest thing I have to family, but they pop in and out of my life when their need for my money expires. Do you see that young man over there, Arnav? We've been working together every single day, and he feels like a son to me. He's a college student who's going to head home as soon as soon as the season's over, and I'll probably never see him again." The grey-haired man paused as premature nostalgia painted his face. "So you see, if you and your sisters want to move on at any point, I won't have an issue with that. I'm used to it, and I just want to know that I made a positive impact while I could, however brief that may be."

Trevain saw that she was staring at him with a peculiar and unreadable expression. Was it wonder? Approval? Well-concealed contempt? Feeling suddenly exposed, he cleared his throat gruffly. "At any rate, if you choose to grace my home with your presence you will always be considered a welcome guest. I'm not a tyrant, and never will be. If Callder ever bothers you, I'll smack him upside the head—but he's a harmless lout, even when drunk. No one will ever tell you what to do—you would choose your every action as you see fit. Go where you want, do as you please. You would be safe. I promise you this, Undina."

"Well, then. I cannot listen to you calling me that anymore," she said softly. She glanced furtively toward the curtain before leaning close to him and putting her lips near his ear. "Please allow me to tell you my real name..."

Chapter 5: A Good Man

"He offered you to *live* with him?" the child almost shouted. "A complete stranger?"

"Hush, Corallyn. I will explain in a moment. I need to rest."

"Of all the ridiculous…" The small girl furiously marched into the bathroom and shut the door behind her.

Aazuria slowly made her way to the bed, trying to keep her sore knees from collapsing. The joints felt like liquid that might give way under her weight. She finally crumpled weakly onto the mattress. A very quiet woman with a long braid rushed to her side and propped her legs up on pillows as she winced.

"Thank you, Elandria," she whispered. "The twins will be here in a moment."

Elandria nodded. Throwing her long braid over her shoulder, she began to knead the other woman's calves.

After a few minutes, the massage seemed to soothe Aazuria enough so that she could speak. She reached out to touch Elandria's wrist. "Do you trust me, sister?" she asked earnestly.

Elandria looked up in surprise. Her large, dark eyes were similar to Aazuria's own, except for the shyness present in them. Before she could respond, the door to their motel room opened. Two identical redheaded women entered. They were laughing and chattering as they shut the door behind them. When they noticed the state of the woman on the bed, it only added to their humor.

"Oh, Aazuria," one of the twins scolded from across the room. "What is the point of having a doctor around if you never listen to my counsel? I told you not to dance on stage. You can make far more money by just lap dancing, and it's much less strenuous."

"Unlike you two, I feel greater comfort in dancing on hardwood than on the laps of men," Aazuria responded curtly, with a small smile.

"You didn't seem to object to spending a little alone time with that captain of yours—and his hospitable lap," the other twin said coquettishly, with a bold wink.

"He is a kind man," Aazuria responded, running her hands over her thighs and groaning, "but he barely even touched me. I certainly did not become acquainted with his lap. You always jump to conclusions, Visola."

"What? You didn't sit on his lap? Why in Sedna's name not?" Visola stumbled over to the bed, revealing in her canter that she had consumed a few adult beverages. She clumsily tossed her purse onto the night table, and a cluster of bills spilled out. She grinned at this and launched herself onto the bed beside the other girls, landing face-first against the mattress. "Tell me everything!"

"He thinks that I am too young," Aazuria responded drolly.

Visola snorted in laugher. "*You!* Young, indeed. Did you tell him how old you are?"

"Yes. He did not believe me; he thought it was a joke."

"Typical," said the other twin. She had been carefully removing her purse and jacket, but now she turned to Aazuria and crossed her arms over her chest. "That's due to the deterioration of the quality of communication between men and women in this society. It's really quite markedly manifest."

"What do you mean, Sionna?" Aazuria asked, trying to focus on her friend's words through her blinding pain. She saw the brilliant doctor tilt her chin arrogantly before speaking.

"You could tell a man anything, darling. Anything at all. Tell him about the secrets which make us unique—our biological faculties. Tell him about our rich heritage; tell him about our beautiful home and how it's unlike anything else on earth. Tell him about your years of captivity, about how long and hard you've dreamed of this very moment when you could be in the company of a kind stranger and reveal all this. He will very likely respond with, 'Och, that's funny dear! Now let me see your titties.'"

Visola chuckled at her sister's cynicism. "So true! So very true."

Sionna nodded. "The same goes for the women. Men and women of this particular period are so used to constantly lying to each other that they are culturally trained not to take the other seriously. It's a mental adaptation everyone seems to have. Ubiquitous distrust."

"Captain Trevain Murphy was so genuine and generous with me," Aazuria insisted. "After meeting him I think it must surely be possible for men and women to communicate candidly, even here."

"You're so naïve, Zuri," Visola said with a yawn. She leaned her head against her friend's shoulder. "For your advanced years, you can be so idealistic. Soon you'll see that we're right."

When Aazuria sighed, she inhaled the combination of Visola's fragrant red hair and alcohol-laced breath. She knew that it was futile to criticize the warrior-woman's habits; among other unsavory titles, Visola was Adlivun's drinking champion. Aazuria glanced down at Elandria who was still rubbing her calves dutifully, but the small woman did not speak. She turned back to the redhead resting on her shoulder with a smile. "Trevain noticed you two hovering around me. So much for stealth!"

"Sio and I have been at your side, guarding you for over five hundred years," Visola said firmly. "We're not going to let any harm come to you. After all we've been through, it would be downright silly if we let you get shanked in a lap dancing booth."

"Shanked?" Sionna repeated, rolling her eyes at her sister. "General Visola Ramaris! Where did you pick up such smutty slang?"

"You ladies forget that I have the ability to take care of myself," Aazuria pointed out in amusement. "I hardly think I was ever in any danger from that sweet, harmless man."

"Harmless my foot," Visola muttered, stomping her foot on the bed for emphasis. "Didn't you notice how tall he was, how broad and muscled his shoulders? He is physically strong and potentially *very* dangerous."

"You grow more paranoid every day, Viso." Aazuria rested her cheek against the wayward red curls exploding from her friend's scalp. "Trevain Murphy is a gentleman. He runs a boat called *The Fishin' Magician*. He works too hard and does not have a large family; I believe he is lonely." Seeing that her silent sister had looked up curiously, Aazuria smiled and gave some more descriptions. "He has sad, tired green eyes and a slight limp. He also has some kind of obsession with age and he seems to think that he is extremely old."

"Proportionately to his lifespan, he is rather old," Sionna pointed out, "although in absolute terms and relative to us, he is but an infant."

"An infant who has accomplished great things," Aazuria told the doctor. "Apparently, he owns a massive home not too far from here. He has invited me to live with him."

"To live with him? To *live with him*?" Visola asked, bolting upright frantically. "You're not considering it? Great Sedna below! You're seriously considering it."

"We need to be practical. He has also offered me access to financial resources. There are five of us. One hotel room with two beds is quite pathetic considering the cavernous dimensions we were accustomed to in Adlivun."

"It doesn't bother me, Princess Aazuria." Sionna's voice was firm. "We didn't come here for luxury. We came here for safety and protection. *I* came here for knowledge and technology to update our infirmaries."

"And *I'm* here in to score superior weaponry for our forces," Visola said. "It's embarrassing to admit, but our weaponry is pretty primitive. I can easily fix everything with some hardcore American dollars."

The door to the bathroom flung open just as loudly as it had been slammed shut. The child called Corallyn emerged from restroom, wringing a cloth between her hands. "Why is he offering you this?" she demanded.

"He feels sympathy for me," Aazuria explained to her youngest sister. Corallyn's physique was similar to that of a nine-year-old. "He wishes to be our benefactor since our father is dead."

Visola's eyes narrowed as she regarded her friend. "I wonder if he would feel that way if he knew that you had killed your father, Aazuria?"

"Please," Aazuria said in a low voice, "please."

The quiet girl with the long braid stopped massaging Aazuria's legs for a moment to use her hands to sign an insult to Visola angrily: *"It is too soon to bring it up so casually! Have you no tact?"*

"I'm sorry. Elandria, you're right." Visola sighed and hugged Aazuria gently around the waist. "Forgive me, Zuri. I forget how much you cared for your pops."

"I am very tired. My legs are burning. I should rest." Aazuria pulled away from the others to curl up into a ball on the small, crowded bed.

"Zuri," said Corallyn, approaching her older sister and placing a damp cloth around her knees apologetically. "I ran a bath for you. Sio mentioned before that I should add something called Epsom salt to heal your legs right up. Please try it; it should make you feel better."

Aazuria remained still for a moment, her eyes closed tightly before she nodded. When she spoke, her voice was hoarse and soft. "Thank you, Coral. I will."

She sat up, and began to move to stand, but once she was off the bed, her knees began to collapse. The twins were at her side in an instant, placing their arms under her shoulders to support her as she walked to the bathroom. They helped her remove her dress and get into the bathtub where she blissfully lay down and closed her eyes.

"I did not know it would hurt this badly. It did not hurt at all when I was dancing on stage," Aazuria admitted.

"That was probably adrenaline," Sionna explained. "Your body had a rush of a hormone which made it think it could do more than it really could. I somehow never experience that sensation at home."

"This place is much less calm than we are used to, Doctor Ramaris," Aazuria said softly to Sionna. Seeing that the young girl at her side was worried, she reached out to touch Corallyn's elbow. "The bath helps. Thank you."

"You're welcome, big sis," the child answered. "I'm sorry that I was rude earlier. Just the idea of living with a man again! So soon after we rid ourselves of Papa! The idea truly frightens me."

"He promised me that we would have our freedom," Aazuria said, stretching her aching legs out underwater. "If you think about it, we may not get another offer like this. We *need* to seize it. His resources could be invaluable to our cause."

"We don't need a man, Aazuria," Visola said firmly. "Do you know how much money we've made in the past week? They say Alaskan king crab fishermen make the most money in the world, but I don't believe it. My sister and I have *each* made over five thousand dollars this week. The shrewd women seducing away large portions of the salaries of the men who make the most money in the world stand in a substantially better position than those fools do."

"She's right. If your main concern is our poor accommodations, Viso and I can easily afford an additional hotel room," Sionna suggested.

"You two would not allow a curtain to come between us. Now you want to sleep in separate rooms?" Aazuria closed her eyes and rested her head against the back of the tub.

"You can't blame us for being cautious," Visola said. "Everything has changed now that Adlivun is being threatened and scouted. Your father ignored the signs of impending attack, but everyone knows what's happening. If you really want, we could get a larger suite. Maybe two joined rooms if we leave the door between them open..."

"All of these solutions are so temporary! We can't revive Adlivun's defenses in a week. We do not have bank accounts, nor do we have any safe places to store the massive amounts of money we are making. We cannot get bank accounts, and we cannot purchase homes or vehicles. We do not have any identification. We do not exist."

"I have identification!" Corallyn interrupted. "We could use mine."

"Yes. You have identification that says you were born ninety years ago in Moscow, but you only look about nine years old by land standards."

"I'll just stay above the surface for a few years until I look my age!"

"By the time you will look your age, you would realistically need to resemble a cadaver. I think the best solution is to take Trevain up on his offer and to live comfortably in his home while we do what we need to do. We cannot survive in this world without connections and allies. Just as we have allies in Adlivun, we must have allies here."

Visola sat down on the toilet seat of the small bathroom and strummed her nails against the ceramic basin. "How about we just kill a few friendless, jobless, women who look like us and steal their identities? People won't notice they're missing. We can hide their bodies in Adlivun and no one will ever find them. Then we can just do everything ourselves."

"Visola!" scolded Sionna angrily, "we are *not* doing that."

"It would be efficient and fast," Visola muttered with a nonchalant shrug of her shoulders. "Spoilsport."

Corallyn had been chewing on her lip nervously. "I think Aazuria's idea makes the most sense," she finally admitted.

Aazuria looked at the young girl gratefully. "I am glad you agree. But if I accept his offer I can only take my sisters with me."

"No," the twins chorused in unison. There was very little the two could agree upon, but this was one of those rare moments.

"Absolutely not," said Visola. "We won't allow you to go. We may not be related by blood, but we grew up at your side. I have hardly ever been separated from you, Zuri. We are as much your sisters as

Elan and Coral are!"

"In almost every respect you two *are* my beloved sisters," Aazuria
answered, sitting up in the tub and turning to cast a stern glare at the
women. "However, politically, and with respect to the government of
our people, I am now your mother. Mother to all of you. I am the
eldest, and I have been educated for this role. Father is gone now, by
my hands. It is my responsibility to take care of all of you, and to make
decisions that will keep us all safe. I will consult you and gather your
opinions, as we often begrudged father for not doing, but I would
appreciate if you treated my ideas with a little more respect."

Sionna sighed and knelt by the bathtub, resting her chin on her
elbows and looking up at Aazuria. "Do you really like him, darling?"

Aazuria pondered over the questions for a moment. She stared at
the olive fleur-de-lis patterned tiles on the bathroom wall before
nodding. "Yes. I do really like him."

"Very well. Just remember this is exactly what King Kyrosed
always warned us against." Sionna dipped her finger in the bathwater
and drew lingering circles. "He kept us imprisoned because he believed
it was dangerous to get too close to land-dwellers."

"And that is exactly why you all wanted him gone," Aazuria
reminded her. "We thought it better to face these dangers as free
women than to waste our lives away in captivity. We thought it better
to have a fighting chance at survival rather than to remain sitting ducks
and be conquered. Now that we are here, what is the point of our
freedom if we are guarded to the point of keeping ourselves
imprisoned anyway?"

There was a small silence, before Corallyn nodded. "You're right.
Besides, if we make mistakes, we'll always have each other to help us to
rectify our errors. Nothing is permanent."

"I still can't agree with this," Visola said. "It sounds too good to
be true."

Aazuria gestured to the doorway where the silent woman stood.
"We have not yet heard what Elandria thinks."

Elandria, who had been fretfully fingering her braid, dropped the
rope of hair. She lifted her hands to answer in sign language. "*I defer to
whatever you decide, esteemed sister. If you say he is a good man, then I believe he is
a good man.*"

"Rubbish," said Visola with a dissatisfied grunt, "absolute
rubbish. There is no such thing."

"I may prove you wrong yet," Aazuria challenged gravely.

"Ha! I certainly hope you do," Visola said. Then after taking a deep breath, she smiled. "I can't say I'm not a little jealous, Zuri! A few days here and you've already been offered to enjoy someone's home and fortune. Basically a marriage proposal. I've got squat!"

"That's only because Zuri gives off that 'refined royalty' vibe, and you give off more of a 'vicious harlot' vibe," Sionna explained.

"Don't forget that we're exactly alike," Visola said to her twin with a sunny wink. She turned to look at the others. "Do you girls mind if I have a private word with the princess?"

When the other three had left, Visola sat on the edge of the bathtub. The two women sat in comfortable silence for a moment before Visola began speaking. "Look, Zuri. I understand if you don't like dancing in that grimy club for money. It was the quickest solution I could come up with that didn't involve pawning our jewels."

"It was a great solution, Viso. It is an impressive way to make money," Aazuria admitted. "But we should also sell the jewels; what use are shiny baubles if we can use the money to save lives?"

"They are irreplaceable heirlooms from our ancestors. Let me see if I can do this without touching our treasures. Maybe we won't need to go that far."

Aazuria nodded. "I should have listened to you and I should not have tried the ballet. My legs were not ready yet."

"I'm not sure about that," Visola confessed. "Your dance was so moving. It almost brought tears to my eyes, and you know that I am as cold as they come. You were so free and... triumphant. I've never seen you let go like that, not once in over five hundred years."

Aazuria reached up and grasped her friend's hand, squeezing it firmly to express her gratitude. Her voice descended to a whisper. "You know me so well, Viso. I have never felt as exultant as I did on stage tonight. Thank you for showing that place to me—it is rough and crude, but there are real people there with earnest passions and sorrows. I could see it in their eyes when I danced. It was almost too much to bear; to feel all those heavy eyes on me, and to feel so obligated to dance their afflictions away!"

Visola's lips twitched. "Only you could turn a strip club into something spiritual."

The dark haired woman sent a sly smile at her protectress. "It was worth all the physical pain I now feel. It was worth taking father's life for. This is one of those days that I do not regret what I have done."

Visola brought Aazuria's hand up to her lips and kissed it gently with respect. "You should never feel regret. You did us all a great justice, but I wish that you would have let me do it for you so that you wouldn't have to live with the guilt."

Aazuria was quiet for a moment. Visola reached out to brush her moist dark hair over her shoulders. "How are your lungs?"

"Perfectly fine. No pain at all," Aazuria answered, forcing a small smile. "I will be in good health as long as I do not attempt to dance like that too often."

Visola continued to stroke her friend's dark hair, sighing. "Poor Zuri. I hardly recognize you with this dark skin and dark hair. How long has it been since you were in the sunlight? Australia, maybe?" She swallowed at the bittersweet memory. "I really wish that you would take me and Sio along with you to live with your captain. It would ease my mind. I'll drive myself mad with worry otherwise. Why don't you just lie and say we're related?"

"We must be realistic, Viso. With my melanin problem, and you two just as fair as ever, there is no way that he is going to believe that." Aazuria gave her friend a wry look, lifting her arms. "I look as though I come from the heart of the Caribbean or Mediterranean, not from the Bering."

"We could dye our hair to match yours…"

"It would not work. Coral and Elandria are also tanning considerably, so it's easy to see that they are my sisters. Let us not lie any more than we need to. Also, I would not want to cause Trevain more discomfort than necessary; bringing two girls with me is far more polite than four."

"Fine," Visola said, reluctantly. "I understand—but Zuri, I haven't let you out of my sight in a very long time. I want you to know I'm not going to be comfortable with this." The redhead slowly stood up, placing her hands on her hips in an aggressive pose. "If you see shadows lurking in the bushes outside your new place, don't freak out. That's probably me. If you see a red laser dot in the middle of your captain's forehead, don't freak out. I've probably just got him in the crosshairs of my sniper rifle."

Aazuria looked up at her friend in confusion. "You have a sniper rifle?"

"Not yet, but trust me: I'll get one soon enough." Visola's turned upwards in her classic mischievous grin. "I'm working on it."

Leaning back in the tub, Aazuria returned a tired smile. "Can you ask the girls if anyone needs a bath?"

Visola opened the door of the bathroom and addressed the other women in the room. She turned back to Aazuria and shook her head to indicate the negative response.

"Do you need one?" Aazuria asked.

"Nope," Visola said, "I showered before leaving the club."

"Great. You four can share the beds. Have a good night. I am going to sleep here in the bathtub." With that, Aazuria sunk down into the artificially created saltwater, and curled up inside the ceramic basin.

Visola refrained from protesting. "Goodnight, Zuri," she said tenderly before exiting the bathroom. She left a crack open in the door and seated herself against the wall just outside.

Chapter 6: The Captain's Manor

"These clothes are itchy," Corallyn complained as the taxi cab drove off.

"The twins did their research and said that these are normal and fashionable garments," Aazuria answered. "Are you alright, Elandria?"

The quiet girl nodded, playing with her braid as she surveyed the house they stood before. It was indeed massive, and there would surely be more than enough room for all three women inside. The house was also very close to the water, only steps away from the seashore.

"So how old is he again?" Corallyn asked.

"Nearly fifty," Aazuria answered.

"Younger than I am," Corallyn mused. "Maybe I'll finally be treated with respect now that I won't be the youngest person around."

"I doubt it. You will be obliged to act as though you are nine years old."

"Delightful," Corallyn muttered, gazing down at her young body with scorn, "simply delightful."

"Remember, he thinks that I am an innocent eighteen-year-old teenager," Aazuria said, making a face. She turned to stare at the massive double doors and asked, "Are we ready for this?" When the other two women nodded, Aazuria marched forward and pressed the button which rang the doorbell.

Before too long a portly but energetic elderly man came to the door. "Come in, come in! Mr. Murphy told me that he was expecting some young ladies. It's a pleasure to meet you girls! My, aren't you all so beautiful!" The short, round man with even rounder glasses quickly ushered them into the house, and looked around in confusion on the porch. "Don't you have any more bags?"

"No," Aazuria answered, gesturing to the sacks that they held. "This is all."

"I see, I see," the old man mumbled, scratching his chin, "well, right this way!"

He bounced into a room with sofas and encouraged the girls to sit down. He rubbed his hands together in excitement. "It's been so long since we had a lady in the house! Or a child! Or even a permanent resident! Mr. Murphy and his brother are gone out to sea most of the time. I do their cooking and housekeeping and laundry and whatnot, but it's awful lonely here in this big house sometimes. My name is Mr. Fiskel, by the way. Where are my manners? What are your names?"

"I am Aazuria, and these are my sisters Elandria and Corallyn."

"My goodness, what unusual names! Aazuria, Elandria, Corallyn. I couldn't believe it when Mr. Murphy told me there were young ladies coming to stay with us! I'll go and let him know you're here and then cook something delicious up for lunch—do you girls have any preferences?"

"We are fond of seafood," Aazuria said with a smile.

"Seafood! Seafood is my specialty," the old man said happily. "I guarantee this lunch will be the freshest, yummiest seafood that you ever did taste!"

This was his claim as he arrogantly ambled away. Aazuria looked at her sisters, exchanging secretive smiles. Corallyn couldn't conceal a small giggle.

"He's cute," Corallyn whispered. "Thank heavens we can eat real food again and don't have to live on those awful things called hamburgers!"

Footsteps echoed on the white marbled floors of the imposing foyer, heralding the arrival of the man of the house. When Trevain Murphy entered the room, Corallyn's judgmental eyes roamed over him languidly from head to foot. Elandria, however, turned to observe her sister's reaction. She was surprised to see the subtle light warming Aazuria's eyes and the creases forming around her smiling lips. She knew without a doubt that her sister was somehow enchanted by this man. She also knew that Aazuria had a way of seeing qualities in people that existed far beneath the surface.

Corallyn observed Trevain's limp and his wavy grey hair. She compared his appearance to the descriptions she had heard from the twins, noting his broad, muscled shoulders. She watched the way he crossed the room, eyes fixed eagerly and reverentially on Aazuria, hands outstretched in warmest welcome.

Aazuria rose and placed her hands in his, pleasantly surprised by the sight of him. In the daylight, he looked much more robust than he had in the somber lighting of the club. Of course, that had also been immediately after he had lost a member of his crew and had been in a very distressed state.

"I am so glad you chose to accept my offer, Aazuria." Trevain was beaming. His face seemed to have been cleanly shaven, revealing a sharp and angular jaw. "I promise you won't lack for any convenience while you're here."

"I cannot thank you enough for your kindness," Aazuria said, inclining her head slightly. She felt the urge to curtsey, but she reminded herself that this was not Europe, and the rules of conduct had changed since she had last been among land-dwellers. "I would like you to meet my sisters, Elandria and Corallyn."

"Hello," said the captain, smiling and approaching them. "I am Captain Trevain Murphy. I hope you will enjoy staying here. The house is huge and empty, as you can see, so I'm thrilled to have some company. You have already met Mr. Fiskel, the cook, but you might also run into my brother Callder once in a while."

Trevain extended his hand first to the younger of the girls. "Corallyn, is it? What a lovely name. What does it mean?"

"I was named after a marine organism," Corallyn explained tersely. The harshness of her tone and the precision of her words did not suit a nine-year-old; she seemed determined to dislike Trevain. "Some varieties of coral are valued as precious gems and worn as jewelry."

Trevain nodded, observing the young girl carefully before asking. "What grade are you in, sweetie?"

Corallyn bit her lip and looked tentatively at Aazuria for assistance. Aazuria moved to the girl's side and stroked her back reassuringly, surprised at how edgy her youngest sister seemed.

"She has been homeschooled," Aazuria quickly offered. "We all have been homeschooled. I can guarantee that her knowledge far exceeds the standard for whatever grade she should belong to."

"Ah, I see," Trevain remarked, feeling tension radiate off the young girl. He swallowed, hoping that it would ease away with time. He could not help but wonder what dreadfulness she had experienced to make her so distrustful of him. He understood why Aazuria had seemed protective of her sisters at first.

"Well, Corallyn," he said lightly, "you can call me Uncle Trevain if you'd like. Let me know if there's anything you ever have need of, and I'll try my best to help out."

"Thank you, Uncle Trevain," Corallyn said politely, glancing at Aazuria with a look of amusement. Aazuria gave her a feeble smile and shrug which went unnoticed by the captain as he turned to address Elandria.

"Elandria, is it? A pleasure to meet you." Trevain reached out to shake the woman's hand. "You look so much like your sister."

Twisting her braid nervously within both hands, Elandria looked up bashfully at Trevain. She peered at his outstretched appendage, too hesitant to accept the offer.

"Elandria does not speak," Aazuria explained to him quietly. "She uses her hands."

"Her hands?" he asked.

Releasing her braid, Elandria deftly moved her fingers into a few communicative formations before returning them to her hair.

Aazuria laughed softly before translating. "She says that she is honored to meet the man her sister spoke so highly of, and surprised that for once I was not exaggerating. She also says that she is humbled by your kindness in inviting us to stay with you."

"You speak very well with your hands," Trevain said with fascination as a slight blush touched his cheeks. He remembered the sign language he had seen Aazuria use at the club with her redheaded friend, and reasoned that Elandria must be the reason they knew how to speak that way. He thought to himself that if things worked out with the girls, and if they decided to stay for an extended period of time, he would learn sign language in order to better communicate with Elandria. That might impress Aazuria. He pushed the thought away as soon as it had come.

"Elandria. I don't think I've ever heard that name before. What does it mean?" he asked.

Elandria hesitated before signing the words, looking to Aazuria for reassurance that it would not give away their secret.

"It means 'she who lives by the sea,'" Aazuria translated with a smile.

"Ah, that's suitable!" Trevain remarked with a laugh, gesturing through his windows at the stunning view they had of the ocean. "I'm sure Mr. Fiskel is working on lunch as we speak. I can show you girls up to some rooms so that you can choose yours and get settled in. I have to go to work not too long after lunch. I'll probably be away for a few days, but please make yourselves at home and help yourselves to anything that you'd like."

The girls rose to follow Trevain to the second floor of his house. As he ascended the staircase, his limp became more prominent.

Corallyn thought she might as well take advantage of her supposed youth by bluntly asking, "What happened to your leg, Uncle Trevain?"

"It was an unfortunate accident at sea," he answered, turning to look at her. "I always point out my bad leg to the sailors in my crew when they're doing something carelessly. It serves as a constant reminder and warning—safety first! You never know when your leg might get crushed or your arm might get chopped off on those dangerous fishing boats."

While Corallyn could not resist a grin at his adorable fatherly lecture, Aazuria frowned, wondering why she felt that she could detect the smallest hint of a lie somewhere in his words. She continued to listen to his voice as he pointed out the available rooms to her sisters, indicating which ones had the best views and the largest closets, but she did not hear the tone again which she thought indicated untruth. Each room was painted in a different color, and Elandria gravitated toward the warm yellow. Corallyn preferred her namesake coral, and was exuberant when she found apricot-colored walls.

Trevain took Aazuria's arm gently as the girls selected their rooms, guiding her down the hall to the room he thought was best suited to her.

"This one is my favorite," he confessed as he opened the door. "I'm not sure if you'll like it, but the walls are painted a rich dark red…"

When Aazuria saw the combination of burgundy walls and dark mahogany wood, she turned to Trevain in excitement. "It is charming!"

He smiled at her reaction, noticing that her accent was far thicker than the one in Corallyn's voice. Perhaps their family had moved around? He gestured further down the hall. "That room on the left is mine, and the one on the right is Callder's—that is, when he decides to stay over, and when he's sober enough to make it up the stairs."

Aazuria smiled, remembering Callder's lamentable display at the club. Trevain grinned at her. "He's still sound asleep there right now. Hung over. I should wake him up before lunch, although I dread it—

he will be grouchy as hell. Maybe I'll have Mr. Fiskel do it."

"Poor Mr. Fiskel," Aazuria said, following Trevain as he continued to guide her through the house.

"He's an old friend of the family. He used to be a sailor on the boats back when my father was alive. When he was too old to fish, I decided to hire him on as my cook and butler."

You are amazing, Aazuria thought to herself, but she decided against saying anything of the sort. Instead she just nodded in acknowledgement.

"There's an indoor swimming pool and hot tub on the main floor," he informed her. "Heated so you can get a bit of exercise even in the winter. There's a solarium filled with exotic plant species. We also have a very large library, although you might find my taste in books eclectic. If you ever want to entertain, maybe invite some friends over like that redhead from the club, feel free to do so. Just let Mr. Fiskel know so he can prepare extra food."

"That is thoughtful," Aazuria said. She could not wait to invite the twins over and show them the magnificent quarters, proving to them that Captain Trevain Murphy really did honor his word. She still had difficulty believing her good fortune.

From downstairs, the sound of the doorbell was heard ringing through the house. Before a second passed, the doorbell was rung again fiercely several times, each loud clangor overlapping the echo of the previous peal.

"Crap," Trevain whispered, growing pale, "not now."

"What is the matter?" Aazuria asked, feeling the muscles in her stomach tighten in apprehension. The doorbell continued to sound wildly.

"Keep an eye on your sisters," Trevain said with a frown. "Don't let them come downstairs. This isn't going to be pretty. I've been dreading this."

Aazuria watched as an agitated Trevain limped downstairs. She rushed to the room where Corallyn and Elandria were discussing their new closets in sign language.

"There may be some kind of danger," Aazuria said, ushering the girls behind her and closing the door until there was just a crack open.

"Danger?" Corallyn asked. "I knew this was too good to be true. I knew it."

"Hush," Aazuria said, reaching into her purse and pulling out a small knife. She crouched by the door with the knife in a ready position and pressed her ear close to the crack to listen for any signs of trouble. The doorbell only stopped ringing when the door was opened, and promptly slammed shut.

"You need to explain to me *exactly* what the hell happened, Trevain!" came a hysterical voice. "I leave for a few days and all of you men forget how to tie your own goddamned shoes? What happened? Tell me! Start talking *now*!"

"Calm down…"

"Don't you *dare* tell me to calm down! Leo is dead! *Dead!* How can I be calm? How could you let this happen? Dammit, Trevain! Dammit!"

"Listen, Brynne…"

"You listen! What the hell is wrong with you? You've never been such a negligent asshole!"

Meanwhile, upstairs, Aazuria was grimacing. "It is just some annoying, irate female," she whispered to her sisters angrily. "No real danger, but Trevain is too nice to stand up for himself. He is letting her rip him apart!"

"Then go do something about it," Corallyn suggested.

"I do not wish to interfere," Aazuria said, although she was sorely tempted to give that woman a piece of her mind. She tucked her knife back into her purse. "I hardly know him. It is not my place."

From downstairs, Trevain's voice filtered up into the room, his tone beseeching. "Please, Brynne, there was nothing that I could have done. Nothing that anyone could have done. We didn't even know when…"

"You didn't know!" the female voice almost screamed. "You didn't know when a man fell overboard? When a man was injured? When a man was *drowning*? How could you *not* know? How could no one have seen or heard *anything*?"

"You know that I run my crew more carefully than any other captain who fishes the Bering Sea. I have never lost a man in my entire career before Leander. I can't explain what happened out there, but we can't allow it to get us overemotional or we risk making mistakes and letting it happen again."

"Why didn't you call me? I headed down to the docks today after doing some grocery shopping for our trip—I got some vegetables in addition to the instant mashed potatoes and chocolate because I was in such a great mood and felt like getting something healthy. But once I got to the *Magician*, everyone looked as though someone had died. Finally, I had to practically beat up Billy to find out that someone *had actually* died. Do you know what it's like finding out that way? Why didn't you tell me?"

"I knew you'd react like this. I didn't want to ruin your time in Florida."

"Fuck Florida! I needed to know this. Dammit! This is your fault, Trevain. I hope you know that Leo's death is on you. This is what you get for hiring such an incompetent greenhorn! No one else is to blame but you."

There was a silence before Trevain wretchedly said, "I know."

Aazuria resolutely raised herself to her feet at sound of the captain's quiet acceptance. Elandria grabbed her wrist and held her fast with both hands, mouthing words to her since she could not use her hands: *Aazuria! Do not be rash!* However, the older girl slipped out of her grasp quickly.

"Stay here," Aazuria commanded her sisters, before opening the door and quickly crossing the corridor to the staircase. Her modestly-heeled black shoes clinked on the oaken staircase as she descended, her posture erect and uncompromising. When Trevain and Brynne turned up to look at her, she was suddenly conscious of her new clothes. The twins had chosen a simple knee-length teal dress for her, believing it would accentuate her new dark coloring. She also wore her extremely long hair wrapped up tightly into a bun. She hoped this styling would have the added benefit of ensuring that she was taken seriously despite her young appearance.

"Forgive me for overhearing your bellowed accusations," Aazuria began steadily, while still descending the stairs. "I did not mean to eavesdrop, but it is challenging to ignore such a deafening commotion."

Brynne assessed the woman with astonishment. She had not expected anyone to be in the house other than Mr. Fiskel and Callder, and was immediately ashamed. She was even more embarrassed by the feminine appearance of the girl, and her elegant mannerisms. Brynne was suddenly conscious of her own ragged jeans, flannel shirt, and manly shouting.

"Who is she?" Brynne whispered angrily to Trevain.

"Be polite," Trevain softly warned the brunette.

Brynne's fists clenched in jealousy. "I'll be as rude as I damn well please!"

"Captain Murphy does not deserve to be verbally attacked," Aazuria stated calmly and evenly. "Do you not think he has suffered enough pain for his loss already? In fact, Captain Murphy has had to be strong for his brother and all of his crew who are equally distraught. They were all present at the tragedy, and they all share the burden of responsibility. Perhaps you should do something positive. Console the men; reassure and support them instead of tormenting them as though you are entitled and blameless just because you're female."

"How dare you!" Brynne shouted, swiveling to face the captain. "Now you're living with some woman, Trevain? Is she the reason you weren't paying attention on the ship and you let a man drown? Is your new bedmate keeping your head in the clouds and distracting you?"

Trevain recoiled and shouted. "Brynne! Jesus, woman. This is Aazuria. I only met her two nights ago, after Leo drowned."

"Two nights ago! And she's already living here? Did you have a Vegas-style wedding? How old is she, nineteen? God, Trevain! I thought you were a sensible man, but it looks like you're having a midlife crisis! The granddaddy of all midlife crises!"

Aazuria approached Brynne until she was standing directly before her. "Excuse me ma'am, but you are mistaken in your obscene suppositions. When Trevain learned that my father recently died he extended his sympathy to me and my orphaned younger sisters in letting us stay in his home. I am sure you can see how offensive it is to hear the character of the man who has offered me such charity and compassion slighted so unjustly."

Brynne was rendered silent for a long moment. She stared into the hard black eyes of the woman who reprimanded her until she had to look away. She looked at Trevain and saw that he was also displeased. "I'm sorry, Trevain. Sometimes I jump to conclusions. And you... sorry about your dad," she said, trying to soften up, but failing to fully let go of her fury. "What did you say your name was?"

"I am Aazuria."

"Aazur—? What the hell kind of a name is that?" Brynne spat.

"It is derived from the word 'azure' which is the color of... the ocean," Aazuria said. She had briefly hesitated, almost having said that azure was the color of her eyes, but she quickly remembered that her eyes had changed with the increased melanin from her high sunlight exposure.

"The ocean? The ocean isn't *azure*, girlfriend, it's *black*, okay?" Brynne snapped. "Black as death. And sometimes, when someone dies in it, portions of it are red. Was there lots of blood in the water when Leo died, Captain?"

"Stop attacking him," Aazuria said darkly. "Also, stop displaying your ignorance. The ocean is azure."

"What do you know?" Brynne asked, advancing on Aazuria until they were almost nose-to-nose. The women were both tall, but Aazuria's low high heels allowed her to tower over sneaker-wearing Brynne by two inches. "What does an adolescent girl like you know about the ocean?"

"Enough." Aazuria's voice was cold as ice, sending a chill through those around her. Her chin had lifted as she dissected the brunette with her glare. Hostility crackled in the air between them, and Aazuria felt so much bile stirring within her that she surprised herself with the force of the emotion. She had never felt so compelled to defend someone's honor, and she almost hoped that Brynne would strike her so that she would have an excuse to strike back.

"You know nothing!" Brynne shouted. "You're obviously a brainless spoiled brat—I am a grown woman who has lived and worked on the sea for over a decade." Each word was laced with mounting resentment.

"A decade," Aazuria repeated with a condescending smile. "Is that supposed to impress me? Poets have been calling the ocean azure for thousands of years."

"Exactly. Romantic, dimwitted poets. I'm a fisherwoman. Don't you dare come into my world and tell me what color the ocean is! I don't care what the poets say. It's black. Black as midnight. Black and awful!"

Aazuria realized that the woman was in pain from mourning—sympathy promptly replaced most of her anger. "You may feel that way right now, but you are only allowing passion to cloud your judgment. Look out the windows and you will see that the ocean is clearly azure."

"Don't you have some audacity!" Brynne hissed, stepping even closer to Aazuria. "I am *intimately* familiar with the water. I'm telling you now, what you see is a goddamned illusion! It looks blue and pretty to your untrained landlubber eyes, but I can see *the truth*. It's actually *hell* that you're looking at. Hell on earth!"

"*Brynne Ambrose*! Settle down," Trevain demanded, putting a hand on the woman's shoulder and trying to firmly guide her away from Aazuria. At that moment, he would have preferred to be breaking apart two giant football players. Brynne seemed out for blood. "Give her some space."

"No! She needs to be taught a thing or two," Brynne barked, shrugging him off and turning back to her adversary.

"Hell on earth?" Aazuria repeated in a whisper. "It is closer to paradise. If only you knew…"

"I'm trying to teach you something, you vexing little virgin. You are a virgin, aren't you?" Brynne snickered, much to Trevain's frustration. "Learn this fast if you want to survive amongst us: the water is black. Do you understand me? Black. You had better change your name."

Aazuria stared at her challenger, her eyes flashing with indignation and pity. "You are gravely mistaken. Your soul is of the earth—how could you know the sea?

"Who knows the color of the ocean better than me?" Brynne released a hysterical snicker. "In case you didn't notice, girl, I'm a fucking fisherwoman. I know *best*."

"I know better—because I am a fucking mermaid."

Chapter 7: A Fiery Fisherwoman

Elandria slid down the wall she was leaning against, her bottom landing against the floor with a little thump.

Corallyn's lips parted in shock. "I can't believe she just gave it all away like that."

"I thought she found the term 'mermaid' offensive and erroneous," Elandria signed with her hands. *"What is she doing? She is usually so tactful. She used to be a diplomat."*

"She cursed too," Corallyn noted. "She never curses. I think we should get ready to leave. It's a good thing we didn't unpack or get too comfortable."

The girls were interrupted by a great howl of laughter traveling up from downstairs. Corallyn and Elandria stared at each other in surprise as they listened to Trevain's gigantic guffaw until it petered down into uncontrollable chuckles.

"It's just like Viso said," Corallyn realized after a moment of confusion. "He didn't even believe her."

Downstairs, Brynne's face had been etched with shock at the other woman's statement. They had stood in a moment of stalemated silence until Trevain had begun to laugh in his good-natured and infectious way. Finally, Brynne felt a smile coming to her own lips, and felt rather silly for being so aggressive to the beautiful young girl. She vaguely wondered why she had been so unwelcoming; there was an unpleasant combination of grief and envy in her chest.

Brynne realized that it had been a long time since a woman had stood up to her like Aazuria just had—perhaps no female had ever done so. Brynne was used to battling with males, and she was used to winning. She had perfected the art of intimidation at a young age, and it had served her well. She argued ridiculous things, claiming that grass was blue while the sky was red. She would have argued for milk being purple if it suited her need to overpower someone. The arguments were always about the same thing for Brynne; establishing and emphasizing her dominance in all of her relationships.

"Well, Aazuria, I guess you win," she said reaching out to shake the woman's hand in a gesture of apology. "I can't compete with a certified sea-wench like yourself. I'm sorry for being such a bitch; I just went a bit crazy after learning about Leo. I really liked that kid, even though he was a bit of a greenhorn. If he was half as tough as you are, he probably wouldn't be six fathoms deep right about now."

Aazuria raised her eyebrows at being called a sea-wench but she returned the woman's handshake and nodded head in acceptance of her apology. Trevain had been observing the interaction between the women curiously. He was used to Brynne's rough ways, but very impressed and amazed by the graceful vigor that Aazuria had battled her with. The girl was young, but she could stand her ground.

Brynne turned to look at Trevain, and lowered her eyes shamefully. "I'm sorry, Captain. I just had to let off a little steam. I'm fine now, and reporting for duty. Let's go catch some crabs."

"Brynne," said Captain Murphy quietly. "I understand if the accident has made you angry enough to want to quit. I can pay you for the portion of the season that you worked, and that will be that. I think you know, however, from experience, that women aren't generally treated very well on most other fishing boats. You'll have to choose your next employer carefully. I'll give you the best of recommendations, of course."

Brynne crossed her arms across her chest, exhaling heavily. "I don't want to quit, Captain. Our crew is a family. I just don't want this to happen again. I feel like I just lost a brother. We've always heard about this happening to other crews, but it has *never* happened to us. I wasn't even there! Goddammit! It's just... I only learned about it a few minutes ago at the docks, and I haven't been able to deal with it yet."

"If you need to take time off, take as much as you need," Trevain said. "The men haven't been dealing with it well either."

"No," Brynne said, her voice cracking. She shook her head violently. "I'm not letting anything else go wrong. You boys need me to keep an eye on you out there."

"Yeah. We do," Trevain said, slapping Brynne on the back in a companionable fashion.

"No more weekends in Miami for me," she joked. "Have either of you been to Florida? It's far too warm, and I simply don't have the right wardrobe; definitely not my cup of tea. My cousin's wedding was beautiful though."

Just then, Mr. Fiskel entered the room, "Captain Murphy, Miss Aazuria, lunch is served. I heard Miss Brynne's voice (it was rather loud) and I set another place at the table. We're having lobster tails!"

"Sounds delicious, Mr. Fiskel! You're a savior," Trevain said with a smile. "Could you do me a favor and go upstairs to—"

"No," Aazuria interrupted, placing a hand on Trevain's arm. She sent him a secretive look before turning to the brunette. "Brynne, do you know where Callder's room is?"

"Yeah," she answered suspiciously, "why do you ask?"

"You seem like the type of woman who would know where men's bedrooms are. Would you please be a dear and go wake Callder to tell him that lunch is ready?"

Brynne looked as though she wanted to hit Aazuria, but she quickly gathered her composure and turned to Trevain with reddening cheeks. "Where on earth did you find this creature? She looks like she's eighteen but she speaks like she's eighty. Goddamned sea-wench!"

The brunette continued to sputter curses as she marched up the stairs to perform the dreaded task of waking a very hung-over Callder. Trevain had to try very hard to keep from laughing at how much Brynne's feathers had been ruffled.

"I am sorry," Aazuria said, turning to him. "I just had to get her back for the virgin comment. Goodness, that was rather fun."

"You've got a *legendary* sense of humor," Trevain responded with a chuckle, shaking his head. "No one ever stands up to her like that."

"She may be a fiery fisherwoman, but she is still just a woman. I know her type. She thinks because she is the only girl tough enough to hang out with the guys that she can disrespect them as much as she likes. This probably grew from issues with her father. Am I right?"

"Spot on. It seems that no one I know has a good relationship with their father," Trevain remarked. "Luckily, bad parentage affects people in very different ways. In your case it seems to have made you stronger."

Aazuria glanced up at him judiciously. "What about you, Trevain? Have you ever had children?"

"No. I've always wanted to, but…" Trevain's brow furrowed and he cleared his throat. "I guess my life didn't work out that way. Probably for the best; as you can see, I'm hardly capable of taking care of a boatful of men. There's no way I'd be able to shepherd little rugrats away from danger."

"You do take care of them," she assured him. "The whole boatload of men and one eccentric, maniacal woman."

Trevain grinned again. "You had me fooled, Aazuria. I thought you were so innocent when I first saw you, but if you can handle yourself around that banshee then I'm not worried about anyone taking advantage of you. Ever."

Aazuria's cheeks felt the strength of her smile. The strength of her smile led to embarrassment which led to heat flushing her cheeks. She turned away from him, murmuring, "I should go and collect my sisters for lunch."

"Wait," Trevain said, moving close to her. "Brynne and Callder and I are probably going to head out to work directly after lunch. We will be away for a few days, depending on the weather. I just wanted to mention one thing to you in private before I leave."

"What is it?" she asked, searching his eyes for clues. She wondrously watched the delicate skin around his eyes crinkle into tender lines of hilarity.

"You were right, my dear. The sea is azure."

*   *   *

Brynne's heavy footsteps echoed through the hallway as she trudged towards Callder's room. "Maniacal banshee!" she grumbled. "Call me more flattering names as soon as I turn the corner, why don't you? Brynne doesn't have ears!" Even though she was making good progress in convincing herself that she was upset with Aazuria and Trevain, she was mostly upset with herself. For a woman in her mid-thirties she sure could be immature at times.

"That's Calzone's influence on me," she told herself. Then she cringed and made a face at the sound of the old nickname. It exited her lips so naturally, creating one more reason for her to be ashamed and upset with herself.

Brynne jumped in fright when a small head poked out from one of the many doors in the corridor. She caught her breath and looked at the child to make sure it was a human being and not a ghostly apparition. Trevain's house was usually so empty that it was shocking to find anything or anyone in it—this was her second such surprise for the day.

"Hi, there," Brynne said, once she was convinced that the child was real. "What's your name, sweetie?"

Corallyn sent the woman an appraising glance. "You were a total dick to my sister."

Brynne winced at hearing such words leaving a child's mouth. "Hey, I'm sorry…"

"You're ignorant. Where I come from, for speaking to a Vellamo like that, you might have been beheaded. Or worse." With that, Corallyn withdrew into the room and slammed the door vehemently.

Brynne flinched again at the loud noise. "A Vella-what?" Her brow knitted in confusion, and she wondered what kind of books Aazuria was letting her little sister read. Shrugging at the child's unusual behavior, she continued down the hall to Callder's room. The hallway seemed to stretch forever. When she finally stood before the door, she knocked hesitantly. Gone was the boisterous Brynne who had viciously rung Trevain's doorbell a dozen times within ten seconds. She swallowed, feeling more uncomfortable to be standing at this door than she had expected; and not just because Callder was cantankerous when hung over.

She cleared her throat and shook her hands out at the wrists to release her misgivings. She knocked on the door again forcefully, in a decidedly more Brynne-like manner. "Hey, Callder! Wake up. Lunch and work!"

"No!" was the grouchy shout heard from the inside.

"Don't make me come in there!" Brynne yelled back. "I will kick your lazy ass right out of that bed."

"Please do," was the muffled invitation which filtered through the door and possibly blankets.

Brynne immediately flushed. "Worst day ever," she whispered to herself. She took several deep breaths before turning the doorknob. "*Callder Murphy!* You useless layabout! *This* is why we broke up."

The man had been facing the curtains. Now, he shifted under the blanket to turn and consider her. Brynne felt a twinge of dismay when she saw the red puffiness around his eyes. He looked far more hung over than usual, and she could tell that he had been crying.

"Wanna come help me wake up?" Callder asked as he stretched.

"No!" Brynne immediately felt her pity disappear. "We have to get out on the water. Some of us adults actually need to pay our bills and can't depend on big brother to do everything for us."

Callder rubbed his eyes and yawned loudly. "But you could. Come live with me and Trevain will take care of your stuff too. I miss you."

"My answer is still the same. Unlike you, I have this little thing called pride, and a few other little things called goals. There's more to life than staying in bed all day."

"I could change your mind in about ten seconds," Callder said with a toothy grin. He lifted the blanket to expose his impressive arousal before pouting melodramatically. "I've got this little thing called morning wood. Bring that pretty ass over here and help me get rid of this! It hurts."

"You filthy pervert!" Brynne said, crossing her arms. She assumed the meanest look she could manage to hide the smile that threatened to appear. "We're co-workers, Callder, and this is sexual harassment. Get *your* lazy ass out of bed and get dressed!"

"Just go away," Callder said grumpily, replacing the blanket and turning to face the window.

Brynne heard the note of sadness in his voice, and released a sigh. Against her better judgment, she crossed the room and sat on the side of the bed. "What's wrong?"

"Don't wanna work today," Callder admitted. He lifted a hand to scratch behind his ear. "I'm not really that hung over. Just don't wanna go out on that boat."

"But we need you out there. We're a man down."

"Is that the only thing you need me for?" he asked quietly. He glanced at Brynne briefly, and for once there was serious sorrow speckling his warm brown eyes. "I have a really bad feeling."

"Everything's going to be fine," Brynne said. She felt the familiar sensation of mothering Callder, as though he were six feet and two inches worth of pure, giant child.

He turned away and grunted. "The *Magician* stinks of death. I can't stop thinking about it. Just find some bright-eyed young kid to do my job, and I guarantee he'll do it better even."

"It's going to be tough on all of us to get back to work today. Please don't make it harder on us."

"That's all I'm good for. I'm a fuck-up, remember?"

"Calz—Callder. Please. It comforts Trevain to have you around. You relieve everyone's stress with your trashy, tasteless jokes. Don't flake out on us; not today of all days." Seeing that her speech was not having the desired effect, she knew that it was necessary to pull the woman-card. She placed a hand on his arm tenderly. "*I* need you out there."

"Leo was ten times the man that I am," Callder said gruffly. "It should have been me. I should be dead."

"No." Brynne's touch changed from affectionate to reproachful instantaneously as she slapped him upside the head. "Don't say things like that!"

"What do you care?"

"I care."

"Then get back together with me," Callder said, propping himself up on his elbow. "How many years are you going to make me beg? I miss you."

Brynne pulled her lips into a tight line. She never knew what to say. Sometimes she wanted to relax and agree more than anything, but a small part of her still hoped that she could find a better man— someone who felt less like dead weight. "Let's talk about it when we get back," she said. "For now, we need to focus on getting through this day. The guys are miserable."

Pushing his torso fully upright, Callder ran a hand through his messy brown hair. "So I guess you need me to rant about booze and whores to cheer 'em up?"

Brynne laughed. He always could make her laugh. "Exactly."

Chapter 8: I Remember 1741

"This library *is* rather eclectic," Sionna observed as she browsed through the titles.

"In the best possible way," her twin added giddily. Visola had been curled up in an armchair with her legs tucked under her as she rapidly consumed the pages of the book she had chosen.

"What are you reading?" Sionna asked, glancing at her sister nosily.

Visola's eyes lit up as she held up the cover for the others to see. "*The Influence of Sea Power on Ancient History* by Chester Starr."

"Non-fiction," Corallyn observed in disappointment without glancing up from the laptop to which she had recently become joined at the hip.

"Always work, work, work with you, General Ramaris. You're totally obsessed with naval warfare," Sionna accused somewhat fondly. "Grim situations aren't supposed to get a person so excited."

"He even has submarines!" Visola sputtered excitedly. "I just thought it was best to do my reading in chronological order and save the best for last."

"Maybe you should start with the titles most relevant to our situation," Sionna suggested as she went back to browsing the section she favored.

"There certainly is a common theme," Aazuria remarked as she studied the rows of spines, thinking of how the carefully shelved volumes reflected on Trevain's interests. She fingered one book idly and read aloud, "*The Beasts of the Sea...*"

"Are we featured in that?" Corallyn joked as she continued pounding away at the keys of the small computer. She had grown addicted to the machine much too quickly.

"No. It just caught my attention because it was written by Georg Wilhelm Steller."

"Steller?" Visola asked thoughtfully. "Now why does that name sound familiar?"

"It's because you slept with him," Sionna informed her.

"No way. Did I really?"

"It's okay, sweetie." Sionna gave her sister a superior smirk. "1741 was a very long time ago. I don't expect you to remember every man whose bed you invaded; especially considering you can't remember the names of people you slept with yesterday."

"That's not true! I remember all the important ones," Visola argued. "There was only one important man in the 18th century."

"He was a writer too, wasn't he?" Sionna asked.

"Shut up," Visola said, rolling her eyes and stretching languidly. "Shut up and find me something with lots of mines and torpedoes."

"You can use this computer to do research if you need to know about a specific weapon," Corallyn suggested.

Visola raised an auburn eyebrow. "Honey, I was born in 1449. Do you really expect me to know what to do with that machine?"

"What she means to say is if it doesn't kill something, she's not interested," Sionna explained.

Aazuria was leaning against the bookcase and looking at her quiet sister thoughtfully. Elandria was avoiding conversation with the others by curling up in a corner of the couch with a book, but Aazuria knew she was listening. Very little escaped her taciturn observation. "I remember 1741," Aazuria murmured as she watched her sister; the years being discussed had not been pleasant for Elandria. "So much began to change back then. Father had just decided that we should stop speaking Aleut and converse mainly in Russian. I began studying ballet under a new instructor on land. My legs were so much stronger back then…"

"I didn't know that Russian was ever exclusively spoken in Adlivun," Corallyn commented in surprise.

"We had a very brief Russian phase," Sionna said, waving her hand in dismissal. "We spoke it for less than a hundred years before King Kyrosed decided that English was the way to go. That man never could make up his mind! By the time he ventured off to impregnate some poor, unsuspecting girl with you, Coral, we had been used to English for quite some time."

"I see. What did you speak before the Aleut language?" Corallyn asked.

"Old Norse," Sionna answered, "but that was a very long time ago, before we came to the Bering Sea. Even longer ago, way before our generation, Latin was the language of choice. We sort of go with the flow of the world above us, wherever we are living. We try to stay current in case we need to spend time on land—like right now. Only our sign language has remained pretty much unchanged and unique to us."

In response, Elandria lifted her hands from her book to communicate, *"I appreciate consistency."*

This drew a burst of laughter from Corallyn. The young girl placed her laptop aside and moved to the sofa that Elandria was sitting on. She curled up beside her sister in a catlike way.

Aazuria continued to browse the library, running her hands along the old volumes as she thought of Trevain. Each title made her more and more curious about him, and about what secrets of acumen he held behind his unassuming demeanor. After several minutes of examining the books, she began to feel guilty about concealing her true origin from him, and slightly nervous about whether the secret could remain hidden for long.

Feeling a warm hand on her shoulder, Aazuria turned to find Elandria looking at her intently and holding out a particular book. Reaching out to accept the offering, she looked down at the blue cover with bold black lettering.

"The Aquatic Ape Hypothesis by Elaine Morgan," she read curiously.

"Are we in that one?" Corallyn asked sleepily from the couch.

"I doubt it," Sionna answered without even glancing at the book, "but I found our section over here. Take a look." A few of the girls gathered to where she had been pointing as Sionna placed her hands on her hips and glowered at the shelves. "He's got probably every book in existence which examines the various European water myths: the Selkie, Melusine, Kelpie, Vodyanoy, and the Rusalka. Take your pick! There are even African folklores about Mami Wata. He doesn't stop there. Here's Inuit lore on Qalupaliks and obscure southern legends about Aycayia and Sumpall. This collection is remarkably extensive. There's plenty of reading on Asian stories about the Ningyo…"

"The Ningyo. Ah, memories!" Visola immediately commented. "I wonder if Queen Amabie is still alive and well. She was the greatest swordswoman I have ever known. Do you remember fighting alongside her in that vicious battle in the 1950s? The last real fun I've had."

"How could I forget," Sionna grumbled. "Your asshole husband tried to kill us and he nearly took my leg off."

"I should pay a visit to those crazy Japanese mermaids," Visola said, completely ignoring the personal remark. "Reinforcing our alliance with them could come in handy in the future. Queen Amabie would definitely help us out if things got rough."

Sionna was reflexively ready to protest and mock her sister, but she found herself relenting. "That's actually a really great idea, Viso."

Meanwhile, Aazuria clutched the book Elandria had given her to her chest as she examined the titles in horror. "This is dreadful. If he is so finely educated in water mythology, how did he not take one look at me and know exactly what I am? I have been imprudent. I will be found out; it is inevitable. He knows what we are."

"Oh, darling, don't worry so!" Sionna said lightly. "All land-dwellers have a general idea of what we are, and the general impression that we're here. They just deny our existence so hard that it wouldn't even cross their minds."

"You mean they know *who* we are," Corallyn corrected from her perch on the cushions.

Visola shook her head. "No. They don't know *who* we are specifically, but they do have a vague conception of *what* we are. They just blow their damned stories out of proportion. They have to say that we have fish tails, sparkly scales, hair made out of smelly seaweed, magical singing powers or other crap in most of these stories."

"I know, right?" Sionna said, firmly shutting a book that she had previously opened. "They're just xenophobic! All of them! Doesn't it make sense that if we have slightly longer lifespans, those of us who are singers will be better singers? There's a limit to the mastery of any art that can be achieved in any single lifetime. Their limits just happen to be much lower than ours!"

"Your extreme nationalist views are showing, Sio," her sister teased.

Sionna made a face. "I'm proud of both who and what I am. I love my country, and I love the woman who will soon be our new queen."

"Yes. Some queen I will make," Aazuria said, laughing derisively at herself. "If Adlivun wasn't already underwater, I swear I would somehow sink it. I have already made a mess. I tried to secure a home on land, and I messed it up by basically revealing us."

"We haven't been revealed!" Corallyn shouted from the sofa, opening her eyes and slamming her fist into a soft pillow. "Sweet Sedna! You worry too much, Zuri. 'Uncle Trevain' is totally enamored of you and you couldn't have said or done anything to screw that up if you tried. He thought the mermaid comment was hilarious!"

Aazuria nodded, feeling marginally reassured by her youngest sister's words. Sighing, she moved over to the sofa and sat down listlessly. She stroked Corallyn's hair absent-mindedly.

"We all look perfectly normal," Sionna reaffirmed. "Sure, we're extremely cognizant of our differences, but the truth is that no one can see the morphological distinctions of our lungs directly through our chests."

"That's a good point, Doctor Ramaris," Visola said, grinning, "and even if they *could* see directly through our chests, they would be far too distracted by the exterior to do so." Corallyn giggled at Visola's indicating hand motions.

"The extra inch of webbing between my fingers and toes is very conspicuous," Aazuria said, self-consciously examining her hands.

"Sweetie, there are varying degrees of webbed fingers and toes even in land-dwellers," Sionna said. "Seriously, they consider excessive webbing a disorder called syndactyly. Some people have *complete* webbing of the fingers or toes that they have to fix with surgery. No one will think anything of it, even if they do notice."

"I saw on TV that girls with partial webbing of their toes get piercings there to accentuate it," Corallyn chimed in. "I thought it was pretty. I kind of want to get the webbing between my toes pierced too."

"It would be hard to wear shoes and walk around while you were healing," Visola commented.

"Maybe I'll do it when I no longer have to wear shoes," Corallyn argued.

"What about my legs?" Aazuria asked. "What if I collapse at some point and have to lie to explain it…"

"Oh Zuri, that's nothing," Sionna said with a laugh. She had always been captivated by anatomy and medicine, and she came alive when the topic of conversation drifted to biology. "Doesn't even Trevain have a limp? Land-dwelling humans are chock full of interesting imperfections. I recently read about a disorder called Sirenomelia which people nicknamed the 'Mermaid Syndrome.' Apparently, on rare occasions, human babies are born with their legs *completely fused together*. That's what they think of us. They think we are radically abnormal and disfigured in some grossly apparent way."

Aazuria frowned. "I know that their notions of us are ridiculous. That is partly what protects us from them; their unwillingness to understand. However, if Trevain has all these legends from across the globe, and I am going about declaring myself to be a mermaid..."

"I told you, men don't believe anything a woman says any longer. The legends could just be a collector-type thing. Maybe he hasn't actually read them."

"Nah, they're dog-eared," Corallyn affirmed. Then seeing that Aazuria's face had fallen, she added, "Maybe he just hasn't read them in years. He's probably forgotten all about anything he ever knew about us. Decades of hard work will suck the magic right out of life."

Sionna scoffed. "Darling, we aren't magic. We're just biologically superior. It's all science, really."

"All life is magic," Aazuria said softly.

"Speaking of life," Visola said, drumming her fingernails on the wooden bookshelves, "this is unbelievable. This guy... who is he? Look at these books."

"What is it?" Sionna asked.

"Underwater birthing. Apparently it has recently become popular with land-dwelling women."

"How fascinating," Sionna said, selecting a book. "Perhaps there's even knowledge in here that could be of some use to Adlivun's midwives."

"I doubt that," Visola said, "but don't you find it strange? All the subjects? It's like he knew we were coming. This guy has every instruction manual you could possibly need if you were planning on falling in love with a mermaid."

"There is something odd about the focus of this library," Sionna agreed. "I don't trust him. He could be allied with whatever enemy forces threaten Adlivun—we don't know nearly enough about our attackers."

"There's only one army big enough to dare," Visola muttered softly.

Aazuria leaned back in the sofa leisurely, studying the suspicious faces of the twins. "Girls, if we really consider it, it makes perfect sense that Trevain would be personally interested in all of these subjects. He's a seaman. Someone who spends his life on the water probably spends a lot of time meditating on the water. Listening to stories, imagining what could be. Maybe he just likes to research mythologies and practices concerning that which he knows best."

"That's right," Visola said. "There was an Inuit man in his crew—maybe this began with a fascination with researching Inuit traditions, and one thing led to another."

"Goodness. We have to be very careful around him," Aazuria said, straightening her spine abruptly. "We may henceforth only curse to generic, non-water-related deities."

"That's right," Corallyn chimed in. "Instead of 'Dear Sedna' we can just say 'Dear God.' It works just as well."

"I'm quite fond of the scintillating phrase, 'Holy Shit,'" Visola offered.

"My sister has charming taste," Sionna said.

"We still need to investigate part of this house which is much more important than the library," Corallyn said, uncurling her small body and bouncing to her feet.

"What's that?"

"The hot tub, of course," Corallyn said with a grin.

"You goof," Visola accused with a chuckle. "Mmm, but it has been a while since I've gotten wet."

Aazuria smiled at the girls encouragingly. "You all should go have a soak. I need to spend some time reading and try to get more caught up on this modern world. I need to know everything that has happened above the surface in the last hundred years if I am going to successfully implement reform in Adlivun."

"Fine, be a bookworm and miss out on the fun stuff!" Corallyn said with a pout. "I sure am grateful that I don't have responsibilities like yours."

"You might someday," Aazuria said to her with a fond smile, "but for now, go relax!"

Corallyn grabbed her laptop and had exited the room almost before Aazuria finished speaking. Sionna smiled and predictably selected a medical volume. "I'll take this along. I can read and soak."

"Sounds like a plan to me," said Visola, trailing after her sister.

The other three having left, Elandria rearranged the throw pillows in the corner of the couch and sat down beside Aazuria. She snuggled in and got comfortable before returning to a weathered leather volume.

"Are you sure you do not wish to go with them?" Aazuria asked.

Elandria smiled and shook her head. Using her elbow to mark her place in the book, she signed to her sister: *"I prefer to stay here and read with you."*

Chapter 9: We Have Been Decimated

It was their second day out at sea, and everything had been perfect. Trevain briskly walked across the deck of the ship, his limp hardly noticeable in his determined stride. He meticulously supervised the work of his entire crew, barking out unyielding commands instead of his usual polite-but-forceful recommendations. He was normally very respectful; he knew that the men were capable of doing their jobs and he did not like to insult them by treating them like newbies and nitpicking over minutiae. However, things had changed—Trevain found himself suddenly searching for the proverbial Devil whom he understood to have a penchant for haunting the details.

He would have liked to exchange a word or two, or better yet, blows with that particular Devil.

The crew responded to his behavior in kind, carrying out their instructions in jumpier, but more obedient form. It had only been a few days since Leander's death, and to a disinterested onlooker the actions of those aboard might have seemed more or less exactly the same as before, (the men were still performing the same routine procedures, and still catching crabs, after all) but the atmosphere had changed significantly.

"Good work, Edwin. Those pots look secure. Careful there, Brynne—if that pitches to starboard you'll get crushed."

"Not my first rodeo, Captain."

Trevain smiled at the woman's lithe movements as she climbed over the pots. She really was an asset to the morale of the team. "Perfect as always, Doughlas. Just rig a few more of those up and we should be ready to start today's catch. Callder, for god's sake! You aren't done with the bait yet?"

"If this herring didn't reek so goddamn bad I could work faster," Callder complained, wiping his forehead with the back of his gloved hand.

Trevain rolled his eyes at his little brother. "Jesus, how long have you been doing this? You should be numb to the smell of fish by now."

Brynne could not help cracking a smile. "The aroma must remind him of the strippers he's been hooking up with lately."

The men all burst into laughter. Doughlas clapped Brynne on the back. "Low blow! I swear; these jokes are twice as funny coming from a lady."

"She's just jealous," Callder said with a scowl as he scooped up great handfuls of putrid bait. "She just needs to get laid is all. She misses all of this hotness."

"Brynne is *way* out of your league, Calamari," Billy said with a giggle. "She could have you in a second if she wanted to."

Callder grinned. "True. Do you want me in a second, Brynne?"

"You can ask me ten times a day, Calabash, but my answer isn't going to change."

Trevain smiled at the antics of his shipmates. "Let's get started, guys. Ujarak, did you remember to bring the..."

He found himself trailing off midstride and mid-speech. The captain's head swiveled sharply to the south, and he felt a keen sense of awareness overtake his body. He felt shivers of trepidation suddenly arrest him, along with a dark feeling that could only be described as dread. He walked to the edge of the deck and grasped the railing, staring out at the giant swells of the sea breaking against the boat.

In the darkness of the wee morning, the water looked black. It felt black.

The color was not for lack of light, but for malevolence. Trevain suddenly felt himself taken by a bout of dizziness. *Am I going crazy? Today looks like it's going to be a perfectly fine day for fishing. The skies are clear, the temperature is mild, and the waves are pleasant. What's wrong with me?* He stared at the water until he imagined he saw large, dark figures just under the surface. He peered down at them, trying to determine whether they were whales or sharks or something of the sort. But something about the silhouette of a certain figure struck him as oddly human—and there was no shape more capable or terrifying. He turned around, observing his men hard at work as his double vision began to correct itself. He felt ill.

"Stop," Trevain said abruptly. "We're turning around at once."

Ujarak's brows knitted together in confusion as he paused, his hands full of ropes. "Captain Murphy? You're kidding right?"

"No. We need to turn around."

"You've gotta be kiddin' me, Cap'n!" Wyatt Wade shouted across the boat. "Billy and I are just gettin' warmed up here! There are plenty more crabs for the catchin'!"

"Everyone stop," Trevain said resolutely. "We won't be fishing today. We're going back to shore."

Brynne frowned deeply. "What the hell, Murphy? I know I only worked eighteen hours yesterday, but I needed a nap mainly due to the jet lag. I'm good to go for another twenty-five to thirty hours today."

Everyone else chimed in with murmurs of agreement.

"Listen," Trevain said gravely. "I may sound crazy right now; I know I'm asking you all to sacrifice potentially fifteen thousand dollars each... but we need to turn around."

The crew members looked at each other in quiet surprise and disbelief. The Wade brothers, Wyatt and Wilbert mumbled to each other in displeasure and bewilderment.

Edwin flexed his enormous arm and scratched the back of his neck in puzzlement. "Look, Captain Murphy. I want to be home in front of the television with a beer in my hand and my feet on the ottoman just as much as the next guy... but we have a job to do. We can't go it alone—we need to stick together as a team."

"We've already taken some unexpected time off," Ujarak added as he crunched down on an unfortunate toothpick. "We lost prime fishing days due to the whole situation with Leander. We have major catching up to do."

"I'm telling you all now—if we want to avoid more unexpected days off, and more anguish and grief, we're not going to fish today." Trevain's voice was inflexible and resolute.

"But Trevain..." Wilbert Wade whined.

"No buts, Billy."

Callder snickered a bit at this, but promptly stopped when he felt Wyatt's elbow connect with his ribcage.

"Trevain," Brynne began, almost frantically, "I know that you feel responsible for what happened. My outburst didn't help. I'm really sorry for attacking you before. I said some awful things. I just didn't know how to deal with it other than to lash out, you know? But please, Trevain... don't give up on us. Be reasonable..."

"Brynne, this is not up for discussion. We're turning around."

"Wow. When did my big bro grow a pair?" Callder questioned

sarcastically. The captain glared at his brother, but their staring contest was interrupted by Arnav stepping between them.

"Guys... look. It occurs to me that we've been decimated."

"What?" asked Wilbert grumpily.

"It's a word that's been stuck in my head for days," Arnav spoke. "Decimation. It's not an easy thing to deal with, and I think we're all a little off our game..."

"Decimation?" Ujarak asked.

"It's a war term. It means that one tenth of our forces have been destroyed," Doughlas answered. "There were ten of us on this boat originally, and one of us was killed. That amounts to exactly one tenth of our unit being destroyed."

"But this isn't a war, boys," Brynne said "We're a crew, not a unit. No one is attacking us. The crabs certainly aren't fighting back. It was just an accident."

"Whatever it was, I won't let it happen again," Trevain vowed.

"It won't. Leo was an anomaly," Wyatt Wade said. "If we get scared now, it's kind of like we just got pulled over for speeding on the highway, and decided to slow down for the rest of the trip out of fear. It's asinine —I mean logically there won't be another cop around for ages. This is Alaska, and it's fucking gigantic. They can't afford to put a cop at every exit."

"That's an interesting comparison, but a little more is at stake here than a speeding ticket. All of your lives are at stake," Trevain rebuked, running a hand through his grey hair in frustration.

"Captain Murphy," Arnav said politely. "I think that's something we all have accepted. I'm sure everyone here has heard the statistics. There are dangers in every job... people die all the time from construction and mining accidents and whatnot. But this is *the* most dangerous job in the world. I came here knowing that I was one hundred times more likely to die doing this as I was doing anything else in America."

"Not on Trevain's boat," Brynne said softly.

"Now you show some loyalty, eh?" Ujarak spat. "That's nice, Brynne. After callin' the cap'n names all day yesterday."

"I needed a nap," she said defensively.

Arnav sighed before putting his hands up. "I know Captain Murphy runs the best crew on this sea, maybe the world, and that's why I begged him almost on my knees to hire me. Still, we're not immune to the elements. What makes up for the danger is the money. If we don't work, we won't make money, and the danger isn't worth it. We can't hide from the danger whenever someone gets a bad feeling."

"I'm with the kid," said Edwin, in his Canadian way. "This job is all kinds of nasty. It's physically strenuous, it's exhausting, and it's wet. But we're here because we prefer to be rich men of action than poor men of cubicles. We're here to get insanely rich. So let's not wimp out because of what happened to poor ol' Leo. Let's catch some more crabs! Let's make expensive, scrumptious entrées out of some poor unsuspecting suckers!"

A cheer went up from the men aboard the boat, and Trevain found himself frowning. "We already have a good day's catch. We can head out again tomorrow when we've all had a good night's sleep at home in our own beds and refreshed ourselves. We need to learn not to be greedy. Let's just take what we've got so far and head back to shore."

"A day's catch isn't bad, Captain," said Doughlas, "but there comes a moment when every self-respecting man has to upgrade the old Toyota. I need a few more bucks to buy that new Audi I've been saving up for."

"Seriously? You're still on about that Audi?" Wyatt said scornfully. "I told you to go with the X6."

"Leo was saving up for a goal too. He wanted to buy a house so he could marry his girlfriend. Now he can't do any of that," Trevain scowled. "When you get too greedy you end up losing everything. Isn't that right, Callder? Isn't that the way gambling works? I *won't* gamble with your lives!"

Callder glowered at his brother, but was prevented from responding by Brynne grabbing his shoulder and shaking her head.

Ujarak sighed. "We're gambling with our own lives, Cap'n. We're already *here*. Other fishing crews aren't going to fish for a day and then go home to rest. They're all out there now, hauling in their pots and catching as many crabs as possible. They're pulling inhuman *marathons* to make the best of the season. They're bulldozing through their setbacks and focusing on the cauldron of gold at the end of this watery rainbow of shit."

"This isn't a competition with the other fishing boats," Trevain argued. "We need to focus on ourselves. I want us to do well, and I want us to make our money safely—we shouldn't be concerned with how much other fishermen are making."

"It totally is a competition," argued Wyatt. "At the end of the day, I want my house and car to be bigger and shinier than my neighbor's house and car. This is my method of achieving that. I don't have anything else in life to aspire to. This is America, you know. Do you expect me to have some kind of nobler intent than competition?"

"And when your neighbors are all also fishermen, you've gotta fish harder than them," Ujarak added.

"Fish *harder*!" Billy echoed, as though it were a prayer in a gospel choir.

"We make a lot of money, but it's in fleeting periods of time. The fishing season is always gone in minutes. Every single day of fishing that we lose is a massive amount of money lost as well, and it hurts," said Doughlas. "I start getting really depressed if I don't make money for a single day—you don't even understand."

"If you lost your life on one of these excursions, the pain of losing potential income would be the least of your concerns," Trevain muttered.

Callder advanced on Trevain threateningly, speaking in a slow and steady voice. "We're not all rich like you, big brother. Some of us need to work in order to pay our bills."

"You mean you need to pay off those credit cards you maxed out gambling, right Callder?" Trevain shot back.

"Look bro—you haven't taken a day off since you became captain. You're a beast! It's downright *weird*. You're like some kind of demonic machine-thing."

"Thanks. I believe you've taken enough days off for the both of us."

"Look, shut up! I'm trying to be nice here. I mean… you're getting pretty old. Someday, eventually, you're probably going to retire, right?"

"What the hell are you talking about?" Trevain asked with a modicum of panic. "Retire? Have you gone mad?"

"No, seriously—listen. You do a lot of other things. You read and you plant shit in your stupid garden. I do nothing except fish during the fishing season and gamble when I'm not fishing. I'm basically nothing if I'm not a fisherman. So just let me do it for once.

Let me take over and be the captain for one fucking day while you relax at home. That way everyone gets what they want. The crew can keep fishing, and you can stay at home where it's safe."

"It's not just about me! I want everyone to be safe. I have a very bad feeling about this."

"About this beautiful day?" Calder asked, making grand gestures around himself. "Big brother, maybe you need a break. A sabbatical. I know you've been taking this Leander thing hard although you're acting tough. Let me be the head honcho for this trip. We'll turn around and drop you off then we'll head over to fish near Kodiak. We're good to go, right crew?"

Many of the crew members nodded. Trevain looked around, making eye contact with all of them and frowning. "You really want to be the captain?" Trevain asked the younger man slowly. "You want to act as my deputy, take charge of things?"

"Why not? I *am* your brother. It could be good practice for when you retire."

Trevain sighed. "And when do you think that will be, kid? I could have retired at thirty if I really wanted to sit around on my thumbs."

"But there's a woman in your life now. Maybe you can relax a little."

"It's not like that, Calder. She's just a girl."

"The same way you were just a boy at her age?" Calder snorted. "She's a woman if I ever saw one. Hell, her vocabulary even intimidates me!"

Doughlas nodded. "He's right there, Captain. You need a woman."

Trevain groaned. "Guys, my personal life isn't up for discussion. Let's keep this work-related. I'm only asking that we take a break for one day."

Brynne smiled tenderly. "That's 'cause you never have a personal life, Murphy. I hate to say this, but I think Calder's right."

"You do?" Trevain scowled, thinking to himself that he would rather put Brynne in charge of his ship than Calder. However, he could see on his brother's face that beyond the confident words the younger man was seeking his approval and recognition. What kind of monster would he be if he withheld it from him? He was the only family that the boy had. Calder was his responsibility.

"Do you guys think he can do this?" Trevain asked his crew.

The first mate Doughlas had a skeptical look on his face, but he only shrugged. "He can't make it worse. We know what our jobs are."

"Let him give it a shot, Trevain," Brynne said gently. She was smiling brightly at seeing Callder show a bit of initiative. Trevain knew that Brynne had always had a soft spot for his younger brother. She liked her men the way she liked her cars and houses—pathetic fixer-uppers that she could feel sympathy for initially and profoundly proud of after the renovations. She had never successfully renovated a man, of course.

"Alright, alright, fine," Trevain said, taking a deep breath in surrender. "Callder, I'll give you the chance to do this. You can run the rest of the excursion."

"Awesome!" said Callder gleefully. "You won't be disappointed. You deserve to spend some down time with your new girlfriend."

"I told you she's not—"

"She will be. I like that Aazuria, even though she talks a bit funny. So go home. Take her out for dinner. Show her your stupid plants."

Chapter 10: *Homo sapiens marinus*

"He is especially well-preserved for a land dweller of his proportionately advanced years. What if she falls in love with him?" Corallyn asked, wriggling to allow the jets of water better access to massage her back.

"She deserves the opportunity to 'fall in love,' but she is much too reasonable a person to lose her head about it. We need her, and she won't neglect us," Sionna answered, flipping a page of her book. She was seated on the edge of the hot tub and only allowed her calves to dangle inside. Her twin sister was, contrarily, completely submerged.

"What if we all mate with regular land-dwelling humans?" Corallyn asked. "We'll… what's the word? Hybridize? All of our children will be mostly human and our descendants will be regular boring ol' terrestrials. They'll live shortened lives and never even have a chance to see Adlivun. I would probably be dead already if I were a land-dweller!"

"There are negative aspects of that scenario," Sionna answered distractedly as she continued her reading.

Corallyn became annoyed at being ignored and pulled Visola out from under the surface. "What do you think about that? Us hybridizing with humans?"

Visola blinked the water out of her eyes with her red eyelashes. "We are human, aren't we? What's the big fuss?"

"You know what I mean!" Corallyn said in exasperation.

"Well," Visola said thoughtfully, "after working at the strip club, I've learned that men generally prefer us to land-dwelling women. If you want to go out and 'hybridize' when you look old enough, you shouldn't have a problem finding a mate."

"Why is that?" Corallyn asked.

Visola grinned. "The buoyancy of water keeps our breasts from sagging. Gravity, man. If I had lived on land for five hundred years my breasts would be dragging on the floor!"

"No. Technically they would be dust. You wouldn't be able to live for five hundred years on land," Sionna corrected.

"Well, hypothetically," Visola explained jauntily. "But look at you, Coral. You've lived ninety years and you don't even *have* breasts yet. Now that's a superior lack of senescence."

"Yes, yes, of course. We're so superior," Corallyn muttered, "but if we're so great, why are there so few of us and so many of them? And why do they have television and the internet, but we don't?"

Visola splashed water at the young girl in response, and they both laughed.

"Hey! Reading here. Don't get my pages wet," Sionna said sternly.

"Sorry," Corallyn said. She leaned her head back against the concrete edge of the hot tub. "I know my questions sound silly to you two, since you've lived on land among humans before. It's all just so new to me. One moment we're calling ourselves human, and the next we're saying that we're superior. I'm having difficulty drawing the line between them and us. Sometimes there is no line. Sometimes there's a canyon."

"*Homo sapiens marinus*," Aazuria said as she entered the room and approached the girls in the hot tub. Elandria trailed behind her with her hands wrapped around her braid.

"What's that?" Corallyn asked.

"It is what I believe we would be identified as if they ever 'discovered' us," Aazuria said with a smile, crouching down beside the hot tub. "We are human, but it is undeniable that we have diverged at least enough to warrant a subspecies."

"Perhaps," said Sionna curiously, looking up from her book. "Yet there are a lot of human beings with unusual traits. There have been Alaskan Inuit families with blue skin. One wouldn't consider a person with that condition, although they look extremely unique, to be of a different species."

"Yes, but that's not really functionally any different," Visola argued. "Our people have lived separate from land-dwellers for tens of thousands of years. Instead of treating our unique traits as a disease or unfavorable mutation, they were revered, preserved, and propagated. Additional changes have happened to our bodies over time, and we've been perfected. I believe it makes sense for us to have our own subspecies."

"There's one problem with that, Viso," Sionna said, closing her book and placing it aside. "We have never really completely been separate from the land-dwellers. Perhaps it's due to some innate nostalgia, or sentimentality, but our culture has always been intricately tied with theirs. We have always interbred with them, even when it was disallowed. Many of us have chosen to live among them, and I would argue that our true differences are much more political than biological."

"Stop, stop. You guys are confusing me," Corallyn complained, putting her hands to her head. "I just asked a simple question, and now my thoughts are even more muddled than before."

Elandria smiled and lifted her hands to contribute. *"That was not even a slightly simple question, Coral. As you can see, there are very conflicting opinions on the matter. Just remember: your mother was a completely human land-dweller. Father said she hated the water with a passion, was afraid of it, and would never go near it. The twins were fathered by a man, a great warrior, who was one of us but chose to live on land and leave his daughters below. That being said, you have lived your entire life, from just shortly after your birth, immersed in the sea with us. Whatever stance you choose, remember to honor the balance of our connection to the land and those who dwell on it in addition to the separation from it which makes us unique."*

Corallyn nodded as she processed the words which rolled off Elandria's fingers. She moved closer to the silent woman who had seated herself on the edge of the hot tub, and leaned her head on Elandria's knees. Corallyn had never known the land-dwelling mother that her sister had mentioned. She knew that she was named after the woman, Koraline Kolarevic, who had been a tall blonde ballerina with whom Aazuria had taken private lessons. However, it had been Elandria herself who had raised and educated Corallyn. Corallyn respected and loved Elandria as much as she could have loved any mother. The two shared a father, but had been born hundreds of years apart to different women.

"You never cease to amaze me, Elan," Aazuria commented. "Balance between separation and unity with humans and the land. It sounds like the perfect purpose to aspire to."

Visola shrugged and asked, "Don't we have that already? We walk amongst them and they can't tell we aren't like them. Some of them probably have our abilities and will never even know they are anything special. Humans look at other humans of different skin tone or gender, or as Sio points out, even political alignment, as far more different than us."

"That's only because they lack knowledge of our people," Sionna said, stretching her arms, "but you know, we truly do not have balance. The Alaskan Inuit families with the blue skinned people—there was nothing really wrong with them, they just appeared different. They were missing a certain enzyme in their blood called diaphorase. In fact, some of them lived longer and healthier lives and had more children than people with regular skin tones. But that trait was so rare that it has been basically lost now. It was preserved when the blue people lived in closed off communities and intermarried with cousins or close relatives who had similar genes... but as soon as they began to travel out into the world, the trait pretty much dissipated. It's too bad. It was rather special."

Visola quickly added, while staring pointedly at Aazuria, "Not as special as being able to breathe underwater."

"Exactly," Sionna said. "That's why we need to be careful, and protect it. It's our gift... we should not throw it away. Do you understand what we're saying, Aazuria?"

"Yes. Yes, of course I do," Aazuria answered halfheartedly.

"Some rather large decisions need to be made rather soon about our future," Sionna reminded her. "I only hope that you will..."

"We will make those decisions together, and as wisely as we can manage," Aazuria said.

"They're both implying that you shouldn't fall in love with Trevain even though he's super nice and has a great house with an awesome hot tub," Corallyn said bluntly. "You will eventually have to return to Adlivun and go through the coronation..."

"I know," Aazuria said firmly, "I know."

"Sweetie," said Sionna gently, "just don't do anything with him physically. It will break your heart if you have to leave him after that."

Aazuria nodded.

"Oh, for sure!" Visola said adamantly. "Considering you've never been with a man—not in six hundred years? No way. You will attach far too much emotion to the first person you sleep with, and if it's a land-dweller then he'll be dead in a few years and you'll be mourning him for centuries more. Gosh, Zuri—do anything but that! The first man you sleep with should be your king. It should be a sea-dweller who

83

can remain in Adlivun with you. Someone who will be around as long as you will be."

"Viso, I get it," Aazuria said with a smile. "I know what is required of me."

"Do you, Zuri?" Sionna asked, looking at her friend inquisitively. "I have never seen you show so much interest in a man as you seem to be showing to this Captain Trevain Murphy. There are plenty of male sea-dwellers at home, hundreds. If no one there suits your taste—and I am quite sure no one does—we could travel. We could go to Japan and live amongst the Ningyo for a time, meet new people. If we need to travel further…"

"Stop this!" Aazuria said, grimacing. "Do I seem that desperate for a man that we must make it a priority and travel the whole undersea world for it? Please. I just killed my father, and a girl does not get over such a thing so easily. Let us focus on what is important."

There was a heavy silence for several lengthy minutes.

Aazuria cleared her throat and began speaking to break the silence. "The book that Elandria gave me earlier was intriguing. It suggested that the main difference between human beings and other apes is that our bodies are so well adapted to aquatic life: because we had an aquatic ancestor. It mentioned the way that our bones and organs are better suited to functioning when submerged."

"That's true. Land-dwelling elderly have issues with arthritis in their joints from chronically moving on land," Sionna added. "They perform exercises underwater because it's gentler."

"Is it any wonder that we live so much longer?" Visola asked. She rubbed her neck idly. "So, your book posits that the secret ingredient which makes all of humanity special is our ancestral connection to the water? Therefore, our bodies and our way of living is closer to the ancestral condition and more natural? I believe the correct celebratory term here is 'boo-yah.'"

Sionna winced at the use of the word and made a horrified face, but with a great effort she refrained from reprimanding her sister.

"I guess that's why they have hot tubs in their houses," Corallyn said with a chuckle as she lightly splashed the surface of the water.

"That is true," Aazuria said. "They find comfort in the same things that we do. They are quite akin to us."

"Yes," Sionna said, "and that's why they're dangerous. They are similar enough to assimilate us completely! Our numbers are dying.

There are hardly any of us left who have all of the *pure* sea-dweller traits like you do, Princess Aazuria. All of our children could eventually just blend in with them, and we would lose our culture and disappear."

"I sometimes wonder… about my daughter," Visola said uncomfortably. Everyone else quieted down, for this was a subject that the warrior never felt comfortable enough to address. She had already begun staring forward vacantly when Aazuria reached out to touch her shoulder. Visola gave her friend a sad smile. "I suppose my little girl already has blended in with land-dwellers."

Sionna closed her eyes, feeling her twin sister's pain as if it were her own. "It is not such an inadequate life, to live among humans," she said softly. "For some, it's what they would choose."

"No," Aazuria said, shaking her head. "It was only under Father's tightening regime that we fell apart. The largest allure of being a sea-dweller is the feeling of freedom. You are liberated from land constraints and borders—or at least there is an illusion of such. If you are forbidden to leave your home whatsoever, the whole 'freedom' aspect severely suffers."

"*It certainly made our charmed life much less charming,*" Elandria responded. "*Even a glorious ice palace can be hideous when you are incarcerated within it.*"

Sionna sighed. She reached out to touch her sister's arm. "Sweetie, we should probably take a cab back to work." Visola nodded, her eyes still empty and forlorn. She was evidently immersed in thoughts of her lost daughter.

"Good luck, you two!" Corallyn said with a shudder. "I'm so glad I don't look old enough to work in that awful sounding place."

Visola forced herself to smile and put on an energetic voice as she rose from the hot tub. "Coral, dear! It's quite a lot more fun than you'd expect—the unparalleled sense of power you get! A bit of breath on a man's neck, just enough to rustle the tiny hairs there, and he's putty in your hands. Quite easy really."

"What if the thought of a man being 'putty in my hands' doesn't appeal to me?" Corallyn inquired with a raised eyebrow.

"Then you just don't understand the delicious manipulatin' goodness you're missin' out on!" Visola teased, drying her auburn curls with a towel.

"Viso, stop trying to act as though you know anything about

being on land or being around men," Sionna scolded as she also dried herself off.

"You're right, sis. I should stick to what I know: knives and spears." Visola's tone had suddenly grown darker and her expression had become hard. "Now, I know you all value my opinion and I must advise serious caution. Trevain has an extremely fascinating library, and he seems to be a clever fellow. The more intelligent a man is, the more dangerous he is. Also, the chances of him being 'good' are much fainter."

"Aw, you should give him a chance, Viso," Corallyn said kindly.

"No. I will not. The moment I relax and expect anything better than the worst is the moment that the worst will inevitably happen. Sio and I have to go to work, but I swear—you two. Look out for Zuri. This is a command. If anything happens to Aazuria while I'm gone, I swear to Sedna, I will hold both of you responsible. I will kill both of you in the most painful fashion conceivable."

Visola wrapped her towel around her body and strode away from the other women. Sionna sent the others an apologetic look and rushed after her sister.

Elandria hesitantly lifted her hands as if she were intending to sign something. However, after a slight twitch of her fingers, her hands fell back to her sides below the water. She was physically speechless.

"I read about the ingredient that makes her like that," Aazuria mused to herself, "I believe it is called 'testosterone.'"

Corallyn turned to Aazuria incredulously. "How many more hundreds of years do you think she's going to carry around that vendetta of hers?"

Aazuria lifted her shoulders and let them fall dejectedly. "I do not anticipate that she is going to become trusting anytime soon. She was atrociously betrayed by the man she loved. She was left alone and with child—she was abandoned and had to raise her daughter by herself. I mean—we were all there for her, but it was not what she needed. She was never the same after that. She had been a strong and formidable warrior before Vachlan... but after what he did to her, she was ruthless. She became fearsome and unforgiving."

Elandria lifted her hands out of the water again. She closed her eyes solemnly as she moved her fingers in signage: "*It did not help when she lost her daughter.*"

"Poor Viso," Corallyn said, hugging herself. "If I ever met that

Vachlan, I would give him a piece of my mind for hurting her like that."

Elandria looked at the small girl in horror. She shook her head fiercely, a harsh look on her face. She gripped her braid tightly until the sinews in her forearms were strained.

Aazuria placed a hand on Elandria's back, massaging in gentle circles to soothe her. She then turned to glare at Corallyn and spoke in an austere tone. "Do not wish it. He is not the kind of person you should ever have the misfortune of encountering."

"That man is an abomination to both aquatic and terrestrial humanity," Elandria viciously signed. *"I hope he no longer breathes air or water."*

Chapter 11: Floating in Stability

Trevain stood on the docks and watched *The Fishin' Magician* depart until it was indistinguishable from a grain of sand on the horizon. His worries accumulated as he watched *his* boat float away, completely without his guidance. He was not sure whether he felt more like his crew and ship had abandoned him, or like he had abandoned them. His brother had been right: he had not taken a break from work in as long as he could remember. Now, as he watched his men head off without him, he felt sick to his stomach. It did not seem right to him that he should be left on the land while they sailed off to sea—his sea. That was where he belonged.

He felt a powerful withdrawal from the comfort that his sense of control had given him. Trevain had never realized that being captain of his ship had not only meant that the crew depended on him, but that he also depended on them. Without his boat and his men, his body did not feel like it weighed the same as before. He did not feel like he was attached to the ground. He was unencumbered and free from burden—he was as light as a teenager, and just as terrified.

He wondered how owning and running a floating vessel could have the effect of making him feel so steadfast and immovable. Why did bowling through twenty-foot-breakers make him feel like his roots were firmly planted? When he was at sea, he was floating in stability.

Turning to the parking lot, he began walking towards his car. There was no use standing on the dock and waiting for the *Magician* and his crew to return. They would probably stay over in Kodiak, and might not return for a week. He glanced back over his shoulder deftly, and seeing nothing as far as the horizon, felt strangely naked. He had been stripped of his boat, his job, and his authority. He returned his gaze to his Range Rover as he approached it.

His eyes fell on the gaudy bumper sticker that Callder had given him for some recent past birthday. Big orange capital block letters against a blue background declared: "EAT. SLEEP. FISH." He had always seen the sticker as a lame product of Callder's juvenile sense of humor, but had sentimentally valued it because it had been a gift from his brother. Now he saw it as almost a clinical diagnosis of an addiction. Callder had been serious: Trevain did little more than eat, sleep, and fish—he felt little joy in anything other than work. He needed a break.

"They disobeyed me, so let them work and carry on as they see fit. It's none of my concern; they're all big boys. They'll be fine."

Unlocking and throwing the driver's door open, Trevain entered the car without even removing his waterproof yellow rubber clothing. He realized he was still somewhat in denial about the whole situation when he glanced in his rearview mirror to see if the boat was returning. He shook his head to clear it and turned the key in the ignition. Putting the car in drive, he placed his yellow-gloved hands on the steering wheel and used his yellow-booted foot to accelerate out of the parking lot.

The world around him seemed to blur as he stared straight ahead in a sort of daze. He went through the motions of driving robotically, without much conscious thought or focus. His latex-swathed fingers clutched the steering wheel tightly as angry thoughts filled his mind. He remembered the negative feelings that he had been unable to shake on the boat—the sinking sensation of dread. He merged onto the Sterling Highway, his foot heavy with indignation on the pedal. His arms locked stiffly as he remembered the way no one would listen to him. He did not understand how he could feel so much galvanizing rage, yet feel so aloof and withdrawn from his body at the same time. It was as though he had split into two separate beings—one was feeling, and the other one was retreating to a distance and observing himself feeling.

He was unable to appreciate the magnificent views of the Kenai Mountains which the highway afforded. The sight he usually found tranquil and poignant had about as much effect on his psyche as a cheesy greeting card would have had.

Trevain gritted his teeth and reached to the center console to turn on the radio. He browsed through his presets, feeling awkward at pushing the buttons with his large yellow gloves on, but at the same time hardly noticing. He really did feel like something horrible was going to happen, and this anxiety was upsetting. He felt like he had left a huge part of himself on *The Fishin' Magician* and all that lingered were the frail remnants of a clumsily functioning person.

A few familiar chords enveloped him from the various locations of the speakers on his car. It was an old romantic rock ballad he had heard when he was younger, and the tune and the sound of the voice roused his memory. His lips began to move along with the long-forgotten words as the song drew the distant pieces of him forth.

These highways just ain't long enough
for my jaded soul to wander.
These oceans just ain't large enough
for my spirit to navigate.

Trevain felt the music pervade his being. His waterproofed fingers began to tap on the steering wheel as his waterproofed toes lightly tapped on the gas pedal—too lightly to make a difference in the speed, which he suddenly noticed for the first time. He had been driving at 110 miles per hour. He took his foot off the gas pedal completely for a few seconds to allow the vehicle to calm down.

Unbidden, Wyatt's words came into his mind: *This is Alaska, and it's fucking gigantic. They can't afford to put a cop at every exit.* He frowned, thinking of the unnecessary and fruitless risk. The risk that his whole crew was now facing without him. He pressed his foot back down until the pedal hit the ground. He glared forward at nothing in particular as he began to accelerate again, feeling a thrill from the wrongness of the speeding. It gave him a sense of control along with a rush of masculinity. Watching the other cars appear to fly backwards made him feel superior to their mellow, listless drivers. The throbbing of the subwoofers added to the experience. He felt alive. He could not recall ever having felt this free on land. Again, he was floating in stability.

He forgot about his responsibilities and only felt his own existence and movement. All awareness of where he had come from and the troubles on the boat slipped his mind. All remembrance of his destination disappeared too, and he just lost himself in the music and the sensation of flying across the road. The smoothness of the rolling wheels over the highway was intoxicating; he wished the highway and the moment could go on forever. He felt the same delirious delight he felt on his boat.

He felt ridiculous.

A lyrical line reminded him of Aazuria, and thinking of her made him feel suddenly embarrassed. Trevain suddenly recalled that he was not heading home to an empty house to wallow in his own distress. He was heading home to where the beautiful dancer and her two adorable younger sisters were now staying, and they would be looking up to him for guidance. There was another ship at home of which he was newly crowned captain. He wondered why for a moment he had been acting like a rebellious youth. He had never even done so even when he had been an adolescent. It puzzled him that thinking of an eighteen year old girl made him feel embarrassed about the puerility of his actions.

"Maybe Brynne is right," he said aloud. "Maybe I am going through one granddaddy of a midlife crisis."

He continued driving, swallowing up the miles until his home. Before long, he found himself pulling into his driveway, and glancing up at the windows to check if any lights were on. Would Aazuria be awake? Seeing nothing, he sighed and entered his garage. It was an ungodly hour, and any normal person would be sleeping. It was too late for anyone to have stayed awake and far too early for anyone to have just awoken—that ominous silent moment right in between.

Trevain exited the Range Rover and entered his house, heading directly for the stairs. It slipped his mind that he had not eaten in quite a while, and it slipped his mind that he was still wearing his waterproof fishing clothes as he headed upstairs. He found himself glancing under doors for any signs of light or life. It was just his luck that as soon as his house was no longer empty, he would still come home to find it deathly tranquil. What had he expected? Someone smiling and greeting him when he walked through the door?

He sighed, heading for his bedroom. He dearly wanted to just lie down and let slumber take him. He wanted to forget all about the emotions he had experienced on the boat, and especially all the ones that had been generated since he had left the boat. When he was steps away from his room, he thought he saw the dim flickering glow of a light under a door. It was the room he had shown Aazuria. He felt a small rush of hope that she was awake. How he wanted to talk to her; if only he could see her face once before he went to bed!

He approached her door, trying to walk softly, but instead having his rubber boots squeak loudly on the hardwood floors. He winced at the sound, and inwardly scolded himself for still wearing his rain gear. (It was the first time he had become aware of it since he had left the boat.) It occurred to him that perhaps Aazuria just slept with a dim light on—a night light or a lamp of sorts. He noticed a flicker again as he stared at the glow, and wondered if it was a candle. Did he even own a candle? Surely she was awake—it was not wise to fall asleep with a candle burning, and Aazuria seemed like a very wise girl.

Trevain felt tempted to knock, but he immediately realized what a horrible idea that was. (He had already lifted his hand to the door, but he abruptly lowered it before it made contact.) There was no sound coming from behind the door, and Aazuria was most likely asleep. Even if she *was* awake, it was rather unseemly for him to knock on her door at this hour! After assuring her that he would be the perfect gentleman, it would be ridiculous to bother her now, in the middle of the night, on one of her first few nights in his home.

She would surely think that he was seeking sex. He shuddered at the foul thought of being considered a dirty old man. He imagined Aazuria's face painted with fear and distrust if she were to open the door and behold him. He remembered what he was wearing. With a little sigh, Trevain turned away to head down to the hall toward his own room. He could be a patient adult and wait until the morning to see his new houseguest and speak with her.

As he walked away, he heard a light shuffling sound. He turned back and saw the light under her door becoming brighter. His hope was instantly reignited and shortly gratified. The door opened to reveal Aazuria's curious face lit softly by a flickering candle she was holding in a candleholder. She was wearing a black robe over her nightclothes. She held a book under her other arm.

"Trevain," she said in surprise, with a warm smile of greeting. She seemed genuinely pleased to see him. "I thought you would not return for days!"

"I've been kicked off my own boat," he found himself saying blithely.

"What?" she asked.

"I was supposed to be out at sea much longer, but I was paralyzed by this awful feeling. I tried to stop the fishing trip altogether, but the men just opted to eject me instead. Callder decided to try to run things."

"*Callder?*" Aazuria asked, before remembering herself. "Oh, I am sorry. I barely know him; I have only met him a few times. I am sure he is quite capable…"

Trevain started laughing. "He's completely incompetent. I'm expecting my multi-million dollar boat to return in several pieces, if at all. The boat's insured of course, but the people can't be replaced. My best bet is if Brynne and Doughlas take care of things. I'm sure it will all be fine."

Aazuria stared at him for a moment before she realized that something about the experience had shaken him; the smiles and laughs were all a cover. She gestured inside of her room. "Would you like to come in and talk about it? My sisters are asleep down the corridor, and I do not wish to wake them."

"Yes. I…" Trevain welcomed the idea of sharing his uncomfortable burden, but then he remembered the sensitivity of the situation. Aazuria was young—impossibly young. It was unseemly to enter her bedroom. He really did not want to make her feel as though he sought to sleep with her.

She cocked an eyebrow at his hesitation. "You really should vent to me about the injustice of it all; it might make you feel better."

"No. I…" Trevain felt heat flush his cheeks, and wondered why he had been suddenly reduced from a successful captain to a bumbling schoolboy. His own nervous spluttering annoyed him. The conversation was in serious need of a change of subject. Or change of location. Before he could think of the right thing to say, he noticed something strange.

"Were you reading by candlelight?" he asked with a frown.

She glanced down at the candle she held with dismay, nearly loosening her grasp on its holder. "I… well, I was…"

"You should have asked Mr. Fiskel for a desk lamp or a flashlight," he said.

"Of course," she answered, "but I did not want to bother anyone so late. I do not mind candlelight."

"What were you reading?" he asked.

"Oh," Aazuria said, squirming a bit as she tried to conceal the book behind her. "It is just a novel. I probably should be reading something scientific or historical…"

"There is nothing wrong with fiction," Trevain said. "Science and history can be easily learned. Fiction leaves you with vague impressions you need to sort out on your own. Human relationships are complex."

93

"I believe you are right," she said softly.

He nodded, reaching up to scratch his head as he looked at the strange young girl holding a candlestick. He thought that the best thing to do was to bid her goodnight and head to bed. He was tired, and stressed, and very likely to say something bizarre or senseless. He did not want to make an ass of himself, and she probably wanted to go back to reading her book. Yes, he should tell her goodnight.

He opened his mouth to wish her sweet dreams, but as he was beginning to realize was often the case when it came to Aazuria, his tongue and body disobeyed his commands. He instead found himself asking, in what was probably the dorkiest pick-up line ever:

"Aazuria… would you like to see my plants?"

Chapter 12: The Baobab Bonsai

Trevain and Aazuria stood quietly beside each other in the solarium. They had opted not to put the lights on, since the room was bathed in the dim morning sunlight streaming in through the glass. Aazuria still held her candlestick. They were an odd pair, with Aazuria in her robe and Trevain in his yellow rubber coat. They both had their arms crossed as they gazed in silence at the central piece of the solarium.

"What do you think of it?" Trevain asked.

"It is very… stout. The trunk is very intricate."

They continued to stare at the small potted plant for several more silent minutes. It was evident that Trevain wanted to say something, but he seemed uncertain of how to proceed.

"What type of plant is it?" Aazuria asked, trying to incite conversation without being intrusive. It seemed to her that there were heavy thoughts on her host's mind, as she was beginning to realize was often the case. She wanted to be involved, but she did not want to cause him discomfort by invading the private space of his mind that she imagined had been sacred for quite some time.

"It's a baobab tree," Trevain answered, as he began to pace. Despite his subtle limp, there was something decidedly dignified in his gait as he slowly circled the small tree. "The species is from Madagascar. The tree naturally grows to be massive. They get so large, and the trunk gets so thick that people can live inside of them. There's actually a *pub* inside of one of these trees in South Africa—a pub that can accommodate fifty patrons."

"That's remarkable," Aazuria responded with surprise as she eyed the tiny plant. She did not know very much about plants that grew above the surface of the sea. In fact, the only growing species in Adlivun were those that did not require sunlight, such as various mushrooms.

Trevain nodded, and the passion in his voice increased as he spoke. "People find pleasure in using the bonsai technique to domesticate them. It should be impossible to stunt the growth of a living thing to one thousandth of its natural size! There's something disturbing about it; almost paranormal even."

"And here I was thinking that it was just a plant." She squinted at the silhouette of the tree in the soft light, and could not help but think of how *alien* it looked. It did not resemble anything she had ever seen anywhere in the world—not on dry land or concealed within ocean depths.

"I hate the idea of bonsai," Trevain said firmly. "I hate the idea of constantly trimming and pruning something to keep it from reaching its full potential."

"Are there not any benefits to the method?" Aazuria asked.

"It can result in an extended lifespan for the tree—it lives a comfortable life, free from disease and drought, well-taken care of." Trevain shook his head. "I am just not convinced that living longer and being safe from the elements is worth the sacrifice of becoming what one is supposed to become. It's just... horrifying. To take a stately tree and inhibit it like this!"

Aazuria looked at Trevain curiously. She held the candle up to his face to better examine his expression. "So what this tree means to you... is hatred?"

"Restriction."

"And yet you let it live. You let it live while pitying its existence. You come here and tend to it, further restricting it while thinking about how much you despise what it represents?"

"No, not exactly. I think about my life." When he saw that she did not follow his words, he sighed. "I think about the human obsession with bringing order to anything wild. I think about control and consumption; about the anxiety that everyone has about the world running out of space and resources. I think about how unnatural it is to tell people they can only have one child. To worry that people will run out of room to live, and food to eat."

Aazuria nodded. "I see. If these trees are allowed to grow and consume everything around them, it is beautiful—a thriving majestic life form, but it is also... uneconomical?"

"Land is limited," Trevain answered. "There is only so much available for us to use for everything we need to use it for."

"Yes. Land is limited," Aazuria repeated slowly. She wished that she could tell him that she had the solution to his problems. A new habitat, an unlimited domain with almost endless opportunity for settlement; but her home did not quite suit everyone.

"I really believe that life will find a way," Trevain said gently. "The challenges push our creativity. Skyscrapers, sustainable farming; there are so many ways. When we allow anxiety about the future to inhibit our lives now..."

"How is it inhibiting life?" Aazuria asked. "You said that these miniature trees might live longer than their gigantic counterparts in the wild. So perhaps a little control can be a good thing?"

"I suppose," Trevain answered. "But think of your own life, Aazuria. You said that you have lived under constricting circumstances—would you have chosen to continue living that way if it meant you would be protected?"

Aazuria closed her eyes as she thought of her father. "Of course," she answered softly. "It was only when Father began to make foolish decisions which placed us all in dire danger that we needed to get away."

"Danger?" he asked.

"I do not wish to speak of it now," she said cryptically. Aazuria was quiet for a few moments. Finally, she glanced at Trevain and smiled at his gaudy yellow jacket. She wondered if she could "bonsai" him somehow and take him home with her. She wished that she could tell him the truth about her kingdom and her past—she did not know how to build a friendship with so many secrets between them. "If you could choose to extend your natural lifespan, would you?" she asked.

Trevain considered it before answering. "I would, but not if I had to be confined in a pot in order to do so. It's not natural for anything to live and die in a pot."

She walked to the windows. She gestured out at the water whimsically with one hand. "What if you could be even more wild and free?" she asked in a musical voice, feeling a bit homesick.

He smiled sadly, thinking of his drive earlier. "Sometimes I feel that way—but it's such an evanescent sensation."

She turned back to him, suddenly serious again. "Trevain, here in Alaska... is it not the only chance of survival for these plants? For the foreign species at least, is it not necessary to be indoors, in your solarium, in a pot?"

"Yes," he said bitterly, "but they shouldn't be here in the first place."

"What do you mean?"

"Why do I need to own an African tree here in Alaska?" Trevain quickly crossed the room to where she stood and carefully picked up a potted plant that was near to her. This one was even smaller than the baobab, and it had needle-like evergreen leaves.

"This is a Giant Sequoia bonsai. Kind of an oxymoron, isn't it? A tree of this species is the tallest tree in the world. Yet I keep mine regulated to fifteen inches tall."

"I do not think the tree minds," Aazuria suggested. "Records and milestones? Those are human fixations. I do not think that trees themselves want to be the largest of the large."

"Then what do you think they want?"

"Just to be," Aazuria said, allowing a genuine smile to possess her lips and eyes. It was all that she wanted too; she was beginning to form a secret hope that he would somehow be part of her existence. "Just to be—alive and healthy, for as long as possible."

"So the important milestone is the age of the tree, correct? It doesn't matter if it's stunted—as long as it lives a long and healthy life. In that case, practicing bonsai on these trees is a good thing, correct?"

"I... I believe so," she answered.

He gently held up the Giant Sequoia until it was between their faces. "We confine them, we constrict them... they could have been so much that we will never know. Their roots feel out gingerly until they touch the ceramic—then it's decided. They must follow the concave surface religiously, having no other choice, until they tangle up amongst themselves, suffocating." Aazuria peered around the plant at Trevain's wrinkled brow as he soliloquized. "The heart knows the immensity it wants to achieve, but it is limited..."

She cocked her head to the side curiously. "Trevain, are you saying you feel like you are a potted plant?"

He chuckled. "Well, when you put it that way it makes me sound ludicrous." He turned around and placed the tree back in its location. "I probably sound outlandish to you—don't mind me. I'm just... not quite myself right now."

"No, please tell me what you meant to say!" she insisted.

He gave her a small smile. "Growing up in Alaska, losing my parents and having to take care of Callder—I had no choice in my career. I really wish I could have done something more rewarding with my life than catch a lot of fish."

"What would you do?"

He hesitated. "I probably couldn't have done much more anyway. You never know these things."

"What would you have done?" she asked firmly.

"Maybe Marine Biology—maybe help to preserve sea life instead of massacring it on a daily basis." He shrugged. He did not know that this answer won him major points with Aazuria since she considered herself to be within the category of sea life. Trevain removed his yellow gloves and tucked them into his pocket. "I don't know. Maybe I'd have studied Cultural Anthropology and traveled more."

"Then do it," she said simply.

"I wish I could," he said with a sad smile. "It's too late to make changes of such magnitude. I'm too ol..."

"No! I cannot listen to you calling yourself old one more time," she interrupted zealously. "You are in the prime of your life! You have accumulated so much knowledge and so much experience—now you are ready to pursue that which you regret not pursuing and be exactly who you wish to be. If you feel stunted or confined, then just break out! Reach out, and explore and grow—you too can be a giant instead of being fifteen inches tall. You are already a giant in my eyes—why should you not be so in your own?"

Trevain stared at her in surprise. In the short time he had known her she had always remained so calm, but she was evidently incensed about this subject. It gave him the impression that she was beginning to care for him, at least in some small degree. Her manner was inspiring, but a few livid words could not undo years of decaying hope.

He reached out and removed the candleholder from her hand. He blew the flame out before placing it down on a table. Reaching out, he gently took both of her hands in his. "I am not young like you, Aazuria. You are a teenager and all the whole world lies before you. I wish that I were standing here a young boy of your age and that we could imagine grand futures together and dream of the glorious years to come; but I stand here a potted plant all twisted up into the prescribed shape of my confinement. Your roots are reaching out in freedom, eager to burrow their own path into the earth for miles around. My job now is to nourish you and help you grow."

She shook her head adamantly. "You cannot cast your life aside as though it is worthless!"

"I am not," he spoke softly. He was moved by her concern for him, and he closed the distance between them, wrapping her up in a fatherly hug. "The better part of my life is over but maybe I can help to make the better part of yours the best it could be."

She was a bit stiff at first and surprised by the proximity, but she took a slow deep breath and relaxed into his embrace. Hesitatingly, she lifted her own hands up to circle his body and return the hug. The fabric of his waterproof clothing was rough to the touch, but the subtle scent of him which filled her nostrils when she inhaled was particularly pleasant.

She could not shake a strong feeling of melancholy at his words; she did not feel comfortable accepting that the better part of Trevain's life was over. He was younger-looking than her father by a large margin, and her father had been expecting to live for several hundred more years. It did not make sense, or seem fair to her. She almost believed that if he somehow chose to continue living the best years of his life instead of resigning himself to being "over"—then it would suddenly be the best time of his life again.

Aazuria pulled back slightly away from his hug. She scanned his face, searching for contours or shadows of hope. "You should leave your pot," she whispered with determination. She did not know what to say or do to convince him, but she would have tried anything. She felt like there was a world between them, and it had nothing to do with the fact that they were from different worlds. It was all in his mind. "You should break out of your prison and plant yourself beside me—if I am in fact planted. How else can our roots grow interconnected?"

He studied her dark eyes, trying to decipher her meaning. Was there a subtle suggestion in her tone—was it a question or demand? He became confused. Even though he could see the truth of what she felt and wanted, he could not completely believe his eyes. He wanted to believe. He wanted to achieve the intertwined roots that she had described, building a sturdy foundation of networked essences. He wanted to build this bond with her and even more. He wanted to grow close at the core, and close at the trunk, and closer still at the branches.

Yet his honor reared its head to remind him that it was wrong. She was his ward now, and she was under his protection. He should not allow a touch of temptation to turn him into the thing from which she needed protection.

"They can't," he answered, pulling away from her abruptly. "I'm sorry I disturbed you at such a late hour and interrupted your reading. Thanks for chatting with me and listening to me rant; I had a rough day. I should probably get some rest."

With that, Trevain turned and left.

Aazuria watched his retreating yellow back with disappointment. She felt the unfamiliar sting of defeat; she had tried to reach out to him, and had found him unreachable. Would he always be so distant and disciplined, so difficult to get close to? She found herself suddenly smiling; she was sure that he was just trying to be kind and gentlemanly.

She walked over to the centerpiece of the garden. She reached out to carefully trace the patterns on the baobab's ceramic pot with the fingernail of her index finger. Harder than any pottery or steel was a person's manner of thinking; if a person chose to be firmly set in his ways he was forever immobile. On the other hand, if that same person decided to seek another way, or several other ways, there was no substance on earth that could stop such ambition.

Aazuria felt like there had been a change in her own manner of thinking. If she could accomplish such a feat after six hundred years, then surely anyone's mind was pliable. Surely anyone's heart was elastic enough to be reached.

Chapter 13: American Sign Language

"Very good, Captain Murphy," said the instructor, closing his book. "You made excellent progress in this session."

"I've never been great at picking up new languages," Trevain admitted. "This seems really difficult. Communicating a simple phrase takes so much more effort than talking."

"You get used to it if you have to," the instructor answered, beginning to gather his materials. "I don't mean to pry, but what is the reason you've decided to learn sign language?"

"There's... a woman," Trevain said, awkwardly. "She's fallen on hard times and she's staying with me. Her sister is unable to speak, and I'd like to be able to understand her."

"Ah, I see," the instructor said with a grin. "Trying to impress a lady, are we?"

Trevain smiled sheepishly. "Well, yes... but when this lady translates her sister's speech it's always very intelligent and insightful. I'd like to be able to carry on a conversation with her without the translations. Maybe it would make her more comfortable with me... we could feel a bit more like a family."

"That's thoughtful of you," the instructor said, nodding. "I'll come by at the same time tomorrow?"

Several days had passed since Trevain had been expelled from his own boat. *The Fishin' Magician* had yet to return from its leaderless voyage. Trevain had received a few phone calls from Brynne and Doughlas, assuring him that they were doing great and that everything was fine.

He wondered if he had truly been worried for no reason. Paranoia—perhaps a sign of old age? He even mused that the crew might enjoy the fishing trip without his authority more than with him there to boss them around. Maybe they would be kicking him out more often.

Trevain had been getting along very well with Aazuria and her sisters. He had taken the girls on trips to museums where he found they were fascinated with only the extremely old artifacts. He had taken them on shopping trips to update their very sparse wardrobes. He was very excited about his idea to surprise Elandria by learning American Sign Language.

Entering the kitchen to grab a snack, he happened to run right into Elandria. He decided that he was finally feeling confident enough to try to use a few phrases with her. Trevain lifted his hands and tried to communicate a few basic words of salutation, and a comment on the weather.

Elandria looked at him in confusion—her eyes darted from his hands to his face nervously.

Aazuria entered the room was immediately puzzled by the look on Elandria's face. Elandria glanced at her with worry before picking up her skirts and rushing out of the room.

"What's wrong?" Trevain asked. "Did I say something wrong? I thought I could manage a simple greeting..." He continued going over the motions with his hands, trying to figure out where he had erred.

Aazuria stared at him for a moment. "You've been learning sign language?" she asked.

"I thought it would make it easier to speak with Elandria..."

"That is so sweet of you, Trevain." Aazuria said softly. How did she tell him that their sign language probably predated any language that was currently used above water? She sighed and rubbed her temples.

"What's wrong?" he asked, approaching her. "Do you have a headache?"

She gave him a small smile, feeling saddened that he had tried to take the initiative to connect with her family, and that it had not worked out. The cultural barrier between them felt suddenly immense. Being from different countries made communication challenging, but being from different worlds was doubly daunting. She knew she must try to explain. "The sign language which my sisters use is a bit different from the common..."

"Damn!" he cursed. "I should have asked you first. The instructor did ask me if I wanted to learn British or American Sign Language, and I just assumed."

She smiled in relief. "That is correct, we use British Sign Language. Perhaps—I could teach it to you?" she asked.

"I could just ask the instructor to switch…"

"No!" she said hastily, reaching out to touch his arm. "Please, do not bother with employing an instructor. It will be my pleasure to teach you."

She smiled, moving her hand in a simple pattern, followed by another. "This is 'hello,' and this is 'how are you?'"

He repeated the motions with his hands, "Like so?"

"Perfect," she answered. "Try that with Elandria next time and maybe she will not run away in fear."

He laughed, and continued to practice to drill the words into his muscle memory.

Meanwhile, upstairs, Elandria was explaining what had happened to Corallyn.

"So that's what he's been doing for the last few days," Corallyn said in admiration. "He said that guy was his stockbroker!"

"*I did not know what to do, and I panicked,*" Elandria said. "*I could not understand him… he probably thinks I am psychotic.*"

"Nah," said Corallyn, poking her sister in the side. "You're the only sane one among us."

*　　　*　　　*

"You seem unimpressed," Trevain remarked as he observed Aazuria's reactions—or rather, the lack thereof. Her youngest sister was bouncing all over the museum, zipping from plaque to plaque to devour every word she could find.

"Oh, no," Aazuria responded as they strolled along. "The exhibit is fascinating. Just staring at the bones of all these creatures which have been dead for so long… I find it a bit macabre."

"You're difficult to please. You are always bored to tears when we go shopping and won't purchase a single thing unless I force you. I thought women were supposed to like shopping! And then you order rice and bread whenever we go out for dinner." Trevain shook his head in exasperation. "I don't understand you."

"Where I come from, rice and bread were very rare," Aazuria explained. "Plus they are usually the most affordable items on the menu. I do not wish to take advantage of your generosity."

Trevain sighed. "I wouldn't have invited you all to stay if I couldn't afford more than rice and bread!"

They came upon Elandria, who was standing before a colossal collection of bones arranged in the shape of a dinosaur-like sea creature. The silent woman had her hands clasped behind her back, and she seemed to be examining the exhibit intently.

"There!" Trevain said, gesturing to the quiet woman. "Elandria seems to like the giant monsters."

"Yes," Aazuria responded. "She keeps several as pets."

"What?"

Hearing them approach, the small woman turned around quite suddenly, her dark braid whipping over her shoulder. She fixed her sister with a puzzled look. *"It says that they believe Steller's sea-cow is extinct,"* Elandria signed. *"I suppose it is lucky that I saved a few."*

Aazuria nodded, observing the skeleton of the gentle beast sadly. *"These people destroy everything they touch. Then they put the lifeless remnants in display cases like trophies…"*

"Trophies?" Trevain asked, squinting as though it might help him to better understand what they were saying. He had barely managed to recognize three words.

Immediately embarrassed, Elandria lowered her head and moved away. She had forgotten that Trevain could now understand some of her speech, and this made her uncomfortable.

Aazuria turned to the grey-haired man apologetically. "She needs to improve her social skills."

"What were you two talking about?" he asked as they began strolling again.

"Trophies of destruction," Aazuria answered. "That is all these buildings seem to be. Some of these lost treasures were defeated by natural causes, but many were wiped out by us—and we cannot just let them go quietly. No, we must celebrate their annihilation."

Trevain stared at the dark-haired woman walking beside him. "Did anyone ever tell you that you can be really uptight?"

"Pardon me?" she asked, as she paused in her movement.

"Yeah. You're just so… stiff. If I hadn't seen you dance I would have believed you were made of harder wood than Pinocchio, and with a harder stick of wood shoved up your ass."

She stared at him speechlessly for a moment. "How dare— "

"I would apologize, but it's kind of a compliment," he explained with a smile. "I like it."

"You like the stick up my ass?"

He reached up to run a hand through his grey hair nervously. He worried that he was being too familiar. "It's just the exact opposite of what I'm used to. The men on the boat are very, very loose with language. They curse like... sailors. Listening to you speak is rather refreshing. I don't feel my brain hurting as it tries to process the rawness into something palatable."

"I cursed that one time," Aazuria reminded him.

"And it was adorable," he said. "I like your language. It reminds me of something... maybe an old fashioned, black-and-white movie. I also like the fact that you never slouch. It makes me feel like I should pay more attention to my own posture and language."

"A stick up my ass," Aazuria repeated, in disbelief. "There is only one person who has ever dared to say such things to me..."

"I didn't mean to insult you," Trevain said, but he was suddenly grinning. He gestured around them to the re-assembled skeletons. "Most of the time, you seem more rigid and emotionless than these guys. So yes, there is a stick the size of a Giant Sequoia, and it is way up there."

Aazuria's eyes widened. "But... I am a..." She felt the need to explain that she was extremely old, and from a royal bloodline, and that there had always been certain things expected of her. But when she tried to finish her sentence, laughter bubbled out of her instead. "A stick! Trevain, you..." The hilarity began to shake her torso. Glancing up at the dead dinosaurs, and picturing that Trevain considered them more passionate than she was, she suddenly found herself doubling over in laughter. Was she that horrible?

Corallyn happened upon them at that moment, and she stared at the spectacle with surprise. She saw the self-satisfaction on Trevain's face, and she lifted her eyebrows. "Wow. You made my sister laugh? I haven't *ever* seen her really laugh like that... but I'm only ninety—er, nine." Corallyn felt embarrassed by her blunder and quickly tried to distract him with a compliment. "You must be a magician."

"No," Trevain answered, looking at Corallyn suspiciously. "I'm just the *Magician's* captain."

In another attempt to distract him, she bounced up on her toes. "Uncle Trevain, will you buy me something cool in the gift shop?"

"Sure."

"Now, now, Corallyn," Aazuria said, having regained control of herself. "I told you that you need to stop frivolously spending the captain's money."

"Don't listen to her," Trevain said to the young girl warmly. "She has a health issue which makes her so snooty. Something about a large tree."

Aazuria was astounded by his boldness as Corallyn pulled them both towards the gift shop. Trevain sent her a playful wink.

"Look. This bottle of lacquer has my name on it!" the young girl exclaimed.

"It's called 'nail polish,'" Trevain explained. "Women use it to paint their fingers and toes."

"Uncle Trevain, will you purchase it for me?" Corallyn asked. "Please! There's a Coral Sunrise and a slightly darker Coral Catalyst."

"Sure," Trevain told her. "Get as much as you like. Maybe you can pick a color for your boring sister to try to liven her up."

"Heavens!" Aazuria said, shaking her head. "You are having entirely too much fun at my expense."

"I'm trying to have enough for the both of us," he told her.

She smiled. "I will make an effort to relax. On one condition."

"What's that?"

Aazuria slipped her hand against Trevain's large palm, weaving her soft fingers between his rough ones. "Show me one of those old-fashioned, black-and-white movies."

Chapter 14: Raine and Storm

"Now introducing an amazing duo who will knock your socks off: *Raine and Storm!* Give it up, gentlemen!"

The redheaded Ramaris twins made their grand entrance, smiling and bowing. Sionna, or Raine, was wearing a tuxedo bodysuit and fishnet stockings, and her hair was pulled back tightly from her face. She was evidently her sister's assistant for the show. She moved to a circular piece of wood which her sister eagerly strapped her against with leather cuffs.

Visola, or Storm, wore a long glittering green dress with long slits up the side, all the way to her waist. There were knives strapped to her thighs, and she held a saber in her hand. Visola brazenly walked up to the edge of the stage, and picked up a champagne bottle that was usually left there for her show. She smiled to the audience, displaying the bottle to them before she used her sword to "cut" off the lip of the bottle. A small uproar of excitement came from the crowd as the champagne bottle burst open.

Personally, Visola found the sabrage trick rather boring and easy; it was a trick of physics more than skill, and it was performed with a blunt sword. Nonetheless, the collective enthusiastic response of the audience made her grin. She followed this by tilting her head back, turning the champagne bottle upside down over her mouth and pouring a few glasses worth of the bubbly liquid down her throat. Much of it spilled over her cheeks and chin, cascading over her chest and over the sequins of her dress. The liquid pooled around her high heels, but she did not care. Visola had no aversion to being covered with liquid of any kind. The audience found this extremely entertaining.

Disposing of the saber and champagne bottle by 'recklessly' tossing them aside, she pulled one of the knives from her thigh strap. She showed it to the audience confidently, walking the length of the stage and causing the men to murmur in interest. She moved forward to a man sitting near the stage, and grabbed his tie, yanking him forward before slicing the tie off. He fell abruptly back down in his chair. Everyone laughed and cheered at the demonstration of how sharp her knife was. She giggled and winked at the man in apology for ruining his tie. He smiled at her, and she could tell he did not mind in the least.

Sauntering towards her sister who was strapped onto the wheel, Visola ran her knife along her twin's neck. Sionna tried to act appropriately scared and vulnerable. Visola took a step back, and set the wheel spinning in one fluid motion. That should have been enough, but the audience did not know her strength. She pushed it again twice for demonstrative purposes, to give the impression that it was spinning even faster.

Moving back to the other end of the stage, Visola proceeded to throw her knife at Sionna. She rapidly chose another from her thigh to throw within a second. The men in the audience stared spellbound in amazement. When the wheel stopped spinning, Visola had thrown four knives at her sister. Two were piercing the shoulders of her outfit, very close to her neck, and another two were piercing her tuxedo coattails on either side of her hips. Finally, she took a fifth knife out from deep within her cleavage, and she aimed and tossed it right between Sionna's thighs.

The audience erupted into applause and cheering. There was a loud standing ovation, as Visola bowed. She pretended to walk off the stage and forget about her sister, but then raised a finger to indicate that she had remembered at the last second. Even this goofy bit of drama earned her chuckles. It was an easy and good-natured audience tonight, for which she was grateful. Visola could comfortably feed off the warmth of a crowd like this one. She returned to untie Sionna. The women held hands and bowed graciously, earning even more accolades and yelling. They walked off the stage together.

When the twins entered the back room, the loud buzz of various power tools was heard. Hairdryers, curling irons, and straighteners were wrangling unruly hair while fancy electric razors were being used to deforest legs. Nail files and nail clippers were being vigorously employed in taming talons. Girls were frantically asking each other to borrow equipment; superglue to fix garments that had come apart, antiperspirant, perfume, and mascara. Noxious fumes were everywhere from the nail varnish, hairspray, and foul, nauseating mixture of beauty products in the air. To the senses, the atmosphere seemed more like a construction site than a dressing room—indeed, each of the women was her own little building project.

The twins tried to find a quiet corner of the dressing room to sit.

"Did you have to nick my pantyhose, Viso? Heavens. Hundreds of years of training and you use it mainly to annoy me! Your poor older sister."

"Only older by a minute, darlin'. Besides, the crowd loved the expression of almost-barely-surprise on your face, and I can't get that unless the knife hits close enough for you to feel the breeze and the vibration. Maybe draw a little blood next time to make you yelp so they don't think you're a statue."

"I just know how good you are. It rather bores me to have you throw knives at me, you know."

"I know. But you don't have to yawn! You can at least act a little impressed!"

"I do not fear for my life or even my skin," Sionna said with a smile. "I do, however, fear for the lives of those who would intend me harm."

"Or even a hint of disrespect," Visola added with a wink. The twins did not share many sentimental moments, preferring the merriment of bickering. They both were entirely secure that they cared deeply for each other underneath the surface squabbles.

"Hey," said a woman with a thick Russian accent, "there is man looking for you."

Visola eyed the woman's sagging boobs disdainfully. They perfectly conformed to her personal stereotypical expectations, and this was disappointing. "Sorry, sweetheart—I am only interested in military men at the moment."

"Why? You are better than everyone else?" the woman spat questioningly. "You are princess?"

"No, tootsie-pie," Visola said in a supremely condescending voice as she rose from her chair and advanced on the woman. "*I* am not a princess, but I happen to be the elite bodyguard of one: and guess what that means?"

"Stand down!" Sionna ordered as she firmly restrained her sister. Then, once she felt Visola relax she made a show of fake gagging. "Tootsie-pie? *Tootsie-pie?* My goodness, Visola! Could you be any more experimental with your language?"

The Russian woman made a disgruntled noise and fished a

cigarette out of her sequined bra, proceeding to light up before the twins.

"You are not allowed to do that," Sionna scolded, eyeing the cigarette warily. "Other people have to breathe this tainted air, which is already killing us rather quickly. I know you have no idea what I'm talking about, but I can *feel* myself aging. Put that cigarette out immediately!"

"Why? I can smoke if I want," she answered stubbornly, jutting out her chin and taking a defiant suck of her cigarette before blowing the air out at Visola's face. "This man is military man. He is asking to see you now."

Visola's green eyes flashed with rage to have smoke blown into her face, but Sionna's arms still restrained her. She processed the words that the annoying woman had spoken. "Really? Where is this man?"

"Why should I tell you, princess?" the Russian dancer asked, raising a thinly plucked and stenciled eyebrow. She pointed her finger at Visola threateningly. "You are rude girl."

"You should tell me," Visola said softly, staring at the offending finger, "because I use knives with great precision."

The girl sized her up before turning to leave. "He is the man sitting by bar, wearing red shirt."

"Score!" said Visola with a grin. She called out to the retreating dancer, "Thanks, lady."

Sionna released her grip on her sister and began rubbing her own temples. "You know, there are ways of getting information from people… and just plain communicating with them which don't involve threatening."

"Why fix it if it isn't broken? It's been my surefire method for half a millennium. Oh, boy! I sure do hope this guy can help me get access to what I need. You never know when your day is going to suddenly become more important than all the other days." Visola cheerfully checked her reflection. "Now how do I look? Wish me luck!"

Visola had disappeared before Sionna could respond. Sionna rolled her eyes skyward before looking into the mirror and responding to herself. "You look exactly like me. Your makeup is a bit trashier, of course. Otherwise, dear sister, you are drop dead gorgeous. Also, you make *every* day important with that crazy charisma of yours. Good luck."

Chapter 15: Brynne's Bad News

The doorbell rang once, demurely.

One of Aazuria's eyes squinted open. She felt an unusual pressure across her stomach, and was startled to see that it was an arm. An arm belonging to another person—a rather heavy arm. Everything was heavier on land, but she was not accustomed to having arms draped across her body at all. Her eyes followed the limb to their possessor and she was further amazed to see a man. This was the most surprising element of the situation altogether. She looked around and took in the couch, the popcorn, the empty bottles of wine, and the television still tuned to the channel that constantly played old black-and-white movies.

This is exceedingly comfortable, she thought to herself with contentment, remembering the movie marathon they had had the night before. She had been swept away in the classic beauty of Audrey Hepburn and Marilyn Monroe, of schoolteachers falling in love with doctors, and millionaires with big boats. (Trevain had jealously insisted that his ship was worth a hundred useless pleasure yachts.) After Corallyn and Elandria had gone to sleep, Aazuria had finally relented to trying a glass of merlot called Pétrus, and had enjoyed sipping on the fruity oak flavor for hours. Eventually, they had needed to open another bottle. She hoped that Visola would never find out about her lapse, for after years of giving the redhead grief about her drinking habits, she would surely seem an awful hypocrite. But she did not regret it—the moment had begged for a touch of abandon.

As the divine dark liquid had caressed her palate with hints of berries and vanilla, her spirits had begun to soar with sensual pleasure. She had not wanted the moment to end, and had requested "one more movie" at least five times, until she was far too tired to sit upright. Her memory was fuzzy about her final hours of consciousness, but she remembered growing comfortable enough to lie against Trevain's chest on the couch. She remembered his fingers lazily stroking her long dark

113

hair, entangling between the strands near the nape of her neck. She remembered how soft and warm, how extraordinarily cozy he had been. She remembered thinking that she would give up her kingdom in a heartbeat for this.

She remembered being so overwhelmed by the beauty beyond the television screen that she had begun crying during one of the scenes. Aazuria had discovered with dismay that the one century she had been confined to the water happened to have been the most incredible century in the history of humanity.

"I have missed it all," she had moaned. "I have missed the entire twentieth century. How can I never have seen a movie? All this technology, all of these new stories. How can he have kept it all from me? I should have been able to experience all of this as it was created!"

"Aazuria, these movies were filmed long before you were born. Some of them even long before I was born. Luckily, they have all been preserved and we can still see them now."

"You are wrong. It is not the same," she insisted, tears cascading over her cheeks. "The world has changed so much that I hardly know it anymore. I do not belong here. I want to survive in your world, but I do not know the first thing about this place."

"I'll teach you everything you want to learn," Trevain promised, wiping away her tears. "The world isn't going anywhere anytime soon. We can go and see anything you want to see."

"Just stay close to me," she pleaded. "There is too much to take in—I am afraid that I will make too many mistakes. I will stumble and fall on these weak legs. I am so lost here."

"I won't let you fall," he had answered.

She remembered Trevain lightly pressing his lips against hers in a reassuring kiss. But she was not sure if that was memory or imagination of what she had wished to happen. She should have felt embarrassed at showing such emotion—Aazuria had always prided herself on being stone-faced, as was expected of undersea royalty. But Trevain's warmth easily melted her icy countenance, and she was not upset with herself for allowing this. It was refreshing to trust someone enough to fully relax in their company.

The doorbell rang again.

Aazuria lifted a hand to rub her eyes. She adjusted herself so that she could stretch her legs before carefully slipping out from under Trevain's semi-hug. She walked out of the room a bit unsteadily at first, but she had resumed her poise by the time she reached the door. She undid the locks deftly. When the door swung open, it revealed that Brynne was standing there.

"Sea-wench," Brynne said hoarsely.

"Fisherwoman," Aazuria responded in greeting. She was suddenly alarmed when she realized how unkempt she was. In Adlivun, she never entertained visitors without first suffering hours of intricate hairstyling and elaborate face-painting. She quickly tried to arrange her disheveled clothing to be more presentable, and lifted her hands to smooth her hair. "Please come in."

"Where's Trevain?" Brynne asked in a quivering voice.

"He is still resting," Aazuria answered. "I apologize—it's my fault. I kept him up all night watching movies."

Brynne chewed on her lip fearfully. "I need to see him. Can you please get him?"

"Shouldn't we let him rest?" Aazuria asked. "I can tell him whatever it is…"

"Please," Brynne said in a hushed voice, completely unalike the brash tone she had used with Aazuria at their first meeting. "Please get him, Aazuria."

Aazuria frowned, but she nodded compliantly. She crossed the house to the family room and spoke Trevain's name while touching his arm to wake him.

"Hmmm?" he asked, groggily.

"Brynne is here. She wants to speak with you."

"Brynne?" he responded, clearing his throat. "Bet she's here to boast about their catch."

"I'm not so sure," Aazuria said in confusion.

"I guess I should find out what she wants," he said, pulling himself to his feet. He rubbed the wrinkles out of his shirt. He left the family room and headed for the foyer, with Aazuria close on his heels.

When Brynne laid eyes on Trevain, she stopped wringing her hands. She was deathly still and quiet for a few seconds before she tried to speak. "Trevain…" Brynne's voice caught in her throat. She paused, and tried to speak again, but no sound left her lips. She tried again. "Trevain, I…" She shook her head, screwing up her face before she burst into tears.

Trevain did not move or speak as he observed the strange

behavior of the brunette. Finally, he turned his back on the women, clenching his fists. "No. I don't want to hear it." He turned around and headed upstairs.

Aazuria was bewildered by the whole situation. She knew that something serious had been silently communicated between the longtime co-workers, but it escaped her understanding. She stared after Trevain's retreating back, seeking understanding in his tired and angry gait, before returning her gaze to Brynne. "What is wrong, dear?"

Brynne was now sobbing uncontrollably, and she had fallen against the marble-topped console table in the foyer. Her shoulder had knocked over a large glass vase holding fresh flowers, and it was rolling off the edge and crashing to the ground. Aazuria knew that she could not catch the heavy vase in time, so she pushed Brynne back to prevent the woman from being cut by the shards of glass. Aazuria felt a few sharp pieces graze her own legs as the container smashed on the marble floor. Brynne fell to the ground a few feet away from the vase, and was whimpering as she stared at the water from the vase spilling all over the floor. The water had surrounded Aazuria's bare feet, tinted with a few droplets of blood from where the glass had cut the woman's skin. The fresh forsythia blossoms lay scattered gracelessly on the pile of broken glass.

"I'm so sorry," Brynne said wretchedly. She began sobbing again.

Aazuria moved to her knees and tried to put her arm around the distraught woman to console her. "Come and sit down," she insisted, using her strength to support Brynne as she helped her up from the ground. She guided the distressed brunette carefully around the floral glass carnage, and deposited her safely in the nearest couch. Brynne moved compliantly along in a daze, and once she was sitting, she collapsed and placed her head in her hands.

"Brynne," Aazuria urged gently. "Will you please tell me what has happened?"

"It's Callder," Brynne said between gasps. She could not seem to catch her breath as her sobs shook her whole body. "Callder's dead."

Chapter 16: The Fall of Bimini

Aazuria was rendered speechless. She remembered the lively young man she had spoken to only a few days ago. He had been full of vibrant energy and blunt, unsophisticated honesty. He had been a slightly more primitive and mediocre version of his big brother. But it did not seem possible that...

"I should have married him. I should have married him," Brynne was moaning. "This is all my fault."

"What do you mean?" Aazuria asked numbly. She had grown confused again.

Brynne tried to control her sniffles enough to speak coherently. "We dated for a while. A few years ago. You know how it is: close quarters on the ship, working together every day... he always made me laugh." The brunette smiled through her tears. "But I thought... I thought he was beneath me—he had a lot of bad habits. Maybe if I had accepted one of his many proposals things would be different. Sometimes men change when they get married, don't they?"

"I do not believe it works that way, dear," Aazuria answered softly.

"He killed himself," Brynne whispered. "At least I think he did. He was acting crazy. He said he saw a woman in the water..."

"What?" Aazuria sat up to attention. She looked at the other woman grimly and infused her tone with hardness. "Tell me *exactly* what happened."

Brynne nodded, wiping her nose on her sleeve and trying to calm her gasping breaths. "I... I was cooking. He took me aside. He asked me if I would reconsider marrying him if he was the permanent captain of the *Magician*. I laughed—I laughed at him and said that Trevain would sooner appoint *me* to that position than a lazy ass like Callder. Then he got angry and said something weird... he said that if I didn't want him, he was going to go with the woman in the water..."

"What did she look like?" Aazuria demanded.

"What? What does that matter? He was just saying nonsense…"

"Any detail you remember matters!" Aazuria responded firmly.

"I think he said that she was blonde," she said, sniffling. "She was wearing a black dress with some strange necklaces…"

"Necklaces?" Aazuria gripped Brynne's shoulders. "This is not a joke. What kind of necklaces?"

"He mentioned shark's teeth… lots of shark's teeth. Callder's always had a thing for them. He said that she had beckoned him to go away with her—and that he would go if I didn't stop him. I just laughed and told him it was his lamest pick-up line yet, and I went back to cooking. He left, and skipped dinner, but I thought it was because he was mad at me. He usually gets moody like that after I reject him. Except no one has seen him since then." Silent tears began to fall over Brynne's cheeks again. "God, it's all my fault."

"It is not your fault, Brynne." Aazuria closed her eyes. *A black dress and shark's teeth. This cannot be what I believe it is. My people wear green, and whoever lured Callder was definitely not one of us. The only sea-dwellers who wear shark's teeth are… but it cannot be them. We defeated them ages ago in Japan! It cannot be the clan I am thinking of—but who else would dress like that? It seems that Trevain and I share a common enemy—whether he is aware of their existence or not.*

"What does it all mean?" Brynne whispered.

"It is not good news," Aazuria told her honestly. "Listen to me, Brynne. Do not go out on the water anymore. Do you hear me?" When the woman nodded, Aazuria sighed. "Thank you for the information."

"Trevain was right. He's always right." Brynne hugged her legs against her chest. "We shouldn't have been so greedy. I should have listened to him. He's going to be so broken-hearted when he finds out. Callder was all he had."

"He has us. We need to be there for him." Aazuria squeezed the other woman's shoulder gently. "I should check on him." She left Brynne and began to climb the stairs to the second floor, already feeling the heaviness of Trevain's grief. When she reached the corridor, she was stopped by a small hand on her arm.

"Is death usually this frequent for these land-dwellers?" Corallyn asked in a whisper.

"I do not believe so," Aazuria answered. "Go down and sit with Brynne. Try to cheer her up a little."

Corallyn nodded and darted off. Aazuria noticed that Elandria was standing in a cracked doorway. The two girls looked at each other knowingly for a moment.

"It is them, is it not?" Elandria asked. Her hands were shaking with fright as she signed the words. *"The Clan of Zalcan. It is happening all over again. They are going to massacre us. The same way they wiped out the Bimini Empire. The same way they razed Yonaguni. Soon Adlivun will join these fallen kingdoms…"*

"Not if I can help it," Aazuria signed back. *"Yonaguni might have been destroyed, and Queen Amabie might have had to perform an emergency evacuation, but she defended her people. We helped her fight them off in the fifties with minimal losses—and if Zalcan did have the audacity to reorganize, we will just disorganize and dispose of his men again. We will send dispatch messengers to ask the Ningyo for help."*

Elandria responded hesitantly. *"Sister, we need to take definitive and immediate action. Perhaps we should also evacuate everyone and move to a different location… it is too dangerous to remain here."*

Aazuria stared at Elandria's hands, unable to respond. She did not know where they would go. Many of her people had never been on land, and were rightly terrified of land-dwelling society. They could not run north, for with the approaching winter, the Arctic would be too cold for even the northern mermaids to survive.

"Aazuria?"

Nodding, the princess tried to display strength on her face. *"Do not worry, Elan. We will figure this out shortly. I am going to check on Trevain."* Excusing herself from her frightened sister, she walked down the corridor towards Trevain's room. She knocked once, lightly. Upon hearing no response she opened the door a tiny bit.

Trevain was sitting on his bed and staring at the wall.

"Trevain," she spoke softly.

He slowly turned to look at her, and lifted his eyes piteously. "Zuri," he mumbled. He had overheard her sisters calling her by the nickname over the few days that they had spent together, but this was the first time that he had used it himself. He shook his head wretchedly. "Please don't tell me. I don't want to know."

She could see that he knew the truth of what had happened, even though he had not heard it himself. How could he be sure if he had not listened to Brynne's story? Maybe he felt that if he did not hear the words, he would not have to accept them. "Are you sure…" she began.

"I don't want to think about it," he said, turning away. His voice cracked as he spoke. "I know Brynne. The wrath of that girl! She gets angry; she rages and rampages. She rips everything apart—but the *only* thing that could possibly make her cry… is if something happened to Callder. She loved him, even though she wouldn't let go of her pride and admit it if you held a gun to her head. I can't face this right now. He's my little brother. He wasn't perfect… isn't! He *isn't* perfect… God!"

Trevain buried his head in his hands. Aazuria went to his side. She could feel despair emanating from his body almost like a physical thing as she seated herself next to him. She put her arms around him, and rested her head on his shoulder. She hoped that her touch was comforting and motherly, but she didn't feel very strong. Elandria's words were floating through her mind. She thought of Bimini.

For thousands of years, the ruins now known as the Bimini Wall had been home to a thriving and prosperous undersea settlement in the Caribbean. That was until about a hundred years ago. An army of anarchist sea-dwellers from various clans and kingdoms all over the world had banded together under a revolutionary leader to form the Clan of Zalcan. They had ferociously attacked the Bimini Empire.

The underwater war had been waged for many years, causing a massive amount of collateral damage in the form of land-dweller casualties. The area became known as the "Bermuda Triangle" to superstitious seafarers. It was a well-known technique that mermaids used against each other, to attack ships or nearby surface settlements and bring huge numbers of suspicious investigators to the area, making it unlivable. In the 1940s, Bimini finally fell. The inhabitants of the empire were forced to relocate to nearby land, or to other underwater settlements. Adlivun had gained quite a few citizens from the fall of Bimini.

Aazuria's thoughts and memories were interrupted as she felt Trevain tighten his grip on her. She was pulled away from her focus on maritime warfare and returned to the second story of this land-based dwelling. She was returned to the sorrow of the terrestrial man of whom she had grown so fond. She felt a consuming rush of anger, thinking of how both worlds and so many lives had been ravaged over the past century due to the cruelty and selfishness of the Clan of Zalcan. She hoped that they were not really the ones responsible for the minor attacks on the outskirts of Adlivun and on fishing boats in the area. There was still no confirmation; it could be anyone. But in her heart, she knew what was coming—just as Trevain had somehow known.

"How did you sense that there would be danger?" Aazuria asked him softly, feeling his soft grey hair under her fingertips.

He did not move from where he weakly rested his head against her chest before he responded in an empty voice. "It was just a stupid feeling. I don't know. I was being irrational..."

"But you were right," she answered. "Did you see or hear anything?"

"I thought I saw some dark shapes in the water. It really gave me the chills."

"Why?" she asked.

"Why?" he repeated blankly. "I don't know. Some old story I heard or something. I... I'm a fool. I shouldn't have let them use my boat."

She bit her lip before speaking. "It is too dangerous out there now. You know this as well as I do. There are forces at work which aggressively seek to cause you harm. You must promise me that you will not go out on the water again. Please say that you will not!"

"I don't think I'm in any state to do so anytime soon, Aazuria," he answered. "I mean, I will have to eventually. People are counting on me. But this... first Leander and now..." The strength seemed to drain from him as he exhaled all of his willpower in a single breath. "I need to lie down."

He pulled away from her and moved to lean back on the pillows. She stood and unfolded the blanket from the foot of the bed, tugging it over his legs to keep him warm. He extended his hand to her.

"Zuri, would you stay with me?"

She took his hand and slipped under the blanket with him, hugging his arm and resting her forehead against his shoulder.

"I never considered leaving."

Chapter 17: Come Home Immediately

A week had passed since Brynne had showed up sobbing at their door. Trevain had hardly left his bed. He found it impossible to accept that his younger brother was truly gone. Whenever there was a noise in the house, he asked Aazuria to check if Callder had returned home. She did everything he asked without question. She took care of him, bringing him meals and encouraging him to eat. The princess spent endless hours chatting with the captain and trying to lift his spirits. She even slept beside him every night because she could not bear to leave his side.

She ignored the worried looks from Elandria and Corallyn's raised eyebrows as her focus on Trevain's life began to overshadow her own priorities. Aazuria knew that he was getting too deep in her heart, but it was too late to stop the flow of such great tides. She tried to compensate by spending a good deal of time strategizing with her sisters and with the twins about how to handle the situation in Adlivun. They argued over whether they should prepare for full-scale war, summoning all their allies to their defense, or whether they should turn tail and run. The very thought of running made Aazuria want to vomit. General Ramaris completely agreed, becoming livid when anyone even suggested retreat. They both knew that if it became necessary, they would need to advocate and implement an evacuation plan. But their pride would not allow them to surrender their beloved home so easily.

Aazuria also found herself quite suddenly in charge of Trevain's affairs. She found herself dealing with the Coast Guard since Trevain wanted nothing to do with them. She had to learn acronyms like SAR (Search and Rescue) and PIW (Person in Water) very quickly, and found it all rather irritating. She knew that Callder had not drowned naturally, and felt that these regulated procedures of the land-dwellers were largely a waste of time, at least in this instance. She found herself answering every phone call, and frequently being addressed as "Mrs. Murphy." At first she had corrected the callers, explaining that she was not married to Trevain, but they still assumed that she was his girlfriend or somehow the woman of the house. Eventually she had grown tired of explaining. It seemed that she had naturally fallen into role of acting as the captain's wife.

Mr. Fiskel helped her to deal with attorneys and death certificates and a whole host of unpleasant minutiae. Aazuria mostly sent people away and told them to call back later when Trevain was feeling better. He had already gone through this once with Leander, and she did not think he was ready to deal with legal responsibilities and press statements again so soon. This was not like before—this was not another workplace accident. Callder had been his blood—someone whom he had grown up beside. He was not prepared to deal with this loss, and he had yet to even truly admit that his brother was gone.

Members of his crew came by to visit with condolences, apologies, and their very hats in their hands; but whenever Aazuria told Trevain that he had a visitor, he was never interested in seeing anyone. The fishermen had been much too terrified to attempt working again. Doughlas had decided that he did not have to buy his new Audi as urgently as he had initially intended. The old Toyota would do.

The tragedy had driven Trevain closer to Aazuria than he had ever intended to become; in his misery he had let his guard down and been completely honest and open. He forgot all about the fact that she was supposed to be too young for him, and he began treating her like an adult and an equal. He saw less through his eyes, since his vision was obscured with grief, and more accurately with his intuition. The walls that had prevented their effortless communication and the development of their friendship were crumbling. Trevain had not placed any labels or rules on what they had become to each other, but they both knew that they had become something more; they were inseparable.

Only Aazuria and her sisters were permitted to enter Trevain's room. Corallyn and Elandria would sometimes sit with the captain and listen to him reminisce about Callder, and tell stories of their youth. The girls were truly sympathetic for him; they all knew how painful it would be to lose each other. Late one evening, when they were alone, Trevain made an unusual suggestion:

"You know, maybe you and Elandria should consider going to high school."

Aazuria laughed. Trevain observed her laughter, but did not

smile.

She was startled when she saw that he was serious. "Trevain—you are in earnest. High school? What can I learn there?"

"It's not necessarily about learning. I know you are intelligent. It's about getting the diploma so you have something to show for it. At least the younger girls should go to school, for the sake of their futures. If you want to succeed in this world, you're going to need at least a high school education."

Aazuria nodded. "I suppose we do need that... in this world."

Trevain did smile then. "I love the way you speak. It's so unusual and puzzling. Watching you is like watching one of those old movies."

"Because my manner of dress is archaic or because I am terribly romantic?" she asked playfully.

They were interrupted by a knock on the door. It was Mr. Fiskel. "Miss Aazuria, there is someone here to see you."

"At this hour?" she asked, sighing. She had received at least five visitors earlier that day. "It never ends, does it? Please, just tell him to come back another time."

"He says it is urgent, Miss Aazuria."

"Fine, then," she said, rising from where she sat beside Trevain on the bed and smoothing out her white dress. "I'll be right down."

Trevain sighed. "I feel so guilty for making you do all my errands for me..."

"Nonsense," she said firmly. "It is my honor. You just rest; I will be back before long."

Aazuria dutifully headed down the corridor to the stairs, but when she saw the man that was waiting in the foyer she had a moment of panic. "Naclana!" she cried, placing her hand on her chest. She descended the stairs quickly, almost at the pace of a run. She felt her heartbeat quicken palpably under her hand. "Sweet Sedna, are we under attack?"

At the sight of the messenger, chaotic scenes had instantly begun dancing through her mind. She saw her kingdom being pillaged. Having listened to Visola's lectures about new technology, she almost expected to hear that torpedoes and missiles were killing her people by the dozens.

"Princess," he responded, striking his chest in salute and bowing. "At this point the attacks are only peripheral. There have been losses—and there will likely be many more. We believe that the Clan of Zalcan has returned in full force. General Ramaris ordered me to escort you home."

Naclana was one of the few males who resided in Adlivun. He was one of a handful of men amongst thousands of women. It had not always been this way, but King Kyrosed, Aazuria's father, had significantly thinned the male population in the past few hundred years by exiling the sea-dweller men and sending many of them away on missions from which they would never return.

"I cannot leave right now," Aazuria said softly. She thought of Trevain, grieving over the loss of his brother. The captain was still an emotional mess, and she did not want to abandon him. She frowned. "Perhaps Elandria or Corallyn could go in my stead?"

"We need *you*, Princess. This is a time of crisis and emergency. An attack is imminent. Adlivun needs *you*."

"Adlivun? Attack?"

Aazuria looked up in horror to see that this was Trevain's voice filtering down the stairs. It was the first time he had left his room in over a week, and it was unthinkable that he had chosen this moment. As Trevain descended the staircase, Aazuria found herself trying to lie.

"Adlivun is my… hometown," she attempted to explain. Naclana raised his eyebrows at this.

"I don't understand. I thought you ran away from your home after your father died."

"Yes. My father was a man with many responsibilities which I suppose I have… inherited."

"And what about the 'attack?'" Trevain asked, coming to stand beside her. "What's going on, Aazuria?"

"Oh… uh. Attack meaning lawsuit… my father's estate. Taxes. Tax evasion. Bequest. Settlement. This man is my lawyer."

"Your lawyer calls you 'princess?'"

Aazuria wanted to slap herself in the face—she was sure that her cheeks were growing quite red. "Naclana has known me since I was very young. He was my father's lawyer. My father used to call me princess when I was a toddler. It was… a whole thing." Aazuria laughed nervously and waved her hand in dismissal.

Naclana cleared his throat. "The point is, er… Aazuria. I have my orders. You need to come home immediately."

Trevain looked stricken. "You're leaving?"

"I must." Aazuria turned to look at Trevain with worry on her face.

"But... I'm sorry—I'm being selfish," he quickly corrected. "You've helped me so much with my brother, and I forgot you have your own family problems to deal with."

"I wish I could stay," she told him, reaching out to squeeze his hand. "I will return as soon as I can."

Naclana cleared his throat, a bit surprised with this display of affection. "Aazuria, you must also bring your sisters along with you. Summon Elandria and Corallyn immediately, and we must depart."

"You're taking *all* of the girls?" Trevain said with surprise and dismay. "Is that really necessary?"

"Yes," answered Naclana. Aazuria sighed and called out the names of her sisters.

"This man gives me the creeps," Trevain remarked, eyeing the male sea-dweller suspiciously and noting his unusually long hair. "Aazuria, I'm not sure if I approve of you going off with this fellow alone. Maybe I should come along."

"Do not worry, Trevain," she said with a smile. "I have known him for four hun... fourteen years. Besides, I am quite certain he is even related to me. A distant cousin of sorts."

"Second cousin, twice removed, on her mother's side," Naclana responded promptly.

"There you go," said Aazuria with a smile.

"Do you come from the kind of village where people marry their cousins?" Trevain asked.

"Why are you being so overprotective?" Aazuria asked with a laugh. "That is frowned upon in Adlivun. However there have been accidents, as with any society, when there has been poor genealogical recordkeeping."

Elandria and Corallyn appeared on the landing, and Corallyn emitted a small shriek at the sight of the messenger. "Naclana!" she cried. "Is everything alright?"

"No," Naclana answered simply. "You are to come home to Adlivun immediately."

"Good Sedna," Corallyn whispered.

Elandria began signing furiously to Naclana with her hands, and he signed back the answers to her questions.

"Sedna?" Trevain asked curiously.

"That is… we had an Inuit grandmother," Aazuria fabricated. She was tired of the mountain of lies that were piling up. "It is just something she used to say."

Trevain nodded. He was surprised at the fact that the messenger also knew the sign language of the girls. He tried to read their hands, but could not follow their speed.

"Are you ready to go?" Naclana asked.

"He's all business, isn't he?" Trevain remarked dryly.

"Yes. Let's get going," Corallyn said, after reading Naclana's hands. She begun heading for the door. "We need to move."

"Don't you girls need to take some things? Clothes, toothbrushes, shampoo?" Trevain asked with concern.

"No," said Naclana. "We are leaving now."

Aazuria saw the look on Trevain's face and understood that he was feeling deserted. He had just lost his brother, and now he felt like he was losing her as well. "Elandria, will you stay with him?" she asked her sister. She added with her hands, *Take care of him for me.*

Elandria nodded, accepting the assignment. *"Please be careful, Aazuria. Make the decisions which are the safest, the boldest, and the most unpredictable."*

Aazuria quickly signed the words, *"I love you."* She reached out and pulled Elandria into a fierce hug.

Trevain comprehended the hand signals for these three simple words, having learned enough to remember the basics. He also recognized that the way that Aazuria embraced her sister was desperate, as though she were heading into some kind of peril from which her return was uncertain.

"Aazuria," he began in a warning tone. "You know I would never try to stop you from doing anything, but I'm beginning to seriously worry. Where are you going? Can you give me the address and phone number so I can reach you? What is this about? Look, I don't like the way…"

She smiled at his concerned face, and moved forward to place her palm against his cheek. She rose to her tip-toes in order to place a soft kiss on his lips. She pressed her mouth against his for several passionate and purposeful seconds.

He was shocked into silence by her bold manoeuver. Although they had been very close over the past weeks, they had not crossed any definitive lines of romantic affection. Every touch and every word, however intimate, could still *almost* be considered friendly. Almost. At least, that is what he had told himself every time he considered her position in his life. But *this* was crossing some conclusive intersection—a junction from which they could not cross back. He recognized it in the devotion which he felt pouring into him through her lips. The kiss was so absolute that it could not, in any way, be considered merely friendly.

And Trevain was very happy about that.

Although he was still tremendously worried, his momentary gladness at this confirmation of her feeling overwhelmed him.

"I promise I will be back soon," she said, giving him a look that was somehow determined and tender at the same time.

"Aazuria…" he began, but she was already walking through his front door with Corallyn and her cousin-lawyer. He turned to Elandria, and saw that the girl's face had gone very pale, and that she was twisting her dark braid nervously between her hands.

"Is something wrong here, Elandria?" he asked firmly. "Is there something I should know?"

Elandria looked at him but could not respond. She continued to dig her fingernails into her rope of hair nervously.

"Where is Adlivun? If we get in my car, can you give me directions?" When she did not respond, Trevain clenched his jaw. "Jesus, Elan! Can you tell me if this town is in Canada or America?"

The woman's eyes grew wide and she turned around completely so that Trevain would not see the answer on her face. Her heart-rate had escalated with the interrogation.

Trevain swore under his breath. "If she doesn't return, I'll go mad!"

Elandria nodded in solemn agreement, staring at the wall uneasily.

"I'm going back to bed," he announced, before turning to drag himself up the stairs.

Chapter 18: It Never Snows, but it Blizzards

Elandria paced nervously in the corridor outside Trevain's room. A week had passed and Aazuria had still not returned from Adlivun. It had been too long.

Mr. Fiskel exited Trevain's room with a bowl of soup in his hands. The old man lifted his shoulders helplessly as he made eye contact with the girl. "I still can't get him to eat, Miss Elandria. He just won't stop talking about Callder. He's also running a temperature. The captain's making himself sick with stress."

Elandria gave Mr. Fiskel a steadfast look before approaching him and taking the bowl of soup from his hands. She nodded to him and entered Trevain's room. She marched to Trevain's bedside and placed the soup down on the nightstand firmly before reaching out to feel the man's forehead.

Trevain's eyes opened slowly, and he blinked at her. "Zuri, you're back. I thought you left forever. Like my brother. It never rains, but it pours. Shouldn't we amend that for Alaska? It never snows, but it blizzards. Doesn't have the same ring to it."

Elandria frowned at his nonsensical rambling. She moved her face closer to Trevain's and shook her head firmly to indicate that she was not Aazuria. She slapped him lightly on the cheek.

He blinked again, several times. "Elan? I'm sorry. What am I thinking. My vision must be… I'm just tired. In my defense, you do resemble your sister."

"How on earth can you be tired?" she asked him with the rapid hand motions *"You have done naught but remain in bed for a week!"*

"I didn't get any of that," he answered, staring up at the ceiling. "Did you know when Callder was a boy he liked fencing? Fencing, imagine that. A rather noble and focused sport for such a lazy and careless kid. Mother caught us playing with wooden swords once, so she signed us up for fencing lessons. He loved it. He really did. Especially when I let him win."

Elandria studied his pallid complexion with worry. There was moisture on his skin which caused strands of his grey hair to cling to his forehead. He had been very quiet for days, sending her away whenever she had tried to speak with him. Now he seemed to hardly notice her presence as he ruminated. He seemed like he was in the beginning of delirium. Having seen many illnesses and much grief in her extended lifetime, Elandria resolutely decided to do all within her power to bring him out of his despondency. She picked up the bowl and spoon, and attempted to coax Trevain to drink some soup.

He turned his head away from the offered victuals and buried his face in the pillow. "Fencing," he mused to himself. He continued mumbling into the pillow. "Put a saber in his hand and he was full of life. Why wasn't he like that about anything else? No self-esteem. Didn't know how great he was, how great he could have been. Should've told him. If only things had been different; if I'd been more attentive to my little brother... but I only cared about myself and my own success. Now what can my money do?"

Elandria placed her hand on his shoulder, shaking her head, intending to object to his self-blame with all the gestures she could muster. Trevain, however, did not acknowledge her touch. He continued to mutter against his pillow.

"The money's worthless," Trevain whispered. "Callder knew it. He knew it more than I did. He always said such negative things about himself. Why? He kept insulting himself until the insults became truth. He'd say, 'I'm worthless scum, and I'm better off dead. You're better off with me dead, and so is Brynne and the whole world!' It wasn't true. I swear it wasn't true."

Elandria reached out to soothingly pat Trevain's hand, but he still did not react. He swallowed and continued speaking softly to himself. "He made it true because he believed it so much! How could he believe those awful things about himself? He was such a smart boy. A kind boy. I should have told him! I should have forced him to know."

Elandria returned the soup to the nightstand. She took some of the fabric of her dress into her hands and began to squeeze it anxiously. She considered Trevain's words and wondered if she should have gone to Adlivun instead of her sisters. Waiting and not knowing was very difficult; it was paralyzing.

"Why did he drink so much? Why didn't he give himself more

credit? Why did he have to be such a damned fool? It should have been me. It should have been me instead."

Standing up abruptly, Elandria walked to the window of Trevain's room. She parted the curtain and gazed out at the serene view of the ocean. Trevain continued to mumble to himself in bed, but Elandria was too far away to make sense of his muffled speech. She raised her fingers to the glass and traced the shoreline with her fingernail. She sighed as she also traced the horizon.

Her lips, which she usually kept tightly shut, now parted. She drew in several deep breaths before finding the courage to release her voice in song:

> *My love has gone to sail upon the sea,*
> *A fortnight has passed without his return.*
> *I cannot smile; I cannot eat or sleep.*
> *I fear the worst and already I mourn.*
>
> *We were to marry come the gentle spring,*
> *In the small church our mothers kindly chose.*
> *I clutch a lock of his hair and his ring,*
> *Watching for signs of him upon the shores.*

Elandria's voice echoed off the walls of the room, filling it completely with her celestial *a cappella* melody. Trevain stopped his muttering and paused, allowing the music to flood his mind and body. It permeated his being in the same way that ingesting hot liquid would have sent feeling of warmth throughout his insides.

He had not consumed any of the soup that Elandria and Mr. Fiskel had tried to get him to drink for days. They had been respectful of his wishes to starve himself. This poignant singing, however, was force-feeding his senses and overloading them with bucketfuls of emotional nutrients and enchantment. Now he discovered for what he had truly been famished.

Elandria's voice was sublime. She moved his blood, sending powerful currents through his stagnant arteries, with ripples that extended all the way to the smaller veins and capillaries. She brought all his pain to the surface, where it simmered on his skin, burning him briefly before dissipating into the air around him. Elandria's voice was…

Trevain suddenly sat up in bed, shocked by the realization. *Elandria's voice?* He looked to where she stood near the window, belting out passionate lyrics in a loud and clear soprano. Yes, it was coming from her throat—the throat of the girl who had not spoken *once* since she had entered his home. He was being serenaded by the speechless girl for whom he had begun learning sign language!

Although his astonishment was colossal, his immense pleasure at listening to the exquisite music easily overpowered his surprise. The sound was breathtaking. He could have sworn that he had heard it before.

O, where is his fine ship? Where is my love?
It was under the great sequoia tree,
He avowed to all the heavens above,
Come hell or high water he'd come for me!
So I ask the skies now: where is my love?

"You can speak," he said dumbly, interrupting her song.

She smiled at him weakly, and gave a small ladylike shrug. He stared at her, dumbfounded.

"You can actually speak," he repeated, in wonderment.

Elandria shook her head to indicate the negative. She raised her hands to answer him with sign language. *"Yes, I can, but I choose not to do so. I can communicate in many other ways. Where I hail from, everyone knows sign language and it is completely unnecessary."*

Trevain frowned as he stared at her fast moving hands. "I am really trying to understand you, but I can only pick up a word here and there. I can't put it together."

She tried to slow down her hand motions so that he could comprehend her signage. *"I dislike the sound of my own voice in speech. It is garish and unrefined."*

"Elandria!" he responded in frustration. "I just heard you use your voice! I'm not going crazy, am I? Please, speak to me. I know you can!"

She paused, clenching and unclenching her hands into fists fretfully.

"Elan?" he coaxed softly. "Please?"

She reached up and began to finger her braid as she gathered the resolve to form a simple sentence. She opened her lips and uttered a simple proclamation:

"Just as it never snows, but it blizzards, I never speak; I only sing."

He nodded then, satisfied. "I understand. I guess you have your reasons. Just like those ultra-holy monks who take vows of silence for personal enlightenment and such, right? Well, I won't force you to speak anymore. I just wanted to know why... your voice! It's magnificent. You're an opera singer... you performed those recordings which Aazuria danced to in the club."

Elandria nodded, her eyes downcast shyly.

"You've been professionally trained," he added. "Just like Aazuria has been trained in dance. No high school diplomas, but professionals when it comes to fine arts. You girls are just full of surprises, do you know that?"

Elandria gave him a small coy smile. *"You have not the faintest idea,"* she answered.

Trevain observed the shy girl curiously for a moment. Then he grunted and crossed his arms. "That whole situation with that man, Naclana, didn't make any sense. What is your sister hiding from me?"

"Secrets bigger than you can imagine," Elandria responded. *"I am sure you know that she cares for you and acts with your best interests at heart; but she has important duties of which you cannot conceive."*

"I see. Actually, I don't. I don't see at all," he said miserably. "Would you sing to me again, Elan? I love the sound of your voice."

Elandria smiled in relief, grateful that Trevain was understanding of her need to remain silent unless it was in song. She was also delighted that he appreciated her singing so much that it had almost made him completely forget for a few seconds that his brother had just died. It was her only gift; if her voice was not capable of reaching him, there was no more she could do.

She closed her eyes, and lost herself as she allowed her soul to pour forth and fill the room.

The skies give me no comforting reply,

Instead they mock me with cruel tempests.
They terrify me, making lightning fly,
And I know I am not one of the bless'd.

I shall hold fast to hope though all seems lost,
I shall think of my love and his kind smile.
To retrieve him I shall pay any cost,
To rescue him I shall sail endless miles.

She continued to sing for several minutes. Every song that came to mind about love and loss, and even some songs she had created herself over the years. The acoustics of the large master bedroom were favorable, and she felt a sensation approaching joy as she allowed her voice to gust forth from deep in her gut and fill every corner and crevice of the chamber.

When her songs ended, she remained motionless and quiet for several seconds. She turned to gaze out the window again, scanning the horizon. She heard a creak of motion in the bed, and turned and saw that Trevain was sobbing.

"Not Callder, not Callder," he was moaning. "I just don't believe it."

He was crying. He was finally grieving and allowing himself to face what had happened. She felt a solemn satisfaction. He would be better before long. Elandria knew that modern medicine was without value in a case like this.

Only music could heal a destroyed soul.

Chapter 19: Eternal Asphyxiation

A few days later, Trevain was scarfing down an omelet that Mr.
Fiskel had prepared while he skimmed through the newspaper.
Elandria smiled at him as she sipped on her orange juice and nibbled
her toast. His health and spirits had improved exponentially since the
night she had sung to him. She could see that he was almost himself
again.

Trevain suddenly closed the newspaper and folded it up. "Maybe
I'm out of line, Elandria—but what would you think of me asking for
your sister's hand in marriage?"

Elandria dropped her fork. It had been tragically halfway to her
mouth with a piece of buttered toast on it. She stared at Trevain in
bewilderment.

"I know there's a gigantic difference in our ages… a gulf really.
But do you think it's too large? Aazuria doesn't seem to notice or care."

It was a moment before Elandria had the presence of mind to
retrieve her fallen toast. She stared at it intently, as if it would reveal the
answers to her.

"I know it seems really sudden. I just thought I'd ask for your
opinion… and your permission, before I go ahead and do anything
stupid."

Elandria thought about the fact that if Aazuria chose to marry
Trevain and live on land, Adlivun would become her responsibility.
Elandria shuddered at this thought; she did not wish to be placed into
such a frightening position of power. Then she thought about the fact
that her sister seemed very happy with Trevain. Happier than she had
been in as long as Elandria could remember.

He waited for a moment, but there was no response. He smiled
nervously. "I thought so. It is a stupid idea, isn't it?"

She still remained quiet, and he sighed. "Elan, I understand the
basic hand signals for 'yes' and 'no.' Do you think I'm an idiot for
considering this? Just tell me what you think."

The hand holding the fork—which had been pierced through a carefully cut square of toast—began to shake. Elandria tried to breathe steadily, thinking about how little Trevain knew of her family. Happiness could never last when there were so many skeletons in the cupboard. How should she respond? This was not an easy question to answer. An idea began to form in the back of her mind. She considered telling Trevain something personal, just to test his love for her sister.

"Should I be worried that she hasn't returned yet?" Trevain asked. "Is that what this is about?"

Elandria stood up and headed for a certain cabinet she had seen the men go into. She grabbed the knobs and flung the doors open. Choosing a bottle, she held it up and looked at Trevain questioningly.

"Uh, help yourself," he said, scratching his head. "But it's pretty early in the day for scotch and I'm not sure you're even of legal..."

He stopped because Elandria had already opened the bottle and was guzzling it down as though it were water. He watched in surprise as she finished a quarter of the bottle before he rose to his feet to wrestle it from her surprisingly strong grip.

"That's pretty potent stuff, Elan," he said with a frown. "It'll hit you really hard."

"That liquid is vile!" she said, wheezing and screwing up her face. She placed a hand against her nose to ease the burning in her sinuses. Her eyes were beginning to water.

"Yeah, it is," he agreed, looking at the bottle. "It was my brother's favorite. Hey! You talked again."

"May I have another sip?" she asked politely. Against his better judgment, but unable to resist the sweet request in the third sentence he had ever heard her speak, he handed the bottle back to her. He watched warily as her sip became several generous gulps.

"Elan..." he began in confusion.

"Trevain, there are a few things you need to know," Elandria said, coughing as she put the bottle aside. She retrieved a napkin to daintily wipe the moisture from her lips.

"I'm all ears," he said.

She hesitated. "Aazuria, and Corallyn and I... we each have different mothers."

"Different mothers? That's unusual. I suppose some people remarry..."

"He did not 'remarry,' as you say," Elandria hissed. "Our

father... he had many wives simultaneously. At least at first. Eventually, he stopped marrying them all together. He just chose whomever he wanted, and he took her...."

"Are you saying your father was a rapist?"

"No. Perhaps not in the legal sense of the term. But also, yes. Very much so. Women simply did not refuse him. He was a man of power, and everyone was afraid to say 'no' to him." She picked up the bottle again and proceeded to swallow several mouthfuls of liquor before looking Trevain squarely in the face. She wiped her mouth with her sleeve and spoke again. Her voice faltered. "Even his own daughters were afraid."

Trevain tried to respond, but found himself failing to find the right words. "I'm so sorry, Elan." He swallowed. "I had no idea..."

"The type of father a girl has creates a profound effect on the woman she becomes," Elandria said softly. "My father is the reason that I prefer never to speak."

As he watched the emotions dance across her face, Trevain felt hot tears sting the back of his eyes. He raised a hand to his temple, and took a deep breath. "God, I wish I could undo what happened to you. Why... why are you choosing to tell me this?"

"I trust you. If you wish to become my brother it is important that you understand what little you can of our lives and past."

Trevain reached for the same bottle in which she had put a remarkable dent, and took a few gulps himself. He understood how the bitter taste made it easier to converse about such topics. "So you're trying to tell me that Aazuria is not in the least bit ready for marriage because of what her father did to her."

Elandria smiled a neurotic little smile. "He did not touch her. She was his firstborn, his pure gold baby. He would have locked her up and kept her in a metal cage forever if he could have done so. He did try to do so a couple times, but the cage was made of ice—and ice always melts. No, he only came to me, and to Corallyn, and to our other sisters. We had a few other sisters, but they have killed themselves."

Trevain felt physically sick upon hearing this. Bile rose in his throat as rage blossomed in his gut. "I didn't know—I didn't know. God. What you must think of me, crying like a child over my brother when you have lost siblings too! I can't believe... why didn't she tell me *any* of this?"

Elandria reached out and placed her hand on his arm as he struggled to cope with the information. It was more challenging for her to speak at all than for her to actually face these facts. It was all in the past, and she knew how to be detached. Trevain was more emotional than she was. In her lengthy existence she had seen and experienced much suffering. She was excellent at being numb when she most needed to be.

"It doesn't matter," he suddenly said resolutely. "That's all in the past. I want to make her life and all of your lives better. I'll help you heal, the way you have helped me heal. Tell me truthfully, Elan. Do you think I shouldn't ask Aazuria to marry me? Is it too soon; should I give her some space?"

So he was not yet dissuaded. Her brow creased in a combination of pleasure and frustration. Elandria looked down at her hands for a moment in silence, as if deciding whether or not she should answer.

"Elandria?" he urged, a bit frantically.

She looked up at him for several seconds, with a decisive and intense expression rapidly consuming her normally timid features. He could feel that her next words were going to be pivotal, but he could not have prepared himself.

"Aazuria killed our father."

"*What?*" Trevain took a step backward as though he had been struck. "She did wha… are you… you've got to be… a joke…" He seemed incapable of finishing his sentences, and temporarily powerless to begin any new ones. He slammed his hand down on the breakfast table as though trying to jumpstart his stalling brain. "Dear Lord! You're serious. Aazuria killed her father? Aazuria killed her father."

Elandria nodded gravely as she observed his reaction with as much mild amusement as she could allow herself to feel.

Trevain took several deep breaths, placing both hands on the table to calm himself and process the information. "Aazuria killed… killed as in murdered. She's a murderer. God. Is that—that seedy looking fellow, Naclana, is he her defense attorney? Is she on trial? If so, she needs a *real* lawyer! Someone who gets haircuts. We can get her off…"

A smile touched Elandria's face. She had already gotten her answer; she knew with whom Trevain's loyalties were aligned. "She is not on trial. Everyone knows that she did it. Everyone begged her to do it."

Trevain had to take a moment to let this sink in as well. "How did she kill him?"

"Why does that matter?" Elandria asked, studying his face carefully.

"I guess it doesn't," he answered. "I'm just curious—and very confused."

"She drowned him," Elandria answered, "with his own blood."

Trevain's brow wrinkled in consternation as he tried to imagine Aazuria doing this. "How?"

"I believe the precise term is 'hemothorax.' She stabbed him between the ribs in a particular spot, severing an artery and causing his lungs to fill with blood in less than a minute."

She saw that Trevain was staring at her rather aghast upon hearing the details of this description. Elandria reflected upon her father for a moment. There were several sacred tenets that every sovereign sea nation abided by—not laws in the sense of the ones enforced on land, but principles of living. Her father had broken the first tenet:

Ye who dwell beneath the sea or above it, know that your breath is a gift. If ye desecrate the sanctity of the liberty and wellbeing of any innocent human without just cause, your breath shall be stripped from you straightaway. Henceforth, you shall become one of the cursed legions of the drowning mermaids and mermen.

The major concept among sea-dweller faiths was that breath was holy. It was what gave life, and it was what took life away. Adlivun's myth of the afterlife depicted that if one lived in a dishonorable way, they would spend eternity struggling for oxygen; struggling to extract it from any medium possible.

Hell was eternal asphyxiation.

"Why do you call it drowning?" Trevain asked. "Wouldn't 'stabbing' be a more appropriate description?"

Elandria considered this. She wished she could articulate the relevant spiritual significance behind the act, but Trevain would not understand without context. She could only explain it anatomically. "I suppose that death actually comes from the loss of blood more than suffocation with blood. This is just the way that our people refer to this… traditional method of execution."

"Traditional," he repeated. He shook his head, almost refusing to believe that it was true.

"You may consider my sister a murderess, but our people consider her a heroine. Aazuria is *my* champion. I needed you to know; she may seem sweet and gentle, but she is also incredibly strong. She is very important to many people. She is not the kind of person that anyone can ever get away with hurting."

"I would never hurt her," Trevain said hoarsely.

"Yes, but in the unlikely case that you did, there would be dire consequences." Elandria gave him a forbidding smile. "I can assure you of that."

"I need some time to process this," Trevain said slowly. "Thank you for telling me."

He nodded at Elandria before exiting the room. He went directly to the library, where he began to briskly pace back and forth across the length of the room. He continued to pace for hours, hardly noticing the passage of time. He was overwhelmed with trying to accept and understand this new information. He knew that Elandria would not lie to him.

He paced the library until his leg was terribly sore. He had not been on his feet for a few days, and his bad leg protested against the sudden vigorous exercise. His limp became very pronounced as he continued to pace, but he did not notice this. He did not know how to accept that the woman for whom he had developed a deep attachment, the woman whose family he already loved and considered his own—the woman whom he wished to take as his *wife* was a murderess. Regardless of how awful her father had been, death was not the solution. He did not know if he could ever forgive her for having done such a savage thing.

Part of him knew that he already had.

Chapter 20: Atargatis is Coming

"Go at once, Naclana," Aazuria ordered, in a tone of voice which could not be disobeyed.

Naclana bowed deeply, recognizing her for the first time in weeks. In the torch-lit volcanic caves of Adlivun, Aazuria's silvery-white hair glistened as it hung down her back, woven with dozens of strands of pearls. Her stern eyes bored right through him, their color having returned to their natural, undersea azure; her namesake.

She was nothing like the fretful, lackluster girl he had seen when she came to answer Trevain's door. His faith in her was restored. She was the same intelligent, refined woman he had always known; she was *more* than capable of leading their nation. Here at home, Aazuria was fierce, judicious, and capable of anything. The difference was palpable even to Corallyn and the twins, who felt great comfort and security in seeing Aazuria's coloring return to the pale, albino-like tones she had sported for hundreds of years. With it, her fortitude seemed to return.

On land, they were all a little awkward and uncertain. Even the regal, confident Aazuria seemed overly-cautious and agitated above the surface.

"I will leave immediately, Princess Aazuria," said Naclana, saluting across his chest with sincerity.

"I wish you a safe journey," Aazuria said, inclining her head slightly in gratitude. Above the surface, her cousin was able to give her orders, but in their true niche, he was an emissary bound to serve her.

"Do not forget to give Queen Amabie my message!" Visola reminded him. "Tell her it's urgent."

"Yes, General Ramaris." Naclana saluted Visola as well before turning and marching away.

"May I please go with him?" Corallyn begged. "I have always wanted to meet the Ningyo."

"No," Aazuria said firmly, and that was that.

"It is far too dangerous, Coral," Sionna said in agreement.

"Naclana will be safer and faster on his own."

"I hope they *do* send reinforcements," Corallyn said with concern. "I would feel so much safer."

"They will, kiddo," said Visola, ruffling the girl's hair. "Don't worry so much; I have scouts everywhere around the kingdom, so if anything goes sour we'll have plenty of notice."

"Since we're nearby, I think we should visit the infirmary caves," Sionna suggested. When Aazuria nodded in consent, the women began to walk there together. "Our warriors were able to save a few lives during recent attacks and we have about a dozen injured in the healing springs. We also have a few wounded captives."

"The easiest kind to work with," Visola said with a smile.

"Viso spent the last few days 'questioning' them and we found some interesting information."

"How bad are our wounded?" Aazuria asked briskly as the three girls navigated the warmly lit caves.

"A few of them are unconscious, but some are not hurt quite so badly. I'm considering staying behind to help take care of them," Sionna said.

"She thinks her talents are better expended in the hospital than in the strip club with me," Visola grumbled.

"And you do not agree?" Aazuria asked her friend.

"There's a war coming, Zuri. We know that now. We need weaponry badly. I've used the gloriousness of my boobs to single handedly triple our defenses. I'm working my ass off—literally, to prevent more people from being injured or killed. Isn't that important?"

Aazuria nodded. "Yes, but we need more." She turned to her sister. "Coral, go to the castle. Collect all of my mother's jewels. Get the guards to raid the royal chambers so we can pawn anything of value. We need to tap every resource and give Visola some real funds to work with."

"Your jewels, Zuri? But I thought..."

"We should have done this long before. We were not certain that it was war—we thought it might be just a few random attacks on our people when they happened to stray too far away from home. Even then we were largely unprepared. Now that we know we might be up against the Clan of Zalcan, we need to fortify to an immeasurable degree. Go now."

"Sure thing!" said Corallyn, saluting across her chest. "I'll go give the orders."

Visola clapped her hands together in delight as the youngest girl left. "Aazuria, my beloved princess! I would grab you and kiss you right now if you didn't have that serious, terrifying look on your face. Maybe I'll do it later." Visola winked at her friend, which caused Aazuria's lips to twitch slightly into a smile. Visola grinned and pumped her fist. "Yes! I'm done with that club, although I can't deny that it was fun and useful. Say goodbye to your pretty heirloom gemstones, and say hello to awesome American firearms. You won't regret this, Zuri."

Aazuria could not resist letting her face completely relax into a smile at her friend's energy, but Sionna rolled her eyes. As they entered the infirmary, Visola immediately went off to the area where the hostages were kept. Sionna placed her hands on her hips and assumed her own air of command. This was her element.

"Right, so we have a dozen wounded; ten women and two men—about three are in critical condition…"

"Two men?" Aazuria asked with concern. It was disturbing to hear that two of the very few men in Adlivun were out of commission.

"Yes. One is Sidnigel, the chef. He was out fishing in distant waters with his wife—he saw her being attacked, and he barely managed to save her. Both of them are seriously wounded."

"That is awful," Aazuria said, her eyebrows knitting into a deep frown.

"Sidnigel said he thought he recognized some of the attackers. They might be some of ours—the people Kyrosed exiled probably want revenge."

"I thought as much." Aazuria balled her hands up into fists and scowled. "It is unfair we have to suffer for everything my father did and inherit his enemies! Who else is here?"

"Here's the funny thing—the other wounded man is not one of ours. He's unconscious so we do not have a name. No one recognizes him, but he was impaled by an enemy harpoon. He was found floating in the middle of the sea, losing a lot of blood, and left for dead. Scouts took him in, figuring that the enemy of our enemy…"

"May I see him, Doctor Ramaris?" Aazuria was intrigued by the unusual situation. Perhaps he was a messenger from a nearby kingdom who had tried to bring them intelligence.

"Sure," said Sionna, leading Aazuria over to the hot springs where the man was submerged. She motioned for a nurse to lift the man out of the water. The woman immediately complied, and entered the spring. She carefully lifted the man to the surface so that Aazuria could see his face.

The princess released a gasp. "Sweet Sedna!" Aazuria exclaimed. She reached out and grabbed Sionna's arm in shock. "It is Callder Murphy! Trevain's younger brother who we thought to be dead."

Sionna stared at her friend for a moment in surprise. "Well, he's not quite dead yet, although he might be before long."

"Neither of you recognized him from the club?" Aazuria asked.

"I only saw him once, and he looks different wet and dying, sweetie." Sionna sighed. "I'm sorry. I don't have any good news for you. This handsome stranger took a harpoon to the chest; I'm surprised he's still breathing. I wouldn't tell your captain if I were you—there's no use in giving him false hope in case he has to deal with losing his brother a second time."

"But he is breathing," Aazuria said, watching as the healer eased Callder's body back down into the hot spring. "He is breathing underwater."

Sionna turned to face her friend and placed her hands on Aazuria's shoulders. "I know exactly what you're thinking, Princess. Stop that train of thought *right now*. Callder Murphy may have sea-dwelling traits but it does *not* mean that Trevain does. These are recessive genes. If both of his parents were our kind, then maybe—but if it was only one of them..."

"But he *might*, Sio. He might," she whispered. Her heart soared, and she tried to calm her exploding insides. "Oh, Sedna, look at me. People are dying all around—yet all I can think about is the fact that this means I might be able to stay with the man I love..."

"You *love?*" Sionna questioned, staring directly into Aazuria's cerulean eyes.

Aazuria felt a shockwave of horror course through her at having said the word aloud. She inhaled sharply and straightened, resuming her composure. "Possibly. Conceivably, though it is neither here nor there. It is wonderful news that Callder has a fighting chance at life; I will do as you recommend and conceal this from Trevain. It would be... so miraculous."

Sionna sighed, knowing that Aazuria's life had just become a lot more complicated. "Sure, darling. Now let's see if any of our hostages are feeling chatty. I'll take intelligence over miracles any day."

Visola had already begun to terrorize the prisoners, and she grinned at her sister and Aazuria when they entered the holding area. "Hey girls, listen to this. Tell me if it makes sense to you!" she said, before jabbing an enemy woman forcefully in her already injured abdomen.

The woman screamed, and took several ragged breaths to assuage the pain and calm down before she spoke in an angry hiss. "Atargatis is coming. Do what you want to me. Atargatis is coming! She will avenge me."

"Atargatis," Aazuria repeated in confusion. "That is an ancient name. I believe it belonged to an Assyrian sea-dwelling queen, several thousand years ago."

"Yeah, there's no way the original Atargatis is alive," Visola said with a frown. "My guess is that some young rebel mermaid chick named Jennifer or Molly decided to call herself Atargatis to make her shrimpy attack on us a bit scarier. Isn't that right, honey?"

The hostage woman tried to spit on Visola, but Visola expertly dodged the flying lump of saliva. "Now, now, that's not nice. Are you going to tell us why evil Miss Molly Mermaid is attacking us, or do I need to beat it out of you?"

"Her name is *Atargatis!* She is coming to exact vengeance because Kyrosed Vellamo stole her daughter!" the woman shouted desperately.

"That hardly narrows it down," Sionna said. "King Kyrosed took the daughters of many women."

"Atargatis is coming," the captive repeated, rocking back and forth frantically. "When she comes she will kill Kyrosed Vellamo and take Adlivun for her own!"

"Ah, I see. It's just your average run-of-the-mill divide-and-conquer attempt," Visola diagnosed, looking up at Aazuria with a shrug. "Pretty standard stuff. Happens every century or so to any nation worth its salt. Keeps things interesting."

"Viso, this is serious," Aazuria said softly. "Our people are in danger; so many are already dead or wounded. We need to find out as much about this 'Atargatis' as possible."

"It would be my pleasure, Princess." Visola cracked her knuckles cheerfully. "I already know the most important thing about evil Miss

Molly Mermaid."

"What would that happen to be, sis?" Sionna asked.

"That I'm going to kill her. I'm going to toss a knife right into her left eye." Visola pointed to the eye in question. "I'm going to bury it deep in her brain, right up to the hilt."

"Let us see if some kind of diplomacy can prevent things from getting to that point," Aazuria said. "Maybe if you release the hostages and send an ambassador to speak with her—if she knows that my father is dead, perhaps it will appease her. We could even invite her to see his body for confirmation."

"Invite her here?" Sionna said with surprise. "That's risky as hell."

"Just her; not her entire army," Aazuria said. "I fear she may be allied with the Clan of Zalcan. Perhaps Atargatis is their new leader."

"You should remain in a safe location," said Sionna. She glanced at the captive and lowered her voice. "Stay with Elandria until all this is over. You will be safe there, Princess."

"I will," Aazuria agreed, "but if I am needed you must send for me at once. Let me know of every single attack on our citizens, however small. Send me word about whether Atargatis accepts our meeting. If you wish—you may communicate with me by telephone. Also, Corallyn says that the 'instant messaging' on her computer is rather efficient."

"I have Trevain's landline and cell number," Sionna said with a nod. "In all likelihood we will send a runner as well. Old habits die hard."

"Diplomacy never works," Visola said cynically, "but if you really want me to try this, I'll give it a shot."

"Atargatis is coming!" the hostage repeated with a hysterical screech.

Visola waved her hand in annoyance. "Duh. Of course she's coming; didn't you hear? We're inviting her over for tea and crumpets."

Chapter 21: Immerse your Body

Trevain looked up from his book, startled by the interrupting sound of the doorbell. Elandria had just left to go upstairs and take a shower, so he would have to answer it himself. He pulled himself up from his armchair, and tossed his book against the cushion. He limped across the library, grimacing at the pain in his leg. He had really aggravated it with his endless hours of pacing over the past few days. He did not want to call a doctor, but he assumed that there was some kind of arthritis developing.

Slowly limping to the door, Trevain unlocked the bolt and turned the knob. When a crack of the sky became visible, he noted that it was already dark outside, heralding that the extremely long nights of Alaska had begun. When he saw who stood outside his door, his heart immediately began beating faster. He forgot about the pain in his leg.

"Aazuria," he said, reaching out to gather her up into his embrace. She still carried no luggage with her, so she could use both of her arms to return the hug. He was glad that she clung to him just as fiercely as he held her. "I thought you wouldn't return," he breathed.

"How could I not?" she asked. She smiled against his warm, dry shirt, rubbing her cheek against the fabric. "I have learned so much that I wish to tell you."

"I guess you two are going to pick up right where you left off and continue smooching," Corallyn said dryly from behind her sister. She had entered the house and shut the door, and was now leaning on it with crossed arms.

Aazuria gave her younger sister a playful look. "Coral, go find Elandria and tell her about our trip. Tell her all the important parts, okay? The 'adults' need to talk."

Instead of saluting respectfully as she had done in Adlivun, Corallyn stuck out her tongue at her sister before obediently scurrying upstairs. Fundamentally, it meant the same thing.

"Will you come and sit down with me?" Trevain asked Aazuria, as he caressed her dark hair. "My leg has gotten really bad lately. I haven't been feeling so great."

Aazuria pulled away from him and looked down at his leg suspiciously. "Your 'fishing injury,' right?"

"Yes, that's right..." he began.

She saw it in his face again and stopped him by raising her hand. "Why do you deceive me, Trevain? You did not really injure your leg while working, did you?"

"How do you know that?" he asked. "I haven't told anyone. It's a congenital bone disorder. I've had it since I was a boy. I just tell people it was a boating injury to make them more cautious."

Aazuria's face was lit with a giant smile, and she laughed. She had to restrain herself from throwing her hands up in the air. "I knew it! This is wonderful!"

"You seem awfully excited about my defects," Trevain commented, but he was enjoying her laughter.

"I have the exact same problem with my legs! I know just how to ease the pain," she said, taking his hand. She beamed in delight. "Do you trust me?"

Trevain looked at her innocent face, and remembered Elandria's words. He tried to imagine that this smiling young girl before him was capable of murder. He inwardly scolded himself for the thought, and easily pushed it away. It did not matter to him.

"Of course, I trust you," he said softly. He was enamored of her smile. She placed her arm under his shoulder to support him as she guided him through his own house. She took him to the room where the indoor swimming pool was situated. She did not turn on the light, because the room was just barely lit by the moon and starlight.

"The first step in healing is undressing," she told him solemnly, holding out her hand. "Your garments, please."

"I don't think that's a good idea, Aazuria," he answered. "I probably can't swim right now, my leg is really..."

"You said you trusted me," she argued. He nodded and obediently pulled off his shirt and placed it in her outstretched hand. She stared at his body shamelessly, taking in the contours of his muscles. Her lips curled as she observed his massive chest and broad shoulders. While clothed, his ultra-nice manner made him seem harmless, but seeing the physical manifestation of his strength made her swallow back a lump in her throat. In the excessive darkness of the

Arctic afternoon, he seemed rather intimidating.

He followed this by undoing the buttons of his pants, and allowing them to fall before stepping out of them.

"I did not realize it was Tuesday," she said with a mischievous smile.

He looked down, and his cheeks flushed as he realized that the day of the week was printed on his boxers. He cleared his throat in embarrassment. "So what is this miracle cure you have for me?" he asked with a bashful chuckle.

Aazuria placed his clothes aside, and shrugged out of her dress as well so that she was also in her undergarments.

"Come with me," she said with a smile before diving perfectly into the deep end of the pool. He admired the graceful curve of her back and the way she hardly made any splash. He could immediately tell that she was experienced with being around and within water. Trevain limped to the edge of the pool and slowly crouched down to a seated position. He dipped his legs in the water first, up to his calves.

Aazuria's emerged from the surface with her hair soaked and matted against her head. She picked up a tendril of her hair and looked at it, and was pleased to see that it was still dark. Not that she was really visible at all in this scarce lighting. She looked back to her patient. "This would probably be better if it were salt water, but nonetheless…"

"Do you think that simply having contact with water will make my legs stop hurting?" he asked skeptically.

"No. You need to come in with me," she said, beckoning him with her hand. "Fully immerse your body!"

He smiled at her enthusiasm and complied. Once he was submerged, he realized that it had been a very long time since he had actually used his swimming pool. It had been one of those things he had been very excited about getting before it had actually been installed. Once it had been neatly added to the house, he had mostly been too busy to enjoy it, or too preoccupied. Trevain gazed at Aazuria's dark cloudy form through the water, and lifted his head above the surface to see her more clearly.

"Race me," she challenged with a laugh, beginning to swim to the far side of the pool. Her enthusiasm was infectious, and he could do nothing except forget his sore leg and follow her. They experimented with swimming using different types of strokes, and Aazuria was surprised to see that Trevain almost always matched her speed.

"You are a *very* strong swimmer," she remarked when they stopped for a break.

"Well, I am a seaman," he explained.

"Yes. Yes, you are…" she answered, sending him a cryptic look.

"I made it to the state finals in high school," he said with nostalgia in his tone. "I couldn't finish competing because I had to work."

"You would have won," she said. "The state finals and more. The Olympics even. You're a natural!"

"Nonsense. If I'm so great how are you beating me every time?"

"I am one of the fastest swimmers in the world," Aazuria said matter-of-factly. "Yet I think that if you spent more time in the water you would be far better than I am. Can you not tell? It is rooted deep in your bones; the water calls out to you until it causes you physical pain unless you come to it."

"You're just trying to make an old man feel better about his ailing body," Trevain said humbly—but the truth was he did feel a bit of an ego boost from her words. He had always prided himself on his skill as a swimmer. He realized suddenly that the pain in his leg had eased almost completely with the swimming, and he marveled at this curiosity.

"Good grief, Trevain. If you call yourself old one more time, I will make a valiant attempt at drowning myself," she declared.

He laughed. "Unfortunately, Zuri, there's no getting around that fact. I'm way past my heyday."

Aazuria pressed the back of her palm to her forehead and mimicked a fainting damsel in distress. "Alas," she said dramatically, "my feeble heart."

She allowed herself to sink to the bottom of the deep end of the pool.

He smiled at her little display. "I shouldn't have shown you those old movies with all of those vulnerable and needy women!" he joked, knowing that she could not hear him underwater. He waited for a moment, and was surprised when she did not reemerge for quite some time.

"Aazuria?" he asked. He imagined that she must be trying to

impress him with how long she could hold her breath. He had often played that game as a child. After some time, he began to glance at the clock in worry. She was really good at this game. He dipped his own head below the surface, and began to dive in search of her. The waters were dark, but he could make out her shape in the corner of the pool. She was in a seated position, and she was looking up at him patiently.

He swam down to her, positioning himself directly before her. He had always been quite skilled at holding his breath as well. She smiled at him under the water, and he could barely make out the curve of her lips in the darkness. His eyes roamed over her body, clad only in her green bra and panties. He returned his eyes to her face, battling the sensations that her state of undress aroused in him.

The two hovered in silence, looking at each other.

Trevain became very conscious of the fact that they were all alone, in a dark corner of the bottom of his swimming pool. He remembered the way that she had kissed him before she left, before her family. She had done so proudly. He realized that he no longer wished to restrain himself; he no longer wished to try so hard to be a gentleman. Here, immersed in the water so close to her, his body hummed with vitality and spirit. He felt just as young as ever.

Aazuria had seen the power in him which he had long forgotten, and she had forced him to see it too. He did not know how he could possibly thank her. All he knew was that he wanted to give every last drop of himself to her. He wanted to love her with every facet of his being.

He reached forward and circled his hands around her small waist, pulling her body against his. He pressed his mouth against hers hungrily. Her small hands immediately wrapped around his neck, and she deepened the kiss without reservation. She found herself wrapping her legs around him to try and get closer to him. The pleasure she felt from this underwater embrace ignited flames of craving within her which she had never felt.

To be a free human being; she wanted to cry.

The flames mounted to a firestorm. She felt his lips trailing down her neck and chest. She had not even realized that Trevain had ripped her bra from her body until his lips found her breast in the dark water and pulled her nipple between them. She felt his teeth graze her skin with his gentle sucking, as quivers of pleasure pulsed through her body.

His hands were everywhere on her at once, and she could not concentrate. She was utterly swept away and lost in his ardor. When his hand explored between her thighs, she gasped at the sensation, taking in a deep breath of water. Trevain felt her chest expand against his body. He looked at her in confusion, not sure if she had really taken a breath or if he was just imagining it. He realized that they had both been holding their breath for far too long, and that he should take her to the surface for her comfort. He wrapped his arms around her and swam to the surface. She exhaled the water from her lungs as they ascended.

When they broke forth into the air, he took a breath. She did as well, mainly to maintain the appearance of needing one. She laughed, clinging to him, and immediately moved to reconnect their mouths in another kiss. He responded, before abruptly pulling away.

He took a few deep breaths and gathered his composure. "Aazuria—I'm sorry. I didn't mean to jump your bones as soon as you returned. I am being way too aggressive with you. I just couldn't restrain myself." He wiped the water out of his eyes. "We need to talk."

His words returned her to reality. She watched him breathing deeply of the air and wondered with horror whether he really could breathe underwater. She pressed a hand against her chest, feeling her racing heartbeat. She had gotten carried away. Testing something like this by trial and error was not exactly safe.

There was no evidence that he did have the ability, other than his legs being perfectly designed for swimming. It was not certain that he shared Callder's trait. In fact, if Callder had been unknowingly fathered by a different person than Trevain, there could be no chance at all of him having the trait. Aazuria closed her eyes in anger at herself for jumping to conclusions. Trevain's limp, and the structure of his legs, could have nothing to do with sea-dweller ancestry. She had heard the stories; throughout history, hundreds of human men had been accidentally or intentionally killed trying to be with their undersea lovers in this fashion.

She had been a breath away from becoming one of those reckless seductive sirens who killed sailors. "I am truly sorry," she whispered. "I meant you no harm. I did not mean to do this but I missed you so dreadfully."

"You haven't harmed me," he said with a laugh. He kissed her again. Although their heads were above water, he traced his hand over the curve of her waist beneath the surface. She seemed to be able to tread water effortlessly, without much movement. He could not seem to stop touching her body, and he willed himself to remove his hands. "Listen; I can't deal with being away from you anymore, Aazuria. These past few weeks I've gotten so attached to you that I felt lost when you were gone. I need to be close to you from now on, always."

She ran her fingers through his wet hair happily. "I feel the same."

"But I need to tell you something. I want you to know that I know, and I don't want you to feel you have to hide things from me anymore."

She looked at him in puzzlement. "What are you speaking of?"

"I spoke with Elandria when you were gone, and she told me some things about your past..."

Aazuria smiled. "You must have really improved in your sign language without me here to translate!"

"No, Aazuria. She *told* me."

Aazuria felt dread mushrooming in her chest. She held her breath, knowing intuitively that something bad was about to happen. "She spoke to you... with her voice," Aazuria said softly, knowing that it had to have been something extremely serious. She could not remember the last time she had heard her sister speak. "Good Sedna. I'm afraid to know what she said."

"She told me your big secret."

She swallowed. "What big secret?"

"How many do you have?" he asked gently. "She told me the biggest one."

"So she told you... that I am about to be made queen of a small sovereign kingdom and that we live in a mostly underwater ice palace carved into a glacier?"

He threw his head back and laughed as he often did when she spoke the truth. When his laughter died down, he reached out and hugged her around the waist, pulling her against him. "I'm trying to be serious here. I just want to clear the air between us."

So, I suppose that was not the secret, Aazuria mused to herself. "Really, Trevain. I am at a complete loss. I do not know what she could have told you."

"She told me about your father."

He felt Aazuria's body instantly stiffen under his hands. "She told you…" Aazuria wanted to ask specifically what Elandria had told him, but she saw the answer written on his face. Her stomach sank. She drew in a sharp breath, placing a hand over her mouth. Her hand muffled an involuntary sob. She fiercely ripped herself away from him, and swam to the edge of the pool.

"Zuri! Don't go…"

"What you must think of me!" she whispered as she climbed out of the pool hurriedly. She realized that her bra was still in the pool, and she covered herself with her arm as she fumbled in the darkness for her dress.

"Wait, Aazuria—we should talk about this!"

She had already run from the room.

Chapter 22: In Moist Despair

Aazuria considered leaving the house.

Her hand was on the doorknob, and she had to decide quickly. She could run out of the house, leap into the sea, and swim home to Adlivun. She would not have to encounter Trevain ever again and hear how negatively he thought of her. She would not have to face Elandria again, at least not immediately.

She had a mental picture of lashing out at the poor girl in anger, and she did not want this to happen. She loved Elandria, even if she had turned Trevain against her. Her fingers tightened around the cold metal doorknob. Why would she have done it? Was Elandria jealous? Did she want Trevain for herself? Had she been hoping to sully Aazuria's character?

She knew this was not the case. Her sister was fiercely devoted and would never intentionally harm her. So what was the reason? She knew that she was far too upset to simply ask. The vicious way her voice would leave her body would scare the stuffing out of her sister. She turned the doorknob and pulled the door open. She had no other choice but to leave.

Trevain was suddenly behind her and his hand was on hers, closing the door which she had just opened. She immediately began sobbing again at the feeling of his skin against her hand. How could he bear to touch her, now that he knew?

"Aazuria, please don't leave me again," he said softly into her ear, slipping his arm around her stomach. "I need you to talk to me."

She felt all the energy drain from her body as she leaned against him. She knew then that she did not have the strength to make the swim back to Adlivun tonight, and her hand fell away from the doorknob helplessly.

"I shouldn't have brought it up right away," he said, kissing her temple, her ear, and her neck. "I just... I'm an idiot sometimes. I want you to know that I don't think any less of you..."

She twisted out of his grasp and moved away from him. She could not believe his words! It was not true. An altruistic, compassionate person like Trevain could never understand murder. "I am… exhausted from my trip," she said, struggling to speak calmly and evenly through her tears. "I need to rest."

"Aazuria—"

She bolted up the stairs, clutching the railing tightly as her weakened legs threatened to buckle under her. Congenital bone disorder, indeed! She ran directly to her room. Crawling into her bed, she buried herself beneath the covers as she quietly sobbed. She knew that he would never want her now. She deserved it. This was the price she paid for being herself. She felt betrayed by her sister for the first time in her life.

Why would Elandria tell him such a thing? It did not make sense.

She shut her eyes tightly to fight back her tears. She was not crying out of remorse for what she had done, or sadness for the loss of her father. No, she had come to terms with that and even wished she had been capable of doing it sooner. She knew that long-term repercussions of her father's cruelty would haunt her people for many years to come. She should have seen this and acted sooner, but her judgment had been clouded by filial love and loyalty.

Droplets of water slid from her wet hair down into her mouth. She tasted the chlorine from the pool. It tasted so unlike the comforting ocean saltwater, or even the fresh glacial drinking water which filled her massive bedchamber at home. She missed the taste of saltwater.

Chlorine just tasted like defeat.

She lay there in moist despair until she felt two strong arms encircle her. She was too weak to protest or to pull away. It was then she discovered how comforting a human touch could be. It was altogether different from when her sisters hugged her—it was more than just affectionate. His warm embrace spoke volumes of reassurance which her body instinctively understood. It was a secret sign language exchanged between souls.

"I asked Elandria for permission to ask you to marry me," Trevain explained, holding her close. "That's why she told me. She wanted me to truly know the woman I was hoping to join my life with; providing she'd have me of course."

Her body had known his intentions before her mind could

register his words. She looked over her shoulder to see the honesty and love on his face. "Trevain," she whispered in astonishment.

"If you want to know the truth, Zuri, it has only made me more in awe of you. To go through what you have experienced must have taken incredible strength."

She examined each wrinkle and pore for the hint of a lie, but his expression was pure. She saw only truth there. She could not believe that he was so accepting and sympathetic. "You are amazing," she said softly, out loud this time.

He smiled. "I was planning to find some fancy, impressive way to ask you… but since you already know I'm going to, it kind of spoils the surprise. I guess I should just do it now." He wrapped his arms around her even more tightly and kissed her cheek. "Aazuria, please say you'll be my wife."

His words created several tiny explosions of emotion within her. She was inundated with euphoria and knew without a doubt that she wanted to accept his offer. Then, she forced herself to ignore the feelings and *think*. Her thoughts raced as she tried to imagine the possibility. She knew that she would have to return to Adlivun, and she was uncertain whether he could breathe underwater. Even if he could, he would think it was crazy. He would never even consider coming to her home; he laughed at the mention of its existence like it was some great joke!

Could she manage to live her life with him here, in his house, on land, and forsake her kingdom? Could she leave everything she had ever cherished behind in order to love him? No, those were not the right questions. She knew without a doubt that she easily could; the strength of her feeling attested to that. The real question was *should* she? She knew the answer to that question as well. She should not.

She had always been Princess Aazuria Vellamo of Adlivun. How could she suddenly be Mrs. Trevain Murphy, Alaskan housewife?

He saw the thoughts and emotions dancing in her eyes, even in the darkness of the room. Her eyes still had that certain subtle shine to them, reminding him again of a cat in the dark. He reached out and brushed the wetness of her tears off her cheeks, now that they had stopped falling.

"You don't have to tell me your answer now," he said. "I know it's crazy and sudden. I'll ask you again and again until you know for sure what you want."

She exhaled a breath that she did not realize she had been holding. She turned over in bed to face him completely, burying her face in the crook of his neck as she embraced him. "I do need to think about it," she said softly, "but it is a rather nice idea."

"I know you may not love me yet, but if you're willing to waste a few years beside me… maybe you'll grow to care for me more." His voice was hesitant but hopeful. "I don't really know how this love thing works, but I know I've never felt this way. I never thought I would, and it's kind of crazy powerful. I can't stand to be separated from you for a few minutes. I'll do just about anything to make you happy, and see you laugh—and it's *really* tough to make you laugh."

She smiled. She did not know how to tell him that she already believed that she loved him. She had entertained, and disdained, many proposals before, but usually from distant strangers who had sent an envoy to her father. Never from a man who was holding her tightly in his arms, and professing that he cared for her in spite of… and *because of* the fact that she was a murderess. This was new.

"Don't run away from me anymore, Zuri," he said burying his face in her hair. "You're all I have left."

She sighed deeply, remembering his recent loss. She guiltily thought of how Callder lay wounded in her infirmary. She wished she could give Trevain some small measure of optimism, and tell him that there was a slim chance his brother might pull through—but there was too much explaining to do. She felt awful at having to keep this from him.

"There is so much about me which you do not know," she whispered.

"I want you to feel comfortable telling me all your secrets," he answered. "I promise that I can handle them. We can get through anything together. Now that I know about your father, nothing can faze me."

"Did Elandria tell you why I did it?" she asked.

"Yes… she told me what he did to her," he said, swallowing. He could not think about it without feeling emotional. The main emotion was anger.

"I let him harm my sisters for years. I did not do anything to stop it," Aazuria said, struggling to vanquish a new onslaught of tears. "But that's not even why I killed him."

"Shhhh, it's okay," Trevain said, rubbing her back soothingly. "You don't have to think about it now."

"I thought his actions were going to destroy us. He did not care about who he hurt or trampled to get what he desired. I thought that killing him would save us. Now, I am not so sure. The damage has been done. The people he wronged… they are already coming after us. I may not be able to stop them."

"Don't worry about a thing, Zuri," he said, kissing her nose. "You're safe here with me."

"I wish that my own safety was all that I needed to consider," she lamented. "That would be easy."

Chapter 23: Take the Twins

Aazuria placed her teacup down violently. "I strongly recommend you do not return to work. Not yet."

"I have to," Trevain said. It had been a few days since Aazuria's return, and he had been catching up on his messages and chatting with his shipmates. He had decided that it was time for a return to normalcy. "It's been a while since we lost Callder and Leander, and the crew is getting restless. Everyone still has to live."

"I *command* that you do not go back to work yet!" she said, leaning forward with both of her hands gripping the edge of the table.

He chuckled at her intense body-language. "Zuri, we've missed most of the fishing season. If my men all go off and join other crews then I won't know what to do with myself in the years to come. *The Fishin' Magician* will be blacklisted and no one will want to join my crew…"

"If you must go off to sea then you will allow me to join you," she insisted. "You are short two men, and surely I can take over some of their duties."

"Aazuria!" he said with a laugh. "It's hard work. Dirty, wet, and exhausting."

"Please," she persisted. "I just want to make sure that you are safe."

"And I want to make sure *you* are safe. You've never been on a crab fishing boat before, have you?" he asked, raising an eyebrow.

"I have been on many boats," she answered, "so many kinds of boats that I cannot remember all of their names. You know that I am a strong swimmer as well."

"It's too dangerous for you," he said inflexibly.

"Dammit, Trevain, that's not fair! I want to be involved in your life."

"Then agree to marry me," he said with a grin as he sipped his tea.

"I will *not* agree if you do not either heed my warning, or take me aboard."

"And you will if I do?"

She shut her lips tightly.

"Very clever, Zuri. Nice try." Trevain smirked at her. "You're already trying to use all the leverage you have over me to manipulate me into doing what you want. I think you're going to make the perfect wife."

The sound of an annoying car horn being honked multiple times interrupted them. "That's Brynne, no doubt," he said. "I'm going to carpool with her to the docks."

"You are in grave danger," Aazuria whispered, putting her face in her hands. "How can you not see this?"

"Look! Wifely concern," Trevain teased, putting his hands on her shoulders, and kissing the top of her head. He gently massaged her shoulders to ease her tension. "Relax. As Brynne likes to say, it's not my first rodeo. I know how to take care of myself."

Brynne's car horn impatiently sounded again, startling both of them.

"Crazy Brynne Ambrose," he said, shaking his head. "I swear that woman will be the death of me!"

"Do *not* joke about the death of you!" Aazuria said harshly. "I have a very bad feeling about this. When *you* have a bad feeling you listen to it, and make your whole crew listen—will you not believe me this time? I am certain that there is a menace out there of which you cannot even conceive. I know these things, Trevain. I am being completely sincere; this is not paranoia."

"I've been doing this my whole life. It's a cinch," he said, giving her a reassuring smile.

She was not reassured. She could see that he also was anxious, but he was trying to push past it and remain calm. She wanted to pull rank on him and tell him exactly what she had been doing *her* whole life, just how long that was, and how much she had seen. She wanted to tell him what had *actually* happened to the boats in the Bermuda Triangle, and to the boats in Japan's Dragon's Triangle, and how it was happening again now, right here. Instead she just shook her head. "I hope you know that I am deeply displeased. Nothing good can come of this, and one of us will surely suffer for your mistake."

He reached out and squeezed her arm before kissing her on the temple. "I'll see you in a few days, okay?"

With that, he left. She let out a huge sigh, returning her head to her hands. She sat there, wallowing in worry for several minutes before she heard her sisters entering the room. Elandria came and sat close to her.

"What's wrong, Zuri?" Corallyn asked. "Still bummed about Trevain heading back to work?"

"I asked him not to go. I strongly recommended him not to go. I ordered him not to go! I demanded he let me come along!" she said angrily. "Why did he not listen to me? How dare he ignore me like this?" She wanted to smash something, but she had enough composure to restrain herself. She had learned to control her temper long ago, in her youth. It had taken three centuries, but she no longer acted on foolish impulse and whim. At least not when anyone was looking.

Corallyn smiled. "This is his jurisdiction. You can't order him around here. Besides, he doesn't know you're a crown princess, and even if he did it would probably make no difference."

"Atargatis is out there," she said uneasily. "I threatened him that I would not marry him if he left, and he still left."

"He must have known that was an idle threat," Corallyn said with amusement. "Do you think you're going to refuse him?"

"Yes! I cannot do this," Aazuria said. "I cannot be his wife. He does not even consider my words significant."

"*You know that is not true,*" Elandria said. "*You must understand that he has obligations to his crew just as you have obligations to Adlivun.*"

"Fine," said Aazuria, standing up and slamming her fist on the table. "Then I will follow him. I will not sit idly by as he plunges himself into dangers unknown to him. The sun sets so early; the fishermen spend most of their time working in the dark." She pointed to her eyes. "I have a tapetum lucidum, so I can see more clearly in the night than they can. I will be beneath the water, so I will also have a better angle of view."

"Sio and Viso won't be pleased about this," Corallyn warned her.

"It is just a reconnaissance mission, really. You know that I am fast, and I will not be seen."

"Then take the twins," Corallyn urged sternly.

"Sionna is in the infirmary taking care of people who are close to death! Visola is busy pawning my jewels and buying illegal weapons on the black market. Both are busy; I do not wish to disturb them."

"You promised Sionna you would stay here," Corallyn reminded her. "This is your sanctuary for now."

"Coral," Aazuria said, looking at her sister with authority, "it might be the Clan of Zalcan out there. Do you know how much fun they have killing unsuspecting sailors and fishermen? It is their trademark. They sunk hundreds of boats in Japan. Hundreds. Do you know how many people died? Those people had nothing to do with the Ningyo—that was just 'while we are in the neighborhood' killing."

"Yeah, exactly—so if they're so dangerous do you really want to run into them without your warriors? Elandria and I would go with you, but if there is any trouble, how much can we really help?"

Elandria placed her hand on Aazuria's arm to elicit her attention. She fixed her sister with a somber gaze. She opened her lips ever so slightly and murmured, "Take the twins."

Aazuria turned to her sister in surprise. When Elandria used her voice to speak, it was always imperative. Aazuria often said that her silent sister was the wisest person she knew, and she would never take any action against her counsel.

"Fine. I will."

Chapter 24: A Million Reasons

"He really proposed to you? Poor guy, I bet he was so devastated when you flat out rejected him! I hope you weren't too mean about it."

Aazuria did not respond, and Visola froze in the middle of wrapping a thick forest-green fabric around her chest. "You did refuse him, right? Zuri?"

"I have not given him an answer yet."

"You're joking right? You're actually considering marrying this guy?" Visola's vivid green eyes widened. She held up her hand in order to count on her fingers. "Here are a million reasons why you shouldn't: one, you barely know him; two, he *barely* knows you; three, you belong in Adlivun; four, I don't like him; five, you're way too pretty; six, you have no idea if he's well-endowed, seven, you don't know if he's any good in…"

Sionna interrupted by throwing an arm around her sister and smiling. "Viso, I think it might take a little while for you to give her a million reasons. We are still mortal creatures and our time on earth is precious. Why don't we talk about this later?"

"Okie-dokie," said Visola, continuing to wrap the green fabric around her midsection. "Strip, Zuri. You get suited up next."

"What is that stuff exactly?" Aazuria asked as she slipped her dress off. The three women stood in a private area of the docks. "It had better not slow me down."

Visola grinned as she began to wrap the fabric around Aazuria's chest. "Relax! It's something innovative and fun."

Sionna assisted, wrapping the material around Aazuria's legs and hips. "Is it truly necessary?" Aazuria asked again.

"Yes, if you're really concerned about your boy-toy's safety. This is fifteen layers of Kevlar: a super lightweight, bulletproof body armor, covered in water resistant fabric."

"It is green."

"Such a lovely deep forest green," Visola mused.

"I call it 'slimy seaweed' green," Sionna said in embarrassment.

"Viso was drunk and complaining that the drab color didn't match her complexion and hair. She dyed all the armor."

"That's not the only reason," Visola said with a blush. "Malachite green has always been our nation's color! And if we ever need… uh, camouflage…"

"We're not supposed to be drinking," Aazuria reminded her friend, feeling guilty for her recent indulgence. "It affects us poorly."

"Lighten up," Visola said, grinning, "and take one of these beautiful babies."

"What is that contraption? How am I supposed to carry it while swimming?"

"Here, I have it all figured out." Visola hooked the instrument over Aazuria's arm, fastening it onto her back.

"You two never answer me when I ask questions! I want to know what this is and why it is important before I allow it to slow me down."

"It's just an underwater assault rifle, sweetie." Sionna strapped one onto her own back and nodded at Aazuria reassuringly. "We probably won't need it, but it's just for extra safety. Shall we do this?"

Aazuria wanted to ask how the twins had managed to procure such weapons, but she thought better of it. "You two really outdid yourselves this time," Aazuria commented. She checked that the rifle was secure on her back and smiled at the other two women. "Let us go."

In one fluid, fishlike motion, Aazuria extended her arms and dived off the docks into the water. Visola and Sionna followed in perfect synchronization behind her.

Chapter 25: Three Against Thirty

"We've been following him underwater for two days and nothing has happened." Visola yawned, opening her mouth widely to take in a huge breath of water. *"We've been down here so long your hair has bleached itself. I think he's going to be safe, Zuri."*

Aazuria pulled a lock of her hair before her face and saw that Visola was right. She looked up at the twins. *"Let us wait a little longer."*

"Fine. But I hate camping out in open water. Eating whatever grows or swims nearby—this is barbaric." Visola and Sionna had followed their leader in search of Trevain's boat for several hours, easily keeping up with her effortless high speeds. They had found several other fishing boats before they located *The Fishin' Magician*. Initially, they had all felt the exhilaration of being in the water again, strength infusing their bones and spirits. However, now that they were just hovering around deep beneath the boat, waiting for the crew to exhaust themselves and head home, they were feeling rather bored.

When a metal cage was lowered nearby, Visola grinned. *"Don't get caught! You'll be used as sushi by the sailors for lunch,"* she signed to her sister as they lurked deep in the shadow of the ship they stalked.

"At least I'm palatable and won't give them food poisoning," Sionna retorted with her hands.

"You're right, but they would probably lose their appetites at the sight of you and toss you out with the bad seafood."

"Viso—we look exactly the same. Quit insulting yourself!"

The sisters were startled out of their mindless time-killing banter by a hand signal from their newly platinum-blonde leader. They were further surprised when she reached behind her and pulled the assault rifle off her back. She stared down at the device in her hands, before looking to the twins for help.

Visola swam forward and quickly mouthed the instructions on how to use the weapon, giving plenty of gestures for rapid training.

"What did you see?" Sionna asked, frowning.

Aazuria pointed above them, to shallower waters, her eyes

squinting in the darkness. The boat was turning around very slowly. Approaching the ship at high speeds, but still at a distance, was what looked to be a school of large fish. Upon more careful examination, and as they drew closer, one could see that they were actually people swimming in a military like formation and diverging around the boat. Their legs were covered with some sort of black fabric which made it look as though they all had black tails.

Aazuria could just barely make out the white glint of shark's teeth strung around their necks. Legend had it that the Clan of Zalcan trained their young warriors by pitting them against sharks in wrestling matches. Every single tooth on their necklaces came directly from a shark that the wearer had actually killed in hand-to-hand combat. If a warrior killed another warrior in a duel of honor, they would take the other's necklaces as a trophy and wear them as his or her own. The greatest warriors wore so many strands of necklaces that their necks were fully armored by them—they also wore them around their wrists, ankles, waists, and around their foreheads.

"*It is them,*" Aazuria said. "*I am sure of it. It is the Clan of Zalcan. Well, a few of them; maybe scouts or raiders.*" She felt her blood boiling and knew instinctively that they were going to attempt to cause some sort of trouble on Trevain's boat. She began swimming up to the surface with the rifle in her hands, but she felt herself restrained. The twins began to hastily pull her back down deeper into the waters.

"*What are you two doing? We need to go and confront them,*" she argued.

"*No,*" Sionna mouthed. "*There are at least thirty of them, and only three of us! They haven't spotted us yet, and that gives us the advantage. We're here for reconnaissance, so let's observe.*"

"*We need to see how they work, and what they want,*" Visola added. "*Take a few deep breaths, Zuri. Your captain will be fine.*"

Aazuria nodded, appreciating the wisdom of her friends. She retreated into the darkness with them, out of sight. She pulled slow breaths of water into her lungs, trying to calm herself down as she watched the mermaids prepare some kind of attack. *Trevain is up there,* she thought to herself, *and so is Brynne and several other innocents.* She had not realized how fond she had grown of not just the captain, but his entire crew in the past few weeks. She had no clue what the enemy intended until she saw that a few of them were laughing and swimming in zigzagging patterns under the boat.

"*Are they drunk?*" Aazuria asked.

"*I don't know, but they're definitely enjoying themselves,*" Visola responded, frowning.

"*Do you think that 'Atargatis' might be amongst them?*" Sionna wondered.

Aazuria saw it then—a blonde woman swung her arm back and launched a harpoon at someone on the boat. The person fell into the water, and several of the mermaids immediately surrounded him, dragging him down. Aazuria's heart began to pound so hard it was painful, and she placed the rifle between her teeth before using her hands to rapidly swim up to the boat. The twins knew that they could not stop her this time, so they grasped their own rifles and followed.

It was several seconds before their enemies were aware of their presence. The black-clad sea-dwellers were so focused on the person they had taken from the boat that they did not even see when their own numbers began to dwindle.

Aazuria had never held a rifle before, but she found it surprisingly easy. Her first shot missed, but she gripped the metal barrel more tightly and tried again. Her second and third shots were slightly more precise, and after that it became easy. Aazuria shot at least five people who had heaped around the man, fearing that it was Trevain they were harming. A dark pool of blood surrounded him and she could not see his identity. Sionna and Visola shot many people on the flanks of the formation until they were too close to use the rifles.

The lifeless body of a man she had shot in the lower abdomen floated close to her. Aazuria pushed the rifle onto her back, and felt the man's waist for more basic forms of weaponry. Scoring a knife, she propelled herself forward into the thicket of battle, engaging in hand to hand-to-hand combat with the remaining mermaids. Her only focus was on fighting her way through the crowd toward the injured man. She was terrified of fighting the skilled Clan warriors, but she knew that she was much smarter than the sharks they had ripped all those teeth from.

She saw with great relief that it was not Trevain they had attacked; the man in the water was Arnav, the young student from New York of whom Trevain had always spoken so highly. She swam toward him, but a blonde woman with countless necklaces intercepted her with a leer.

Aazuria was caught off guard for a moment, for she thought she recognized the woman. She did not have time to remember who she was, for the woman seemed intent on gouging her eyes out. She would not allow this to happen easily, and used her knife to defend against the woman's strikes. When her blade bounced off the woman's waist, she discovered that the shark's teeth did serve as effective armor. As she struggled to keep the woman from gashing her body open, she realized that the woman was obviously the leader. Her black garments were the most ornate, and she was the most skilled fighter. Aazuria was kept on her toes in dodging the woman's attacks, and trying desperately to get in a few of her own. She silently prayed that each thrust of her arm would be the last. The woman's sword hit Aazuria squarely in the thigh, and Aazuria flinched, expecting a huge laceration. She was stunned when the blade of the knife did not penetrate her soft armor.

Visola saw this, and tried to get away from the fight she was having with three people at once to help her friend. She hacked at them mercilessly, but they were very fast. Sionna was in a similarly overwhelming situation. The blonde woman that Aazuria was fighting was annoyed that her blow had not wounded her opponent as much as she had anticipated. She reached out and grabbed a handful of Aazuria's hair, but Aazuria used the opportunity to drive her knuckles into the woman's soft breast. The woman recoiled in pain, and Aazuria lunged forward, using her other hand to slice open the woman's throat—but her opponent just barely evaded the blade. The blonde woman fought valiantly. Before both women knew it, their fight had broken the surface of the water. Their gasping and yelling was now audible in the air.

The men on the boat above began to take notice of the action, and began to crowd to the starboard side of the *Magician*.

"What in the bloody hell?" Ujarak exclaimed.

"It's pretty dark, but it looks like there are two women wrestling in the water," Doughlas observed.

"It's fucking cold down there! What's wrong with them?" Edwin wondered.

"*Help!*" Aazuria screamed, in a piercing voice which she hoped that none of them would recognize. She continued to fight with the blonde woman as she yelled to the men. She figured that if she screamed at the top of her lungs her voice would be adequately distorted. "One of your men—he is in the water, injured and drowning!"

"What is she talking about? We're all right here," Brynne said in confusion.

"Where's Arnav?" Trevain said very suddenly. Everyone began to look around frantically. The captain began to pull off his boots so that he could dive into the water.

Meanwhile, the giant blonde woman had placed Aazuria in a headlock and was proceeding to choke the life out of her. "So you know those people, do you, sweet pea?" she whispered.

Aazuria froze in her struggle for a moment, recognizing the voice and the pet name. "Koraline?" she gasped out in a labored voice as her neck was crushed. The woman had been one of her ballet instructors many decades ago. She was Corallyn's mother. Aazuria tried desperately to pry the muscled arm away from her throat. The pointy shark's teeth on the woman's bracelets which covered her arms from wrist to elbow were digging painfully into Aazuria's skin. She was sure that she was bleeding, but she did not care; her focus was on survival at this point.

"No one has called me that in a while. I go by the name of 'Atargatis' now. It rather suits me, don't you think?" Koraline further tightened her grip on Aazuria's throat, causing her to grow dizzy from the strangulation. She desperately tried to free herself, hammering her elbow back into the woman's ribcage. She reached behind her to press her nails into the woman's eyes, but Koraline seemed to anticipate her every movement. Aazuria knew that unless Visola or Sionna could fend off their own attackers and come to her rescue, she would be unconscious within moments.

Aazuria was startled when Trevain was suddenly in front of her, and his fist was flying into Koraline's face. She darted beneath the surface as soon as she was free of the woman's grip, breathing deeply. She saw that the twins were still alive and fighting. She dove down to where she had last seen Arnav. She slipped her arms around the boy when she found him and rapidly swam to the surface, carrying the boy. Once they had broken through to the air, she pressed her fingers against his jaw, checking his vitals. Finding nothing, she gasped and pressed her ear close to his nose and mouth. There was no sign of life. He was already dead. "No," she whispered. She closed her eyes, feeling powerless. She turned to Trevain in despair.

"I could not save him," she spoke softly, holding Arnav's dead body mostly above the surface in her arms. She suddenly remembered to incline her head downward, using her white bangs and wet hair to conceal her features.

Everyone was curiously peering off the side of the boat. Trevain moved towards Aazuria in the water. She assumed that he must have killed Koraline or at least knocked her unconscious, for no one was immediately attacking them for the first time in several minutes. She extended her hands to offer Arnav to the captain. She was eager to swim away before someone could recognize her identity under the paler skin, hair, and eyes.

Suddenly, a look of alarm came to Trevain's face. "Look out!" he shouted, diving forward. "*No!*"

Aazuria screamed at the violent impact of something colliding with her body and piercing right through her. A searing pain shot through her back. A frenetic female laugh mocked her agony; Koraline had thrown a javelin directly at Aazuria, aimed precisely at her heart.

Trevain had moved swiftly towards her within the water and pushed her aside just in time, or it surely would have hit its target. The javelin intended for the center of her torso had gone through her right shoulder instead. She moaned with the blinding pain, and felt Trevain's arms around her. She looked up at him through dizzy, blurred vision. She had let go of Arnav, whose body was now sinking. She clutched Trevain tightly, blinking and trying to focus. She was about to say his name when she caught herself.

"That's just a taste of things to come!" the blonde woman shouted. "I won't rest until I have my daughter back—and until every one of you is dead. Tell Kyrosed Vellamo that I'm coming for him!"

Aazuria flinched, wondering if Trevain knew her last name. "But he is…" She could not speak through the blinding pain. Her head spun, and she struggled to stay conscious. The world was fading, but she firmly dug her fingers into Trevain's upper arms for support. She used his strength to stay grounded and awake. Her head, neck, and shoulders which were above water were covered in a cold sweat from the severe pain. Her hand immediately moved to grasp the javelin, instinctively trying to rip the offending shaft out of her body.

"Atargatis, you bitch!" shouted Visola, bursting out of the surface of the water. The redhead grabbed the woman around her neck and dove down into the depths of the sea.

Aazuria felt a rush of relief, knowing that Visola had fought off her own attackers. She prayed Sionna was also safe. She sighed; it was over. Tears had come into her eyes without her permission because of the excruciating pain. She tightened her grip around the javelin in her shoulder, knowing she must pull it out, but finding it too unbearable to do by herself. She would surely pass out if she tried, or at least end up screaming unattractively. Instead she gritted her teeth and used both hands to break off the narrowest part of the stick which had been protruding from her body. She looked up at Trevain who had bravely risked himself in order to save her, and still held her protectively. He had even allowed the body of his friend to sink into the sea in order to save someone he believed was a complete stranger.

"You're hurt badly, Miss," he was saying. "You have to come aboard the ship and let me take you to a hospital." He found himself suddenly stricken by the idea that it might not be an injured woman he held in his arms, but a legendary creature. "Who are you?" he asked breathlessly.

She smiled through her pain. The bleeding coming from her shoulder was profuse, but she knew it was not a lethal wound. She felt a rush of gratitude. She had been impressed with the speed and vigor with which Trevain moved in the water. It had been brave of him to jump off the ship to help her, when none of his crew members had. She could not believe that she now lived with this valiant man, and that he was hers to go home to. She also could not believe that he did not recognize her—but she was glad for this.

"Thank you for saving my life," she said softly, before slipping her hand behind his head and kissing him. At first his mouth was tense and unresponsive, and he displayed surprise more than anything. She wondered with amusement if he felt guilty for cheating on her. A second later, his lips softened, but she had already ripped herself away from him and disappeared under the water.

"Wait!" he shouted fruitlessly. He submerged himself under the water, intending to follow her, but she was already too deep beneath the surface for him to see where she had gone. He looked around in every direction frantically, but the injured white-haired woman had disappeared. Only Arnav's floating lifeless body, and the bodies of several of the other attackers floated in the ocean around him.

Meanwhile on the boat, there was a silent confusion. "Did you guys see what I saw?" Edwin asked softly.

"Weird chicks fighting," said Ujarak with a clueless shrug.

Wyatt cleared his throat. "Uh... Arnav was killed by a bunch of people wearing black, but then some females wearing green kicked their asses for it?"

"They had APS underwater assault rifles strapped to their backs," Doughlas said. "Probably some military training thing... they probably came from a stealth submarine which we can't see somewhere around here..."

Everyone began peering off the side of the ship and looking for the aforementioned vehicle. The captain had just been helped back onto the deck by Brynne, and he heard the submarine comment. Trevain grabbed a towel and began to absorb the water in his hair. "A sub... that makes sense. I don't know why that didn't cross my mind."

"So Arnav is really gone?" Billy asked quietly.

A flash of rage darkened Trevain's face. "I don't know why any of us should be surprised. Three fishing trips. Three deaths. They say one man dies per week during the fishing season but this..." Everyone jumped in surprise when the captain grabbed a handful of heavy metal rigging and violently hurled it across the ship. It smashed against the metal cages with a loud clangor. "What the *fuck* is going on?!" Trevain shouted, as tears filled his eyes.

"Shhh," Brynne said, moving to his side. She had never been scared of the kind captain in her life, but it seemed like something had broken in him. After a moment's hesitation, she reached out to hug Trevain. He immediately softened and returned the hug. She felt how wet and cold he was, and she shivered. "You need to warm up downstairs and get some dry clothes."

"Yeah," he said. It was all he could do to stay standing. Callder may have been a freeloading loafer, but Arnav had been a brilliant young man with a future. Trevain felt dizzy with disgust, and had an urge to empty the contents of his stomach all over Brynne. She must have sensed this, because she stepped away. He realized then that he had scared her with his display of violence. "I'm sorry I cursed and yelled."

"I curse and yell in front of you all the time, Murphy," she responded. "So who was that albino chick you made out with in the water?"

Trevain shook his head, completely oblivious. "All I know is that she was on our side. She tried to stop it from happening."

"They had to be marine forces," Doughlas was saying. "That's the only explanation."

"Or they could have been…" Billy trailed off, knowing that he could not reasonably finish that sentence.

"What? They could have been *what?*"

"Mermaids," Billy mumbled softly.

"Don't be fucking ridiculous," Trevain said angrily. He resisted the urge to toss more large pieces of metal across his boat. He resisted the urge to scream at the top of his lungs. Instead, he allowed Brynne to guide him downstairs so that he could get warm and dry.

Chapter 26: Diplomacy Never Works

"My mother? My *mother* did this to her?" Corallyn asked. "*She* is Atargatis, our great new enemy?"

Sionna had finished cleaning and disinfecting Aazuria's wound, and was administering a tetanus shot to her as a precautionary measure. "It would seem so."

"I thought she was a land-dweller; I thought she was dead!"

"We thought so too." Sionna began applying a poultice to Aazuria's shoulder. She had also sustained a few injuries, but she had quickly stitched them up herself. "Coral, Elan, you girls have to watch Aazuria closely to monitor her temperature, alright?"

Elandria nodded silently in a corner, with her hands folded in her lap. She looked fearfully at Sionna and Aazuria's wounds.

"It's not a Jennifer or a Molly—it's a Koraline," Visola said gloomily, "and I let it get away."

"I'm sorry, Viso. It was my fault," Sionna said with a sigh as she bandaged Aazuria's shoulder. "I should have handled myself better. You had her until I distracted you."

"Are you kidding? You were in trouble. I'm not going to let my sister get killed if I can prevent it."

"I like assault rifles," Aazuria said weakly, her head spinning with pain. It was the most complex contribution she could manage to make to the conversation. Sionna smiled and patted the sweat off her forehead with a damp cloth.

"That's right! Let's look on the bright side of things," Visola said. "We fought *three against thirty* and we won. When does that ever happen?"

"Four... if you count Trevain," Aazuria said, grimacing. "He punched... Atargatis in the face for me. And he did not even know it was me."

"I *do not* count him. He could have prevented you from having to follow him in the first place if he had listened to you. Then he could have prevented you from getting injured if he had killed the bitch—but he just pushed her away from you and thought it would help! Was he trying to break up two kids on the playground or save his potential fiancée's life? What a jerkwad," Visola muttered, earning a death glare from her sister. "Anyway, it was a good fight. We killed at least half of them, and wounded at least ten—and now we know who Atargatis is and why she's pissed off. Frankly, I'd be pissed off too if someone took a cutie-pie like Coral away from me."

"Thanks," said Corallyn, a bit downcast. "I guess I *would* kind of like to meet my mother. She didn't have to start a war about it. She could have just visited and said 'Hi, I'm your mom. Would you like a cookie?' Even if there wasn't a cookie involved, I would have been okay with that."

"She still has not been informed that the king is dead. Did you send someone, Visola?" Aazuria asked, through clenched teeth.

"I did send a representative out to look for the Clan of Zalcan… but she never came back." Visola sighed. "I will try again… but it seems like a useless sacrifice. Diplomacy never works."

"The ones who got away will tell the others not to take us so lightly," Sionna said. "Atargatis has a black eye, and a few of the others have bullets lodged in them. Maybe things will be different, and they will be a bit more communicative. I think assault rifles have that effect on people."

"Viso," Aazuria whispered. "I can never repay you for the armor and weapons. I am alive because of you. Adlivun will remain safe because of you."

"Aw, shucks, Zuri," Visola said, bashfully yet proudly. "What's a right-hand-woman for?"

Chapter 27: Aquatic Guardian Angel

Trevain trudged up the stairs after returning from his fishing trip. He was having difficulty processing what exactly had happened. All that he knew for sure was that Arnav Hylas had been killed. The Coast Guard had told them that it was just a bad season. The same thing had been happening to many other fishing boats. Two other boats had been *completely* lost. There was no sign of them at all, and nothing had been recovered. The press had not even heavily covered these tragedies; it was just the way things sometimes happened in Alaska. It had been that way for dozens of years. *"Count yourself lucky,"* the man at the docks had said.

"Just a bad season," Trevain repeated bitterly, pausing halfway up the staircase. His hand on the railing tightened its grip. "Count yourself lucky!" He felt bile rising inside him as he smashed his fist into the railing of the staircase, causing the wood to break and splinter. He was immediately upset with himself, remembering that a child now lived in the house.

He tried to calm himself down, but failing, he decided to take some sleeping pills. He just wanted to talk to Aazuria and go to bed. It had been a long few days. He needed to *not* be awake for a while. When he reached the landing, he saw that Corallyn was sitting on a chair in front of Aazuria's room with a book in her hands. This set off alarms of concern in his mind. He moved across the corridor quickly, with a worried expression on his face.

"Corallyn, what's wrong?"

The young girl closed her book and stood up. She responded rapidly as if the sentence had been rehearsed. "Aazuria has become very ill and cannot see you at the moment."

"Does she need a doctor?" Trevain asked. "What happened?"

"My sister has already seen her own private doctor. Mr. Fiskel also gave her some of his pain-relief medication. She will be healed before long. We must allow her to rest."

Trevain stared at Corallyn with puzzlement. He had never seen her act so formal and cross. She was completely serious, and almost unblinking in the deadpan stare she gave him.

"I think I know what this is about," Trevain said with a sigh. "She's still angry at me for not listening to her and going to work."

Corallyn remained expressionless.

"Well, she was right. I should have listened. I need to apologize…" Trevain had started to move forward, and Corallyn stepped in front of him, blocking his path.

"Stop. Aazuria does not wish to see anyone. She is unwell and she needs to rest."

"Coral, please. What's going on?" He reached for the doorknob with a frown.

Although Corallyn was perhaps a third of Trevain's massive size, she resolutely placed herself in front of the doorknob, and pushed her hand into his abdomen to restrain him.

"Uncle Trevain! She is extremely ill. She cannot receive you now. Please respect her wishes and go."

"Fine," Trevain said, with slight annoyance. He turned around and headed for his own room, slamming the door behind him. He ran a hand through his hair. He felt a slight pang of concern for Aazuria, but he also felt suspicious that she was not sick and just avoiding him. Yet, he wondered why she had placed Corallyn outside her door standing guard as her pint-sized sentinel.

Trevain walked across the floor to his window, and placed his hands on the wall on either side of the glass. He took deep jagged breaths, causing the window to fog up. He felt anger, not sadness. He had not been able to understand why he had lost Leander and Callder, but now he did. It had not been natural. It had been the work of men, not the sea. Arnav Hylas had been a clever, animated young man with a bright future. He would have achieved great things someday. Trevain had been tremendously fond of the kid. He needed to find out exactly what was going on, and who those women from the submarines were. He wanted revenge.

Submarines. Although Doughlas had been in the navy, and he knew about things like this, Trevain was somehow not completely sold on the submarine theory. He only wished he could come up with some other sort of feasible explanation. The image of the white-haired woman came to mind. He saw her holding Arnav up sorrowfully in the water. *"I could not save him."* Although her hair had been the color of snow, he knew that she was not old. It had been dark, but he remembered that her ivory skin had been perfectly smooth. As smooth as cream-colored satin. He vividly remembered her striking steel-blue eyes and the dark limbal ring around her irises. She reminded him vaguely of Aazuria.

Heck, who was he kidding? Aazuria was lovely, but she had nothing on this woman. Maybe it was the mysterious circumstance which was clouding his judgment. Being thrust into a dangerous situation together, having to fight to defend each other—it was a rather thrilling way to meet. Trevain remembered the rush of adrenaline he had felt when he punched the blonde attacker in the face to save the white-haired woman.

Atargatis. That was the name he had heard a third woman call her. He vaguely recalled the name, and had looked it up on his smartphone on the boat as soon as he had been dried off and warmed up. He found that it was the name of a Syrian sea goddess. When he informed his crew of this, Doughlas had shrugged and easily explained it. *"Yeah. No big surprise, Captain. The military likes to use fancy code names like that for their covert ops. People always turn to old mythology for naming new technologies. Even new discoveries or whatever—planets, comets, spaceships, and etcetera. You know."*

Trevain had nodded, for it made sense. The women in the water had just been women; strange women with weapons, but women nonetheless. Despite this, he believed that the white-haired woman was the closest thing to a sea goddess which he had ever beheld. She had been trying to protect him from the woman called Atargatis. She was his aquatic guardian angel. Something about her albino-like coloring had been unquestionably supernatural.

Beyond her appearance, there had been such an ethereal quality about her. And her kiss! Her kiss had been voracious. He had never felt such passion from any touch or caress as he had from that one modest, momentary contact. She was a confident woman, not a timid adolescent girl.

Trevain stared out of his window, lost in thought about the enigmatic lady for several minutes. It was a while before he realized what he was doing. He immediately began to scold himself for fantasizing about this stranger he had briefly seen. She had only kissed him to thank him for saving his life—even though she had still gotten badly hurt. He hoped that she was not in too much pain, wherever she was. If he had the faintest clue where she came from, he would be heading there now to make sure she was being well cared for. The look in her eyes, and the sound of her voice were both so unforgettable.

He wondered if he would ever see her again.

He drew a large X in the fog his breath had created in the window. So what if he did see her again? Would he forsake Aazuria, to whom he had grown so close, along with her sisters whom he considered his own family at this point, for a complete stranger? Was he that fickle? No—his fishing trip had been dreadful and he wished to speak to Aazuria to calm his nerves, and she would not even see him. *She* was the one forsaking *him* in his time of need, just as she had done before when Callder died. No wonder he was wishing to be with another! He knew this was faulty logic, and that his thoughts could not be justified. He immediately reprimanded himself for holding the unknown woman in higher regard than Aazuria.

Maybe I'm not ready for marriage if I'm going to spend all night thinking about the mysterious woman in the water. I don't think it would make a difference if I was married to Zuri... I'd still be mentally cheating on her right now with the silver-haired sea goddess.

Trevain cursed and swung the back of his hand into an expensive lamp sitting on a nearby night table. He watched the lamp smash to the ground, and he swore repeatedly in anger at himself and his own inconstancy. Aazuria was sick; that was why she would not see him. He was being completely insensitive to her condition. He hardly recognized the callous person he was becoming. But wouldn't three deaths do that to anyone?

He turned and walked across the hardwood floor briskly, exiting his bedroom. When he was in the hallway, he saw that Corallyn was still guarding Aazuria's room—he supposed that she would be doing so all night, or until her sister was better. He sighed, admiring the young girl's devotion. "Coral, will you do me a favor? Tell Zuri that I'm sorry; I should have listened to her. I shouldn't have gone back to work so soon."

Corallyn gave him a soldier-like nod. "I will tell her when she wakes up."

"Also... could you please tell her that I love her and I miss her?"

The young girl gazed at him for a few seconds, observing his expression. Finding only sincerity there, she allowed the smallest of smiles to barely touch her lips. It was the first time that the hard expression on her face had broken since she learned that it was her own mother who had tried to kill Aazuria. She nodded.

"She loves you too, Uncle Trevain. So for God's sake, listen to her in the future when it comes to anything regarding the water and fewer people will get hurt... uh, emotionally."

Chapter 28: *Freewheeling Through Space*

Aazuria was restless.

She had been confined to one small room for weeks. Only Elandria and Corallyn had visited her to tend to her wound; they had each taken shifts guarding her to make sure that Trevain did not find out about her impaled shoulder.

Trevain had gotten the hint that something was very wrong a few days after her injury when he saw Elandria leaving Aazuria's room with a pile of blood-soaked clothes and bandages in her arms. When Elandria made eye contact with him and her face froze in fear, he knew that the girls were hiding something. Fearing for Aazuria's health and well-being, he had headed for her room. Elandria had tried to put herself between Trevain and the door, but he would not be stopped.

Reaching around Elandria for the doorknob, he had aggressively turned it. Finding it locked, he had frowned. "Aazuria, open this door!" he had shouted. "I'm coming in! I need to know that you're okay!"

"Please do not do this," Elandria had asked him softly.

He had frowned at the quiet girl. He always paid close attention when she spoke. This was probably the first time he had heard her voice since he had asked her for advice on proposing to Aazuria. This was perhaps the only time that her silent, gracious plea would go ignored.

The pile of bloody clothes in her arms was more convincing than even her heavenly voice. "Aazuria!" he had shouted. He looked at the doorknob, and saw that it was impossible to pick the lock or open it from the outside. Even the hinges of the door were on the inside. He scowled and did the first thing which came to mind. He slammed his shoulder into the door. After doing this several times, he managed to break the door open.

Aazuria lay in bed, with the blanket pulled over her up to her chin. There was a slight blush on her face. "Trevain, what is the matter?" she had asked him softly.

"You tell me!" he said, walking over to her quickly. "Why is

Elandria smuggling bloody clothes out of this room?"

"Well… it is… a female thing," she lied. Her cheeks were
flushed, and she hoped that her visible embarrassment would help to
validate her story. Even though she was wearing a conservative
nightgown that covered the fresh bandages over her injured shoulder,
she was terrified that he would somehow find out.

"Aazuria, you've locked yourself in here for almost two weeks.
I'm worried. What's going on? You have your sisters guarding you like
you've got some deadly virus…"

"I do. I do not want you to get sick as well," she quietly lied. She
wanted to talk to him; she wanted to see how he was handling Arnav's
death. She wanted to hear how he had made sense of what had
happened in the water. She wanted to reach out and touch him. She
could not believe he had broken her door down. "Trevain, please go."

"Tell me the truth, Aazuria; are you physically injured in some
way? Because you're clutching that blanket to you pretty tightly, and
I'm starting to think you may have lost a limb or something."

She laughed, realizing that she was indeed holding the blanket so
tightly that her knuckles were white. The laughter caused her torso to
move, jostling her shoulder and sending fresh pain through her body.
She sucked in a sharp breath, and exhaled slowly, trying to keep from
wincing. "I am fine. Please, just let me be alone for a while."

He saw that her laugher had caused her pain, and he pried the
blanket away from her fingers. He pulled it back, and looked at her
body for any visible injuries.

"See? Two arms and two legs." Her own weakness frustrated her,
and she looked up at him miserably. "You had better go wash your
hands before you get the bubonic plague, smallpox, cholera, or the
Spanish flu."

"She means swine flu," Corallyn corrected, sticking her head into
the door. "Smallpox was cured like fifty years ago, Zuri! Even I know
that."

"I had forgotten," she said tiredly, "but they still have bubonic
plague, right?"

"I think so!" Corallyn chirped.

"Okay, good. It might be that one, then." Aazuria groaned,
turning to lie on her good shoulder. Her movements were
uncomfortable and awkward. She had been running a temperature

which caused her whole body to ache.

Trevain had observed the strange way she moved, and he saw the angular protrusion of her shoulder and hip through her nightgown. "You've lost weight," he accused with concern. She had been slender to begin with. "I need to call a doctor."

"No!" Aazuria protested. "Please. I have a doctor, and she said I would be fine. She also said I should be temporarily quarantined."

"Is there anything at all I can do for you?" he asked, growing more upset by the minute. It bothered him to not know what was wrong. "Can I get you any medication or…"

"I just need to be alone. I do not want you to see me when I am unwell," she said dejectedly. "Forgive me for being reclusive."

"You know… you're denying me the opportunity to take care of you when you're ill. I'd like for that to be my job."

Aazuria sighed, and looked at the ceiling with vacant eyes. "I just need time."

"There has been a lot of death in my life lately, Aazuria. I'm not strong enough to deal with another. You had better not dare…"

"I can assure you that hell is not on my itinerary."

Trevain leaned down and planted a kiss on her cheek. "Come to me when you're feeling better," he told her. "I miss you like mad."

Now, she lay in bed, staring up at the same ceiling she had been looking at for weeks. It had been a while since Trevain had broken down her door, and she wondered if she was feeling better. She had long since memorized every inch of stucco and had come to the conclusion that stucco was not very interesting; neither did it hold the secrets of the universe. She had stared at the dancing shadows around the corners of the curtains until she started to attribute characters and personalities to them. Every corner of the small room had been cemented in her brain.

When the wound had closed up, and Aazuria was positive there was no risk of infection, she had begun to move about the room and do gentle exercises. She had dismissed Corallyn and Elandria from guarding her, and she had begun to take baths on her own. She wore only extremely conservative clothing with turtlenecks and long sleeves in case Trevain ever happened to see her. She kept the curtains open, and stretched and massaged her arm and shoulder while sitting in the starlight. She knew that the bones and muscles needed more time to heal, but she could not help trying to push herself every day until she could do nothing but lie in bed writhing in pain. She frequently swallowed the maximum dose of Mr. Fiskel's prescription painkillers. Even more frequently, she exceeded the maximum dose.

Aazuria knew that if she had been in Adlivun's infirmary her injury would have already been completely healed. The rejuvenating hot springs suffused the body with all kinds of nourishing minerals while the heat improved circulation. She often felt like a complete invalid on land even when she was healthy; she was not used to having so much pressure on her legs and such a lack of buoyancy. Now the feeling of feebleness was increased fiftyfold.

Worse than the frailty was the loneliness. Aazuria could sometimes hear Trevain's footsteps as he passed by her room. Her hearing was not special like her eyesight or lungs, but she could easily discern his heavier stride in comparison to others in the house. She wanted to go to him, but she was afraid that he would somehow find out about her shoulder. She was afraid he would touch her in some casual way, and she would flinch, and he would know. Part of her liked to ask: *So what if he knew? He saved my life that night. He let me kiss him even when he thought I was a stranger. Does he not deserve to know?* Another part of her would always find ways to negatively answer these questions and counter every argument until she was deflated and dissuaded from telling him, or even being around him.

Aazuria now sighed. She could see the bottom half of the crescent moon from where she lay. The winter sky was incredibly clear. Sea-dwellers often named their children after stars and constellations. Orion the hunter shone brightly right outside her window, forever chasing the Pleiades. Was there any more inspiring constellation? It was over, she suddenly decided. She was releasing herself from her own mental penitentiary. She was going to stop hiding, and she was going to stop using her injury as an excuse to seclude herself like a leper or criminal in solitary confinement. Life was short—even shorter here on land, and she would not waste any more days.

She raised herself off the bed, carefully using her good arm to support herself until she was in a seated position. She tossed her legs off the side of the bed, and straightened herself until she was standing, dissolving the ninety-degree angle between her knees and calves. She swayed on her feet for a second. Grasping the furniture, she carefully walked over to the dresser mirror. She pulled her nightgown away from her shoulder and studied it in the dark reflection.

The puncture wound was not that visible. It was also not that bumpy and discernible to the touch. The only damage remained deep underneath the skin, where no one else could notice. No one else could feel it but her. As long as she pretended that the injury was not there at all, no one else would ever know that it had been inflicted.

Trevain would never know. She smiled at herself in the mirror with determination as she pressed on the wound with her thumb, and practiced maintaining the calm smile on her face and showing no outward expression of pain. She was successful. That was it—it was over, and she was healed. The decision had been made, and the documents had been stamped.

She opened her door (the broken door had been fixed shortly after it lost the battle with Trevain's shoulder) and walked soundlessly into the hallway, closing it gently behind her. She tried to tiptoe as lightly as possible down the corridor, blushing and hoping that her sisters would not hear her footsteps.

When she reached Trevain's door, she turned the knob and opened it carefully, slipping in with the liquid stealth of a lynx before closing the door behind her. She stood in the room for a minute, silently listening to the sound of his breathing.

After a minute, he sensed her presence and stirred from his slumber. "Aazuria?" he asked drowsily.

"I am feeling better," she said softly.

"Then what are you doing way over there?" he asked with a yawn.

She slowly walked across his hardwood floor, her bare feet making hardly any noise. She slipped into bed with him, and lay on her back, staring up at his ceiling. It was the same position that she was in before, but there was a world of difference—and not just because of the unfamiliar stucco. She could feel the sweet warmth and energy radiating from his large body beside her. She felt such soothing security in his nearness. It was divine just to listen to his tranquil breathing.

Aazuria knew that he was still half-asleep—she did not want to bother him with conversation or cuddling, although she had been starved for both. All that she allowed herself to do was to reach out and gingerly graze her fingers against his hand. His fingers immediately closed around hers, sending waves of heat throughout her body. She closed her eyes, with a blissful smile on her face. That had been all she needed. She was content now.

But his fingers began gently stroking the palm of her hand. They slowly, methodically travelled from the tips of her fingers to her wrist, drawing rivers and waterfalls across the sensitive skin. This kept her from the sleep that she thought she would find. The more he caressed her palm, the more awake she became; her fingers tingled with the sensation, and soon her whole body was buzzing to life. Her eyes opened, and she stared at the foreign stucco with confusion. Something had changed in the way he was touching her. Or had something changed in the way she experienced his touch?

Trevain turned over onto his side so that he was facing her. He draped his hand gently across her stomach. She held her breath as she felt his fingers lightly brush her abdomen through her nightgown. She did not understand why she was suddenly so sensitive to every small administration to her skin. It was not as though she had never been close to him before. His fingers continued to play along her abdomen until they lightly brushed the undersides of her breasts. Little prickles of electricity danced through her flesh, and it was completely unnerving. Her breathing was shallow, and she was sure he could feel the way he was affecting her in the irregular rhythm of her chest's expansions, or in her quickening heartbeat.

She felt that his lips were on her shoulder, and she closed her eyes. Although it was the shoulder that was injured, the idea of his kiss overpowered the idea of her pain. She swallowed, feeling very affected by his attentions. When she felt his breath and his lips on the side of her neck, she could not resist turning her head to face him. She looked at him with a question in her eyes which he immediately answered by capturing her lips.

Aazuria forgot everything once her lips were joined with his. She found herself turning to face him, even though it meant lying on her injured shoulder. She resisted crying out, allowing the pain to mixed in easily with the pleasure—they were two elements of the recipe to a perfectly spiced dish. Their bodies fused together perfectly. They remained there like that, entwined and kissing for an unhurried, leisurely stretch of time. Aazuria did not understand how a sensation could be so relaxing and yet so exhilarating at the same time. The only thing she knew with a similar aspect was the sea.

Trevain kissed her with the temperament of the ocean itself.

He did not seem to know it, as he pulled her leg over his and caressed the underside of her thigh. He did not seem to know his touch tormented her insides, flinging all the calm places into the tumult of a tempest. He did not seem to notice how his closeness subdued all of her strength, and liquefied everything that was frozen and hard in her self-possession. The warmth and demanding pressure of his lips against hers destroyed her cool composure. She had seen this power in his eyes the very first time she had beheld him, but she had not understood exactly what it meant.

Aazuria suddenly did not know herself. She did not know this frantic, desperate woman who was governed by bodily pleasure. She could feel his male hardness pressing against her, and it thrilled her to imagine that he felt the same way that she did. Could he? Was it possible? This was the most pleasurable thing she had ever felt. She wanted the sensations to continue forever, and she wanted more. She stared into Trevain's jade eyes, which always seemed more compelling in the dark.

"Make love to me," she pleaded. There had never been such a fine line between begging and ordering for Aazuria; she was not sure whether the words leaving her lips embodied a request or a command. She played it over in her mind, and she still could not decide. Luckily, she was far past the point of caring in the least. She felt so possessed that she might even beg if it was necessary.

He was in a state of similar need and urgency, but still just barely able to think clearly. "Have you ever done this before?" he asked her.

"No," she answered. "Have you?"

He laughed a deep throaty laugh. "You always forget that I'm almost fifty years old."

She did not know what this meant, but she assumed it attested to his great experience. She wondered why land-dwellers placed so much significance on age.

"There could be consequences," he told her. "I don't want you to regret..."

"Regret!" she repeated incredulously. She clutched his hand decisively. "I may live one more day. I may live a hundred, or a hundred thousand more days. But I will never once regret being with you tonight."

He returned the pressure of her hand, almost as if silently praying that she meant these words. "Zuri," he said in a suddenly serious tone.

"Many people do these intimate things with each other and then they become strangers. I don't want that to happen between us, okay? I can't... I can't deal with that."

She nodded, surprised at hearing the emotion in his voice. "I will never be a stranger to you." She wondered who had hurt him so deeply in the past to make him so guarded. She hoped she would someday hear all of his stories. She leaned forward, pressing her lips to his again.

Trevain was the first man she had met in six hundred years with whom she truly wanted to be. She did not give her heart or body away as effortlessly as he seemed to think; neither did she intend on trampling his. Her father had left a string of broken hearts behind him wherever he went, and she did not want to do the same. She knew there were repercussions to every action, and if she hurt Trevain he could someday end up being far more dangerous than Atargatis.

"If you knew everything about me," she whispered against his mouth, "you would not think this was such an easy decision."

"I want to know everything about you," he said, pressing his forehead against hers. "I know your past may be hard to face right now, and I'm not asking you to share it... but I do need something from you."

"Me too. I need you," she said softly, crushing her body against his imploringly.

He held her firmly an inch away, and looked down at her with resolve. "On one condition, Aazuria."

"Anything."

"If you want to do this with me—you must agree to marry me. I am not young anymore. My heart is not strong enough to bear losing you. It would kill me. I have already lost too much."

She stroked his grey hair tenderly. She looked into his melancholy green eyes. Her own heart broke to see what sadness he felt underneath the strong, successful man that he seemed to be on the surface.

"My time for playing games is over," he said. "I can't do this unless you give me your word."

Aazuria considered this carefully for a moment. She thought of Adlivun. She felt herself torn down the middle, divided by her love for her kingdom and her love for the man before her. She could not have both at the same time. "I could be called away at any time to attend to my other duties. If that happens I will have to go... I may have to leave for periods of time without notice. Would that be acceptable?"

"Aazuria, small things like obligations and duties shouldn't present any challenge to love. I want to be with you because I have come to care for you, and there is nothing you can do or tell me that will change that." He propped himself up on his elbow as he looked at her fixedly in the darkness. "If you believe you can love me regardless of any job or responsibility you have, regardless of how much of your time is tied up in doing other things, regardless of where in the world your life takes you and how far away from me you might be at the time—regardless of how many attractive young men throw themselves at your feet and beg for you to disown me, regardless of how miserable I get when I am so old I can no longer walk, regardless of whether I lose my boat and fishing license and get my pants sued off for..."

"Shhhh," she said, putting her fingers on his lips and smiling. "That's easy. I do love you like that. Is that really all you require?"

"Everything else can be figured out with a bit of work."

"Then you have my word," she said to him earnestly. "I will be your wife—on one condition."

"Anything," he echoed.

She smiled. "When the time comes, if the time comes—will you be open to a concept which you currently consider impossible? Will you allow a new idea into your mind, and will you trust me?"

"I will. I have learned my lesson about not trusting you," he answered. "I will listen to you, and I won't waver from now on."

"Good," she said. "Then it's settled. Can we get back to what we were doing?"

He smiled and closed the inch of distance between them, which had felt like much too far. Aazuria realized the importance of the words she had just spoken. In a delayed reaction, she felt a dam break inside of her—excitement and happiness flooded through all of her mental channels, and into the furthest reaches of her soul. She had not realized how badly she had wanted to agree to marry Trevain until she had actually agreed.

His joy seemed to overshadow hers as he covered her face in kisses. "I'm the luckiest man on earth," he whispered as he returned his focus to her mouth. She allowed herself to be wholly swept away in the comfort of his arms.

They made love all night. Her shoulder smarted like a red-hot poker was being stabbed into it repeatedly, but she hardly noticed. Her spirit was busy soaring to skyscraper-height elevations while her body was discovering that it *was* possible to feel uninhibited on land. She did not feel like she was on land or sea—she felt like she was flying through the air. She was freewheeling through space.

It was utterly worth the pain.

Chapter 29: Gold Unicorn Trident

She woke up in the morning, and found that she was naked. There was dim dawn light was streaming in through the blinds. She immediately looked down at her shoulder and had a mild attack of panic upon seeing that the wound was so exposed and conspicuous. Then she remembered that her eyesight was far better than his in the dark. She felt around for her nightgown, and quickly slipped it over her head. The movement woke Trevain and he turned to look at her through half-closed eyes.

"Good morning, Princess," he said lazily. When she only looked at him with surprise, he smiled. "You said it was your nickname, wasn't it? I can see why. It suits you."

She could not resist a small laugh at this, and she leaned over to kiss him. "Good morning, Captain," she teased. When he gave her a funny look, she tousled his hair and said, "It also suits you."

He pulled her against him, burying his face in her dark hair. She snuggled against him, thinking how this was probably the best morning of her life. She wanted every subsequent morning to just as sublime. Aazuria was sure that her sisters, the twins, and all of Adlivun would understand her engagement. It was her decision to make. She would not allow it to change anything.

"Oh, I almost forgot," Trevain said, turning away from her and reaching over to his night stand. She watched as the muscles in his chest and arm rippled with the stretching motion. She wondered how he could ever call himself old. It was ridiculous—he had the body of a twenty year old combined with the humility of a man on his deathbed. In her eyes he was beyond perfect. He picked up an object and turned back to her. "This is for you, Aazuria."

She saw that he was holding out a small ring box. She felt a few ounces of anticipation creep into her neck. After giving the orders for all of her precious heirlooms to be sold; hundreds of thousands of dollars' worth of irreplaceable jewels, she felt like she deserved a new treasure. As she took the box from his extended hand, she wondered about what his taste in jewelry was like. She inwardly speculated whether it would be something simple or opulent.

"The style is unusual," he was explaining, "but it was a ring that belonged to my mother. When I visited her in the hospital a few years ago she gave it to me. She told me to give it to the woman I would someday love."

When Aazuria flipped open the lid of the ring box, she had been expecting anything from the daintiest, most unimpressive ring to a gigantic glitzy rock. She had been expecting anything except what was sitting there in the velvet box. Aazuria nearly dropped it in surprise.

On either side of the diamond was a gold trident. Not just any gold trident, but one that Aazuria recognized intimately. Her first thought was that he must have gotten his hands on one of the rings that Visola pawned.

Her head snapped to look at Trevain, and she saw that he was smiling at her. She felt waves of confusion. He had said that the ring belonged to his mother, and she could see that he was being honest. She looked back to the gold patterns.

"Are you sure that *this* was the ring that belonged to your mother?" she asked. There had surely been some sort of mix-up in his jewelry box.

"Yes," he responded. "She wore it for decades—for as long as I knew her. Why do you ask?"

Aazuria stared at him in speechless disbelief. "Ramaris," she finally managed to whisper. "This is the Ramaris seal."

"How do you know that name?" he asked her with amazement. "My mother's maiden name was Ramaris."

"Oh, sweet Sedna below," she muttered. She had lifted a hand to press it against her chest. "Truly, Trevain?"

"Yes," he said curiously. "Why are you looking at me like that?"

Aazuria had risen to her knees and was peering keenly into his face. She had seen his eyes before, but she had never recognized them as *Ramaris* green! She suddenly understood why she had been drawn to him. She reached out to touch his grey hair, looking for a stray strand of color.

"Hey! What are you doing?" he asked with a chuckle. "I don't have lice."

"What color was your hair when you were a boy?" she

demanded.

He grinned. "You know, it's too late to back out of this engagement just because you didn't consider that any potential children of ours might have my glaring old red hair."

"Red!" she shouted, bouncing up to her knees. "Red!"

"Yep. And not just the pale orangey-ginger type. A really vivid hue that looked…"

"Like fire," she breathed. She ran her fingers through the locks lovingly. "I can imagine it so clearly. Why didn't I see it before?"

Trevain squinted, a bit puzzled by her behavior. "What's wrong, Zuri? Don't you like the ring?"

"You have no idea," she said, moving slightly away from him in awe. Pressing her hand against her chest again, she could feel the rapid pounding of her heart. She realized that she was also slightly hyperventilating. "Trevain, it is a magnificent ring. Do you know… do you know what the trident means?" To her, it meant that Trevain must be related to the twins in some way. Whether he was a distant relation or a more direct descendant, Aazuria did not know; but she had a hunch.

"I'm not well-versed on the meaning of symbols in women's jewelry," he admitted with a shrug. "I hope it's something good."

She smiled at his innocence. And of how very much he was innocent! She retrieved the ring and moved to sit beside him. "This particular style of spear is ancient. It is called the unicorn trident—it appears on the Ramaris family crest and coat of arms, and other various emblems…"

"My family has a coat of arms?" Trevain said with a large smile. "That's really neat, I didn't know that."

"The Ramaris family includes some of the bravest warriors who have ever lived," she said slowly, with honesty. She wished she could tell him that her dearest friends were descendants of this lineage. But was he ready to know? Keeping this exciting secret inside made her chest feel like it would burst. "This trident is a symbol of great virtue, power, and victory. There is no insignia I could possibly feel more pride in wearing." As she traced her finger over the intricate tridents—surely the work of Adlivun's goldsmiths—tears came into her eyes.

"Zuri, hey!" he said, putting his arms around her and kissing her temple. "What's wrong?"

"Is it possible for us to visit your mother?" she asked softly.

"Yes," he said with surprise. "I suppose so."

"Please take me to meet her, Trevain," Aazuria said, pulling away from him. She got off the bed, standing up abruptly. "Now." She gazed down at the ring in the velvet box. She had to know who had been its previous owner.

"I am not sure if that is such a good idea," Trevain said, sitting up in the bed. He was puzzled at the thoughtful, disconcerted look on Aazuria's face. "I would love to go and see her, but she is very ill."

Aazuria realized that she should curtail her excitement and refrain from jumping to conclusions. There was no history of mental illness in the Ramaris family, and if his mother was in a psychiatric facility—perhaps she was not a relative. Perhaps she had even stolen the ring, or purchased it herself somewhere. The red hair and green eyes could merely be a coincidence—such traits were common among certain pockets of land-dwellers. She had seen other red-haired and green-eyed individuals in her brief stay on land. But then there was his height—and Callder could breathe underwater! She needed to know.

"Illness or not, she is your mother. You should tell her that you intend to marry me." Aazuria removed the ring from its box and slipped it onto the appropriate finger. She held out her hand and showed it to him. "She should know about this."

Trevain shook his head sadly. "I don't know if she'll even be cognizant enough to understand that."

"Can we please try?" she implored. "I would love to meet her."

He nodded. "I'll set it up. Visiting hours are Tuesday and Thursday afternoons so we'll have to wait until after the weekend." He loved his mother dearly, but it always upset him to see her depressed and deteriorating in the hospital. For Aazuria, he would try to be strong enough to endure it.

Chapter 30: *Visiting Alice Murphy*

"Have you ever considered going blonde?" Trevain asked as he glanced over at her in the passenger seat.

"What? No." Aazuria hastily grabbed a curl to make sure it had not somehow begun to blanch. She breathed a sigh of relief when she saw it was still dark. She wondered if he was thinking about their encounter in the water. "It would look too fake on me; my skin is too dark."

"I think it would look nice," Trevain said, as he turned off the street into the driveway of a building.

"This is the psychiatric hospital?" Aazuria said as she stared up at the rundown old building they were approaching. There were bars on the windows. "It looks so cold."

"It's not my favorite place in the world," Trevain responded sadly. "They don't offer much comfort to the clinically insane."

While Trevain parked his Range Rover, Aazuria found herself looking up at the building curiously. He walked around the car to open the door for her, and she stepped out nervously.

"Do you really believe that your mother is insane?" Aazuria asked.

"She tried to do a few strange things when we were younger," Trevain answered. "They think that she just lost touch with reality. I try not to think about it too much. It hurts so much to be apart from her, even after all this time."

Aazuria slipped her arm around Trevain's as they walked through the door. She unconsciously caressed the engagement ring on her finger. "What did she try to do?" she asked.

"She tried to drown my little brother in the bathtub," Trevain explained. Aazuria paused for a moment, looking at Trevain with horror on her face. "I know," he said, rubbing her arm. "It's ghastly. She had tried to kill herself a while before that, but we weren't sure it was a suicide attempt. Father thought it might have been an accident."

Aazuria took a deep breath and swallowed. "How did she try to kill herself?"

"She had begged my father to bring her aboard one of his fishing trips—it was shortly after Callder was born and she said she was lonely and unhappy. She didn't want to be left at home." Trevain shrugged. "I was a kid back then… maybe six or seven. I don't remember the details, just a sense of panic and fear. Mom had jumped off the deck of the boat into the freezing cold water. We nearly lost her."

"Good Sedna," Aazuria whispered softly as she entered the elevator with Trevain. She found herself moving closer to hug him gently. She buried her face against his chest, afraid of what she was about to learn. Part of her already knew what she would find, but she needed confirmation. It was too unbelievable.

The elevator doors opened, and Trevain guided Aazuria to a nurse's desk. "I'm here to see my mother, Alice Murphy."

"Go right ahead, sir."

Aazuria did not realize how nervous she was until she noticed that her hands were shaking. Before she was conscious that she was moving, she found herself standing before a door with the number 201 on it. Trevain was opening the door for her. She mechanically entered the room, allowing her eyes to fall upon the small elderly creature staring through the barred window, surrounded by bright white walls and white linens. Aazuria exhaled a breath which she had not realized she had been holding since the elevator. She did not know this woman. It seemed that Alice Murphy was just a normal, mentally unstable old lady after all.

There was *no way* that that tiny, shrunken woman huddled on the bed had the blood of the Ramaris line in her. Aazuria knew that she had been silly for thinking it—it had been a hopeful whim. Visola and Sionna's ancestors had lived amongst the Vikings, and the Nordic seas had been their playground. It was loosely possible that Trevain's deceased sailor father had been a Ramaris descendant, and had given the ring to his wife. More likely, it had been purchased in the same way that most of Adlivun's royal fortune was now up for sale in various Alaskan pawn shops.

"Mother, I've come to visit you. It's me, Trevain…"

The woman's head turned to face them, and Aazuria inhaled sharply. Heat spread through her neck, and the hairs on the back of her neck stood upright. She stared in shock for a moment at the aged woman's sunken features. The glass-colored transparent tendrils which framed her oval-shaped face in tired wisps. The high cheekbones, the defiant green eyes.

Aazuria's memory rapidly matched pieces of an ancient puzzle together.

"Alcyone!" she gasped, running forward and flinging herself down upon the woman's breast. She clutched the frail old woman tightly, sobbing.

The old woman stared down at her visitor in wonder. "Aazuria," she whispered. Her voice shook with age and emotion, but was weighted with dignity and eloquence. She picked up strands of Aazuria's hair between her fingers and stared at them in confusion. "It cannot be you. I must be hallucinating; you're just a divine mirage in this sterile desert."

"I am real. I am here." Aazuria could not stop weeping. She hugged the old woman tightly, as though she were embracing her own lost mother. It was several minutes before she could speak. "Alcyone! I never thought I would see you again—and to find you like this! Sweet Sedna, there is nothing wrong with you. How could you allow them to keep you in this place?"

Trevain watched this exchange with amazement as the two women displayed recognition for each other. For a moment he had felt defensive, as if the young and vigorous Aazuria was going to attack his old feeble mother. When instead, they conversed like old friends, and his mother erupted in tears and struggled to put her shaking hands around his fiancée, he began to feel clueless and confused.

"My mother's name is Alice," was his feeble contribution—a half-hearted objection that changed into an admission of ignorance on its way out of his mouth. He could plainly see that Aazuria somehow knew his mother better than he did. He could see it, but he could not understand it. He had been extremely close to his mother for his entire life, and he had never heard mention of Aazuria.

"Princess Aazuria!" breathed Alcyone, crying and touching her long-lost friend to be certain she was real. "Please tell me you have come to rescue me. How have you found me?"

Aazuria smiled through her own tears, forgetting, or choosing not to care that Trevain was in the room. "Accidents and coincidences have led me to you. I recently had to leave Adlivun..."

"Oh, but look at you darling," said Alcyone, raising her trembling arthritic hand to Aazuria's face. "You are just as lovely as ever. You have aged hardly a year or two since I last saw you—and look at me. A haggard useless crone!"

"No! No, your eyes are as piercing as the day I bid you farewell," Aazuria said, touching the woman's wrinkled cheek. "Such bright emerald green... they are exactly like your mother's eyes. Oh, Alcie! Your mother is going to have a coronary. I have to call her right away. Do you know how heartbroken Visola was when she lost you? You were her whole world."

"Oh, heavens," said Alcyone, bringing both of her hands to her cheeks as her eyes brimmed with fresh tears. "My mother is here? I've missed her every single day of this wasted lifetime. I need to see her as soon as possible! Oh, but what will she think of me? I look so ancient and decrepit..."

"She will thank the stars that she was reunited with you—and maybe she will stop being so grouchy all the time," Aazuria said with a smile.

"I have a living grandmother?" Trevain asked in confusion.

Both women swiveled their heads to look at him then. Alcyone was the first to speak. "Forgive my manners! Trevain, my boy, it's good to see you. Come give your mother a hug. How did you come to meet Aazuria? I'm sure it's an interesting story."

He had been moving forward to embrace her, but he paused, not wishing to tell his mother that he had been in a strip club, regardless of the fact that he was a grown man. He had contrived many possible stories, but now that it turned out Aazuria and his mother were old friends, the situation was further complicated.

Aazuria laughed, and held up her hand to show Alcyone the ring. "We are in love. We are engaged to be married."

"*What!*" Alcyone shrieked. An enormous smile instantly transformed her features and she shook her head in disbelief. "Married? *Married!*" she exclaimed with an incredulous look. She began to giggle at the prospect. "My boy is engaged to the princess of Adlivun! Imagine that... but wait. Where will you live? Here on land, or underwater?"

Aazuria and Trevain looked at each other. It was a tense shared look of unease and unfamiliarity. She was concerned about her secrets being revealed. He was concerned about his mother embarrassing him with her crazy talk.

"Sorry, Zuri," he began, "my mother thinks…"

"My goodness," Alcyone suddenly said. "What of your father, Aazuria? How is it that…"

"Shhh, it is all okay," said Aazuria, stroking the old woman's hand. The skin covering Alcyone's bones was paper thin. "We took care of it. He's dead."

"Dead?" she asked, blinking. Then she threw her head back and allowed a burst of laughter to surge forth from her throat. "Dead! Kyrosed Vellamo is dead! Those are the most beautiful words I have heard in decades."

Trevain stiffened. He remembered the name spoken by the angry blonde woman in the water. The people who had killed Callder, Arnav, and probably Leander, had spoken the name of this man who was apparently Aazuria's father. He began to try to assemble his own puzzle within his mind to figure out exactly what was going on. He knew that he must finally admit that one bizarre thing was indisputable; too many people had called Aazuria "princess" and in too formal a manner of address for it to be a childhood nickname.

Perhaps his mother had not lost touch with reality as much as he had been led to believe.

"So of course you will live in Adlivun!" Alcyone said, clasping her hands together and sighing happily. "We will have a traditional sea-dweller wedding, and there shall be thousands in attendance. There will be an aisle of icebergs! You two will reign as King and Queen over a new golden age and give me many adorable grandchildren!"

"Alcie… I do not believe we will be living in Adlivun," Aazuria said softly, as she glanced nervously at Trevain. His arms were crossed, and there was an expression of bafflement and displeasure on his face.

"Why not?" Alcyone asked, her smile instantly disappearing and her disposition diminishing. "You mean—you intend to live here on land? *Here*, Aazuria, in this awful place?" The old woman raised her finger and pointed at both of them angrily. "No—I won't allow that! You can't marry my son. I forbid it."

"Why?" Aazuria asked in surprise.

"Darling, look at me: I'm dying!" Alcyone shouted. A chill ran through Aazuria, for she could see Visola's passion mirrored clearly in the woman when she was angry. "I'm practically a corpse! I am hundreds of years younger than you are, and look at me! It is too much to sacrifice. I will *not* have you forfeit your youth!"

"I am not immortal, Alcie. I will age and die eventually too. It happens to all of us, just at different rates."

"Aazuria—you think you understand, but you do not. The incapacitating pain, the endless agony, the humiliating weakness of old age; it is not worth it! No man—forgive me for being callous, but not even my gallant eldest son is worth surrendering yourself for."

"But I love him," Aazuria said softly, staring into her friend's viridian eyes. "I want to spend my life with Trevain, and this is his world."

"Sedna preserve me! This world is *not* yours," Alcyone said firmly. "It never will be. Take it from someone who has gone down that road: I loved a man, and I bore him children… and look where I ended up! Look what they did to me, and how they repaid me for my sacrifice! If only I could go back in time to that day when I 'escaped' Adlivun, I swear to you—I would just turn around and swim back home to you and my mother."

There was a silence in the room after she said that. Aazuria closed her eyes, imagining the suffering that her friend had experienced. She could not even handle a few weeks cooped up in a comfortable room with her injury; she had no clue how Alcyone had lived through years of stark confinement. At least in Adlivun they had all been confined together—they had been able to move around the palace, and had experienced a sense of basic freedom. Sixty years ago, they had thought they were offering Alcyone a chance at a better life, and instead they had thrust her into an inferior dystopia.

"Aazuria, you are a princess—oops, my apologies—I'm a bit behind on the current affairs," Alcyone said with a bit of a giggle. "You are the *Queen* of an extraordinary, noble race. You cannot forsake your people to live on the land with Trevain."

"I will never forsake them altogether…"

"I love my children, Aazuria, but I never see them. All I see are these white walls, day after day. Most of the time I close my eyes and fantasize about what life was like when I was a child. I yearn for Adlivun more than I ever believed anyone could yearn for any place." She was overwhelmed with nostalgia. "Oh, Aazuria! I miss my old life. I miss my mother. I miss my auntie Sio. I miss you and Elandria. I miss Coral—Coral was my best friend. How is she? Please don't tell me she looks exactly the same as the last time I saw her. What will she want to do with an old woman like me?" Alcyone put her head in her hands.

Aazuria put her arms around the old woman, hugging her gently. "Coral loves you to death, Alcie. You two grew up together; you did everything together! A friendship like yours could never be destroyed by a few wrinkles, silly. Coral will be horribly jealous of the dangerous adventures you have had while she was cooped up in the castle with us."

"Corallyn… is my mother's childhood friend?" Trevain asked, swallowing. "The same little Corallyn that lives in my house?" It did not make any sense to him, and yet it made perfect sense. He thought of all the times he had looked into the young girl's eyes and heard her speak, and had gotten the impression that it was not the soul of a nine-year-old in that tiny body.

Aazuria gave him a small sympathetic smile before turning back to Alcyone. She spoke in an authoritative tone. "We will take you back home at once. Once you are in Adlivun your health will be restored and your lifespan will be extended by dozens, perhaps hundreds of years. Your spirits will be lifted to be amongst those who love you and those whom you love. Visola will set everything right again."

"I would wish nothing more than to go home to my family," the old woman said mournfully, "but they won't let me leave this place. Every step I make is monitored."

"You are really trapped here?" Aazuria asked with a deep frown.

"I wasted forty years of my life rotting and rapidly aging in this hellhole. I'm a 'danger to myself and others' apparently, so I need to be kept under lockdown." Alcyone made air quotes with her wrinkled fingers. "What an enviable existence!"

Aazuria rubbed her temples to soothe her growing anger. "No. No. We smuggled you out of one prison and directly into another!"

"Chin up, sweetie," said Alcyone, reaching for Aazuria's hand. "The few years in between my two incarcerations were quite lovely."

"Were they worth it?"

"No. If I'd been able to see my two sons grow up into strong young men, it all would have been worth it, but…"

"About Callder…" Trevain interrupted carefully.

"Not now," Aazuria said sharply, raising a hand to silence him. She did not feel it was necessary to tell Alcyone of Callder's injury unless he completely succumbed to his wound.

"Aazuria, my children were taken from me! They were turned against me. I think I was fated to understand the pain my mother went through when she lost me."

"She was out of her mind," Aazuria said tenderly. "She never fully recovered."

"It is the Ramaris family curse," Alcyone said sorrowfully, "to lose our children and miss most of their lives." She looked across the room at Trevain. "At least my mother knows I had no other choice but to run."

"Mom…" Trevain began, hurt by her truthful accusation. "I didn't know…"

"You didn't know that I was a fugitive sea-dweller displaced to land?" Alcyone asked sharply. "You didn't know that I could breathe underwater just as Aazuria can? I told you everything, Trevain. My good, smart boy! I told you my memoirs when you were a baby and you thought they were magical fairytales. I read you countless volumes I had collected for my personal library. I told the stories again when you were older, and you believed I was schizophrenic."

He stood in dazed silence as everything came together in his mind. The accent. Aazuria's accent which he had detected when he first met her was the same accent in his mother's voice. *She looks like she's eighteen but talks like she's eighty.* The familiar kiss of the white-haired woman in the water who looked nothing like Aazuria and yet everything like her. *I am a fucking mermaid.* His legs and the swimming pool. *I am one of the fastest swimmers in the world.* Her mysterious disappearance for weeks to an unknown destination, leaving no address and taking no luggage. *I have been on many boats; so many kinds of boats that I cannot remember all of their names.*

He gazed at her as though seeing her for the first time. *It is rooted deep in your bones; the water calls out to you until it causes you physical pain unless you come to it.*

"He did not know, Alcie," Aazuria said softly as she watched the realization dance across Trevain's face.

"Oh, God. You mean he didn't know that you were…" Alcyone was frantic. "I thought that since you were marrying him… Aazuria, my dear! How could you not tell him?"

Aazuria had been looking at Trevain with fear in her eyes. "I thought that he would find me to be crazy. I think I was right," she whispered.

"Mrs. Murphy!" called out a fat nurse who entered the room. "Time for your medication, dearie. Oh, I see you have visitors! Well, they're going to have to leave before you get too excited! We wouldn't want you to get overexcited now, would we?"

"God forbid," Alcyone said sarcastically. "The grotesquely bland white walls of this room are already too much excitement for me to handle. They don't glisten quite like your ice castle, do they Aazuria?"

"She's always been the funny one. I think a double dosage is in order today since she's on about that ice kingdom again. Out, out you two!" said the nurse, ushering Trevain and Aazuria out of the room.

Before Aazuria allowed the heavyset nurse to bowl her over, she exchanged rapid hand signals with Alcyone. A brilliant smile illuminated every crease of the old woman's face, and she responded in sign language, while nodding vigorously.

Aazuria smiled too, and continued signing until the nurse had pushed them out of the room and shut the door between them. Aazuria leaned on the door, thinking about what a strange thing fate was. She thought about all the coincidences that had led to her being here, and she thought of the smile on Visola's face when she would first see her daughter again. It was all she could do to keep from getting teary-eyed again.

"What did you say to her?" Trevain demanded. What he imagined he saw her sign was something along the lines of, *"if she knew... burn this place down... rip it apart."* But he was sure that he had misread their hand signals. He did not think that his kind Aazuria would ever—but then he did not know her very well after all.

The angry sound of his voice snapped her out of her dreamlike state. She straightened, and erased the smile from her face. She thought about the fact that Alcyone was being given medication at that very moment because she missed her home. She thought of how cruel the land had been to her friend.

"I do not wish to speak about it," she answered.

"That's my mother in there—my sick, elderly mother. I have a bad feeling that you're going to..."

"*Sick?*" Aazuria snapped, in the most vicious tone she had ever used with him. Then, realizing how she sounded, she brought a hand to her head and exhaled. "I am sorry. Trevain, let us not talk about this right now. I am upset and I fear I might lose my temper."

"Whatever," he responded indignantly, turning his back on her and heading for the elevator. "You're the princess."

Hearing the hatred in his tone turned her stomach over. She feared that she had lost him with all of her lies. But that was hardly her greatest concern at the moment; she had found Alcyone Ramaris.

Chapter 31: *Terrestrially-Challenged*

Trevain and Aazuria had driven the entire way home from the psychiatric hospital in silence. He occasionally shook his head in disbelief and sighed. She noticed this motion out of the corner of her eye, although she chose to keep her posture erect and regal.

She was angry.

The more she thought about it, the more she felt nauseous. He had kept his mother locked up in a tiny room for his entire life because he thought she was insane. All the books about mermaid lore in his library had belonged to Alcyone—it all made sense now. She had been trying to educate him, and share this essential part of her heritage, but he had been unwilling to listen. If he would not listen to years of his mother's teaching, what made her imagine that he would ever grow to accept her for what she was?

Aazuria gazed at the sea as they drove along the street to his house. Every time her thoughts drifted to the mess between her and the man driving the Range Rover, she quickly steered her focus back to Alcyone. She needed to take action. Looking forward, Aazuria managed to observe Trevain's motions out of the corner of her eye. She observed the way his hands moved rigidly and jerkily on the steering wheel. She observed the way his foot alternatingly slammed down on the two pedals. He was evidently angry too.

She jumped a little when he finally stopped the car and slammed the gear shift forward to put the car into "Park." Aazuria eyed his massive fist, clenched tightly around the head of the shifter. His veins were bulging, and each sinew was taut. Despite the latent aggression apparent in the situation, she could not help thinking about how attractive his hands were. She pushed the thought away and watched him turn the keys and rip them out of the ignition.

He waited until they had entered the house before he said what was on his mind. "You expect me to believe that you are a *fucking mermaid?*" His voice boomed throughout the house.

She crossed her arms over her chest. "I said those precise words months ago and you failed to believe me."

"God, Aazuria. Do you seriously think… An underwater kingdom! *A mermaid!*"

"What is so surprising about this?" she asked impertinently.

"How about the fact that I can't comprehend such things *exist* at all!"

"And whose fault is that?" she asked. "We learned today that even after being presented with literature on the subject for years—carefully educated by a highborn sea-dweller, you still failed to believe or understand. What could I have done?"

"How about telling me the truth about what's been happening in the water! If you had told me exactly why you didn't want me to go to work that day—maybe a man wouldn't have died!"

"Would you have listened? I said everything I could to make you hear me, Trevain! Every time I have mentioned Adlivun you laughed at me. So I followed you to try and keep you safe, and *I* nearly died because of your insubordination!"

"Wow! Well, excuse me, your majesty, for not obeying the commands of your royal highness." He bowed mockingly, infuriating her immensely. "I would have acted differently if I knew you were the fucking queen of mermaids."

"That is *not* the technical term," she informed him in a deprecating tone.

"Do you want a euphemism?" he asked. "Should I call you terrestrially-challenged?"

"This isn't a disability," Aazuria whispered through clenched teeth. "It's a blessing. We are aquatically-gifted. I am a human being! I may come from a different country, but that does not give you the right to be so disrespectful."

"Your people are the reason that three of my men are *dead!*" Trevain shouted.

"Those were not my people! Those were auxiliary enemy forces."

"You expect me to just take that at face value? Not only are you the queen of some imaginary kingdom that no one has ever heard of—but you're at war with some sort of enemy. Forgive me if I'm having some difficulty processing this information; you haven't been very honest with me up until this point."

"Good Sedna, you said you would trust me!" she shouted. "This is... oh, it is impossible! I cannot take this."

"Okay, let's cool down. We've never had a fight before." Trevain moved over to the console table which was kept stocked with fresh flowers. He pressed his hand against the marble surface and stared at the blossoms in order to calm himself. "We need to talk about this."

"You are damned right about that," she retorted, "but sometimes one must act first and talk later." She turned around and left the room rapidly, heading upstairs.

"Do not walk away from me, Aazuria!" he yelled after her.

Corallyn and Elandria were already out in the hallway, having heard the raised voices. "What's going on?" Corallyn whispered. "Why are you fighting?"

"Come with me," Aazuria told them, heading directly to her room. They complied, following until she sat down on the chair before her vanity table. "Elandria, please braid my hair. Corallyn, pack our things. Just the necessities."

Both girls immediately started doing what she had asked. Aazuria stared at her reflection in the mirror as Elandria gathered her long hair together and began expertly braiding it. In the past she would have adorned Aazuria's braid with strings of pearls, or ribbons, but she could intuitively tell that this was meant to be a practical hairstyle, not a decorative one.

"Corallyn, I need to know the number to call Visola. Immediately."

"May I ask what's going on, Zuri? One minute you're happily engaged, then we're packing our bags?"

Aazuria took a deep breath. "Alcyone is his mother."

Elandria paused in the middle of the crossing two ropes of hair. She looked into the mirror to gauge Aazuria's state of mind from her expression, and grew alarmed by what she saw. Corallyn's hands lingered inside an opened drawer.

"He kept her locked up in a psychiatric facility for forty years," she added, trying to control her rage. "I am going to break her out. Tonight."

"Holy shit," said Corallyn blankly. "Little Alcie? My best bud, Alcie? She's Trevain's *mother*? She grew up and had babies and I still don't even have boobs?"

"Pack our things, Corallyn. And please call us a cab."

"Are you leaving, Aazuria?" Trevain asked from the door,

frowning. "Where are you going?"

"Home," she answered, as Elandria continued to braid her hair.

"We cannot go home, Zuri!" Corallyn argued. "It's far too dangerous with Atargatis…" Corallyn realized that she was saying too much and closed her lips tightly.

"Atargatis," Trevain repeated. "She's the woman I punched in the face. Is she… a big problem?"

Corallyn turned to look at him, and decided that if her Aazuria's safety depended on it, she would disobey her sister. If Alcyone was Trevain's mother, then surely he was one of them—he should know the truth about everything. She thought about her own mother and her small hands clenched into fists.

"Atargatis wounded Zuri so badly she couldn't get out of bed for weeks," Corallyn said, almost on the verge of tears. "We can't go home now. Please stop her, Trevain… she's hardly in any condition to *swim*— how can she possibly fight?"

"Then we will go to Visola's motel. Visola will protect me," Aazuria said, standing up. Her hair had been braided, and she was ready to help Alcyone escape. "Corallyn, Elandria, gather your things!"

"A motel, Aazuria? Do you hate me so much?" Trevain asked angrily.

"*I think you need to calm down and talk this out with him,*" Elandria signed. "*The situation with his mother sounds awful, but perhaps it was just a misunderstanding. You know that he would never intentionally…*"

"You did not see her, Elandria! She was so unhappy! She was so alone!" Aazuria glared at Trevain and switched to sign language. "*How is what he did to Alcie any different from what father did to us? I would rather die than leave her like that.*"

"I agree with you, Zuri," Corallyn began, "but…"

"But? *But?*" Aazuria snapped. "Fine. You two can stay here. I have a responsibility to take care of my people—anyone who was born in Adlivun is a citizen of my country, and they may not be held against their will in any other dominion. I have to attend to the well-being of one of my subjects—and even if I were not the leader of Adlivun, I would have a responsibility to do so as a human being."

Aazuria left the room, walking past Trevain without giving him a second look. There was war on her face. "Zuri," he said, following her. "Please stop and tell me what you're going to do. Please don't be reckless. Talk to me; don't just rush off…"

She continued through the corridor and down the stairs, heading for the door. Trevain began to feel frantic as he followed her. He had never seen her this angry. Also, having met Atargatis, he did not like the thought that Aazuria might be in danger. Corallyn had asked him to stop her.

"Aazuria, you can't just leave… you gave me your word that we would be married. Doesn't that mean anything to you?"

She did turn to look at him then. She was upset, but she still loved him and believed that this storm would pass. "We will talk when I return. I have to go." Her voice was soft yet resolute. "I'm sorry."

When her hand turned the doorknob and the door began to open, Trevain began to feel sick with worry and loss. He could not lose her! "Please don't go," he pleaded desperately. When one of her feet had stepped over the threshold, he felt as though barbed wire had been ripped across his insides. He opened his mouth to beg, but instead found himself threatening: "If you leave this house, don't you ever think of coming back!"

Aazuria froze. When she slowly turned her chin toward him, he could see how much his words had hurt her. "You said you would never restrict my freedom," she whispered. She swallowed back the bitter aftertaste in her mouth, knowing that she had made a grave error in judgment. The new life she had begun to build was already in ruins. Her chin rose proudly. "Fine then. Do you think I have no dignity? I will do as you wish. I will never return." She placed her second foot on the other side of the threshold.

He panicked and reached out to grab her arm. It just so happened to be the arm attached to the shoulder which had been pierced with the javelin. She cried out and clutched her shoulder in pain. He realized in an instant what Corallyn had meant about the injury that had kept her in bed for weeks. Was it possible that she really was the white-haired woman in the water? They looked so different. Could she have been wearing a wig of sorts?

She was gathering her composure after the bout of pain, and she glared at him. "I cannot believe you just grabbed me!"

"God, Aazuria! You're badly injured. Get back in this house right now. You are not going anywhere! I can't let you put yourself in danger. Why didn't you tell me about your shoulder?"

"Leave me alone, Trevain." She began to walk away, blinking

away tears of pain that were not from the physical injury. She knew it was not could not allow the emotions from fighting with him to distract her from what was important. She needed to help Alcyone.

"Come back in here right now!" he shouted desperately. "I won't let you risk yourself. Come back or I—I will make you!"

Her eyebrows furrowed as she instantly pivoted. "Then make me," she said with a challenge in her voice. She walked up to him, putting her face very close to his and giving him a defiant stare. The barrier of the doorway was directly between them, and Aazuria seemed to be giving him a chance to carry out his threat. Before he realized what was happening, she had deftly taken his car keys from his pocket and had punched him in the face with her good arm.

Trevain found himself thrown roughly to the ground, back into his house. He lifted a hand to his smarting jaw, pressing his tongue against his teeth to check if they were loose. Seeing blood on his hand, he looked up at his fiancée in shock. Standing just outside the doorway, Aazuria gazed down at him with condescension.

"How dare you try and control me this way?" Her voice was laced with venom. "You said that if I came to stay with you I would be able to go where I wished. But now you seek to keep me confined, just like you kept Alcyone in that small white room—and you call *me* dishonest! Who is the liar among us, Trevain? You knew that all I needed was freedom—you promised me safety and said you loved me. That was all a lie. You are *just* like my father!" With that she left and slammed the door behind her.

"Aazuria," he said weakly, looking at the closed door. He felt like he had been robbed of air, and struggled to breathe. He felt like all of the blood had been instantly drained from his body, leaving him empty of warmth and life. "I was just a boy," he whispered. "I was twelve years old when she was taken. The doctors said she was… I didn't know. I just didn't know." He tried to lift himself off the ground, but he was too weak to stand. Falling back to the cold marble floor of his foyer, Trevain put his head in his hands. "I still don't know."

The last thing he had ever wanted to do was remind her of her father. He felt a soft, warm touch, and he realized that Elandria was kneeling beside him and embracing him. He leaned against her chest and cried. Clumsily putting his arms around her small body, he clung to her for sanity. Trevain was windswept and overturned, but Elandria was a solid anchor in the tempest. He cried for the lost years with his mother, and he cried for the fact that he was sure he would never see Aazuria again. He did not know why he had threatened her so rashly with inane ultimatums.

Chapter 32: My Little Girl

"Will she remember me?" Alcyone asked.

"If you have to ask that, then you have forgotten her," Aazuria said gently. The princess was dressed in plain hospital scrubs, while Alcyone wore several layers of sweaters to protect her against the cold night air. Aazuria protectively held an arm around Alcyone's frail body as she helped her to the door of Visola's motel room. "Are you ready to do this?"

The elderly woman nodded, unable to speak. She tightly gripped Aazuria's hand, betraying her apprehension. Giving her a reassuring smile, Aazuria reached forward to rap her knuckles against the door. She winced, discovering that her hand was still quite sore from its earlier encounter with Trevain's face.

A shuffling was heard in the motel room before a light switched on. They could hear someone approaching to answer the knock, and Alcyone's grip tightened.

"What's the password?" asked a sleepy but playful voice from behind the door. Aazuria and Alcyone shared a confused glance.

"It is me, Visola," Aazuria said. "Please open the door."

"I'm not letting you in unless you tell me the password."

Speechless in dismay for a moment, Aazuria tried to think of a word or phrase that Visola might favor. She stuttered as she answered, "Uh... octopus testicles?"

The woman on the other side of the door erupted in giggles as she undid the lock and bolt. "I knew I could get you to say something ridiculous, Zuri." Visola grinned as she flung the door wide open. "Why aren't you with your captain at such a late... oh, hello." Seeing that there were two visitors, Visola smiled in surprise. "Zuri, who's your frie..." Her voice descended to an open-mouthed hush.

Visola's face displayed recognition, and she took several steps backwards. There were suitcases littered all over the room, doubtlessly filled with weapons and cash. The warrior stumbled over them, barely regaining her balance. She gawked at the old woman with a mystified expression—she looked as though she was seeing an illusion from deep in a hallucinogenic trance. Her limbs felt paralyzed, her breaths became shallow.

"Viso, you had better sit down," Aazuria recommended. Visola nodded, but she had not heard or processed her friend's words. She was too frozen to follow the simple command. Aazuria brought Alcyone into the room, and closed the door behind her.

"Do you recognize me, mama?" Alcyone asked with a quavering voice. Tears began to slip down her wrinkled cheeks as she watched Visola.

"Sedna save me," Visola whispered, trying to control her emotions. She stared into the visitor's eyes, which were the only unchanged and identifiable part of her appearance. "Little jade jewels. Alcie, baby... is that really you?"

"Yes, mama," Alcyone said, her shoulders and her voice trembling with her sobs.

Visola crossed the room in an instant, wrapping her daughter up in her arms. She pressed her face against Alcyone's cheek, instantly overcome with weeping. She crushed her daughter against her desperately, as though she would never let go of her again. "Alcie. Alcie," she moaned. She had spent countless years hoping that she would see her daughter again. She could scarcely believe that the day had come, and that her fondest dream was being realized—long after she had given up hope.

"I forgot how gorgeous you are, Mama," Alcyone said, although she was crying so hard she could barely breathe. She clung to Visola with every ounce of her might as she wept. "Your hair is still such vivid scarlet! All the beauty faded from mine long ago."

Visola could feel that her daughter was distraught and feeble. She tried to find her own strength. The emotions erupting inside her were overwhelming, and she felt like she was about to collapse—but no; she was a mother again. She had to be strong. She had spent her entire life being strong, and she was not going to fall apart now. She gently guided Alcyone over to the bed to sit down, before taking a seat beside her. She placed her hands on her daughter's face and looked at her for a moment. She kissed Alcyone's cheeks and forehead before embracing her again and shutting her eyelids tightly closed.

Aazuria could not keep her own lashes dry as she watched the

DROWNING MERMAIDS

poignant reunion. She had single-handedly and easily managed to free Alcyone from the psychiatric facility. She had considered telling Visola beforehand to enlist her help, but she knew that the warrior would go into the place with guns blazing, eager to rip the hospital apart. She imagined that Visola would zealously kill every nurse, doctor, and innocent janitor in order to retrieve her daughter, and would make sure all that remained of the place was a pile of ash. To avoid this unnecessary carnage, Aazuria had stolen a nurse's uniform and security badge. She figured that her method would be more discreet and efficient, even if it was not as dramatic.

"How did you find my little girl?" Visola sobbed, looking at Aazuria over her daughter's shoulder. She had spent several minutes squeezing the life out of Alcyone before she remembered that her friend was in the room.

Aazuria swallowed before answering. "Trevain took me to see her. He gave me an engagement ring with the Ramaris seal and… it turns out Alcyone is his mother."

"*What!*" Visola cried. She let go of Alcyone and recoiled, studying the woman's face. She threw her hands up in the air, flabbergasted. "Are you serious?"

"It's true, Mama," Alcyone said with a small smile. "Trevain is my son."

Visola looked at them both for a minute before she began to laugh. She doubled over in hysterical laughter until she fell off the bed onto the ground.

"It is not quite so funny, Viso," Aazuria said, but she knew that it was.

"Zuri!" Visola said, clutching her stomach as she giggled uncontrollably. "I get it now! You fell in love with that charming bloke because you saw so much of *me* in him!"

"That's right, Viso," Aazuria said with a sigh, opening her palms in a gesture of surrender. "This whole situation is a merely a testament to my clandestine lesbian desires for you."

Visola laughed even harder at that. "I should have known it! He's so strong, brave, and handsome. I should have seen it right off the bat!" She slapped her hand gleefully on one of the suitcases on the floor.

"Are you okay, Mama?" Alcyone asked with concern.

"No!" shrieked Visola, crossing her legs as she sat on the floor. "I just learned that the dude I've been insulting for months is my own grandson! Good Sedna! I called him so many nasty names…"

"Did my mother just say 'dude?'" Alcyone asked, cringing visibly.

"She tries to be cool," Aazuria explained. "Do you remember her fondness for slang? Sadly, that has not changed. Every time we go to land, she immediately finds the sleaziest, seediest hangout for thugs and felons with multiple convictions so she can pick up their lewd language and use it to torture us for a time period resembling eternity."

"But murderers, rapists, and conmen have the most fascinating vocabularies," Visola protested defensively.

Aazuria made a face. "She also likes to invest herself in neologisms so that she can later say that she was saying a word long before the word was officially a word, and long after it was never a word."

"That's right, and Aazuria likes to speak like a dictionary from the 1800s," Visola said glowering at her friend. "Hasn't changed it up since she *learned* English! It's her supremely royal way to never use contractions because she's so fancy and proper. If only everyone could fit a huge stick up their ass like you, Zuri, the world would be a better place. I've tried, but my bottom is too full of hot air."

Alcyone laughed, clapping her hands. "You two are delightful. How I've missed you bickering and insulting everyone, mama!"

"How I've missed you, baby! You're the only person who has ever appreciated my sense of humor."

"Sedna, I can't believe you're still calling me 'baby' when I look like a wizened old hag," Alcyone said, with a bittersweet smile.

"Oh, sweetie, you're the most beautiful thing I've ever laid eyes on," Visola said earnestly. "We have so much catching up to do—you have to tell me everything that I missed. I can't believe Aazuria is going to marry my grandson!"

"I—I do not think I will," Aazuria said emotionlessly. "We have separated."

"Separated? No, I won't allow it. You said you loved him and thus you must marry him. I can think of a million reasons why you should. One, he's my grandson; two, he totally saved your life, I mean, how heroic is that? Three, he's so tall and dreamy…"

"It is over, Visola." Aazuria held up the keychain. "Look, I even stole his car."

"Do you even know how to drive, Zuri?" Visola raised both red eyebrows.

"I figured it out on the spot. It was not that difficult. How do I give the car back without seeing him?"

"Just give me the keys. I'll take care of it."

"Thanks, Viso," Aazuria said despondently. She tossed the metal ring across the room, and Visola's hand swept the jangling pieces of metal from the air. A sad smile settled on Aazuria's face as she walked over to the second motel bed and collapsed on it. "So this is what a broken heart and punctured shoulder feels like. Rough."

"You two will get back together, dear," Alcyone said. "My son is completely smitten with you—of this I'm sure."

"He *was* until he learned who I really am. Then ordering me around and I snapped and hit him in the face. When did I become a vindictive man-abuser? This is surely your influence on me, Visola. I am so ashamed; he probably hates me."

"If you hit him then he deserved it," Visola said. "Grandson or no grandson, I've always warned you to be careful of men. This is the way they work. They get into your heart—they say or do anything to make you fall in love with them, and then once they're confident that they have you, they start to treat you like shit. At least you didn't sleep with him."

Aazuria did not respond.

"Zuri! Did you…"

"Please. We will speak about this another time. Let us focus on Alcyone's needs right now."

"That's right! My little girl. Is there anything I can get you? Soup or hamburgers or…"

"There is only one thing I need," Alcyone said quietly. "Mama, can you please take me back to Adlivun? I'm sick and tired of being on land! I feel so old and miserable. I want to go home."

Visola raised herself to her knees and touched her daughter's cheek. She examined the familiar face, and studied the woeful emerald eyes peering out from under the wrinkled skin. It was like looking into a mirror which showed the future and the past all at once. Visola felt something inside her ache.

"Whatever you want, baby. If we leave now you could be sleeping in the ice palace tonight."

Alcyone breathed a sigh of relief. "Do you know that they tried to tell me Adlivun wasn't real? I almost believed them."

"I'll prove them wrong," Visola said angrily. "When you're returned under the waves; when you're safely tucked behind ice and stone—then you'll know what's fu... er, *fully* real."

"Thank you, mama. I knew all would be well once I saw you again."

Visola smiled at her sadly. "Your little boy is in Adlivun, but he's not doing too well. He could probably use a mother's touch right about now."

"Callder?" Alcyone asked with surprise. "Callder's in Adlivun?"

"Yeah. He's hurt real bad. He might not make it."

"Oh, goodness. Please, let's not waste any time."

"Don't worry, Alcie," Visola said, as droplets of determination clouded her vision. "I have an amazing feeling. Now that I have you back, nothing can go wrong *ever* again."

Chapter 33: Love is Worthless

Since they had arrived in Adlivun, Alcyone had mainly stayed in the infirmary tending to Callder and helping Sionna out with the other wounded. Alcyone was happier and more alive than she had been in decades, even with the threat of impending war. The numbers of the injured had been growing until Sionna had enforced a strict curfew. No one was to venture outside of Adlivun until the threat had been cleared—excepting extenuating circumstances and only if approved by Aazuria herself or one of the twins.

Visola had concentrated all of her efforts on training and preparing Adlivun's army for the worst case scenario. She even enlisted a civilian militia to inflate the numbers of the regular defense force in case they were needed. The volcanic caves of Adlivun extended in miles of labyrinths snaking through the bowels of the Aleutian Islands. It was a natural fortress where an endless supply of food was available to citizens. There were many safe refuges where the elderly, the pregnant, and the ill could stay to avoid any menace that might come. Visola organized everything to the best of her ability, but her worst fear was that her husband, Vachlan, was allied with the enemy troops. He knew Adlivun intimately, and he knew her and her battle strategies just as well. He had fought against her before, but never on her home turf.

Aazuria felt that her shoulder was showing great progress in healing after just a few nights in the hot springs. She would have felt physically rather rejuvenated by her home environment, as she always did after a brief sojourn on land, but the recent fight with Trevain still plagued her. She kept going over and over everything they had said to each other in her mind. She had not yet removed the ring he had given her. She could not accept that it was over.

Aazuria had been in Adlivun for a week when a messenger had showed up to inform them that Atargatis had accepted their terms. Corallyn's vengeful mother intended to visit them peacefully to see Kyrosed's body as proof of his death. If he had truly been killed,

Atargatis said she would consider withdrawing from the area.

This was positive news, but Visola considered it suspicious. She told Aazuria to leave Adlivun and stay at Trevain's house while Atargatis visited, just in case anything went wrong. Aazuria refused. At the persistent urging of Visola and Alcyone, however, she relented to the idea of paying Trevain a visit. Her sisters were still with him as well, and she used this as an excuse. If she was going to go up against Atargatis, she should kiss and hug her sisters goodbye in case anything happened. Visola said she would come along, for she had business to attend to on land.

Now, Aazuria stood outside Trevain's door, her hair darkened with the sunlight. She stared at the door with great anxiety. She was more fearful of ringing his doorbell than she was of facing the woman who had thrown a javelin through her shoulder. Yet she knew she would do both, regardless of fear. She pressed the doorbell.

She expected Mr. Fiskel or one of the girls, but instead Trevain himself answered the door, almost instantly. Aazuria felt low. She was not accustomed to the feeling. It always seemed that the higher her elevation rose with respect to sea level, the lower her self-esteem sunk. Her pride hurt to return to a place where she had been told she was no longer welcome.

Perhaps Trevain was worth deserting her pride. She had forgotten how kind his eyes were. Now that she knew his lineage, she could see that he did resemble Visola and Alcyone—she imagined that the ladies must have flocked to him in masses when he had been a young redhead. They both looked at each other for a moment wordlessly. She wondered what he could be thinking. He broke the silence by moving forward and putting his arms around her.

"Aazuria, I was so worried. I'm so sorry for all those things I said, I didn't mean a single word..."

She closed her eyes against his cotton shirt as she listened to his heartbeat against her ear. "I am sorry that I hit you and stole your car."

"That's some swing you've got there," he said with a faint smile. "I wouldn't have grabbed your arm if I knew you were hurt—but I shouldn't have grabbed you at all. I'm so sorry..."

"It is in the past," she said, pulling away from his hug. "May I see my sisters?"

"They're not here," he told her.

"Where are they?" she asked with a worried frown.

"I was under the impression that they had gone to see you."

"What?" she exclaimed, her composure disappearing for the first time since he had answered the door. "No! They cannot come to Adlivun. They are safer here with you. Why did they leave? I need to go…" She turned around, looking out at the water.

"Aazuria, will you come in and sit down for a moment? You look like you're about to run off again. Please…"

"I hope my sisters did not go home," she said anxiously to herself. Then she realized she had been invited in to the house. She saw the desperate look on his face and she swallowed. "Yes, I will sit for a minute."

He took her by the hand and led her over to the nearest sofa. "Zuri, I know I can't unsay all the things I said… but will you give me a chance to fix things between us? I just want to get back to where we were before."

"When you did not know who I was?" she asked bitterly.

"I still don't know who you are," he admitted, "but I still love you."

She hesitated. "You really want things to be like they were before?" she asked. "You still… want to marry me?"

"Of course," he said, taking a deep breath. "Elan and Coral have been telling me a little bit about Adlivun. I am trying to believe such a place exists, but it seems so outrageous. It feels like someone is playing a huge joke on me."

Her eyes narrowed. "So many people would not lie about the existence of a country," she told him.

"Yes, but… they all say it's underwater. I have a hard time imagining that." He cleared his throat. "Were you really the woman I saw in the water the night that Arnav Hylas died?"

She nodded. "When you would not listen to me and stay home from work, I took two of my best warriors… incidentally, your grandmother and her sister, and we followed your boat to try and keep you safe. There were only three of us against thirty of the enemy, or else we would have been able to save Arnav…"

"I should have listened to you," he said softly. He looked at Aazuria and frowned. "I just don't understand—how can you be the woman from the water? You look so different…"

"You did not recognize my kiss?" she said with a small smile.

"My name does not come from the ocean—it comes from the color of my eyes. They resemble the mineral azurite when I have been in the water for a while."

"The water changes them?" he asked. "And your hair?"

"No," she responded, knitting her brows. "Did my sisters not explain this? It is basically tanning; advanced tanning and blanching based on exposure to the sun. Not all sea-dwellers have this trait. Your grandmother always maintains her red hair, even in the deep sea."

"I see." His expression was thoughtful yet bewildered.

"I suppose it used to be an important adaptation, for the sake of our health. Having fair skin would have been necessary for deep water life, facilitating vitamin D absorption."

"I can't wrap my head around it," he said honestly. "Those weeks that you said you were ill—that was because…"

Aazuria reached up and grasped the fabric of her dress at her neckline, pulling it off her shoulder to expose her scar.

"God, Aazuria!" he said, moving forward. "Why did you hide this from me? I could have taken care of you."

She watched his reaction, and she could almost see him remembering what had happened in the water. He gently rubbed his thumb over her bare shoulder. Leaning forward, he pulled her close and embraced her again, kissing her forehead. "Thank you for trying to protect my crew."

"Thank you for saving my life. If that spear had landed a few inches to the left we would have been unable to argue at all."

"We would have been unable to do a lot of things," he said with a smile as he gently rubbed her back.

She relaxed into his embrace. "The truth is that I was afraid you would not understand. Land-dwellers never understand. Trevain, I want you to know that your mother is happy now…"

"What do you mean?" he asked, pulling away from her suddenly.

"You do not know? You were not informed?" she asked.

"Informed of what, Aazuria? What did you do?" he asked frantically.

She looked into his face, and saw that he was about to grow angry with her again. She exhaled slowly, looking at her hands. She knew that the best thing she could possibly do was to get up and leave *now* before this escalated any further, but she somehow could not pull herself away. He deserved to know. "I took Alcyone from the mental hospital weeks ago. I took her home to Adlivun."

Trevain closed his eyes and shook his head. "You *kidnapped* my mother?"

"Kidnapped? Trevain! You saw how unhappy she was. It was her choice to leave! She is an adult and she has rights." Aazuria waited for his response, silently praying that he would understand this. She hoped that he would remember how passionately his mother hated the land and yearned for home.

"You took her out of the country. Without telling me." He ran a hair through his grey hair in frustration. "How could you do this, Aazuria? Now I'll never see her again. Now I have no clue where the *hell* she is, and whether she's dead or alive!"

"Dead or alive?" she said slowly. "Good Sedna. You honestly think I would hurt your mother?"

"No, but..." He tried to regain his composure. "How do I know anything? You killed your own father, didn't you? As far as I know, you're capable of anything. You concealed so much from me—how do I know what is true and what isn't?"

Her pride was crushed by his words. "You do not." She tried to calm her racing pulse; her insides ached knowing what little faith he had in her. She was hovering on the fence between despair and wrath.

Trevain was glaring at her. "I can't believe you took my mother from me!"

These words tipped her firmly off the fence and she landed on the side where she was welcomed by a rush of pure rage which brought her to her feet. "You did not even notice she was gone! You had not visited her in years! Some compassion you land-dwellers have for your elderly! She's with her real family now."

"Her real family?" Trevain asked, slowly. "Her *real* family?!"

"Yes—she is with those who will never leave her to be alone and scared in a despicable little room! She is with those who love her, and have faith in all that she says and does, regardless of how *insane* it seems."

"Is that all?" he asked, getting up from the sofa and raising himself to his full height. He looked down at her angrily. "Are you finished insulting me?"

She saw the pain on his face, and imagined that he might feel the same way she did. "Trevain..."

"Why the hell did you come back here, Aazuria?" he asked her violently. "You said you would never come back."

She nodded. "Yes. I apologize. I will go." She looked down at his shoes, struggling to fight back her tears. "I just need to tell you one last thing."

"What is it?" he asked, swallowing the saliva in his mouth. He did not really want her to leave, and he had no idea why he was being so cruel to her. He supposed that it was partly because his pride was hurt, and partly because he believed she was going to leave anyway, and he might as well pretend that it had been his decision.

"Do you remember when my cousin came with an urgent message and I had to go away for a few days?"

He nodded.

Aazuria took a deep breath. She expected the worst. She expected him to lash out at her. "When I got home, I saw that Callder was in the infirmary. He is alive, but barely alive. He is unconscious and being taken care of to the best of our ability—your mother is helping to tend to him now. He was stabbed in the chest with a harpoon, much like they tried to do to me..."

Trevain stared at her uncomprehendingly for a moment. There was a long silence, and she dreaded what would happen when it ended. Finally, he spoke quietly. "My brother is alive? Callder is alive and you *didn't tell me?*"

"I did not tell you because he may not live. He may no longer be alive now, for all I know. He is hanging on by a thread."

"I don't care, Aazuria! You know how much I suffered! You know how much I loved my brother!" Trevain was at the point of tears, and his voice was rising higher and higher in volume. "Anything you could have told me, any hope you could have given me, would have made a world of difference! How could you keep this from me?"

Her mouth was set in a grim line. "We considered moving him to a hospital on land, but the move surely would have killed him. He is being cared for in a special hot spring cave under the Aleutian Islands."

He placed a hand on his head as he began to pace in small circles around the area he was standing. "God! What kind of person lets a man think his brother is dead? What kind of *monster* would pretend to be innocent when she has information which she knows will change his life for the better? I was dying inside every day, Aazuria! It was my little brother. I loved him more than anything—and you knew... all this time, you *knew!*"

"I thought it would hurt you more if you had to lose him twice," she whispered. "I wished I could tell you, but our head doctor recommended that I should not."

"Your *head doctor?* Let me guess, some charlatan that calls himself a shaman or something? Dammit, Aazuria. Where the fuck are you keeping Callder and my mother? This 'Adlivun' is not on any map or Atlas! For all I know it's some cult of crazy people..."

"How can you say such things?" she asked. "You promised me—that night I agreed to marry you. You promised that when the time came you would be open to a new concept which you currently consider impossible. If you want to see your family, why do you not come to Adlivun and verify its existence for yourself?"

"Because I'm an adult, and I don't entertain children's fantasies. You need to get Callder to *a real hospital* as soon as possible!" he yelled. "I will never forgive you for keeping this from me. You may be considered royalty in whatever Hicksville you're from, but here, you're just a person. You're not above the law! You are just a woman; just a *stripper* I thought I would show some kindness to, and you've ruined my life!"

She took a step back, wounded by his harsh words. "I never meant to cause you harm…"

"You've taken away everything from me," he told her. "Before I met you, I had a good job where I was respected. Now I can't work because my whole crew is afraid of dying. You called yourself a human being—but this, whatever you're involved with—you people are murderers and inhuman beasts!"

She nodded, trying to release all the pain and negative tension in her head. "I should not be surprised." Her tone was nasty and abrasive. "A man who could forsake his mother should be easily able to forsake the woman he supposedly wished to marry."

"Watch the way you speak to me, Aazuria!"

"Are you going to threaten me again? Go on. How do you want to hurt or control me this time? Inflict physical harm on me— and then tell me how *I* am the inhuman beast!"

"You're the one who punched me in the face! I didn't know your arm was hurt or I wouldn't have been so rough. Corallyn told me to stop you from leaving because you might be in danger. So yes, I would hurt you again if it meant saving you from the dangers of whatever stupid underwater thing you have going on."

Aazuria stared at him in wonder and disgust. "How can a man who is so intelligent in so many ways completely refuse to listen to reason?"

"What is reasonable about a submarine society of people who can breathe underwater?"

"Everything." She clenched her fists. "You have seen enough proof, Trevain! The evidence is in your own body! How can you be so daft?"

"I know you can hold your breath for a really long time. I know you are a really strong swimmer. I know you have convinced a whole lot of people in some commune that they have some kind of special abilities and ancestry—some kind of complex delusion..."

"You are being *such* an American." Grinding her teeth together, Aazuria turned and began to walk out of the house. "I will not stand here and be slighted."

"We're not finished speaking," Trevain informed her angrily. "I *am* American—and you are from your own special country, right? I bet you have your own flag and everything?"

"It is malachite green with a golden triple moon symbol in the center," she responded curtly. "But I will not suffer the shame of justifying our existence to you any longer. I concede defeat to your pigheadedness." She dipped her body in the most sarcastic curtsy she had ever performed; it said farewell for her, and she resumed her retreat.

"Aazuria, stop. Please don't go. I don't want to fight with you like this." He had moved to intercept her departure. He reached out hesitantly and placed his hands on her waist. "Just come home and stay with me—we were so happy for a moment and I would give anything to get back to that place and make it last."

She closed her eyes, melting at his touch and gentle tone. She was eager to agree, throw her arms around him, and ask for forgiveness...

"Let's forget all of this mermaid nonsense," Trevain was saying. "Let's not talk about all of this sea-kingdom crap and just..."

She stepped back, ripping her body out of his hands. The look on her face was simultaneously horrified and indignant. The redness of fury began to creep into her cheeks. "I do not understand why you will not believe me. I am not asking you to believe in some kind of intangible god. I am asking you to witness and accept that a nation of several thousand citizens exists. It is there. We have been established for longer than your own country! Men, women, children, and even their aquatic pets! Doctors, lawyers, masons, poets, singers, dancers, architects! All you have to do is see it for yourself. Instead you choose to stick your head stubbornly in the sand and remain oblivious!"

"Are there humans who can breathe sand too?" he asked harshly.

"Good Sedna. Your mother was not mentally ill, Trevain—but you are! You are willfully ignorant and utterly *mad!* We could have been together, but you refuse to…"

"Let you enlighten me with your watery wisdom? I've had enough of this bullshit, Aazuria."

She closed her eyes briefly. "I am not sure why I wasted so much time here today," she said softly. When she opened her eyes, they brimmed with tears. She quickly turned away to hide her emotion, moving away from him as she delivered one last barb. "You can fuck a woman, but you cannot listen to her!"

Trevain felt a tremor of rage run through him, and before he knew what he was doing, he had vehemently lifted his hand. He reached out forcefully to grab her. Later, he would think back and wonder if he would have had the resolve to stop himself from whatever he was about to do. He would never truly know—had he intended to physically force her to stay? How far would he have gone? He had not been in complete possession of all his faculties. This moment would haunt him for the rest of his life, and would be the first thing which came to mind every time he questioned whether or not he was a good person.

The sound of breaking glass was heard.

Trevain heard the whizzing of a bullet and he felt the impact of the projectile ripping through his body at the exact same time. Through skin, muscle, nerve, and ligament. He froze, and stared at his arm in shock.

His hand was inches away from seizing Aazuria by the neck.

The bullet had pierced precisely between the bones in his forearm, perhaps just grazing the insides of his ulna and radius. Trevain had a moment to appreciate the marksmanship before he was overwhelmed by pain.

Aazuria's world spun. She had turned sharply at the sound, feeling the distortion in the air. She was taken aback too—not due to the bullet that had gone through Trevain's arm, but due to the fact that he had actually been intending to manhandle her. She looked at him in confusion and disbelief. She did not think that he was capable of such cruelty. She had difficulty accepting that the kindhearted man with whom she had trusted her sisters would ever intend to harm her— especially over a few harsh words! But now that she knew he had Ramaris blood in his body, it was easy to understand the darker parts of his character. Also, the vicious Vachlan *was* his grandfather—it seemed he had inherited great rage and did not possess the experience to know how to drive it safely.

Maybe he had *not* been intending to grab her vehemently. She tried to convince herself of this. Maybe he had only meant to lay his hand lightly on her shoulder—he had probably had forgotten about her injury. It could all just be a misunderstanding. But she knew in her heart that her defender would not have taken such action unless she had deemed Aazuria to be in severe danger.

Seeing the blood dripping from his arm, all her thoughts immediately focused upon concern for him. She knew that the bullet had probably hit a vein, and he required medical attention to stop the bleeding. Her first instinct was to try to help heal him, and she found herself about to move forward. Instead, she reminded herself that he had been reaching for her neck and tried to make herself step backwards. The conflicting thoughts resulted in her brain sending her body mixed signals which caused her to sway slightly on her feet.

She straightened her posture, and steadied herself. She looked at Trevain numbly. "Did you wish to harm me?"

Trevain blinked, pressing down on the wound and looking to the window which the bullet had entered. There was only water in the distance—there was not even a boat visible on the water. "What the hell just happened?" It took him a moment, but upon noticing the hole in the glass, he immediately moved so that the wall was between him and the distant sniper. "Who are you people?" he cursed in pain. "I should have known that you were psychotic when Elandria first told me about your father."

Fresh crimson blood continued dripping from his arm. She wanted to ask him again if he had intended to harm her, knowing that in future memory the situation would be distorted. It was not important anymore. Aazuria found herself withdrawing a small dagger from her thigh and cutting strips of fabric from the hem of her dress. She approached Trevain, disregarding his anger. "Here, let me bandage that up for you," she said softly, touching his arm.

"Get away from me," he whispered brokenly. He could not seem to control his vicious tongue. All he really wanted to do was hold her close and apologize. He just wanted to forget the fighting, forget the bullet, and taste her lips. He wanted to carry her to the couch and make love to her until they forgot all the pain and emotional distance that had been wedged between them.

Aazuria's hands shook as she tried to bandage his arm. "I am not very good at this, but it should help to slow the bleeding. You must go to a hospital."

"You should just kill me now and get it over with, Aazuria. First Leander, Callder, Arnav. Now my mother. Everyone has been taken from me. I can see that you are going to leave me too; I will have nothing left. So go on, and make it fast. Break my heart and get it over with."

She knew that this was the moment that he needed her most. But she was not strong enough to cast aside her dignity and nationalism. She stepped away from him and nodded. "I agreed to marry you on one condition: I asked that you trust me—I asked that you allow a new idea into your mind." With great mental effort, Aazuria reached down and removed the Ramaris ring from her finger. She placed it on the coffee table along with all of her hope. "As long as your mind remains stubbornly closed, that is the only piece of Adlivun you will ever possess."

"Make it final this time," he said hoarsely. "Don't come back and dig open these wounds."

"I can assure you that you will never see me again," Aazuria said. "If Callder recovers from his wound enough to be moved, I will send him to you with a heavy military escort, several hundred warriors strong. They will arrive on the beach just outside—you may then transport him to preferred facilities with your vehicle. Similarly, if Callder dies, I will send his body to you in the same way. In either case, I will not be with the convoy." She swallowed as she repeated her decision. "You will never see me again."

She always abided by her declarations. Once decreed, it was a matter of honor to fulfill her own pronouncement. Her words would become cheap and empty; their power would be diminished if she used them carelessly—and if a woman did not have her words, what did she have? She turned to leave.

"Aazuria," he groaned, clutching his bleeding arm. "Just know that I love you."

"Love is worthless without trust and acceptance."

Right before she crossed the threshold she turned back to him, feeling pity for his injured state. She had desperately needed to gaze upon him one last time; in spite of all that had happened, she treasured the sight of him. His face still affected her body like a good meal, delivering nourishment and energy where she was deficient. She knew that she would spend her life pining for him, and wondering what she could have done differently to change their ghastly fate. She had never really loved someone before, not like this; she had never known what it was like to be romantically attached to a man. She was sure that she had made all the wrong decisions, but she did not know how to remedy anything. It was all destroyed.

She wished she could say all this to him. She allowed her lips to part, and let the words which chose to flow forth choose themselves. She had relinquished all control of the situation. "In five hundred years, I have never seen Visola show mercy to someone who tried to hurt me. There are two reasons that you are alive right now. The first is that I also love you. The second is that the woman who shot you is your grandmother."

With that she marched out of the house, and strode out of his life permanently. He never saw the tears streaming down her cheeks. She continued walking across his front lawn, and across the road which ran in front of his house. When she reached the beach, she kept going until she stepped off the land permanently. Moments after her tears had begun gushing forth, they were washed away and absorbed by the ocean.

Chapter 34: A Stranger's Kindness

Trevain did not know whether he wanted to go out to sea because he was hoping to find Aazuria, or because he was hoping to find Atargatis. He just knew that it was the only possible option for him. It was the only thing he knew how to do remotely correctly. And if they lost another man? He did not mind as long as *he* was the man.

He had called up his crew, and no one had agreed with his idea. "It's the last fishing week of the season," he had coaxed, "we won't get to fish again for months."He had pulled every string, called in every favor, and begged for them to assemble. He needed this.

Now, as they all stood on the docks, the hesitation hung in the air like a foul stench. Everyone looked as though Trevain had asked them to step into the waiting jaws of a hungry creature known to chomp down mercilessly.

"I don't know if I'm really in the mood," Doughlas said.

"It's not sex," Trevain said harshly. "It's work."

"Are you sure about this, Cap'n?" Ujarak asked, chomping on his cigar more uneasily than ever before.

Trevain turned on his men angrily. "I gave you all what you asked for! I let you take my boat and fish. And now my brother's gone. You convinced me again! Arnav was killed. This time *I* want to go out and catch crabs, just to relieve stress because I've lost everything. I lost Callder, my mother, and my fiancée. I don't have anything left. So give me this."

"What happened to Mrs. Murphy?" Edwin asked with concern.

"She escaped from the psychiatric hospital," Trevain answered bitterly. "She's as good as dead."

Brynne recognized this destructive behavior as more characteristic of Callder than of his older brother. She felt extremely jittery about this emergency fishing trip; it was evident that something was about to go horribly wrong. It always did lately. Going out to sea was inviting Death over for supper and expecting her not to feast on the other dinner guests. Now, with three empty place settings at the table, Brynne felt foolish about having a dinner party at all—but her captain had polished up the utensils, and Death remained on the guest list. Brynne wanted to hit him.

Nevertheless, it was true that they all owed it to Trevain to be there for him. She knew from Mr. Fiskel that he had also recently sustained a serious injury to his arm. *It never snows,* she thought to herself.

When all the men walked off muttering to prepare the boat, Brynne approached Trevain privately. "For what it's worth, Captain," Brynne said, putting a hand on his back and speaking to him gently, "I think that Aazuria was a lunatic to let you go."

He stood on the dock, staring out at the water vacantly. "I was really hostile to her, Brynne. I said some awful things. I was even rough with her." He rubbed his arm absent-mindedly.

"No way! I don't believe that," Brynne said with a frown. "You're the kindest guy I know. You don't have a mean bone in your body."

"Apparently I do," he said wretchedly. "I'm not this great person everyone thinks I am. I'm just a brainless fuck-up like any other guy."

He walked away. Brynne sighed and glanced after his retreating form. She sat down on the edge of the docks and dangled her feet off the side. She had never seen the reliable and mature Trevain act this way. She supposed that love and loss could turn even the most solid fortress into pudding. She could feel that he was heartbroken. She could also feel that he was hoping to join his brother.

Brynne pulled her knees up to her chest, hugging her calves and resting her chin on her kneecaps. She could not say that she did not understand the way Trevain felt. Since Callder had died, she had often entertained such thoughts. She had often wished that she could go off to sea, and be part of some "accidental" accident. She had never realized what a huge part of her life Callder had been until he was gone. She had always pushed him away and pretended she had not needed him, and she had done so knowing that he would be there smiling at her the next day. She had wasted so much time that she could have spent with him, and now she was suffering for it with no end in sight.

She could see in Trevain's eyes that he felt the same way; perhaps even worse. She vowed to herself that she would keep an eye on him closely on the fishing trip; she would not allow anything to happen to him. He would never leave her watchful care. She almost did not care what happened to anyone else, but she knew she owed it to Callder to take care of Trevain. Brynne hugged her knees tighter as she gazed out at the water. She wondered how she could never tire of looking at the sea.

"Hey, sweet pea," came a caring female voice. "I heard about what happened on your boat a while back."

Brynne was about to snap at the woman for calling her "sweet pea" but then she relented. It was rare to see another woman on the docks. It was also nice to hear a kindly voice and see a vaguely familiar face. She was not sure who the woman was, but she thought she recognized her, possibly from a local bar. "Yeah. We haven't been out to sea since then. We lost three men this year—is that crazy or what? One of them was my ex-boyfriend."

"It's been a bad season, love. I'm so sorry for your loss." The blonde woman sighed. "Did you know two boats have disappeared *completely?* What horrible luck. I pray for my husband like three times a day when he's fishing. It's so dangerous out there. Is there anything I can do?"

"Nah," said Brynne, waving her hand dismally. "Unless you've got a time machine."

"Sorry, sweet pea. Haven't got one of those." The woman managed a small smile. "I do have some extra rice and beans though. I was just down here delivering some food to my husband's boat. I swear, if I didn't do something about it, these men would live on potato chips."

Brynne laughed at that. "God, I know what you mean! Sure, I'll take whatever you've got. I've been in kind of a crappy mood and have slacked off on the grocery shopping."

"I'll be right back, sweet pea—let me just grab some stuff from the trunk."

Brynne smiled at the woman's generosity. Sometimes the kindness of a stranger was all one needed to lift their spirits and brighten their day.

Chapter 35: *Murder in the Mausoleum*

Aazuria knelt on the carpet before her father's frozen tomb, staring up into his colorless face.

The royal mausoleum was one of the few rooms in the ice palace which was not filled with water. The bodies of ancient kings and queens were entombed in ornately carved, vertically positioned ice coffins, and preserved here so that future generations could look upon the faces and bodies of their ancestors. It rather reminded Aazuria of Trevain's macabre museums.

Barefoot, and bare-legged, wearing a sea-foam green tunic with a short sword strapped to her hip, this was the first time that Aazuria had physically faced what she had done. She had been sitting in the respectful position of *seiza* for many hours. Her whole body was numb. When she had first come to the mausoleum, she had tried to kneel respectfully before her father, but her body had refused to comply. Instead, she found herself doubling over until her forehead and arms rested on the carpet, as she wept. This was *balasana*, or more appropriately, child's pose. She was kneeling prostrate and in deference.

"Papa," she had sobbed. "Papa, you were right. What have I done?" With her forehead against the carpet, she could see the world more clearly. "It is better here. It has always been better. I should have left things as they were. If we all stayed and died here it would have been easier than going out into that awful world, with all those awful people." She had cried for hours until the carpet became soaked, and her warm tears began to freeze in a small radius around her face. "I'm so sorry, Papa." She continued to cry until there was a small sheet of ice beneath against her forehead and nose.

She had not moved from this spot since she had returned to Adlivun. Once she had seen that her sisters were safe, she had come directly to this chamber to wallow in her lot.

When she could no longer rest her face on the frozen carpet, she forced herself to cease her sniveling and straighten into *seiza*. Aazuria felt suddenly rejuvenated. She was still on her knees, but not in the same pathetic way as before. She was on her knees not as a servant, but as an equal. Not as a beggar, but as a warrior. Aazuria closed her eyes. She imagined her organs untangling themselves from the jumbled mess in which they had been knotted, and aligning themselves properly. She imagined the natural ease with which her breath and energy traveled through her body; all the channels which had been blocked with the rocks and lumber of anguish and the caulk of vitriol opened one by one as she willed it. She sat for hours more in long solitude and reflection, until she felt healed.

She opened her eyes and saw the small sheet of ice on the carpet that had been created by her tears. She smiled at it, knowing that she had cried all the weakness and negativity out of her system. She looked up at her father's body, and she smiled at him too.

"What happened with Trevain made me question everything I knew, Father. The truth is, I have made peace with what happened between us, and I know that I did the right thing. If not for me, for everyone else. I loved you every day of my life, and will continue to love you for every day that remains—but you were a dark shadow on the brilliant light of Adlivun. Everyone stands a little more proudly, everyone breathes a little more freely now that you are gone. You were my father, and you were good to me; but for too long that blinded me to all the other elements of your character."

Aazuria gazed up at her father until she was interrupted by a sound from behind her. She turned around to see that Elandria had entered the room.

"*Aazuria, you cannot stay here all day and all night,*" her sister signed. "*It is not healthy to reminisce about things like this.*"

"*I am feeling much more clear-headed now,*" Aazuria responded, also using her hands. "*I really needed to come here and confront my guilt and shame.*"

Elandria looked up at the man her sister was kneeling before. "*I think I need that too. It is funny. I see him now and I feel only sadness, pity, and regret; yet when he was alive I felt only fear of his next motion or word.*"

"*I know what you mean,*" Aazuria responded. "*I am sorry it took me so long to do what was needed to be done. A hundred years sooner and perhaps we would not be in the situation we are right now; preparing for war.*"

"*Everything happens exactly when it is meant to happen, sister. Perhaps if things had been different you would never have met Trevain, and we would not have Alcyone back.*"

"Yes. A good thing did come from all this mess."

"Aazuria, I do not know what happened with Trevain, but he is honorable; he just needs time to adjust to our ways. There is no one that I would rather have as my brother." Elandria gave Aazuria an affectionate smile as she signed this. *"Please promise me that after the war is over you will try to make it work with him."*

"I do not know if I can…" Aazuria looked back up at her father pensively.

A sound pierced the silence of the mausoleum; the whizzing of an arrow.

Aazuria turned back to her sister just in time to see Elandria's eyes go wide. The silent woman placed a hand to her chest, gasping as she began falling to the floor.

"Elan!" Aazuria yelled, scrambling off the ground and rushing to catch her sister before she fell. "No!"

Elandria felt the softness of her sister's breast against her cheek. Her hand reached up to grab Aazuria's arm in a vise-grip. She looked at her sister with horror in her eyes. "Aazuria…" her voice rasped. She was too weak to use her hands, and her eyes were filled with the fear of impending death. "Forgive him."

This was all she managed to say before she slipped out of consciousness.

Chapter 36: Any Sane Person

Aazuria felt the heavy fiberglass arrow protruding from her sister's back. It was meant for underwater bow fishing. She could not break it or remove it without causing Elandria further injury. She firmly pressed her hand to skin around the arrow's point of entry, feeling powerless to help her sister. There was nothing she could do. Elandria would be dead within minutes. She took several calmative breaths before lifting her burning eyes to see the face of the attacker.

A tall blonde woman was leaning against the door frame with a smug look on her face as she appraised her handiwork, callously gauging the degree of damage she had caused.

"Koraline," Aazuria said in a quiet voice, "how could you do this?"

"The name's Atargatis now, sweet pea. For the record, it was pretty easy. I just pulled the string and aimed."

"Elandria never hurt anyone!" Aazuria moaned in a distraught voice as she cradled her sister's body against her chest. "This is not fair. This is not right."

"At least it got your attention," Atargatis said, casually strolling around the mausoleum. She stopped when she was standing before Kyrosed's transparent casket. "Oh, lookie here. What a sight for sore eyes. My ex-lover, frozen solid in a brick of ice! So he really is dead. You really did off your pops!"

"Yes," said Aazuria, closing her eyes tightly. She felt for Elandria's pulse, and it was still there, but weak. "Please, will you let me take my sister to the infirmary? She could still make it if I hurry."

"Nah," said Atargatis, turning to Aazuria and aiming an arrow directly at her head. "I need some important information from you first."

"Ask," said Aazuria, seriously. When Atargatis just smiled at her, she raised her voice and shouted, *"Ask!"*

"Cool down, sweet pea. You know, you were such a pretty

237

ballerina in your little tutu. All I want to know is exactly how you killed Kyrosed Vellamo. Every detail—tell me how much he suffered, and describe the look in his eyes. I've spent so many years imagining it that I'm rather miffed that you denied me the honor."

"If you were so angry that he took Corallyn from you, then why are you not embracing your daughter right now?" Aazuria asked furiously. "Why are you here, killing Elandria, instead of taking what you came for? This is the woman who took care of your daughter, someone who was as much a victim of my father as you were! This will not go unpunished."

"Did I ever tell you how flattered I am that you folks named her after me? Anyway, I have captured my daughter already, and she is held in custody by my men. But I want a few other things. Revenge; on Kyrosed and anyone he held dear (that includes you and the dead girl in your arms, sweet pea) and—damn, what was the other one? Oh, yes. All of Adlivun. Can I have it? Pretty please?"

Aazuria frowned. Atargatis still held the arrow pointed directly at her eye. Elandria was dying or dead in her arms; she was too terrified check her pulse again to find out. Visola had been guarding her, and obviously Atargatis had somehow gotten past Visola. Aazuria did not want to admit to herself that Visola was probably dead. If Visola was slain there was no hope at all; taking an arrow to her brain would be the best case scenario. There should have been dozens of other guards in the castle as well. It seemed that her nemesis really did hold all the cards. Would it make any difference if she surrendered now?

She thought of Trevain. Her chest constricted with grief. How foolish she was! Here she knelt, holding her dead sister in her arms. Corallyn was in the hands of enemy forces while the worst could have happened to her dearest friends, Visola and Sionna. To top it all off, it looked like Koraline was eager to release the arrow pointed at her head—and all she could think about was Trevain. Memories of his face filled her mind in full color, and she ached at the thought of never touching him again. She thought of the last words that she had spoken to him, and how awful the fight had been.

"You look conflicted. I will be nice and give you some time to think about that, sweet pea," said Atargatis gently. "Why don't we have a little story-time first? You ought to fulfill my request and tell me *all* about how you killed daddy! Precisely—every word and every sound."

"I… I told him that I was going to do it," Aazuria said, hugging the body of her sister against her. The body was still warm, and she could not believe that Elandria was gone. Even so, her sister's blood was seeping forth, creating a large dark stain on Aazuria's green dress and dampening her skin underneath the gown. "Father said, 'You cannot solve death with more death.' No, that was not what he said. It was, 'You cannot prevent death by causing death.' Wait, no. 'Killing me will not save your sisters from being killed.' Something like that. He said it in such a poetic way… I thought would never forget his exact words."

Aazuria looked up at Koraline with frantic eyes. "Why can I not remember exactly what he said?" she asked her enemy hysterically. "I am trying so hard to remember."

"Wow, sweet pea. You're more than a little messed up in the head, aren't you?" Koraline asked in a mockingly pleasant voice. "Don't worry, I'll put you out of your misery soon enough. Now tell me, what did you say to him in response to the words you can't remember?"

"I said, 'No, but it will give me the power to protect them.' I was wrong. I obviously cannot protect them. I have already failed. I cannot protect my sisters, or any of the citizens of Adlivun." Aazuria looked at Koraline through her dazed double-vision. "What did you do to my guards?"

"They were just *guards*—what do you think I did with them? I painted your pristine white walls with their vital juices. Now tell me the rest of this story! Get to the look in his eyes."

"I took my knife and I pierced his chest in the traditional manner. I told him I loved him, and I watched the sorrow on his face as he died. His eyes were like Elandria's. They both died very similarly, in my arms. My father told me with his last words that he was proud of me for doing what I felt was necessary." Aazuria lovingly stroked Elandria's hair. The thick white braid had always been a sign of the younger woman's modesty. "He used to abuse my sisters. They were glad when he was gone. I think he was glad to be gone as well. I was hoping… I believed that things would become better for Elandria and she would finally feel safe enough to begin speaking again."

"Bravo! Excellent story." Koraline lowered the arrow that she had pointed at Aazuria. She began clapping joyously. "That's all I really wanted to hear."

"Can I take her to the infirmary now?" Aazuria asked in a shaking voice.

"Let me think about that for a moment. How about no?" Koraline laughed. "It's too late for her, sweet pea. I shot her through the heart. She's gone."

"No," Aazuria whispered. She placed her palm against Elandria's cheek, trying to feel the warmth of her sister's soul. Her hands had been covered in the blood leaking from Elandria's artery, and she impressed a bloody handprint on her sister's pale face. A sob rocked her chest. "Please, no."

"This isn't amusing me anymore," Koraline said. She walked to the doorway and shouted into the corridor with enthusiasm. "Hey, boys! Get in here. I've got some treats for you."

A few male Clan warriors entered the room, dressed all in black with copious shark's-tooth adornments. If Aazuria had been in a proper state of mine to acknowledge her surroundings, she would have deduced that these were Koraline's elite forces.

"Nice work, Atargatis," said one of the men. "There will be a huge payout for this. Prince Zalcan will be pleased."

"Forget the prince. I'm more concerned about his daddy. *Emperor* Zalcan will be pleased," Koraline said smugly. "Can one of you boys put a collar on Princess Aazuria? I want her on a chain so I can yank her around like a little dog. That would amuse me."

"It would be my pleasure, Atargatis," said one of the men. He pulled a metal collar from where it hung against his waist and moved over to Aazuria.

She hardly felt it when the man tugged her silver hair aside brutally in order to strap two interlocking pieces of cold metal around her delicate neck. She did not notice when the he placed a padlock on the shackle and yanked it to make sure it was secure. She could only stare down at Elandria, consumed by grief and anguish.

She did not hear a man's voice gruffly ask, "What about the other one?"

"I don't care what you do with the other one," Koraline said with a frown. "She's dead."

One of the warriors laughed. "There's dead and then there's *dead*. This one's warm and fresh. Possibly wet and sticky. Mind if I have a go at her?"

"Ugh. You men are disgusting," Koraline said, but her tone was almost affectionate. "I don't care what you do with the dead one, so enjoy yourselves. But I want to make a public spectacle of Princess Aazuria getting raped repeatedly for the next few months. That would amuse me. So don't mess her up too much."

"Thanks, Atargatis!" said one of the warriors happily. He reached out and forcefully ripped Elandria from Aazuria's arms.

"No!" Aazuria screamed, as tears flooded her eyes instantly. She tried to move to reclaim her sister's body, but the chain around her neck prevented her from getting very far. "Don't touch her!"

Koraline laughed. "This is seriously entertaining, boys." She moved forward to take the chain attached to Aazuria's neck from the warrior who had it wrapped around his fist. Pulling on the chain, Koraline dragged Aazuria across the icy floor until the princess was lying at her feet. "Does it bother you to see your sister's body desecrated? Watch! I want you to watch." Koraline cruelly slapped Aazuria across the face, causing her lip to burst open and bleed.

She slapped again and again, until Aazuria complied and turned to watch the soldier's hands roaming over Elandria's small waist. She saw another warrior push his friend aside before ripping at the bodice of Elandria's gown. She sobbed as one of the men began to unbuckle his pants and kneel over her sister. Aazuria reached up to rip at the collar around her neck, but it was futile. "No!" she begged. "Please stop, if you have any decency!" She tried to move to Elandria, but Koraline yanked at the chain, throwing her off balance.

"That's going to happen to you next," the blonde woman sneered. "Kyrosed's precious little virgin flower should suffer what her father did to so many other women. I'm going to enjoy this more than I've enjoyed anything in the past century."

"This one's not putting up much of a fight," one of the warriors remarked as he grabbed Elandria's braid and wiggled it violently, causing her limp head to roll back and forth. "I like it better when they're loud."

"Ain't much of a change, brother. I hear she used to be the silent type."

Aazuria wished for death. She was sure that if she wanted it badly enough, death would be kind and take her. She began counting down the precious hours until she died from dehydration. She would not accept any water she was offered. She had no reason to go on.

Koraline was having the time of her life. "Boys, when you're done can you grab Kyrosed Vellamo's corpse for me? I want it displayed in my bedroom as a trophy of victory. I want to wake up every morning and laugh at the fact that he is dead and I have destroyed everything he ever loved."

"Sure thing, Atargatis," said one of the men with a chuckle. "Taking Adlivun was far easier than we thought it would be."

Aazuria had to face the fact that she had lost. Once she admitted this to herself, there was a certain kind of liberation in the acceptance. She did not know if there was any such thing as the afterlife, but she needed to believe she could be with her sister again there. She needed to believe that Visola would be there. It was over for her, but perhaps it was not over. She knew her father would be there waiting—he would not be upset with her. He would hold her and forgive her.

"Oh, one more thing, sweet pea."

Koraline's voice sounded like it was far away in the distant background. Aazuria could hardly process the words through the haze of her emotions. Pain was carrying her to a place far removed from this world; perhaps her mind was already resigning itself to death. Her soul was withdrawing from her body, preparing for forthcoming moment when it would no longer be tormented.

"Are you listening to me, girl?" Koraline yanked on the chain and tried to drag Aazuria's spirit back into her body. The physical pain in her neck did startle Aazuria into consciousness for a moment, but she was optimistic that it would soon fade away. The princess was determined to be numb and unresponsive. She was over; she would soon be far away from here.

"A little while back, a pesky crab fisherman broke my fucking nose," Koraline was saying. "I believe he was the captain of a boat called *The Fishin' Magician*. What a stupid name."

Aazuria felt awareness returning to her in painful lumps and pieces. She focused on Koraline's face until her double vision had gone. Her nose? She saw the small, pointed nose that was so similar to Corallyn's. She tried to focus on the voice which grated her innards like nails on a chalkboard. A fisherman had broken her nose. Koraline was speaking about the one person Aazuria loved whom she hoped would escape this war unscathed.

"I tried to kill you that day, right then and there, but I didn't succeed. That foolish man saved you. I would have let him be, but he involved himself in our business. I just want you to know that he is going to pay the ultimate price for meddling with my whims."

"What do you mean?" Aazuria asked, looking up sharply.

"Your captain has a lovely surprise waiting for him on his boat right now. Perhaps we should refer to it as *The Sinkin' Magician.*" Atargatis emitted a chuckle. She extended her finger and pointed at Aazuria unyieldingly. "No one saves the daughter of the man who stole mine from me!"

Aazuria felt her blood freeze. "He's not even a sea-dweller. He's not part of this!"

"He's part of your life. Hurting him is just another way to hurt you, and therefore worthwhile."

"You intend to hurt Trevain?"

"I don't know, sweet pea," said the blonde woman with a self-satisfied smirk. "Do you think blowing him up will hurt a teensy bit?"

"You would not dare!" Aazuria said with a warning in her voice

"I already have."

Something shattered in Aazuria's brain. She felt a floodgate open. The white-haired princess slowly rose to her feet. "You took my sister's life. You took my kingdom. You took everything and I knelt here and accepted it." The princess jerked her arm and grabbed the chain attached to her neck. "But you cannot take him." Yanking on the chain, she wrenched Koraline forward. In an instant, she had used Koraline's momentum to dash the woman's head into the floor. Aazuria rammed the heel of her bare foot into the base of Koraline's skull.

The warriors who surrounded Elandria's body had been groping at her flesh like vultures. They had been arguing over who would have her first, but now they turned to Aazuria in surprise. The woman's icy-blue eyes flashed with spikes of steel as she advanced on the men who meant to vandalize her sister. Using the chain attached to her collar as a whip, Aazuria lassoed the man who had already lowered his pants. She pulled him viciously, moving forward in time to crush his face into the sharp point of her knee. She felt his nose and cheekbone fracture under the blunt impact.

Aazuria felt two of the other warriors grip either of her arms, and one of them reclaimed the chain around her neck. "You better hope Atargatis wakes up, Princess," an elite soldier snarled. "We won't be half as kind to you as she asked us to be."

Struggling hysterically, Aazuria tried to twist free. She felt the metal collar dig into her neck painfully, bruising her sensitive skin and interfering with her breathing. When one of the warriors leered at her and grabbed her jaw to plant a sloppy wet kiss on her face, Aazuria felt her stomach turn in revulsion. However, when he shoved his tongue into her mouth, she used the opportunity to pierce her teeth deeply into the wet protrusion. She clenched her jaw and yanked her head sharply to the side in order to rip the man's tongue out. The man let out a bloodcurdling scream and recoiled as Aazuria spat out the tip of his tongue.

One of the other warriors could not help laughing at his friend. "Serves you right, mate! That should teach you to bite your tongue. Get it? 'Cause she just..."

Having freed one of her arms, Aazuria slammed her elbow into the gut of the man who had been talking, causing him to double over. She retrieved the chain attached to her collar and wrapped it around the neck of the third man, pulling it taut behind him. She used the chain to crush his windpipe until the man crumpled to the floor. Reaching into the boot of one of the injured men, she withdrew a small but sharp knife. She moved first to the man with the wounded tongue, who was writhing in pain. She hastily slit his throat before doing the same to his companions. Wasting no time, she retrieved the key to the padlock on her collar and freed herself.

Aazuria threw herself down on her sister's body with a sob. She pressed a kiss against Elandria's forehead. The younger woman's pale skin was already beginning to grow cold. "I love you," Aazuria whispered. She rearranged Elandria's blood-soaked dress to provide some decency before launching herself to her feet. She knew that she should check to make sure that Koraline was dead, but she was too fuelled by the thought that Trevain was in danger to pause. She needed to move quickly.

Aazuria ran from the room with her bare feet pounding the carpet. She quickly navigated through the castle, ignoring and vaulting over the bodies of the guards with which Atargatis had, true to her word, painted the walls. Plunging herself into the cold water, she considered heading toward the area she had last seen Trevain fishing. It occurred to her that she had no way of finding him in this vast sea. She knew the general route of the crab fishing boats, but where would he be? Would he listen to her? There was no time to think of that—only time to move forward.

As soon as she was out in the open water, a decision was forced upon her. Aazuria had to stop swimming when she saw what lay before her. She stared, forgetting how to breathe and extract her vital oxygen from the frigid liquid. Her body floated motionlessly in the dark depths as her limbs became immobile from shock. Her mouth went very dry.

There was an army waiting outside.

Aazuria's heart sank. Her eyes traveled down the line of thousands of armed sea-dwellers garbed in black battle gear. They were all holding lances and javelins, sneering at her through their visors. Their black helmets bore the crest of Zalcan, and their armor bore his emblem; the ominous shark's tooth. If there had ever been an omen of destruction, it was the contrast of that white tooth against black armor.

Dread and disbelief coursed through Aazuria's veins. It seemed impossible to her that her she would feel such a huge surge of hope only to have it immediately snuffed out. *There is no way around this,* she thought to herself, but she did not fully believe the thought. She tried to force herself to face the bleakness of the situation, but the ranks of undersea soldiers stretching before her seemed too grim to be real. *I have truly lost. I have lost everything. My father, my fiancé, my sisters, my friends… and now, evidently, my kingdom. I may lose my life, or they may keep me alive to torture me until I lose my dignity. There is not much more a woman can lose.*

She felt a hand on her shoulder, and was stunned to see that Koraline was beside her, grinning madly. Aazuria knew that she should have checked to make sure her enemy had been killed—not that it mattered now. The blonde woman used sign language to communicate with her.

"It seems I've erected an army between you and the man you love. What are you going to do about it, sweet pea?"

Aazuria's chest ached as she drew short ragged gasps of water. Her heart rate had doubled, and her vision was darkened. She knew that at the very least, if she was to go down she could take Atargatis with her. She still held the knife from the boot of the man she had killed; Koraline must still be at least a bit dazed from the blow to the head she had suffered. Lifting her arm to chest level, Aazuria prepared her body for one last mêlée.

Her lips parted as she mouthed an answer to Koraline. *"I shall do what any sane person would do in this situation: fight."*

Koraline lifted her eyebrows before she moved her hands sarcastically. *"One lone woman against me and my whole army? That doesn't sound too sane to me."*

"Luckily, I do not care what you think." Aazuria was about to lunge at her enemy when she saw a reflection glinting off the blade she held. Koraline noticed it at the same moment she did, and both women turned their heads sharply toward Adlivun. What had been a flash of green in the corner of Aazuria's eye was quickly blossoming into a field of green.

It was the most welcome sight she had ever beheld. All of Adlivun's infantry was up in arms, exiting the volcanic caves in droves. The men and women were wearing their traditional malachite-green battle garb, except that the material had been updated to Kevlar. The armor and helmets were emblazoned with the golden triple-moon symbol which was on Adlivun's flag. Dozens—no, *hundreds* of the sea-warriors on the front lines had been newly equipped with underwater assault rifles.

General Visola Ramaris was leading the charge. Her red hair ballooned out around her as she swam forward, bare-headed and grinning maniacally. Aazuria said a silent prayer, thanking Sedna for the mad genius of her best friend. It had been over fifty years since Visola's last battle, and she could see that the woman was gung ho for combat. Aazuria imagined that her friend had been informed of the approaching attack by her scouts, and had been able to rally the troops just in time. Not in time for Elandria, but perhaps in time for everyone else.

It looked like the troops were sprinkled with civilian militia to bolster their numbers. There were even children ready to launch their bodies into the fray. Her army was extremely outnumbered, but they did have the advantage of new technology on their side, thanks to Visola's unconventional efforts. Aazuria swallowed. The pounding of her own heartbeat in her ears drowned out everything else, but it was not from fear any longer—it was from witnessing the zealous thirst for battle visible on Visola's face. It was in times like these that the warrior-woman came alive, and Aazuria knew that her friend was about to create magic with her body. The princess felt a rush of adrenaline immeasurably greater than the one she had felt while dancing on stage—dancing and employing the technique in which she had been instructed by Koraline Kolarevic.

It would not be the first time that a student had bested her teacher; Aazuria was ready to dance. Trevain was in danger. She knew that she could do anything thing she needed to get to him. She would do anything necessary, and then she would go ten steps further and do everything conceivable beyond that. If it was the last thing she did, she would break through that stalwart wall of Clan warriors clad in black, and she would fight her way to Trevain.

She turned back to face her enemy and mouthed to Koraline confidently. *"It appears that I am not alone, after all."*

With that, Aazuria swung her arm back, and tightly gripping her stolen knife, she lunged at Koraline's face.

Chapter 37: Outnumbered and Outmaneuvered

Visola raised her arm, signaling the troops forward. Once the infantry was heading steadily toward their attackers in the formation she had recommended, Visola broke away from their numbers. She headed directly for Aazuria to aid her in the hand-to-hand combat. Koraline had pulled a sword from her side and was expertly hacking and stabbing at Aazuria who was deftly dodging strikes and trying to deliver her own.

Many of Koraline's elite fighters did the same, rushing to join the fight and protect their leader. Visola quickly intercepted them, using her rifle to riddle them full of bullets. Once they were dealt with, floating motionlessly in the water, it seemed like no one else from the Clan of Zalcan was bold enough to approach the skirmish. She turned her attention back to Koraline. She saw that Aazuria was fighting with unusual tenacity and precision—she had not been prepared for the battle and she was not wearing armor, so she could not afford any mistakes.

Visola pointed her rifle at Koraline, aiming between the blonde woman's eyes. She made tiny adjustments for the moving target, and positioned her finger over the trigger—but she did not shoot. Koraline was doubtlessly the younger and stronger of the two women, although she looked to be older. Her height and weight were both greater than the Aazuria's, but she did not possess the speed and the experience. Aazuria had not been joking when she told Trevain that she was one of the fastest swimmers in the world; her whole fighting technique was based on speed. Visola knew that she should take advantage of this free moment to interfere before she had to focus on the main battle again, but she saw the wild look in Aazuria's cobalt eyes. She instinctively knew that this was the kind of fight that she could not interrupt.

Aazuria was fighting like a woman possessed, and this chilled Visola. She knew that there must be some reason for the noblewoman's unusually vicious strikes and the indomitable hardness of her expression. Visola feared that something had happened; she knew her princess too well to avoid assuming the worst. Visola accidentally gulped a mouthful of seawater. She could sense that something had happened to Elandria. She felt bile rise in her throat. Adjusting the rifle's aim as the women spun around each other, she yearned for it to be her turn.

It was rather poetic to watch two ballet dancers fight—Visola could see the way that their art worked itself seamlessly into their swordplay in their powerful spins and kicks. Their posture was flawless. It was natural that the way one used their body the most would be the way they became accustomed to moving. Visola made a mental note that if they managed to survive this, she would take some dance lessons herself and see if it improved her fighting at all.

Not that my technique needs much improvement, Visola thought to herself smugly. She wondered how she had found time to be arrogant in the midst of such a chaotic battle. People were dying all around her, and she was entertaining conceited internal quips. But then, Visola always had time for arrogance. She was positive that even if she was seconds away from death, her final thoughts would be private declarations of superiority. She did not think that today was the day on which she would discover the precise nature of those thoughts.

Visola nearly squeezed the trigger to fire a large caliber bullet into Koraline's brain when she saw that Aazuria was leaving the right side of her body open. Unfortunately, she was interrupted by an ambush of three warriors at once. She had lost the moment to interfere, and she could only grimace in the middle of her own battle as she saw Aazuria's mistake. Koraline had managed to thrust her sword directly into Aazuria's shoulder—the same shoulder, the very same spot where she had impaled Aazuria before. Visola could see glimpses of Aazuria recoiling and quickly switching her knife from her right hand to her left. There was an angry look on her face—Visola knew that Aazuria was conscious of her grave error. To get stabbed in the same spot twice was a surefire sign of a flaw in method. Aazuria had a gigantic blind-spot around her upper right side, and it would surely get her killed.

Having to focus on her own fights for several minutes, Visola missed most of the battle between Koraline and Aazuria while trying to protect her own skin. She swung her rifle onto her back and withdrew the heavy unicorn trident which hung from her waist. Underwater, this weapon was manageable, but on land it was almost impossible to wield.

She swung the staff expertly, the way her father had trained her to do hundreds of years ago. Visola aimed at the softest, most vital parts of her attackers' bodies, shoving the prongs between the strands of shark's tooth necklaces and using her foot to press against their bodies and rip her weapon out. She gritted her teeth as she used the carcasses of the men she defeated as ladders, stepping on them for leverage in order to position herself better for the next fight.

While she was happy to embrace new technology, the old trident had sentimental value to her. The enemy soldiers were not wearing Kevlar, so it was easy to pierce their clothing. There were just too many of them. Even as she was swamped by the flood of soldiers around her, she did not fear for her own safety. She was Visola Ramaris, and she was born to fight. She was only half-focused on her own struggle, and completely focused on Aazuria. Every time she needed to look away from Aazuria's battle for a second to deliver a killing blow, she felt fear that she would turn around and see her friend's head severed. It was no secret that Aazuria was not a great warrior. She did not have as much of a zest for training as the Ramaris sisters—even the medically-inclined Sionna was a better fighter than the princess! Aazuria's expertise was grounded more firmly in the political realm. Visola finally was able to fend off the bulk of her swarm of attackers and turned to swim toward the princess.

She saw Aazuria's knife strike Koraline firmly in the throat, but the myriad strings of shark's teeth around the blonde woman's neck protected her from this blow. Surprise registered on her face, however, and Aazuria exploited this moment to ultimately subdue the woman. Aazuria plunged her knife into Koraline's gut, and the woman doubled over, clutching her bleeding abdomen. She held her stomach in a vain attempt to stop her dark blood from spilling out into the water. Koraline's mouth opened in dismay, and dark swirls of blood were emitted from her lips. This meant nothing; the enemy would not stop because their leader was down—she surely had a second, a third, and a fourth in command. That was the way the Clan of Zalcan worked.

"That's my girl," Visola signed proudly as she reached the scene, before taking some plastic handcuffs off her belt and using them to restrain Koraline.

Aazuria looked at her friend with panic still painted on her face. *"Trevain is in danger! I need to go to his boat—can you spare some troops to come with me?"*

250

Visola frowned, thinking of her grandson. *"They massively surpass us in manpower. I can't spare anyone or we risk losing. The benefit of the rifles is mostly gone since our soldiers are fighting at close range. Now it's all down to pure skill, and I've got my reserves out there. They hardly have any training. We could lose Adlivun today."*

"Actually, sis," signed Sionna with a smile, having just joined the fight, *"look over there, and reconsider that."*

The three women looked in the direction that Sionna was pointing. The most welcome sight that Aazuria had ever seen in her life was quickly dethroned by this one. Hundreds of sea-warriors clad in red were diving off boats which were rapidly arriving on the scene. They all wore the *kamon* of the Ningyo clan, on their armor and helmets. The emblem of a pearl-white *mitsudomoe* was their symbol; three spirals connected at the center. The swirls in the symbol had always reminded Aazuria of waves, but like their very own triple-moon, the *mitsudomoe* had complex spiritual significance to the clan. The colors of red and white had never looked so magnificent to her.

The Japanese reinforcements had arrived, led by the eminent Queen Amabie. Naclana was at the side of the illustrious woman.

The enemy forces had been flanked.

Visola's eyes began to shine with almost reptilian delight. *"Well, that changes everything. The enemy is outnumbered and outmaneuvered."* She kicked the wounded Koraline aside and nodded to her sister. She quickly signed a few words before returning her hands to her assault rifle.

"Go save my grandson. As long as our enemies are still breathing, I have work to do. When you return you'll find a necropolis, and I expect a bonus." Visola's green eyes were so predatory that they sent a chill through Aazuria. Even Sionna could not recognize the exuberant, battle-hungry animal that had been unleashed in her twin sister. *"Go!"* The red-haired warrior signed a few final, jubilant words before returning her capable hands to grip her assault rifle:

"There will be a fucking bloodbath of drowning mermaids tonight!"

Chapter 38: *Unfamiliar Ultramarine Orbs*

"Why are we here, Brynne?" Trevain asked, leaning against the wall angrily.

"I wanted a snack," she said, rummaging through the cupboards.

"I didn't."

"Well, you need to eat dinner," she said, with her mouth full. "We've been fishing all day."

"I'm not hungry. Look, Brynne, is there a reason you haven't left my side this whole trip? Do you think that I'm emotionally vulnerable because Aazuria left me and I'm going to fall into your arms or something?"

"Here, just relax and let me cook something good for you."

"I appreciate your concern for my health, but I already told you that I'm not hungry…"

"Hey! That's funny. Why is there sound coming from this bag of rice?" Brynne placed her ear against the bag. "Weird. It sounds like a clock."

Trevain frowned and moved over to the bag of rice to listen.

Brynne shrugged and continued gathering cooking utensils. "Reminds me of that story about the captain and the crocodile—he could always tell the crocodile was near because it had swallowed a clock, and he could hear the ticking…"

"Shut up, Brynne." Trevain pulled a knife out of the drawer she had opened and slit the bag open, causing rice to spill out all over the floor.

"Hey, Trevain! You're making a mess!" Brynne scolded. "Just because you don't have to clean anything up around here since you're the high and mighty capt…"

"Where the *hell* did you get this?" Trevain yelled, staring at the strange homemade bomb which was nestled in the rice.

Brynne had not turned around, and was continuing to gather ingredients. "Oh, some sweet blond lady on the docks gave it to me…"

"Dammit!" he cursed. "There's no time."

"No time?" Brynne asked in confusion. Trevain grabbed her

hand and was pulling her into the next room. "What are you doing, Murphy?"

"Get in the bathtub, Brynne!"

"What? Why? I'm not into kinky…"

"Down, now!" Trevain grabbed Brynne and dived with her into the bathtub, covering her body with his and waiting for the sound.

The next second, all that they heard was—nothing. The sound of the explosion was so deafening that there was a moment of intense pain in their ears before they lost the ability to hear. They felt, however. They felt the intense pressure of the bomb exploding. They felt the unbearable heat of the explosion burning their skin and singeing their hair. They felt the bathtub being ripped from the ship, and pieces of debris colliding with their bodies. Trevain felt large objects colliding with his head and back painfully, and he felt his skin being punctured in several places. Finally, he was aware that they were surrounded by water.

It was several seconds before the heat subsided to the cooling water, and a moment later he was finally able to open his eyes. He could barely make out the scared expression on Brynne's face in the darkness. There was debris everywhere; pieces of the broken ship. *His* broken ship. Trevain was completely disoriented. It was difficult to figure out where they needed to swim. He could tell that sections of the boat floating near the surface were burning. He looked around for the other members of his crew, trying to get his bearings.

The flames were growing stronger. The ship's diesel was leaking from the ruptured gas tank. They could not swim to the surface, or they would be burned. Brynne's face was lit by the flickering firelight as she panicked and tried to communicate with him, but they could not understand each other. As he frantically made hand signals indicating for Brynne to calm down and stay close to him, he was met with only mystification on her face. He appreciated the need for sign language more than ever at that moment. Brynne was freaking out, and she began swimming off in one direction. He was sure that it was not where they needed to go. He tried to reach for her, but he was feeling dizzy from the lack of oxygen flowing to his brain. He looked around, trying to figure out where to go and what to do. He could not help panicking as well.

Trevain tried to swim away from the flames, but he could not get very far. The burning diesel had leaked out over the surface of water for what must already be a square mile, and he could not swim that far without taking a breath. Without several breaths. He needed air badly, and finally realized that he was going to drown. He could not breathe underwater; he did not have the ability. He simply did not know how. What Aazuria and his mother were talking about—he wished it was all true, but it was not. Not for him.

He knew that he was about to die. His lungs painfully begged him to take a breath, but he knew that the moment he did, he would drown. Although he had almost wanted something exactly like this to happen to him when he had set sail earlier, he now realized that he had been fooling himself. As demented as he had been feeling, as self-destructive as his intentions, it had all been just a farce. He did not really want to die.

He tried as hard as he could to hold onto his last few moments of life.

A glimmer of white caught his eye, and he saw that an exquisite creature was suddenly before him. Long white hair fanned out around her face, and the purest eyes of blue sapphire stared at him. The lovely phantasm was smiling as she reached out to take his hands; he knew it must be an angel.

It was his angel. He knew her, although she looked nothing like before. She was his Aazuria, his mythical heroine. In the dancing glow of the oil blaze, she was simply too dazzling to be real and he knew that he must be on death's very threshold. He had heard that people often hallucinated in moments such as these, seeing what they most yearned to see. As she hovered in suspension before him, her skin and hair were almost luminous in the dark water; almost phosphorescent. Perhaps she never had been real. It did not matter—she was firmly grasping his hands, and it sent a feeling of comfort and tranquility through him. He knew that she loved him.

He could see forgiveness and acceptance in her expression. None of the turmoil between them mattered any longer in this pacific moment. In her benevolent gaze, he could finally forgive himself. He smiled at her. Although his vision was fading and the world was disappearing, he could only smile. He tightly gripped her hands to thank her for coming back for him. He could not bear the thought of letting go; he did not want to be robbed of her touch. He tried to keep his eyes open for as long as possible—he tried to keep gazing into the salvation of those unfamiliar ultramarine orbs. So this was what she really looked like, in her element. He wished he could have known her true form. It was mystical.

Trevain could imagine no better way to die. No better sight to see in the final moments during which he was capable of vision. He was wholly happy and blissfully complete. A peaceful expression descended on his face, and the captain's tired eyes closed for what he knew to be the last time.

Chapter 39: Who Gets to Kill Atargatis

"So this is the troublesome female who caused all of this?" Queen Amabie mused in perfect, just barely accented English. She towered over the woman in chains at her feet. "This is the fearsome 'Atargatis?'"

The blonde woman struggled and tried to scream out insults, but the sound was muffled by the gag in her mouth. Visola smiled down at her captive with satisfaction. Although her own body was bruised and battered, she found this moment of victory thoroughly fulfilling. The battle had not continued for many more hours after the Ningyo reinforcements had arrived. Adlivun's losses had been far fewer than expected, and they had managed to capture many of the enemy warriors.

Assault rifles were magical. All in all, it had been a thoroughly successful day and Visola was basking in the glow of fulfillment. There was a large gash just under her ear from where a harpoon had nicked her, but the beautiful thing about a harpoon was that once it was thrown, the attacker was rendered defenseless and open. She had cut down at least two dozen Clan warriors this way. Their battle technique seriously needed refurbishing. Visola she would not have felt like she had properly done her job unless there were trails of sticky blood leaking out of various wounds. Various nurses had offered their attention, but Visola had chosen to treasure her scratches for a little while longer while they tended to those with more life-threatening lesions. Her sister would stitch her up once she returned with Aazuria.

"This woman's real name is Koraline Kolarevic," Visola explained to the Japanese queen. "She was a dance instructor that King Kyrosed developed a liking for in Moscow about a century ago. She is Corallyn's mother."

Queen Amabie had been slowly circling Koraline, her regal crimson robes skimming the floor as she walked. With a hand on the hilt of her katana, she frowned in consternation as she examined the face of her enemy. "What a pity your attack on Adlivun should fail so miserably, girl," she said magnanimously. "You should have known better. No one has ever beaten the magnificent warrior standing before you. This is General Visola Ramaris; she has the blood of the Vikings within her."

"Aw. You sweet-talker!" Visola affectionately smiled at her friend as a rosy blush began to tinge her cheeks. "I can't believe you remember my Viking Uncle Sigarr. Really, Queen Amabie, if you had not shown up when you had, the outcome would not nearly have been as certain."

"Nonsense, my friend. You had it all under control—you will have to tell me how on earth you procured those mighty weapons."

"You'll never believe it." Visola grinned, thinking of how best to tell the story, when the door to the dungeon opened.

Aazuria entered, dressed in full formal attire. She wore her silvery hair woven with pearls as was the custom, and a rich malachite-green dress which hung off of one shoulder. (Her other, bare shoulder, had been freshly dressed with bandages once more.) The airy fabric gathered at her waist with a wide jeweled band before continuing all the way to her toes. The waistband was embroidered with gemstones in the shape of Adlivun's triple-moon symbol. The style of the garment was Grecian and stately.

Aazuria made the traditional salute across her chest before she curtsied deeply, touching the fingertips of her left hand to the floor. "Queen Amabie, I am forever indebted to you for providing reinforcements in our time of need. Please forgive me for having to leave the battle. Atargatis had placed some friends of mine in danger, and I needed to try to save them."

The Japanese queen walked forward, her arms extended in greeting. "Queen Aazuria, why do you curtsy to me? We are equals, my good friend."

"I am still but a princess. I have not yet had my coronation."

"Formalities, my dear, formalities. In the fifties when I was in trouble, your father the 'king' did not come to my rescue—you did. You brought an entire army to save me without his authorization! You have always been the Queen of Adlivun in my eyes. You have always been the one willing to make the tough calls that no one else could handle."

Aazuria placed her arms in Amabie's outstretched ones. When

she looked into the older woman's wise dark eyes, she was reminded of Elandria, and she faltered. Every judgment she had ever made had been done so with her sister's guidance. Elandria saw things from a different perspective than the average person, and she had always been Aazuria's voice of reason. *Make the decisions which are the safest, the boldest, and the most unpredictable.* Her constant vigilance, her quiet virtue, and her levelheaded reflection could never be replaced.

She tried to feel the strength of having her arms linked with her fellow queen to celebrate their triumphant alliance. "I thank you for your confidence in me, Queen Amabie."

The Ningyo leader stared at her curiously. "And why are you not confident in yourself? Aazuria, dear friend; each victory is bittersweet. We sea-dwellers are an archaic bunch who resist change and cling fast to tradition. You listened to your people; you embraced the need for new technology and innovation! I should be imitating your example."

Aazuria gave Amabie a weak smile, allowing her hands to fall limply to her sides. She felt the first small ripple of relief run through her. "I suppose... it all turned out for the best."

"Oh, Aazuria. Do you not know what you have done? By ridding the seas of Kyrosed Vellamo, you have saved your nation. Your bravery and doggedness in doing what needed to be done is unparalleled. You will be honored for countless years to come—long after your body is entombed in ice, sea-dwellers will speak of the brave woman who killed her own beloved father so that they might be free."

In gratitude, Aazuria bowed her head respectfully. Her eyes were stung by tears as they fell upon the three ivory spirals emblazoned on Amabie's scarlet breastplate. It was the Japanese version of the Celtic triskelion; the symbol which represented man's natural balance with earth, air, and sea. It was only in moments like this one that Aazuria could grasp the meaning of such symbols. She was filled with sudden insight into why their ancestors had chosen these ambiguous *kamon* and emblems.

"Okie-doke. I hate to interrupt my two favorite ladies, but I need to know." Visola cleared her throat and leaned on a rifle impatiently. "Princess Aazuria, did you manage to save my grandson?"

"Yes," Aazuria answered, sending her friend a genuine smile. She exhaled in one airy gush. "Trevain is alive."

"Thank Sedna below," Visola said softly. She cleared her throat. "Well, I have some news for you too. Corallyn has been recovered.

While we fought, Alcyone managed to get Elandria to the infirmary. Her wound is serious, but she may pull through."

Tears immediately flooded Aazuria's eyes. She was embarrassed to be so emotional before the imperial Amabie, and she immediately tried to regain composure and stop the droplets from spilling over. Everything that had been taken from her all at once seemed to be falling right back into her lap. She felt a second, more substantial rush of relief.

"It is over," Aazuria said, just to hear it spoken aloud. She lifted her hand to brush her tears from her white eyelashes. "We won."

"We shall always win against the dishonorable Clan of Zalcan," Queen Amabie assured her. She turned and looked to where Koraline was bound on the floor. "What kind of general wages war but never sets foot on the battlefield? Forgive my slandering, but this omnipotent Zalcan fellow must be the puny runt of his litter."

Koraline began to struggle again, attempting to scream out insults against her muzzle.

At that moment, Sionna entered the room. She saluted the other women, and curtsied deeply to Queen Amabie. "I took care of the land-dwelling female, Princess Aazuria. I am happy to report that Trevain's injuries are superficial and that he should be awake shortly. I have to return to the infirmary at once to tend to our wounded, but I have been sent to petition you for mercy. Young Corallyn Vellamo is requesting that she be allowed to look upon the face of her mother before the execution."

Aazuria considered this for a moment. "General Ramaris, please unbind Koraline's mouth."

Visola moved to do this, and the prisoner spat at her. "My name is Atargatis!"

"Honey, you only get to choose your nickname if you *win* the war," Visola informed her.

"Red hair. Green eyes. Big guns. Visola Ramaris," Atargatis mused from the ground. She smiled. "So you are the world famous whore."

Visola's eyes narrowed and Queen Amabie had her katana pressing against the woman's throat in an instant. "You should apologize to my friend if you know what is good for you."

Atargatis completely ignored the pressure against her throat, and even the wet feeling of blood trickling down her neck from her broken skin. "You know, Visola, you and I are exactly alike. I know that you have a daughter too, also fathered by Kyrosed Vellamo…"

"What in Sedna's name are you talking about?" Visola frowned deeply. "Look, bitch. My daughter was *not* fathered by Kyrosed. The mere concept of sleeping with that man makes me want to vomit. Do I seem like a spineless doormat to you? I would have castrated the creep if he ever touched me, and he knew it."

"I have a reputable source," Atargatis said. "I intimately know the man whom you betrayed."

"Betrayed!" Visola spat. "I have *never*…" Her sentence trailed off with a small hitch in her breathing. She had only been married once. She had been completely faithful to her husband. Visola had never understood why he had abandoned her shortly after she had become pregnant, but if he somehow believed that she had slept with Kyrosed Vellamo…

"Do you know my brother-in-law?" Sionna asked Koraline, turning to glance at Aazuria nervously. The women shared a glance of foreboding, for both harbored a healthy hate for the love of Visola's life. The man left destruction and suffering in his wake wherever he went; Adlivun had been no different.

When Koraline responded with only hysterical laughter, Aazuria frowned and turned to Sionna. "My instincts tell me that I should not permit Corallyn to meet this woman. Do you agree, Doctor Ramaris?"

"Yes," Sionna said immediately. "Let's protect her from any harmful memories. I'll go tell her."

"No!" Koraline shrieked. "You will let me see my daughter, you imbecile! You are all fools!" The blonde warrior struggled to sit up in her chains. "You really think this is over? I would not celebrate so soon!"

"And why should we not?" Queen Amabie asked.

"Because I was supposed to fail." Koraline began to cackle madly as she pressed her shackled wrists against her wound. "I didn't know, but I can see it now. They sent me ahead to test your defenses. Emperor Zalcan himself orchestrated this attack on Adlivun. He likes to send several waves with increasing numbers of soldiers to weaken a country before unleashing his final, conquering blow."

"He has done this before?" Aazuria asked softly.

"Like the ocean. The power of the ocean is not in one lone

current, but in many massive waves. That is the way our leader fights."
Koraline smiled through her pain. "You don't stand a chance. Zalcan
will send his forces until you are ultimately beaten down. He has
leaders far more experienced than I am; prominent warriors with
vendettas against this atrocious northern kingdom. Guess who the next
wave is led by, Visola Ramaris? The Clan's most venerated son... you
may know him as the Destroyer of Kingdoms."

"Vachlan," Visola said miserably. If all of the women she
respected most in the world had not been in the same room with her,
she might have sunk down to her knees. Instead, she just stared ahead
blankly. Sionna moved to her sister's side and squeezed her twin's
hand. Visola did not respond, for she was already mentally preparing
for battle with the mighty Vachlan Suchos.

Everyone was startled by a noise when Corallyn burst into the
room, awkwardly holding a gun. "Is that her?" she asked, her face
streaked with tears. "Is that the woman who shot Elandria? I want to
perform her execution."

"No, little one," Queen Amabie said in a soothing voice. "That is
not your job. Queen Aazuria will do it tomorrow before all the
assembled citizens of Adlivun and my Ningyo people."

"She is *my* mother and *I* deserve the right to kill her!" Corallyn
said, before lifting the gun shakily and pointing it at Atargatis.

Aazuria grabbed her youngest sister, physically restraining
Corallyn and lowering the firearm. "Coral, no. Shhhh. You should not
have to experience what it feels like to kill your parent. I will do it."

"Parent? She is a stranger to me, she is nothing! Elandria was my
sister and my friend! Elandria was the kindest, most gentle woman who
ever lived, and now she might die because of *her!*"

"It's not my fault," Koraline whimpered. "Sweet girl, he stole
you away from me. I have been fighting for years to get you back.
Please, have pity! I am but a lowly pawn."

"Why was it so difficult?" Corallyn cried. "I've been here all
along, and nothing was stopping you from just coming here and
meeting me! I know my father was a horrible man, but you are worse!
You are worse, because you shot Elandria!"

"Dear girl, I am but a lowly pawn," Koraline said, begging for
understanding. "None of this was my doing."

Aazuria felt pity spread in her chest, and briefly considered letting the woman live. It was true that Kyrosed had used many women, and many people as pawns.

"This attack," Koraline said, gasping at the pain in her abdomen. She pressed on the wound, groaning to elicit sympathy. "It was not my idea. The details were all sketched out by Vachlan. He wanted information before he led his own forces against Adlivun. Blame Vachlan Suchos!"

"So you know him?" Visola asked in a deathly quiet voice. "You know my husband?"

"*Your* husband?" Koraline said with a small laugh. "He may have belonged to you once, you red-haired slut. But that was over five lifetimes ago. That was before antibiotics and automobiles. That was before the fucking light bulb. He isn't *yours* anymore."

Visola inhaled, her fingers twitching. When she spoke, she paused between each lingering syllable. "Do you know Vachlan Suchos?" she asked slowly. Electricity seemed to cackle in the air around her voice.

Koraline smirked. "He's been sleeping with me for the last fifty years; I think I should know him."

Before half a second had passed, there was a knife buried to the hilt in Koraline's left eye-socket. The woman stared at Visola with her other eye wide open in terror as she crumpled to the floor. It had happened so quickly that only two of the women in the room had been able to register what had happened.

"Bitch," Visola muttered as she walked toward Koraline. She put her boot on the woman's face and yanked the knife out of her eye. Then she looked back to the horrified Corallyn. The young girl had sunk to her knees, and was staring at her mother's corpse in shock. "Sorry, kid." Visola shrugged as she wiped the knife clean on her soft Kevlar armor. "I know you had a better reason to kill her, Coral. Oh, well. Guess I win."

"Goodness, Visola." Queen Amabie shook her head, astonished that after centuries, Visola's temper was still so volatile at the slightest mention of her husband. "This is not the appropriate manner of doing things."

"She surely had more information about the Clan of Zalcan!" Aazuria said in dismay. "She was so chatty—we could have kept her talking."

Visola lifted her wrists out to Queen Amabie and Aazuria. "Well, here I am. I humbly submit to either of your sentences. Lay it on me. Prison, torture? Want me to scrub the floors with a toothbrush? I'm game."

Aazuria turned to look at the regal Queen Amabie, hoping that the older woman would be more strict and authoritative than she. For although Aazuria knew that Visola's disobedience needed to be punished, she could not find it within her to declare a price. She knew that she owed her life and her kingdom to Visola—she owed the woman everything, several times over.

Queen Amabie sighed. If it had been anyone else, she would have immediately issued the sternest of reprimand. If it had been one of her own people they would have been harshly penalized for such rash behavior. However, the Ningyo leader had a great fondness for Visola's skill as a warrior and her affable charm, and all she could manage was a pitying smile.

"Oh, good grief!" Sionna exclaimed as she watched the fearsome women become soft as teddy bears when faced with her sister. Yet again, Visola had proven her worth. She was above the law. She was more powerful than a queen. She could melt stone with her charm. "Viso—for Sedna's sake. We were supposed to have a formal execution to raise the morale of our people. You just made things a lot more difficult for Aazuria."

"So then *you* punish me, Sio," Visola challenged. "What are you gonna do about it?"

Sionna sighed, turning to glance at poor Corallyn. There was a lot that she *could* do—she had no doubt about that. But she was even more biased than the other two women in favor of her twin. Visola could do no wrong in her eyes, even when she had obviously done very much wrong. "I would never hurt you, Visola. Just know that I am disappointed in your behavior; I believe that our father would be disappointed in you as well. We are always expected to act in the best interest of our country."

"Excuse me, but what part of me *winning a war today* did you not notice?" Visola shot back.

"Love, you won *a battle*. As we just learned, the war is yet to come."

"Never any pleasing you, sis." Visola turned her back and briskly exited the room.

Chapter 40: Just One Single Breath

The vaulted cathedral ceiling was decorated with intricate patterns carved into ice. Soft lighting illuminated the white substance until it sparkled like stardust. All of this was viewed through a foggy filter, almost like looking through thick glass.

Trevain blinked to clear his distorted vision until the fuzzy images sharpened. Strangely, the ceiling remained as resplendent as it had been through the haze. Scenes danced across his mind and he could not tell if they were from dreams or memories. He remembered an explosion. He remembered drowning. He knew that he had died, but he did not know how long ago it had happened.

When he lifted his head from what felt like a soft downy pillow, he looked at his body and saw that the angel was with him. She was lying against him, resting—her white hair was draped out across his arms and chest. He wanted to touch her translucent ivory cheek, but he did not dare, fearing she would disappear if he did. White eyelashes fluttered gently open, barely revealing pure sapphire irises with a dark limbal ring around them.

"I prayed that I would see you again," he whispered. "I have never prayed for anything in my life, but I prayed for you to any god that would listen."

She smiled up at him sleepily though half-lidded eyes. "Good morning to you too."

He fully raised his head and looked around at the room. Everything was made of ice, even the furniture. There were ornately carved ice torches which lit the area.

"Is this heaven?" he asked breathlessly. "Or maybe Atlantis?"

"Atlantis!" she mumbled, taking offense. "That place was a dump."

Trevain was surprised when she pulled herself upright and he felt a heavy weight leave his chest. It occurred to him for the first time that all of this could be real and earthly, including the woman. It occurred to him that she could be made of flesh and blood. She was stretching and yawning now, with her eyes still closed. She was lifting a hand to rub her bandaged shoulder.

"Aazuria?" he asked, staring at her in awe.

"Mmmm?" she asked, turning to him. She frowned, reaching up to touch her cheeks. "Do I have something on my face? Pillow lines?"

He reached out and touched her white hair, letting it slip through his fingers. "You're real. This is all real. I'm alive... but how?"

"Oh, Trevain," she said, with a light laugh. She clutched her shoulder as her torso shook with mirth. "You did not drown, my love. You just held your breath until you passed out. Once you were unconscious, your body started breathing naturally again."

"My boat," he said, sitting up abruptly. "There was an explosion... is my crew okay? Everyone was on the *Magician*..."

Aazuria's laughter had abruptly stopped. She reached out to take his hand in both of hers. "I am so sorry. Only Brynne was saved. She was taken back to land."

"Everyone's gone," he said blankly.

She slowly nodded in response. She scooted closer to him to wrap her arms around his neck, sighing against his chest. "Forgive me. I could not get to you fast enough. She shot Elandria and... I did not know what to do. She might not make it. I lost my people by the dozens. My whole body aches from fighting and I just want to sleep for days. Maybe when I wake up Elandria will be better."

"I like that plan," Trevain said, stroking her hair, "as long as I get to sleep beside you. Elan's a tough girl—incredibly tough. I'm sure she will be fine. Why were you fighting?"

"War was waged upon us last night. A fanatical woman attacked us with a sizable army.

"Atargatis?" he asked. He rubbed Aazuria's back soothingly. "That blonde woman I punched in the face?"

"Yes. Her rage had a righteous source, but she channeled it poorly. She made a grave error when she tried to hurt you." Aazuria winced when Trevain's hand skimmed her wound. "She liked stabbing me in the shoulder, apparently. It's my fault for not being a better warrior. It never snows, but it blizzards."

Trevain gently began to unwrap the bandages to examine Aazuria's injury. He frowned when he saw the huge gash that had been stitched up, crisscrossing over an old scar. He lowered his face to plant a kiss on the bluish skin near the stab wound. "Shouldn't you be in a hospital? Getting antibiotics or something?"

"My personal doctor is the best there is," Aazuria assured him. "She gave me various needles and said that as long as I got plenty of rest I would be fine."

"Where is the monster who did this to you?" he asked as he rubbed his thumb along the swollen red skin around the lesion. "Eight of my men are gone because of her. My whole crew."

"Seven," she corrected.

"Seven?" he asked with a frown. "I thought you said that only Brynne…"

"You forget that Callder is here. He is alive, and it looks like he will make a full recovery." She squeezed his hand reassuringly. "We can go visit him if you like. I heard that he regained consciousness right after you lost yours."

He looked at her for a moment. "My brother's alive. Are you sure this isn't heaven, Zuri?"

She responded with a halfhearted smile—her own sister's life still hung in the balance. He saw her grief and he reached out and pulled her against him, pressing his face into her cheek. She allowed her body to melt into his embrace with a sigh, turning to press her lips against his. When he kissed, her it eased her mind and caused her to momentarily forget; it was blissful. She felt a void when he pulled away, and was about to protest—but she could see the questions and confusion on his face.

"So this is your ice palace?" he asked her. "It is so warm here."

"Of course," she said, resting her palm on his thigh. She could not stop touching him, for it seemed to ease the pain inside her. "It is warm inside igloos too. My family was inspired by the simple functionality of Inuit architecture, hundreds of years ago when we first migrated to the Bering Sea."

"Everyone lives in ice?"

"Just the royalty: aristocratic families, warriors, scholars, and such. Most of us live in submerged volcanic caves under the Aleutian Islands."

"Why aren't we underwater?" he asked.

She was growing impatient with his questioning. She just wanted him to hold her. "I did not want you to freak out upon waking up and stop breathing again," she explained. "I figured it was best to ease you into it."

He nodded. "So Aazuria, your age is really..."

"I am six hundred and three years old; just like I told you when we first met. I have never been fond of lying. Do not ask me to explain the biology behind why our lifespans are extended underwater; your great-aunt Sionna will have to tell you about that."

"Six hundred and three," he repeated.

"Yes, I am truly an old, old woman," she said sadly, but there was a glint of mischief in her eye. She drew circles on his chest with her fingertip. "I know that there is no possible way that such a *young* man like you would be interested in an impossibly *old* woman like me..."

"Are you mocking me?" he said, but he could not keep a smile from his face.

She moved her good shoulder in a dramatic sigh. "No, I just feel awful. I feel as though I have taken advantage of you. Trevain... am I a pedophile?"

"You!" He burst out laughing and tackled her gently back onto the bed. He followed, positioning his body over hers and kissing her soundly. When he pulled away, she smiled up at him. He noticed then that the massive bed was also ornately carved from ice. Everything was suddenly new and miraculous to him; it was like being reborn. "Tell me about your world. Tell me about your people."

She seemed ready to protest, and request that he just lie down and rest with her, but she knew that she would eventually need to indulge his curiosity. "I believe that showing is always more effective than telling," she said, pointing to the staircase carved from ice which led out of the room. "Would you like to take the tour?"

"Aazuria... there's water there."

"Of course. Much of the glacier is submerged."

"Can I really breathe underwater?" he asked her hesitantly.

"Yes, silly," she could not resist a smile. "Just relax and let your second set of lungs do what they were meant to do."

He was still doubtful. He raised a hand to his chest skeptically. "Wouldn't they go dormant—even if I do have them (which I suppose I do) from lack of use?"

"The body is magical—many of its parts can be very patient." She placed her hand on his, resting gently against his chest where he was suddenly very conscious of the possibility of having special organs.

Yet he did not feel them, just as he did not feel the lungs he had used for his entire life. She smiled. "In all of my centuries of existence, I have never borne a child, and yet I believe that such a thing would be possible. I think my body would know what to do."

"Maybe I'll have to test that theory," Trevain told her with a smile.

"Please do not delay these tests," she said with a laugh, but her face quickly became serious. "You once told me that life would find a way—and it does. Your lungs know how to breathe water to sustain you should they have to, just as my body knows how to conceive. That life knows how to grow itself without any persuasion or urging on my part. It is effortless. You should try to take a breath. Just one single breath."

At her urging, he rose to his feet and walked over to the staircase. There was carpet running along the center of it so that one would not slip on the ice. He stepped tentatively onto the first stair, turning back to glance at Aazuria. He felt a rush of boldness at her calm expression, and he walked down the staircase until he was completely submerged. He held his breath for a few seconds, before gathering the nerve to attempt it; even if he did not trust himself, he had confidence in Aazuria.

When he inhaled his first breath of water, it was a revelation. The cool, refreshing liquid filled his chest in a new sensation that was close to euphoria. He continued half-walking, half-swimming down the staircase, taking deep enthusiastic breaths until he reached a corridor. He looked to either side of the lit ice-hallway, and saw that guards and other palace residents were swimming about and communicating in sign language. It looked like a normal society. A few people glanced at him, and inclined their heads in greeting.

He smiled like a kid who had discovered the ultimate candy store. He swam back up the stairs, and emerged from the water laughing. "I can't believe this! I can actually do it," he said between bouts of laughter. It was the greatest blast of excitement he had ever felt. He looked at her, his eyes sparkling with enchantment. "For the first time in my life, Aazuria, I don't feel like I'm fifteen inches tall. I feel like I have something special."

"You were special even without this ability," she said. She smiled, carefully pushing herself off the bed and clutching her shoulder as she approached him. "The joy you feel is due to the fact that this is where you originate from. Being on land is uncomfortable for we who know the freedom of the waves. You are the bonsai tree returned to the earth of Africa; this is the country of your mother. Here in Adlivun, you are more than a giant. You are a warrior; a descendant of elite Viking sea-kings."

Her face darkened, and her pale blue eyes became hard and determined. "This empire is my little bonsai tree, Trevain. My father kept it trimmed and circumscribed, but I need to find a way to change that. I want to let the magnitude of life that wants to exist, exist. I need to encourage and facilitate it, while keeping everyone safe." She began to pace across the carpet, anxiously. Her green robes, which had seemed modest when she was horizontal, now trailed behind her to reveal their majesty. "Trevain, there are those that would threaten us with their greed, hatred, and revenge. I need to safeguard Adlivun against that. People just want to live their lives in peace and freedom. I should have realized it sooner, but now I understand—it is *my* responsibility to protect them, and to ensure that they are able to grow and thrive. Will you… help me?"

"I'll do anything I can for you, Aazuria." He approached her, looking down at her in confusion. "As I understand, you are a princess. Well, I am yours. If I can be of any service, I will serve you for as long as I live."

She reached out to touch his hand. "I feel stronger just having you beside me. Can we lie down now? Every inch of me aches."

"Wait," he said softly. "Do you really forgive me for the way I treated you? I can't tell you how sorry I am, and how awful I feel about it. I called you names, I refused to understand, I was rough with you…"

She held up her hand to silence him. "Let us forget that. It is in the past. Besides, you were shot in the arm for it."

He rubbed the scar from the bullet gently. "I deserved it. Although it did scare the crap out of me."

"Your grandmother is my defender. She is an amazingly skilled and somewhat crazy warrior. She makes Brynne look like a bunny rabbit. You will have to meet her—well, technically you already have, twice, but you did not know her. She was the woman keeping an eye on me in the club when we first met, and then she was the woman who attacked Atargatis right after you saved me from getting impaled more accurately by that harpoon."

"That's my grandmother? But she's... young and beautiful. She looks decades younger than I do!"

"That's the gift of the sea. Just imagine how your mother feels!"

"Can you take me to see them? My grandmother and my mother? And Callder too?"

"Yes, of course." She was tired, but she could not deny the excitement on his face. "We can go right away if you like."

"Yes! But Aazuria... I just need to know. Is everything really fine between me and you? I just don't know how you can forgive me so easily."

She looked at him with puzzlement. "Of course. I bear no ill will toward you."

He placed a hand on her un-injured shoulder gently. "I still want you to be my wife. Now more than ever. I just... I don't know if I'm worthy of marrying a princess with her own ice castle and army and..."

"Trevain, when you asked me to marry you above the surface, I was indeed just a girl. There, in your world, I am nothing..."

"You were *never* just a girl, Aazuria," he said firmly. Then he paused, giving her a shy smile. "Although I must confess that the night Arnav was killed... I mentally cheated on you."

"You did what?" she asked, stepping back from him in confusion.

"Well, when I came home and you wouldn't let me see you—you had Corallyn guarding your room..."

"A spear had just been thrown right through my body!"

"I know that now, but back then I thought you were just pissed at me and well... I spent all night fantasizing about the mysterious woman in the water with the white hair and blue eyes. I felt *really* guilty for it too."

Upon hearing this, she could not prevent a small giggle from escaping her throat. She lightly smacked him in the arm. "I like myself more when I am underwater as well. You have my permission to cheat on me with me anytime. If you are in the mood for brunette, just add sunlight."

"Will you marry me in the way my mother wanted? The traditional sea-dweller wedding? Although I have no idea what that is."

Her smile disappeared instantly. Her eyes fell to the ground. "It is not so simple any longer."

"Why not?" he asked. "I will do anything I need to do to make it simple."

"Will you lead Adlivun into war?" she asked, with eyes narrowed into small slits. She crossed her arms across her chest austerely. "This nation is being threatened and attacked by another sea-dwelling clan. As king would you be prepared to lead us into battle?"

"King?" he asked.

Her eyes fell to the ground. When they finally lifted, there was something unreadable in them. Her voice was firm when she spoke. "If we marry in that manner, you will be the King of Adlivun. There is no divorce under the sea. Our marriage contract would last until one of us is dead. Are you ready for that level of commitment to a woman you barely know—and to a country you barely know?"

He observed her erect, unyielding posture, and felt the gravity of her words. Trevain suddenly understood why Aazuria had always appeared so stiff and unnatural. She had been raised in a royal family, and she had been subject to the rigorous training of an upbringing he could not even imagine. Everything odd about her suddenly made sense to him, and was suddenly ten times more endearing. He returned his focus to her words. She was asking for his full and complete dedication to her world. He did not know anything about Adlivun yet, but he knew that it was where he belonged. Aazuria lived there. Nothing remained for him on land.

"Zuri," he said with a smile, "since you stepped into my life, my old life has lost all its charm. Now that I have stepped into your world, and taken my first breath—I hardly think anything else can compare to what you've given me. You must be mad if you think I'm going back to live on land—and even *madder* if you think I'm ever letting you go again."

Her posture relaxed a smidgeon and her face softened. "I was so worried that you would not agree."

"King is easy—you could have asked me to declare myself as God, the Devil, or the Dalai Lama. As long as I am by your side, I will do anything," he vowed.

Her lips curled into a smile. She moved forward and slipped her arms around his waist, inclining her head upwards to kiss him. "Then we have nothing more to speak about. Others may object, but with time they will relent."

"You will have to teach me everything about your nation, Aazuria. I will feel a bit silly and unworthy to have an important position in a realm I know so little about—and where I am considered an infant."

"Nonsense. You have often called yourself a seaman! You spent all of your life working on the sea and building your empire on the water. Now you will have an empire to rule beneath the water. It is not quite so different."

"As long as you have faith in me," he said uncertainly.

"You have so much knowledge and experience to bring to Adlivun. You are introspective and humble, yet powerful and commanding—most of all, you have the most refined sense of intuition I have ever witnessed. All of Adlivun will welcome you as their king at our coronation."

"How do you still think so highly of me after all the things I've said and done?" he asked sadly. He wished for the umpteenth time he could take back all of his momentary lapses; how much more he would enjoy this moment. How much more worthy he would feel of being given this new chance at life.

"You are a real person, a real human being," she said softly. She knew that she must accept all sides of him, not just the ones she preferred. Both kindness and rage were part of the man; she had ample allotments of each as well. She laid her cheek against his chest and closed her eyes in contentment. "I still cannot believe that you are one of us. I thought that I would be separated from you forever. Even when we were at our best, when we were first engaged, I thought that I would only be able to love you for your brief lifetime. I believed I would have to live hundreds of years without you. But now that you are here, you will live just as long as I will. My impending disaster turned into a fairytale."

Trevain returned her hug gently, resting his chin on the top of her head. "I don't care much about living longer, but I'm just thankful I get to live all of those years with you. I thought I had screwed things up for good. I promise I will make up for how terrible I was."

"Of course you will. I have an army to keep you in line," she said. She did not want to pull away, but she knew that she should. She stepped back and took his hand to lead him into the splendor of Adlivun. "Let us go meet your grandmother. I should warn you in advance that Visola will probably give you some sort of threatening speech about how she would not hesitate to shoot you again. Then she will proceed to demonstrate the way her rifle works."

"I'm looking forward to it," he said, kissing her hand. He suddenly paused, holding her at arms' length and looking earnestly into her face. "Aazuria—I need to apologize for some of the awful things I said. I know that you weren't responsible for the deaths of my men. I know you tried to save Arnav, and if I had listened to you he would not have been placed in danger." He sighed. "Also, you rescued both my mother and Callder. I should not have wrongfully accused you; I know you didn't take my family from me."

"We do not have to speak of that now," she said, reaching out to caress his cheek.

"Yes, we do. Somehow, everything that came out of my mouth that day was the opposite from what I really meant. Aazuria, you have reunited me with my loved ones. In you and your sisters I have found even more family. You have given me access to a heritage more mind-blowing than anything I could have imagined. You have reunited me with all the courage and hope I thought I'd lost along with my youth."

His words and manner reminded her of the nobility she had seen in him from their very first meeting. She gazed at him lovingly, thinking that he had not really changed at all. He only saw himself differently now, and it was closer to the way she saw him.

Perhaps the issue had been his discord and disharmony with his surroundings. Perhaps now that he was where he was meant to be, all would be well. But he was still apologizing.

"Aazuria..." On an impulse, he stepped back and looked at her gratefully before bowing forward from the waist. He held the position for several seconds of sincerity before straightening. He met her eyes with an intent gaze.

"You have reunited me with myself."

Available now, Book 2 in the
Sacred Breath Series...

Fathoms of Forgiveness

By Nadia Scrieva

There is no divorce in the undersea kingdom of Adlivun. Marriage is a bond that lasts until death—even if death comes in several centuries, and in that time your spouse happens to become your sworn enemy. This is the conflict that General Visola Ramaris faces when she learns that the mighty Vachlan is behind the attacks on her kingdom. She has sworn to protect Adlivun with her life, but long ago, she also swore to love and honor her husband...

Chapter 1: Tremendously Effective Threatening

"If you ever attempt to harm her, I swear on the souls of my Viking ancestors that I will not hesitate to shoot you again."

He swallowed. "I believe you... grandma."

Visola snorted at being called this. She moved her slender fingers up to fiddle with the barrel of the rifle on her back. "Young man," she almost sneered. "Don't you dare think that just because I'm now aware that you're my grandson anything is going to change between us. I have been Aazuria's defender for five hundred years, and she is more than a job to me. She is my friend, she is my mentor, she is my monarch, and she is at the top of my list of females I would totally experiment with if I ever happen to develop lesbian curiosities. The last time I shot you? Consider it a warning spank on the bottom. Next time I won't be so forgiving."

Trevain lifted a hand to scratch under his ear sheepishly. This encounter was not going as smoothly as he had hoped. He glanced at Aazuria, who only gave him half of a shrug (one of her shoulders had been badly injured) and a half-encouraging smile. He still was not accustomed to the changed appearance of his fiancée. Aazuria's snowy-white hair had been garnished with dozens of strands of freshwater pearls, and gathered into a stylish side-ponytail which hung over her good shoulder. He could not look into her newly cerulean eyes without feeling a small jolt of electricity travel through him. It was silly and superficial that the melanin draining from her body would have such a profound effect on him, but it was what they represented that thrilled him most: her true self was bared to him, all her secrets exposed in her new skin.

They would be married soon, but not soon enough for his liking.

He realized that he felt a bit jealous of his grandmother; he wished he could have been at Aazuria's side for five hundred years. The loyal bond between the women was so fierce that he could hardly understand or relate to it. He had never loved anyone that hard, or for that long. There was his younger brother Callder whom he had taken care of for most of his life, but that relationship had been strained even at its best. As Trevain beheld Aazuria's stately posture he realized he was hoping to learn what it was like to be devoted to someone for centuries. He was only a normal almost-fifty-year-old man, and not too long ago he had considered himself elderly. How quickly everything had changed.

Aazuria sent him a puzzled smile, and he realized that he had been staring at her, lost in thought. He cleared his throat before turning back to Visola. "I'm very sorry to have stolen your woman, grandma." He was lying. He was not really sorry.

"Okay, cool it with the 'grandma' shtick. It's making me uncomfortable. Just call me 'General' for now." Visola grimaced. It was a peculiar situation, because the red-haired warrior woman still looked like she was in her twenties. "For the record," she said, "I'm completely straight, and so is Aazuria, but I was just trying to demonstrate the unparalleled breadth and intensity of my love for her. She is as close to me as my own sister—and my own sister is my *identical twin*, in case you haven't noticed!"

"I noticed," Trevain said, glancing at the other green-eyed redhead in the room. The quiet doppelganger was leaning against a wall with her arms crossed, rolling her eyes at her sister's temper and unobtrusively observing the conversation. He feared having to deal with another overbearing and aggressive matriarch like Visola. (One was truly enough.) However, his curiosity and politeness won out, and he extended his hand in greeting to the woman in the shadows. "We haven't been introduced."

The woman straightened and moved towards him to accept his greeting. "I am Sionna," she said simply. He was immediately surprised by the difference in her demeanor. Although she was a duplicate of Visola, her expression was infinitely calmer, and her voice was infinitely more tranquil. It was impossible that anyone would confuse the two sisters after a few seconds of hearing each of them speak. Once Sionna clasped his hand, she seemed to realize that it was not affectionate enough, and she smiled and gave him a gentle hug. "I'm delighted to meet you. Aazuria has told us great things, but some of us did not believe them." She glanced at her sister dryly as she said this, momentarily forgetting that she had been just as suspicious and disapproving.

"Should I have believed her, Sio?" Visola immediately snapped. "He did try to hurt her. Several times. If I hadn't been there..."

"I doubt he really meant to... but it does not matter. The past is in the past," Sionna said to her sister. She turned back to Trevain with a warm smile. "Don't bother calling me great-aunt. That would be strange. Technically I have the same DNA as your grandmother, so I could be considered—oh, never mind. I sometimes ramble on and on about everything biology-related, so just stop me if I get boring. You may call me Auntie Sio if you like. That's what your mum used to call me when she was a wee thing."

Trevain was a bit surprised at the thought of his mother being young; he had never known anyone from his mother's side of the family. Now that he was in Adlivun, he could fill in the pieces of his life that had always been missing. "It's great to meet you, Auntie Sio."

Visola frowned. "Don't get too cozy with him, sis. He may have our blood, but he was not raised among us. We have no idea what large, crucial fragments of common sense he's lacking. He put my little girl in an insane asylum for forty years!"

"Psychiatric hospital," he corrected, but he had lowered his voice and head shamefully.

Aazuria stepped in then, seeing his discomfort. She slipped her arm around him gently. "This has been a rather touching family reunion. Thank you both for so warmly welcoming Trevain."

"Welcoming?" he asked her in an undertone. "Warmly?"

"Darn, I forgot to pop a fruitcake in the oven." Visola said, snapping her fingers. "I was too busy winning a war." When Trevain sent Aazuria an awkward look, Visola cheerfully took her rifle off her back and pointed it at Trevain. "Hey, grandson, do you want to see how my underwater assault rifle works?"

"No, thank you." He rubbed his arm, remembering the impact of the previous bullet which she had shot between the bones of his forearm. The wound had not completely healed, but he knew that he had deserved that bullet. Long after the scar had faded, it would still be depressing to remember his own actions which had earned him the sniping from his grandmother.

"She's just bluffing," Sionna informed him. "That particular gun fires a heavy tungsten dart and it's only meant for shooting underwater—it doesn't aim as well in the air due to different dynamics."

"Don't tell him that!" Visola hissed at her sister. She moved forward, placing the muzzle directly in front of his face. "Can't miss from this range. I will shoot you, kid. I will shoot you in a much more painful location than before." As she said this, she glanced down at his nether regions and wiggled her eyebrows menacingly. Visola's threatening stare had been expertly honed over several generations of threatening, and it was tremendously effective.

"Uh, I…" Trevain took a step back warily.

Aazuria could not hold back a chuckle. She gently elbowed her husband-to-be. "Do not worry so. Your grandmother is the most terrifying thing in all of Adlivun. That is why she is my undefeated general."

"She still has a gun pointed at my face," Trevain said matter-of-factly.

"Oh, sweetie. Forgive my impolite sister," Sionna said, putting her hand on the weapon's barrel and lowering it. "She's just very, very new to being a grandmother. Just give her some time, Trevain, and she will warm up to you."

"I'm warming up to him already," Visola said with a frosty smile.

"I can see that," Trevain muttered.

"Dear, how about we check on your mother and Callder?" Aazuria asked, trying to ease the tension in the air. "Sionna will give you a tour of the infirmary."

"Sounds great," Trevain said. His head had jerked towards Aazuria at the mention of his younger brother, and he was fairly confident that if he had been a dog his ears would have perked up in recognition of a word that he was particularly fond of. Trevain had not seen his brother in weeks, and he had missed the drunken lout much more than he thought he ever would.

Poor Callder. The Coast Guard had declared him dead months ago.

Chapter 2: My Boat Exploded

"When you said that the commoners lived in 'volcanic caves' I imagined... well, I imagined plain old caves," Trevain said, looking around in awe as they navigated the ornate corridors.

"They are caves, are they not?" Aazuria asked in confusion.

"Yes, but they're..." he looked around, trying to find the words. "They're..."

"Did you think we lived in primitive Neolithic dwellings with stick figures decorating the walls?" she asked him with amusement. Her indigo eyes and silvery hair glistened in the firelight of the gilded candelabras they passed.

"I just didn't imagine *this!* I feel like I'm walking through the hallways of the Palace of Versailles."

Aazuria nodded once, not missing a beat in her brisk stride. "That structure is exactly what our designs are based on. My family moved here from Europe around the same time that Versailles was being expanded. It was the popular palatial style, and Papa was partial to it."

Trevain shook his head, smiling. "I have to admit that when your sisters first told me about your underwater world, I didn't expect such a high quality of life. Libraries, schools, mines, marketplaces and hospitals. You're pretty much self-subsistent. Growing acres of mushrooms and farming huge pools of fish and domesticated manatees—which, by the way, are delicious."

"We even have a natural reserve for a tame, lovable creature that humans hunted to extinction everywhere else. Have you heard of Steller's sea-cow?" Aazuria asked him. When he shook his head, she smiled. "Of course, like land-dwellers, our people still fish and hunt for sport and for delicacies, but we try to respect the purity of the Arctic waters and sustainability of life here. We are a very independent people, with hardly any trade or commerce between the various undersea nations."

"This is all so mind-blowing. I have always fished so close to these islands, and I had no clue all of this was under here," he said with wonder. He turned to glance at her again, observing the proud silhouette of her nose and chin. "If I had known that such treasures existed, I would have gone hunting for them in my youth."

"Do not even begin lamenting your youth again. You are but one twelfth of my age!" she said, shaking her head. "Your own home is of comparable grandeur, just with a modern layout. Besides, you know that what is mine is now yours to share." She glanced at him, and saw that he was looking at her with admiration. She had misunderstood. He did not mean the treasures of her kingdom. She felt her cheeks flush with heat—she knew that her blush was exponentially more visible through her now-pale cheeks.

"I just wish I had met you sooner," he said softly.

A smile came to her lips. "Each meeting occurs at the precise moment for which it was meant. Usually, when it will have the greatest impact on our lives."

"We're here," Sionna called out to the couple. She and her sister had been walking ahead of them and conversing quietly. The candlelit corridor extended out into the infirmary. "We have unusually high numbers of wounded at the moment due to the recent battle..."

"And it was only the first wave," Visola added with a frown. "We have to get everyone healed and start preparing immediately for the next. It could be at any time."

Sionna nodded. "The infirmary isn't usually this chaotic and crowded, but we have some of our allies from Japan here as well. The Clan of the Ningyo."

"Ningyo?" Trevain asked curiously as he followed the twins. "Like the weird fish-people from the folklore?"

Sionna regarded the ceiling with exasperation. "Please, Trevain. You're an intelligent young man. Just forget everything you know about sea mythology. They're exactly like us: just people, no tails."

"They have incredible fighting skill though," Visola said. "Many of them trained with the samurai. They still follow the code and teach it to their young. So be respectful when you run into them. *Especially* Queen Amabie! You want to bow deeply when you greet her. She was known and feared by the samurai—speaking of which, her millennial is coming up in a few years, and we're going to have a huge bash. I have no idea what to get her... what do you get for the queen who has everything?"

"Her millennial?" Trevain asked in disbelief.

"Her thousandth birthday," Aazuria explained to him. His face registered surprise. How could he possibly bow deeply enough to honor a thousand-year-old samurai queen?

"Intensive care is through those doors," Sionna said, pointing. "If you ever need me and I'm not at the palace, this is usually where you will be able to find me. There are a few other wings over there, but Callder is in... hey! Zuri, get back here."

As soon as Sionna had turned away from the intensive care wing, Aazuria had tried to slip away from them. She paused and turned back to face Sionna with a distressed look on her face. "I need to see her," she whispered. "I held Elandria while she almost died in my arms."

Trevain understood her position, having recently gone through the experience of believing his own brother dead as well. He still urgently needed to see Callder's face for confirmation that it had all been a lie. He moved to Aazuria's side and slipped a hand around her waist comfortingly. She sighed and leaned her head against his shoulder. It was her injured sister, Elandria, who had helped him to cope with his loss, however blissfully false it had ended up being. Elandria was a quiet girl who never spoke with her voice, but only used sign language—despite having the angelic voice of a professionally trained opera singer. He loved her like she was already his own sister, and he could not imagine life without her. She had to pull through, or Aazuria would be inconsolable and he would be devastated.

Sionna frowned. "Elandria only just got out of surgery. Her right ventricle was damaged. She has all kinds of tubes placed in her, and an apparatus helping her breathe. We need to allow her to rest, and I won't allow any contaminates in the water. She lost a lot of blood, and she can't risk infection. Aazuria, trust me. Just be patient for now."

Aazuria closed her eyes and nodded. "Fine. Take us to Callder."

The twins began moving through the infirmary, and Trevain followed with his arm still around Aazuria. He observed as many women in simple green dresses rushed around, carrying various implements. It was the strangest hospital he had ever seen; it looked more like an exotic luxury spa. Picturesque hot springs were scattered throughout the massive candlelit room with mossy paths between them.

"Where are all the patients?" Trevain asked in confusion.

"Submerged," Sionna explained. "In individual 'pods' of water. The minerals have healing properties that expedite recovery. That's not hogwash either, it's fact. By the way, Aazuria should be soaking her shoulder."

"This little stab wound?" Aazuria asked, trying to be flippant. Her tight grip on Trevain's arm betrayed to him that underneath her carefree words she was rather tense. "Why bother healing it up when I will surely just get impaled in the same spot again as soon as it is better?"

"That was hilarious," Visola said with a grin. "Stabbed *twice* by the same enemy! We should name the whole battle after that. 'The Shoulder Skirmish.' Or perhaps 'Shoulder Scuffle' sounds better. "

"Wonderful. I shall be mocked for this mistake for the rest of my breathing life," Aazuria said. She lifted a hand to absentmindedly prod the bandages around her wound. Talking about it seemed to make it hurt more.

"Adding insult to injury is my sister's specialty," Sionna said. "We're here." She turned into a corridor and threw another set of double doors open.

An unexpected sight greeted them. Callder was bare-chested, with bandages wrapping much of his chest and midsection, while two nurses fawned over him. One had her lips attached to his, while the other sat in his lap with her dress hiked up around her waist.

"For Sedna's sake!" Sionna shouted, throwing her hands into the air. "Both of you! Who authorized coitus with the patients? You're both fired!"

The nurses immediately ripped themselves away from Callder and arranged their clothing before facing Sionna shamefully.

"Please, Doctor Ramaris... he is just a lonely war hero..."

Sionna extended an incredulous finger towards Callder. "Him? A war hero? Is that what he's been telling you?"

The other nurse turned to Aazuria, curtseying deeply. "My dear Princess!" she pleaded, knowing that Aazuria had a reputation for being far more merciful than the Ramaris twins. "Take pity on us! He was so charming..."

"No. There are *dozens* of war victims in need of assistance," Aazuria said evenly. She did not raise her voice, but it was laced with authority. "This is no time for dallying. You both will go at once to aid the other nurses. Once the volume of patients is reduced, your employment here is terminated."

"Yes, Princess," they both said softly.

"And your employment with me begins," Visola added with a gleeful nod. "You both have been recruited to Adlivun's military. Yay! Now get back to work."

The two nurses scurried from the room, their heads lowered in embarrassment. Aazuria felt a small pang of remorse for them—there were hardly any men in Adlivun, thanks to the destructive impact of her father's long reign as king. She observed Callder's state of undress and she had to conceal a smirk. She found him as handsome as his older brother, but decidedly more coarse and jagged around the edges; both men were almost impossible to resist.

"Now why'd you all have to go and do that?" Callder complained, pointing at his bandages with a pout. "Can't you see I'm in need of some serious sexual healin'? Those ladies were just..." Callder trailed off when he saw his fourth visitor. He slowly raised himself from where he was seated. He took several shaky steps forward, with his hand clutching his bandaged chest. "Big brother?"

Trevain felt tears prick the back of his eyes. He shook his head and cleared his throat gruffly. He did not know what to say. It was true; the Coast Guard had been wrong. The death certificate needed to be ripped up into tiny shreds and cheerfully trampled. His little brother was really alive and well. Very well. He looked at Callder affectionately, trying to think of the appropriate greeting for this situation. He uttered the first three tender words which came to mind.

"You whoring buffoon!"

Callder crossed the room as quickly as he could, and ignoring his injury, he seized his brother in a manly embrace. "I'm so sorry, Trevain. I should have listened to you. I'm so sorry."

Trevain hugged him back strongly, needing to feel that he was really made of flesh and blood. "You fool," he said, trying to fight back his tears. "Callder, you foolish... fool!"

"I love you too," Callder said earnestly. He winced, but did not complain that Trevain's arms were crushing his still-healing ribs.

Sionna and Visola exchanged small smiles with each other. Aazuria looked at them, and she could see that they both were thrilled about the newest additions to their family. Although the Ramaris twins were tough on the exterior, they were the most loving siblings that she knew underneath their crass manner. She turned back to the embracing men, and felt emotion brim up inside of her. It seemed that the bond between Ramaris siblings had stayed strong throughout the generations, even though the Murphy brothers had a different name and overseas upbringing. How uncanny it was that the relationship between Trevain and Callder was so similar to that between Visola and Sionna, even though they had not grown up around them to be influenced. *Nature is powerful,* Aazuria thought to herself. *Nurture is important in determining the path we take, but nature is what defines us, and defines exactly how we will traverse that path…*

"Where's mom?" Trevain asked Callder. "I thought she'd be here with you."

"She's sleeping in the hot springs," Callder said, gesturing to the pool. He punched Trevain in the arm and grinned. "Hey, did you know we can breathe underwater? How cool is that? And all this time you had mom locked up because you thought she was crazy…"

"Callder, my boat exploded."

"What?" Callder frowned. "How? Well, that's no big deal, right? You have insurance."

Trevain closed his eyes.

"Hey, what's wrong big brother?" Callder hit him again playfully. "We'll just get a new boat with a better name than the stupid *Fishin' Magician.* You know what would be epic? Let's call it *The Master Baiter.*"

A burst of laughter shot out of Visola's throat. Aazuria bit her lip to conceal the giggle that was threatening to erupt; she knew that this was no time for laughter. Sionna's eyes had widened. "Whoa. This is unbelievable; he has Viso's sense of humor. It skipped a generation."

Trevain opened his eyes. "Callder, the boat exploded with the *whole crew aboard.*"

"No." Callder's face darkened. He took a step back from his brother, and looked him squarely in the eyes. "No. No! You'd better not be saying what I think you're saying. Were you on the boat when it happened? Is… is everyone okay?"

Trevain shook his head. His fists clenched and unclenched. "Only Brynne survived."

"Thank God!" Callder said, throwing his head back in relief. He exhaled a huge gush of wind. Then he realized how callous his words sounded and he cleared his throat. "I mean… that's horrible. It really is horrible, but I am just so, so glad Brynne is okay…"

"Leander. Arnav. Doughlas. Edwin. Ujarak. The Wade brothers." Trevain slowly listed the names between breaths, gritting his teeth. "They're all gone."

Callder shook his head, swallowing. "I guess we're way past decimation now, huh? I wonder if Arnav would say we've been obliterated or annihilated. Which one would be more correct?"

"Neither," Visola said firmly. "You are alive, young man. You were pitted against a mighty enemy, and you survived. You joined with us, your mother's people, and what you are is *victorious*. We have succeeded in defending ourselves, despite suffering losses—the first wave of the Clan of Zalcan has fallen."

Callder was carefully observing the woman who had spoken. Captivated by the gorgeous redhead, he cleared his throat and tried to put on his best charming smile. "Victorious, huh? Well, I can assure you of one thing, you beautiful sex goddess. Although I may have been harpooned like the wild animal that I am, every part of my body is still fully functioning. I'm just as virile as ever—and I can take you (and your lovely sister if she's interested) to heights of pleasure you've never imagined! So if you're looking to do a little celebratin' of this great victory…"

Both of Visola's eyebrows lifted in amusement. Aazuria placed a hand on her bandaged shoulder, looking around a bit awkwardly. Sionna screwed up her face and made a gagging noise.

"Callder…" Trevain said with a sigh, placing a palm against his forehead. "You're not going to believe this, but that woman you're shamelessly trying to get into bed with is actually our grandmother."

"*What?*" Callder erupted in laughter. "Yeah, 'cause I have a grandma who's younger than I am with the juiciest pair of tits and tightest little ass…"

A small gray-haired and wrinkled woman had just shakily raised herself out of the hot spring in time to hear her son speak these words. She immediately wanted to sink back down and bury her face in the sand. "Ugh," Alcyone said, cringing in horror. "Callder, that's disgusting! That's my mother you're speaking to. Mama, please forgive him, he doesn't know. Apologize this instant, Callder!"

"Are you kidding?" Callder saw that the expression on Alcyone's wrinkled face was humorless. He looked from his mother to his brother in disbelief and confusion. "You're both joking… how is it possible?"

"It's okay, kid," said Visola winking at Callder. She approached him and lightly slapped him on the bottom. "I'd rather be called 'sex goddess' than 'grandma' any day. I'm way more accustomed to it. I didn't even know I was a grandmother until a few days ago, but I've known I was a sex goddess for a few centuries."

"Mama!" Alcyone complained in a dismayed whine. "Stop flirting with my son!"

"Sorry, Alcie. He started it." Visola looked at Callder curiously before poking his cheek. "Hey, I like this one. He's got spunk. A bit slouchy though…"

"What? I have no clue what the hell is going on here," Callder admitted blankly, "but I do gather that I've done something wrong, which is a familiar and comforting feeling."

"Straighten yourself!" Visola commanded in her General-voice. Callder found himself following her command without really intending to. Visola walked around Callder slowly, sizing him up. "I'm going to train both of you boys to be warriors in the Ramaris tradition. Callder will shadow Elandria's personal guard once she is healed."

"Warrior? Sounds like fun," Callder said. "I know how to use a sword—mom signed me and Trevain up for fencing lessons when we were little."

"Aw, really?" Visola asked her daughter. "That's so smart of you, baby." Although Alcyone looked like an elderly woman, Visola still spoke to her as though she was younger—which she was.

"He's always had a passion for it," Alcyone explained. "He is quite skilled and relaxed with a sword in his hand."

"It's because I've had so much practice," Callder joked.

"Okay, Callder. You're going to have to cool it with the masturbation jokes," Trevain cautioned in a fatherly tone of voice. "You're in the presence of a princess."

Callder turned to the white haired woman who had remained rather quiet throughout the conversation. He studied her face, and thought that she looked vaguely familiar. "That's right, those pretty nurses called you 'Princess' and begged you for mercy. Mom explained to me that this was a different type of place with an old-fashioned monarchy. I just want you to know how awesome I think it is that you're powerful and stuff. People respect you." He approached her, taking her hand and kissing it while bowing. "You're also ravishingly lovely, Miss Princess of Adlivun—are you single?"

Aazuria smiled. "I am engaged to your brother."

"*What?*" Callder exclaimed. "Oh, snap! Trevain is boinking a princess!"

"Boinking?" Alcyone shrieked, pointing a wrinkled finger at her son. "Callder! Show some respect."

Sionna had brought a hand up to her neck in horror. "Good Sedna, preserve me. He speaks exactly like Visola. I may be forced to slice my own head off if I must listen to more blasphemous vocabulary."

A deep blush had come to Aazuria's cheeks, but she kept smiling. Trevain had been studying this exchange angrily—he did not like the way his brother held Aazuria's hand a little too long. He also felt a pang of jealousy at the amused look on his fiancée's face. She was normally so stern and impassive, but when it came to his brother's antics she always became too lenient and forgiving.

"When did this happen?" Callder asked eagerly. "Jeez, how long was I unconscious? Tell me everything! How did you two meet?"

"I should thank *you* for that, Callder," she responded warmly. "It was you who introduced me to Trevain. I am Aazuria Vellamo—do you not remember me?"

"No way," he said, stumbling backwards. "The... the stripper? Undina? But... that's impossible. You don't look anything like her. She had black hair and dark eyes... but your face! Yes, your face is exactly the same. You're Undina. You were a princess going incognito?"

"I chose the stage name Undina because it was my mother's name," Aazuria said softly. "She was the descendant of a Celtic warrior clan."

"Wow." Callder's brow furrowed as he turned to his brother. "If this is true, Trevain, then you owe me big time for making you talk to her. Imagine that I hadn't forced you to get off your lazy, antisocial ass and talk to the pretty girl? You would have been miserable and alone forever. Say it. Say that I'm your hero!"

When Trevain frowned and his lips parted to protest, Visola jumped in. "No way! It was all my idea," she said with a grin. "I needed money for weapons and I chose to work in that bar. Who knew that a little strip club in Soldotna would reunite long lost relatives? Regardless, I should get the credit for this."

"I give all my gratitude to Princess Aazuria," Alcyone said softly, dipping into a solemn curtsy. "Zuri killed her own father to make Adlivun safe for us. She freed me from my white-walled prison and brought me back to my family and my best friend. While Callder was unconscious I had a chance to catch up with Corallyn, and it just reduced me to tears. I hadn't spoken to her in sixty years, but it was like not a single day had passed. This is where I belong. This is where I need to be."

"Corallyn?" Callder asked. "Aazuria's little kid sister who wasn't even a pre-teen? I'm so confused. Mom spent all of yesterday just explaining to me where we are and why I woke up underwater. It took her hours to convince me that I wasn't dreaming or dead. This is a lot of information to take in all at once."

Trevain put a hand on his brother's shoulder. "Vikings, Samurai, and Celts. I know it seems outrageous, but let's just go with it."

"My boys need to learn sign language so they can communicate with us in the water," Alcyone said.

"We'll assign them private tutors," Sionna said. "They'll be fine."

Visola nodded. "I hate to have to leave my two favorite new grandsons," she said, "but I have an important meeting at the palace. Are you coming, Aazuria?"

"Of course. We have serious matters at hand, and thousands of bodies to dispose of."

Chapter 3: Napoleon of the Undersea

"…And he implied that in exchange for his help getting those guns off the black market, he wanted me to sleep with him," Visola said, taking a long swig of the warm sake, "so I did."

"No!" Queen Amabie gasped. "Earnestly, Visola?"

"Why would I lie to you? You're my hero," Visola said. She exhaled ecstatically. "I just can't believe that in all the mayhem of battle you managed to remember to bring my drink!"

Aazuria had left the war council seven beverages ago. Once the conversation had gone from concerning the good of the nation to drunkenly catching up on the gossip of the last fifty years, she had excused herself to see to other affairs. She knew that her general had a special fondness for Queen Amabie, and she thought that the two women should have some alone time.

"What are allies for, good friend? Besides, you know I only brought my army to help defend your nation because I wanted a rematch. I need to prove that I *can* win against you in a drinking competition. You have wiped the floor with me in days of yore, but it shall not happen again, General."

"My power is constant like the waves," Visola boasted with a smirk.

Amabie frowned and leaned forward keenly. "Truly, Visola. How could you sell yourself like that? Is it not difficult for a weapons master to do such a thing? You are so connected to your body."

"Why would be difficult for me?" Visola asked, with a halfhearted smile "Over the years I have come to see my body as little more than a weapon. An inadequate one at that! If I can sell the temporary access to one inadequate weapon and use the proceeds to purchase ownership of more effective weapons which will protect the lives of innocent people and their innocent bodies, then I think that's a great deal."

"Your logic is as flawless as your firearms are mighty." Queen Amabie studied her friend's face carefully. "This is about Vachlan, is it not? Everything you do has always been about him, Visola."

Visola suddenly found the floor very fascinating. Her fingers played nervously with the unicorn trident attached to her hip. After several seconds of silence, she reached for her sake, and doused her throat with it. The warmth of the drink was comforting. It even inspired a creative response.

"If what you mean by that is I went to extra, possibly unnecessary measures because I thought he might be the one attacking us, then you are correct. He might have sent a first wave led by that crazy woman, Atargatis, but he almost certainly knew she would fail. He was behind this all along—he sells his loyalties to the highest bidder, and now he is Zalcan's little bitch. Shouldn't even a mercenary have morals? That's the textbook definition of a whore!"

"It is all okay, Visola…"

"I do all I have ever done for Adlivun, for Aazuria, and my daughter. I would do anything to stop him! Anything; whatever it took to defeat him. I would do much worse than anything I have ever done. So, yes. It's all about Vachlan"

"That is not what I mean, dear," Amabie said kindly. "I am not speaking to the warrior in you. I am speaking to the woman."

"Then you are speaking to no one at all." Visola looked up at her friend with vacant eyes. "Not much of that remains."

"I saw her yesterday," Amabie said, reaching out to stroke her friend's wild red hair. "You knew that we were supposed to have a formal, public execution for the leader of the enemy forces. It is hallowed tradition, the formal drowning in blood. Yet all Atargatis had to do was mention that she had slept with your husband, and you threw a knife into her eye. Do you not think that was a tiny bit impatient of you, Visola?"

Visola slowly nodded. "I'm sorry, Queen Amabie. I know. I know it was rash. I'm so sorry… I just lost it and I couldn't control…"

"You were just being a woman."

"I always am when I make my greatest mistakes!" Visola said fiercely. "I mustn't allow it any longer." Her eyes narrowed with focus as she declared, "I am a warrior, first and foremost. I cannot afford to make any more foolish decisions based on my heart."

Amabie observed her for a moment before responding. "We may be the fortunate ones with the gift of dual breath," she said gently, "but yet we are human. We cannot sacrifice all that we are by nature to fill the artificial roles society has created for us."

"Oh, it's not artificial," Visola said, shaking her head. "I refuse to believe that. If my position at the head of Adlivun's army were completely arbitrary; if my birth into a warrior family was merely coincidence; if my heritage and destiny were not somehow intricately linked... who would I be?"

"You would be Visola."

"No! I would be nothing. I am only what I am, and nothing more! You—you were meant to be the Queen of the Ningyo. There is no one more suited to that role than you. It is in your blood and your spirit... just as Aazuria is meant to be our leader. We can all be only what we are."

"Darling, you are burying yourself in your job and sacrificing your identity. The only reason that you are at odds with yourself as a woman is because you keep shutting that part of you down and pushing it away. It is not healthy. You are building up all this anxiety and tension..."

"Oh, don't be silly, Queen Amabie!" Visola said with a carefree shrug and smile. "I'm perfectly fine..."

"You have not been fine since Vachlan left you."

Visola's shoulders slumped suddenly forward, as though the puppeteer who had been controlling her had dropped the strings. "Did you hear what Atargatis said? Vachlan thinks that I cheated on him. That's why he left when I was pregnant with Alcie. He thought... but *why* would he think that? How *dare* he think that?"

"King Kyrosed Vellamo planted a lot of strange ideas into people's heads," Amabie answered. "He was a manipulative bastard. Do not blame yourself for this. It is not Vachlan's fault either..."

"Two hundred years apart. Two hundred years he has been my sworn enemy. He has joined forces with the Clan of Zalcan, the worst brutes who breathe beneath! He has killed thousands, he has destroyed nations. He commands legions, and intends to throw them all against me... all because of a lie told by Kyrosed?"

"It is almost sweet in a way," Queen Amabie said pensively.

"What?" Visola asked in confusion. "My husband wiped out a whole kingdom under the Bermuda Triangle. He tried to do the same thing to you in the Dragon's Triangle. Now he's coming here, to finish what he's started. He's been practicing a systematic methodology. Now he's ready to ruin Adlivun too—he's ready to crush me. How is that sweet?"

"It demonstrates how much he loves you. Your betrayal, although only a false idea, was so intolerable and unspeakable to him that it drove him to insanity."

"Very sweet indeed," Visola said, gripping her ceramic cup tightly as she ingested more sake.

"Truly, Visola. No man or woman dedicates their life to a vendetta of revenge upon the object of their affection *unless* that affection was once so great that it was the crimson burning sun of their whole existence."

Visola paused for a moment. "That's it? That's the silver lining? That's your positive spin on things? You think telling me you believe that he is raising hell because he *loves me* is going to make me look on the bright side and gain perspective?"

"Is it working?" Amabie asked, lifting a thin, arched brow.

"Damn you!" Visola said, furiously. "Of course it's working! But only because you have gotten me exceptionally drunk."

"I told you I would win one of our drinking contests someday," Amabie said cheerfully.

"I am easy to defeat when I am overemotional," Visola admitted. "That is why Vachlan has been two steps ahead of me this whole time. I am fairly certain he is going to kick my well-toned and rather shapely ass."

"No! I do not appreciate the tone in your voice," Amabie said sternly. "You almost sound like you feel you deserve his wrath. You sound like you are welcoming this!"

"Perhaps I am," Visola grumbled softly. "I do deserve it. Remember my father? He always used to make these jokes about being psychic... having this great mystical intuition. When Vachlan and I travelled to Bimini to inform my father of our engagement, my father told us that he could not approve. He said he saw only heartache in the future for us. Our marriage would not last; he said I needed a man who would follow me, not one who would compete with me for control. Vachlan was too strong."

"It is necessary for a man to be powerful in his own right, yet to always honor his wife's decisions. My husband was like this."

"Your husband was a marvelous man," Visola said mournfully.

"He was always right beside you, always helping and supporting you. He would never do the dishonorable things Vachlan did; he would never have left you when you were *pregnant*. When he vanished, I nearly lost my mind… Aazuria took care of me, and she probably saved my life. She told me that my baby would love me more than Vachlan ever had, and more than anyone ever could; because that was the way a child loved their mother. She was right. Having Alcie made everything better, and made everything worth it. I spent years searching her face for signs of Vachlan. I would see his ghost in her expressions when she was happiest. When she smiled so wide that her cheeks dimpled. Those proud high cheekbones of hers, and her angular jaw. It was like having a little part of him still with me, you know? My little Alcie… everything was fine until I lost her too."

"You have found her once more, Visola. As mothers, we all must deal with the pain of separation from our children. Most men do not feel this connection to their young as strongly. Pain can either break you down, or give you great strength."

"I'm not sure whether I experienced the former or latter." Visola gave her friend a small smile before taking another drink of sake.

"You wonder this?" Amabie asked with a laugh. "Ask anyone whether you are strong, Visola. Ask anyone whether they know anyone stronger than you. Then you shall know."

"Maybe. I really wish I were more like my sister," Visola said. "When we were little, I used to lie in bed beside her for hours before we fell asleep. I would look at her, and think about how strange it was that she looked exactly like me. I would put my hands and feet beside hers and search for the slightest differences." Visola stared off at the wall, lost in remembrance. "Most of all though, I would wonder if her thoughts were the same as mine. If her dreams were the same as mine. I had no way of knowing. Did we both have the same aches and pains at the same time, the same pleasures and joys?" Visola refilled their cups. "Now I know we don't. Sionna has all the light inside of her, and I have the darkness. She has all the purity, and I have the dirt. She likes to talk about how we were once both the same cell. Well, when that cell cleaved itself in half, it may have resulted in identical chromosomes, but the soul… the very soul of that cell did not separate identically. She got all the good stuff. She's a fucking paragon, and I am a… parasite."

"No, dear friend. Sionna may be a paragon, but if so, you are a *paradigm*. You are the quintessence of everything a victorious general, friend, and mother should be…"

"Mother!" Visola barked. "I ruined my daughter's life! Because of me she was in a mental institution for forty years…"

"And because of you she fell in love and gave birth to two strong sons. Both of whom are now in training to carry on your family's great tradition! Everything happens for a reason, Visola. You cannot deny this. Every decision you make cannot be the right one, but as long as the positive repercussions balance with or outnumber the negative ones, you are making progress. Progress is all we can hope for, and it is what you are best at achieving."

"You are just saying that…"

"No!" Queen Amabie said, standing up and raising herself to her full height. She swayed slightly on her feet, indicating that she was a bit tipsy. "You are like the great Empress Jingū!"

"Who?" Visola asked curiously.

"Empress Jingū was a great Japanese warrior who conquered Korea after her husband died! Legend has it that she battled for three years while carrying her husband's unborn child—she waited until she was victorious before giving birth."

"Impressive," Visola mumbled.

"Cheer up! You, my friend are the Boudicca of the Deep! Our Joan of Arc, our Tomyris…"

"Only as good as the women," Visola lamented.

"No! You are the Napoleon of the Undersea!"

"Not a big fan of Napoleon," Visola said as she fumbled to pour herself more sake.

Queen Amabie's eyebrows creased in thought. "Alexander the Great. Gilgamesh. Genghis Khan. Attila the Hun! Name the warrior, and you are his very equal, his aquatic counterpart."

"Okay. Now I'm feeling a bit better," Visola said with a sniffle. "Not fair. You know how to stroke my ego better than anyone."

"You need to acknowledge your own brilliance. I am lucky to have you as my ally, for I would not want to ever be pitted against you."

"Dawww… I love you, Queen Amabie," Visola said with a sleepy smile. "I wish it changed the fact that Vachlan is going to defeat me."

"Oh, darling. That's the sake talking."

"No, I mean it. I do not have the will or energy anymore. If I could just cast aside all of my memories, I could take him on. If he were anyone else but my husband, I would wipe the floor with him and make him eat his own shit while laughing condescendingly. I would carve my name into his flesh. I would jump rope with his intestines, or wear them as necklaces and bracelets while asking him casually how they looked. I would dance upon…"

"Then do it," Amabie said. "Cast aside your doubt and do it."

Visola reached out and placed her hand on Amabie's hand. She would normally never be so familiar with the woman, but due to her drinking, the lines of courtesy were blurring along with her vision. She blinked and squinted in order to see more clearly, but this only led to the realization that it was her mind which was clouded more than anything. She sighed.

"I can't beat him, Amabie."

Both women were startled when Aazuria burst into the room, dripping wet, her feet pounding the carpet. "Queen Amabie, General Ramaris—have either of you seen Corallyn?"

"Not since yesterday when I killed her evil mother," Visola slurred. "Why?"

"I cannot find her anywhere," Aazuria said, brushing locks of wet, white hair out of her face. Corallyn was her youngest sister, whose body was of childlike proportions, although she was nearing a hundred years in age. "I had the guards sweep the whole palace. She is not in her quarters, nor anywhere else…"

Visola frowned. "Have you checked intensive care? She probably snuck in to see if Elandria was better."

"That was the first place I looked!" Aazuria reached up and grasped her wounded shoulder, battling a bout of pain. Blood was seeping through the bandage due to her vigorous exercise. She was evidently distressed and frustrated by her missing sibling. "What if she ran away? What if she was angry with us?"

"She's probably just sulking in a corner because of the stuff with Atargatis," Visola spoke with a slight slur. "When your mother shows up out of the blue and kills a whole bunch of people, it's never easy to deal with."

Queen Amabie lowered herself carefully to her chair. "Princess Aazuria, some of my elite warriors said that they were heading to your

Mirrored Caves for festivities… to celebrate vanquishing our common enemy. Perhaps your little sister is amongst them?"

"I do not think Corallyn would be celebrating the death of her mother," Aazuria said with a deep frown. There was terror in her eyes. "I feel within me that something is gravely wrong."

Chapter 4: Elegant Crimson Calligraphy

It seemed that all of Adlivun and all of their Ningyo allies were in the Mirrored Caves, dancing, chatting, and enjoying themselves in the water. They had changed out of their armor, and they all wore brightly colored flowing fabrics which floated in the water behind them like the swirling ribbons of rhythmic gymnasts. The Alaskans wore their malachite green while the Japanese wore bright red or white, depending on their rank.

Aazuria swam through the cavernous rooms, frantically searching for her little sister.

Although many of the people in the room did not share the same spoken language, it did not matter. Everyone communicated with their hands in the universal sign language. Speech was a garbled, incoherent burble underwater. The only thing easily discernible was laughter. The sound of distorted, joyous murmurs reached Aazuria's ears from every part of the Mirrored Caves. Her shoulder throbbed as her bone rotated in the joint, swimming quickly through the rooms. Lights bounced off the mirrors, and she was frequently met with her own troubled reflection. She tried to remember the last words she had exchanged with Corallyn, for any clue to where she might be.

"Well, that's just peachy," Corallyn said with her hands on her hips. *"My biological mother tries to kill everyone I love and I'm not allowed to execute her? Why is Visola allowed to do anything she wants?"*

"Hush, Corallyn," Aazuria answered firmly. *"It was for the best that it happened this way. Believe me."*

"Whatever, big sis. Your mother was some majestic lady, so you don't know what it's like…"

Aazuria placed her hands on her sister's shoulders. *"I killed Papa. Now I have to live with that. I do not wish the same for you."*

"He deserved it. He was a…"

"Coral, your mother was not always like this. When I first met her, she was an ambitious, dedicated young performer. The worst villains are created from the kindest people when bad things happen to them."

"So it's all Papa's fault," Corallyn said quietly.

"No. Your mother's actions were her own."

"My actions would have been my own as well!"

"I cannot allow you to make mistakes that you will greatly regret."

Corallyn gritted her teeth. "Fine. Damn you! Go make more smoochies with 'Uncle Trevain.' Damn Visola too! I'm going to sulk in a corner."

Now, which corner could she possibly be sulking in?

Many of the people Aazuria passed, both warriors and civilians, bowed deeply to her and saluted across their chests before congratulating her bravery and sympathy for her shoulder. They offered condolences and wished Elandria a rapid recovery. Aazuria's hands automatically formed the gracious signs necessary to acknowledge all of their kindnesses and pleasantries. Her head nodded, and her mouth smiled, but her eyes remained unsettled and anxious.

Whenever she was engaged by someone who might have known Corallyn, she asked if they had seen her. She described the girl's appearance and small stature to many of the Ningyo warriors, who shook their heads, profusely apologizing and bowing. Aazuria was growing increasingly agitated, and the swarm of celebrating sea-people only added to her frustration. She turned to exit the Mirrored Caves, and found herself swimming directly into someone.

Caring green eyes assessed her hysterical state with concern. She felt a small wave of relief run through her because of his understanding gaze. Aazuria reached out and placed a hand on his arm, as if trying to draw strength from him.

"Did you find her yet?" he asked, slowly and carefully forming the words in sign language. He did not yet have much confidence in speaking with his hands.

"No," Aazuria said, shaking her head. "I am going to check the labyrinth. She could have gotten lost in any of the intricate channels of caves under the Aleutian Islands."

"Wait, Zuri," he signed. He frowned as he moved his thumbs and forefingers, trying to remember all the correct hand formations. "If I understand correctly, these caves stretch out for hundreds of miles... you can't possibly cover all that ground swimming with your injured shoulder! My great-aunt Sionna sent me to tell you that you have to take it easy, and spend some time resting in the infirmary. She seems like she really knows what she's doing."

"I have rested enough. I must find Corallyn," Aazuria insisted, swallowing. She reached up to touch her shoulder gingerly. She felt extreme embarrassment and growing annoyance at the fact that Koraline Kolarevic, the woman who had called herself Atargatis, had managed to stab her in the same location twice. The first time had been with a javelin that had gone clean through her shoulder; Trevain had saved her life by pushing her to the side just in time, or it would have pierced her heart. The second time was in hand-to-hand combat.

"*Your bleeding hasn't even stopped,*" Trevain pointed out, grimacing at her darkened bandages. The blood that had dried on the cloth in the air had not completely washed out in the water. He reached out with his thumb to caress her skin very close to the wound, and he frowned when she winced. "*If this gets…*" He paused, not knowing the signal for 'infected.' He tried to substitute a word. "*If this gets dirty, it could get worse and you could lose your whole arm…*"

"*I will be fine. Sionna gave me a tetanus shot when I was stabbed the first time,*" Aazuria quickly signed to him as she moved through the caves.

He followed her, confused. "*Tetanus?*" he asked, imitating the hand signal she had formed. "*I'm not sure what that is, could you spell it out for me?*"

"*I need to hurry. I am going to pass by the kitchens and collect some basic food to sustain me while I search for her. Can you go to the palace and organize the military to help me search? Your grandmother is drunk, or I would ask you to go to her.*"

Trevain felt nervous as he tried to make sense of her rapid hand motions. "*You want me to organize your military? Why would they listen to me?*"

"*They will. Go at once.*" Aazuria continued swimming through the caves, with long pieces of her dark green dress trailing behind her.

Trevain ignored her command and swam to block her path. He moved his hands in a series of gestures. "*I'm not letting you go off on your own, wounded and emotional. What if you get lost? Rash decisions could make this even worse. Is there a map? Let me come with you.*"

"*I will not get lost,*" she responded, trying to swim around him. "*I have lived here for centuries. I used to play in these caves when I was Corallyn's age.*"

"*Aazuria!*" he responded. "*You're not thinking rationally. We need to weigh our options. What if Coral went back to land? She could be at my house right now. You remember how fond she was of the internet and television.*"

"*This is true,*" Aazuria conceded. Her hands paused for a second in fear. "*Oh, Trevain. I am so worried about her. Could you send Naclana to check and see if she is at your home?"*

Naclana was Aazuria's distant cousin, who served as her messenger. Trevain shook his head. *"I am just as concerned about her safety as you are, but rushing off alone into miles of dark caves isn't going to help the situation. Aazuria, come back to the palace and let's find Naclana and tell him together…"*

"No. If you will not help me, I shall help myself." Aazuria swam around him, rushing past him in a fraction of a second. All he saw was a blur of green and white. He turned, and immediately swam after her, but he could not catch up for several minutes.

By the time he was close enough to speak to her, she had already arrived at the waterless caves in which food was prepared. He was surprised by the true extent of her athleticism, and her tolerance for pain. He could not believe that she could move at all with her injured shoulder. He entered the room after her and climbed the carved stairs just in time to see the cooks saluting and bowing to her.

"I need basic provisions for a trek into the caves. In a watertight bag."

"Yes, Princess Aazuria."

"My youngest sister Corallyn is missing. Can you please pass my orders to the castle guard to dispatch a search party? Also, if you could tell Naclana…"

"Aazuria," Trevain interrupted. "Please. You need to think twice about this."

"Listen, Trevain," she said, turning upon him with a hard look in her eyes. "This is not up for discussion. My sister could be…"

"Princess!" shouted a male voice.

Aazuria was surprised and turned to see her cousin entering the room, dripping wet. "Naclana. Just the person I wanted to see…"

"Corallyn has been abducted," Naclana gasped, as he tried to catch his breath.

Aazuria stared at him for a moment, blankly.

Trevain felt fleeting disbelief. He almost wanted to smile as though it were some sort of joke, but he could see that the messenger was serious. Naclana had always given him the creeps, and now he imagined that he knew why. The man's very presence was a harbinger of danger and disaster. It was painted permanently in the shadows of his grave, heavy expression.

"We just received a ransom note," Naclana said, straightening his posture and giving a half-hearted version of the appropriate salute to his cousin. "From the Clan of Zalcan."

Murmurs of horror rose up from the kitchen staff. Trevain moved to his fiancé's side, and wrapped his arms around her. Aazuria felt the urge to lean against him for support and shut her eyes tightly, but she could not do this with everyone watching. She could not do this at all. The moment she allowed herself to show her weakness, even to herself, it would overcome her and she would lose her composure. She knew that if she had been paying closer attention to Corallyn's whereabouts after the battle, this would not have happened.

"What do they want?" Trevain asked Naclana. "They aim to exchange her for something?"

Aazuria twitched, moving suddenly out of her frozen state. "That's right. A ransom. All is not lost. Anything they want—I will give it to them."

Naclana cleared his throat. "The note was written in Corallyn's blood. Would you like me to read it, Princess?" When Aazuria nodded. He reached into his vest and withdrew a metal cylinder. He uncorked it and pulled out the heavy paper. The demands had been penned in elegant crimson calligraphy.

When the women on the kitchen staff began to cry, Aazuria lifted her hand, and tried to speak soothingly. "It is just meant to scare us. Do not worry—whatever is requested shall be given. She shall be returned safely. Whatever price is stipulated shall be paid."

Naclana hated his job. He cleared his throat again before reading: "Dear Administrators of Adlivun…"

Aazuria did not realize that she was clenching Trevain's hand tightly, or that her palms had become very sweaty. Administrators! The person writing the note had been exceptionally sadistic if they had chosen to bleed her sister for such long, unnecessary wording. Every syllable had caused Corallyn anguish. Every syllable ignited vengeful anger within Aazuria.

Naclana swallowed before he continued reading:
"Fine weather for this time of year in Alaska, is it not?"

"Vachlan!" Aazuria shouted, ripping herself away from Trevain to drive her knuckles into the solid rock wall of the kitchen. "Only he! Only he would…"

"Shhhh," Trevain said, catching Aazuria's small wrist and gently rubbing it to soothe her. He could feel that all of her tendons and muscles had grown extremely taut with her rage. He knew that the rest of the note did not matter; Aazuria would not let this man live. If she ever found the opportunity (and he knew that she would seek it relentlessly) she would gut this man, as she had gutted his predecessor, Atargatis.

Unless, of course, Trevain got his own hands on him first. Trevain had never killed before, but as he imagined Vachlan using an inkwell of young Corallyn's blood to write this note, he suddenly knew that he was capable of it. Corallyn was *his* sister too.

Naclana struggled to keep his own voice even as he read the note. "Deliver my wife to me at Zimovia by noon Sunday, or I will drain every drop of blood coursing through the veins of this lovely little girl. I will then proceed to write volumes of vicious letters to General Ramaris with my new ink. She will know that little Corallyn Vellamo's death is on her hands. I shall continue in this fashion of persuasion until you are ultimately persuaded. With Immeasurable Sincerity, Vachlan Suchos."

There was a silence in the room. The temperature of the atmosphere seemed to have quite suddenly fallen by several degrees. The only movement was the blood dripping from Aazuria's knuckles. The gentle gurgling noise of a stew beginning to boil along with the sizzling of a dish which was ready to be pulled from the stone oven interrupted the silence.

"So he wants Visola?" Aazuria asked in a poisonous whisper. "Over my breathless body."

Novels by Nadia Scrieva:

ABOUT THE AUTHOR

Nadia Scrieva was born and raised in Toronto, Canada, where she grew very strong from carrying heavy bags filled with books back and forth from the library. She attended the University of Toronto, graduating with a B.A. in English and Anthropology. She likes knives. Her writing always features powerful females and (mostly) honorable male characters.

Nadia loves receiving feedback from readers, so feel free to contact her with any of your comments, questions, ideas, or just to say hello.

www.NadiaScrieva.com

Made in the USA
Las Vegas, NV
01 December 2020